DISCARDED HORSE FEATHERS

SCOTT LUTHER LARSON

Founder's Edition ISBN: 978-1-7372416-0-7

First Edition Paperback ISBN: 978-1-7372416-1-4

eBook ISBN: 978-1-7372416-2-1

Book design by Scott Luther Larson

Cover Model: Amelia Milbrett

www.vestigialvoice.com

www.discardedhorsefeathers.com

❀ Created with Vellum

To Mom, for always being my cheerleader, long after the stadium lights went out...

PROLOGUE

Pendulums timelessly tick on frictionless bearings while God finishes his cigarette. He dwells in a cold place where temperature doesn't exist. Everyone's tale begins and ends in no one's favorite color just as every symphony begins and ends in silence.

Nightmares uncoil an imaginative boon of plot twists, leading its witness toward an unhappy ending. Strangely, most pivotal moments don't happen with a radiating explosion. They seldom gasp with the dead or undead. Beings are not quiet victims of circumstance or unpredictable natural disasters.

Eyes unsquint. Hormones frantically scurry through a fractal, neuroendocrine network the way mice cross cold, hardwood floors in a catless home.

A pair of fingerprints delicately pinch the end of his knife's grip. Morning light splashes across his attic bed through slanted blinds while he tracks the tip—back and forth. It dangles with curiosity in three dimensions above his crossed eyes.

The end won't come at the crescendo of a night's sweaty passion. It will begin with a whimper or whine and beg for a mercy that used to exist. It will suffocate. It will starve. It will bring out the worst from sinners and dim the halos of saints.

Temptation whispers like cave wind to ask his cortex, *"Has anyone ever heard the sound of one's own piercing eye?"* The blade waves. His focus quivers, afraid to blink. Sweat buds his brow and he imagines his hands slicking.

Is it so difficult to believe the end will come with our own hands clutching our own throat? Glory locks herself in a trunk.

The need for others rapidly vanishes. *Why visit a friend or family member, when they can be called? Why call them, when electronic messages can be exchanged? Why write a message, when a selected symbol can be transmitted to summarize one's thoughts?* Rounding the edges. More impersonal. Less personal. Less human. Captains of a digital intelligence.

Some will be prepared. Most will not have even put down the landing gear. The end punctuates, not with a period or a question mark or an exclamation point, but an uncommitted ellipse.

The ground shifts. He blinks—almost in time.

CHAPTER 1

BEFORE THE AFTER

An unlit diode compels Remy to wish there was one unplucked petal in her game of: *he loves me not.* Unrequited love pills taste chalky.

She curls a strand of soft, shoulder-length blond hair behind her ear. *Then again, look at him and look at me. The fit would be... too cozy.* Remy slips a cool hand beneath her shirt. Her tiny belly bounces to the beat of the road and her fractured heart. Her cheeks flush, but no one cares. Self-esteem shrinks in the company of popularity.

Why would he pretend to like me and then not? Hope distorts reality's lens to fit its owner's sockets. She addresses her mobile device —no messages from him.

She sprays her vulnerability on a social stage without a proper audience. *If only he got a chance to know me,* she thinks along with every other lonely teenager. *I would make him happy.* Change is temporary until a goal is met. *He may not be mine forever, but, for a little while.*

With one hand, she taps and swipes, with the other she palms her stomach. It bends and bloats in cycles with the lesser light. Misunderstanding and kindness string a sad violin. Hormone pools finger-paint uncalculated strokes that perpetuate the rawest of offspring.

CHAPTER 2

WE, THE DOMESTICATED PEOPLE

Silly is the idea of pledging allegiance to anything: a plot of dirt, a group of people, a team, an army. Peacock feathers glued in the caps of old men. Why endow strangers the power to orchestrate the impressionable toward carnage on their behalf? Promoting aggressive competition on an unmet someone before mixing words and exchanging pleasantries only exemplifies irresponsibility.

Lines in the sand gather an audience. *We* are different than *them* is fundamental brainwash. A grown-up's playground. Mentality for prosperity in the shape of failure.

A time for choice comes in every evolution. It defines the future. Faltering erases all. Hands must gather, not for selfish causes, but for the benefit of forever.

The belief that success of one comes at the throat of another is shortsighted. It is okay to be happy for a fellow man. Take turns. Rivers flow. Winds calm.

Some stand behind symbols with pretentious passion. Some

put on stoic faces of war to intimidate. Onlookers from foreign rocks wouldn't understand. It is a shame that *We, the people* do.

CHAPTER 3

HAPPY ABOUT EVERYTHING EXCEPT MY LIFE

Mom and Dad's laughter-duet rattles the front seats as if to mock Remy with a perfect love-recipe. Her body slumps its empty core. The seatbelt snags her chest through her thin, white cotton shirt. She can't even seem to pull off the "embarrassed kid" routine. She untucks her breast and slinks deeper into her assembly-line-manufactured cloth seat to connect with the world's webs.

There comes a time in unsuccess that a chauffeur opens the door of change to a limousine filled with "*screw its*." When, despite persistence, one opportunity turns out not to be, all arrows point toward a blank drawing board. Remy uncommits her deviled heart from him and tries new bait.

Her feelings spread across a page to an audience of her, hoping to catch a him. A good him. A funny him. A cute him. A checklist of him. She sighs. *I would even take a kind of cute him.* Before publishing her editorialization of today's life, she reads it back, mends a couple spelling errors, edits out a few intimate insecurities with teasing pictures—just in case she'd have to explain this to a future concerned companion. Self-promotion voluntarily guides her fingers to send information across invisible wires to meet unbridled eyes.

The skyline pushes their home city closer, leaving exhaust on vacation. Modern technology quiets hoofbeats. *One last round of mandatory school,* she dreads. Looking over at the neighboring seat, her brother's tall, slender frame awkwardly fits. *Cub's so lucky to be finished—free.*

Outside the vehicle, the adopted highway stays relatively clean. A white Styrofoam cup met the business-end of an industrial strength lawn mower, scattering its beaded white particles, which statically cling to natural nothingness. Outside's nature is not allowed inside.

Dad points toward the other side of the road. Outbound traffic is gridlocked. "Something's going on. I'm sure glad we're driving this way," he tells Mom. The earth begins to quake. Dad slows, pulling to the roadside as if showing courtesy to emergency vehicles. The brief rumble passes, and he accelerates toward home.

Dad toggles a switch. He keeps two hands on the steering wheel, "out of habit," he tells Mom. "For safety," he tells us kids. "Out of distrust," he tells himself.

MILLENNIAL SLOUCH

A filter fan kicks in as their vehicle flattens the conclusion of a cow's meal. Cub raises the crook of his arm to his nose like a vampire concealing incisors until the odor fades. No one else seems bothered by the scent. The fan's engine slows and so does the whine in its bearings. Cub's arm falls, and he returns to watching the outside hurry.

If he never hears another recycled dad-joke, he'll consider

himself content. Each one, a creeping dash of collapsing freedom. *My friends are so much more interesting. I can't wait to get away from this. There are plenty of girls to meet that haven't said, "No."*

CHAPTER 4

THE SUN CARES NOT WHICH EYES RECEIVE ITS CHILDREN

Arms stretch before they have formed. Ether compiles countless reluctant participants. Blue-white glitter in a colorless space.

Electrons excite, hybridizing orbitals to change their stripes in ways restricted to laws invented by created minds. This becomes home, for a little while. Foreign fabric licks film from the eyes—revealing monsters to honor. They behave as they believe they should, but none can compare to the relaxed state. This new vehicle doesn't respond in a natural way. Techniques must be trained. Experiences replace memories. *I have forgotten what God looks like.*

Tiny pieces work to keep expending energy. Many toil before dying for what they presume may be a greater good. Little machines in bigger places compose slightly bigger machines in slightly bigger places. They divide and separate in pleasureless copulation.

The seams disappear in a gaussian blur, concealing its maker's tracks. Some believe there is, others believe there never was.

CHAPTER 5

OPEN LIMBIC SYSTEM

"I'm so glad you two came on this family trip," Mom says peering through the rearview mirror. "Too bad it is coming to an end." Her eyes pinch together in kindness.

Remy watches Mom's eyelashes flicker. *It is easy to trust her love. She is genuine and unwavered by the awful things Cub and I have done to each other.* At first, Remy misinterpreted Mom's affection as stupidity. *Stupid Remy. Mom's is a warm, but not hot, hug. Her enjoyment can be felt in the squeeze. The way Mom caringly stroked the fringe hair along my neck before releasing a deep breath... Perhaps her lungs wanted to hold in my scent long enough to remember.*

The vehicle leans into their slightly inclined driveway. Dad pulls the parking brake, which sounds like a chiropractor aligning a robot. Cub's door swings open before the final vertebrae is in place. He has had his hands on the safety belt since before they entered town. Cub dashes for the garage and liberation.

Mom exits next. She has to go to the bathroom. She *always* has to go to the bathroom.

Looking down, Remy has no new messages and no social traction, but she checks anyway—in case she missed the audible notification letting her know she is important.

Remy counts. Three doors slam shut, and a trunk pops open. Her posture slumps with poor self-esteem. She is the only one left in the vehicle.

Outside, neighbor boys' chatter is broken up by a young girl's scream, closely followed with laughter until a different girl's voice shrieks. Uvulas vibrate.

Through the open trunk, Remy hears the rustling of plastic bags the paperboy used as protection from the elements. Lifting her nose above the window's half-open pane, she watches Mom struggle to unwind the newspaper body-bag from their front door's knob.

Frustrated, Mom peers at Dad who is arranging the trunk. He pauses to volley her glance. She returns her attention to untangling the plastic-bag knot. She tip-taps her toes to keep her underwear dry.

It doesn't matter. Two concussive explosions echo in rapid succession. The first signals impact, splintering the entryway door —inside-out. The second bursts a pillow-sized hole through its center.

Aged lumber inoculates Mom's lap. Fragments of white-painted wood spray in rotating slow-motion entropy. Second hands tick.

Neither bullet misses. Remy watches her mom's feet lift before falling backward. Eyes dilate. Sound warps. Memories deeply carve horror in a cellblock, forever sentencing its prisoner of consciousness. The blackness of closed eyes will replay this film —real to reel.

Motion slows. Mom blinks, or so Remy imagines. A right foot patters to the porch with gravity. Maybe she imagines this, too. Broken fibers of long murdered trees fall to earth at the same acceleration as the recently deceased. Dusty debris lingers in a dirty, brown cloud above her—a soul goalie. A slat of door frame slides down, finding access through the porch's wood grating.

Remy doesn't hear anything after the blast. The echo. The gasp. The echo. The neighbor's piercing shout. The last echo. She shivers in stunned fear. The air in her throat has been snatched away. She gags as if breathing water.

Like traveling through a long tunnel, sound phases back to catch the muffled finale of her father's angry commands. She forgives all past conflict toward him, her forever role model.

Curled fingers tremble, fumbling at the door. Remy pulls the black, molded-plastic latch. Blunted commotion becomes highly defined. Dad's dress shoes slide like cat's claws grabbing for traction on smooth kitchen linoleum. His hand drags across the hood in an act of balance, drawing lines with each finger in the new sawdust.

Remy reflects. *When the shot rang off, why was I more concerned about my own safety than about Mom?*

Seeds of remorse require very little watering.

On heels, Cub creeps from the open garage's shadow. Below wide eyes, his lower lip hangs open. He looks guilty but hasn't even seen the carnage.

Remy slinks through a narrowly opened, backseat door. She watches the bottoms of Dad's loafers. They flash smooth black, like an eel's underbelly, except for the area beneath the balls of his feet, which have been worn to a thready white.

Dad hoists himself up the handrail, up the stairway, up to the entry door. An oily-black barrel-tip pokes out of the pillow-sized opening in their front door. Remy spots it and screams what starts to be "Dad," but drags the 'a' in a vibrating shrill. If she had to file a report, she would guess: a shotgun.

The volume gets turned way down, again. The second hand hesitates. Maybe this is a blessing in runny Halloween mascara. Maybe. Tragic imagery etched in grey matter is difficult to erase.

Point-blank bullets don't ever graze. The first explosion

connects with Dad's arm. It tugs his shoulder-socket backward like a nagging toddler, too big for their age. Remy is surprised at the number of ejected embers. They singe Dad's clothes like hungry, invisible moths.

Dad reels from the impact, but recomposes, spinning himself straight toward the assailant. He lurches for the broken front door in time to turn the other cheek. The second strike connects with his stomach. Contents escape. Hanging in a plastic cocoon, the newspaper still hangs from the doorknob.

Remy hears her name being called as if from a sewer tunnel. She feels her name ripple. Sounds re-focus like the opening seconds before awakening from sleep. Cub snatches her wrist and pulls her behind their parked vehicle.

CHAPTER 6

UNCALLUSED FEET FOLLOW BRAVERY

People are just that. The fact that one person can hatch a plan over the weekend and create thousands of victims should terrify.

Lines at public gatherings will lengthen until libraries burn. Technology lied. Lives aren't simpler. Workweeks didn't shorten. Single income families are drying up like chivalry. The first chicken never worried about the first egg or even crossing roads. *Be a good little lily pad.*

CHAPTER 7

EGGSHELL WALKING

She can't sense her feet beneath. Clear, focal vision is surrounded by a stretching blur. She watches her hand in his. Grass, then pavement, then grass. She adjusts her hand in his for a tighter grip.

Cub shoots her a glance. "Come on!" Toward the dead-end street, his pace quickens. Hers follows.

"Wait, Cub! Where are we going?" He doesn't answer but she already knows.

The Hen.

Remy can't recall her real name, but this lady ran the local daycare. In a way, she ran the neighborhood. *She knew everybody, and everybody knew her—relied on her. Working parents dropped kids off at sunrise, and then later, usually before sundown, picked them up. Neighbors leaned on Hen's generosity for the spaces in between. "Take care of the people who take care of you," she used to say. Probably still does.*

She seemed more like a friend than a babysitter. As we grew up, we had little need for her anymore. Friendships bend and flex like dry lungs.

It's healthy. Forcing friendships only tarnishes them, right? Then again, friendships shouldn't be built upon "needs."

They approach Hen's home. Remy can't remember the last time she was here, but she remembers it always being unusually dark. *This house haunts from the outside.* Upturned children's toys and trash litter the unkept lawn. The home's pale-blue wooden siding with deep blue shudders reminds Remy of black-eyes. A leafless tree overhangs the pulverized-gravel driveway. Thorny and ignored weeds spring tall, thick stems. If Hen owned a vehicle, it would leak oil.

Cub vaults the cement-block steps, adjacent to the driveway, leading up to the black-eyed house. He bangs a closed fist against the flaking door. The loud rattling startles them and Cub's bangs calm to a knock.

Sixteen. Seventeen. Eighteen. She counts. *I'll wait until twenty.* She finishes waiting. He knocks again, listening close. A warm, dwelling odor seeps through seals.

Remy stands at the base of the stairs with her arms crossed. She leans around the corner of the black-eyed house. She can almost see their own house. The back end of their vehicle sticks out. *The trunk is still open. Were we followed?* She ducks out of view of her home.

Cub presses his nose against the nearby windowpane, shielding his eyes to remove the glare. Condensation patches collect and evaporate the way breaths walk across mirrors.

Remy looks in, too. Thready grommet curtains rustle on the inside of the unlit home. A silhouette thinks it's hidden. A long, white, dirt-packed fingernail slips through the crease. Olive-green-colored curtains slide to reveal a wide, unblinking eyeball. It pans from Cub down to Remy. Remy waves at the eyeball and the fingernail disappears, leaving the curtains to settle.

A muffled older woman's voice can be heard through the building's thin walls. *It sounds like scolding.* Hard heel-stomps precede a fumbling at the slide lock on the other side. Remy hears a chain clang against the door before coming to rest. The scuffed, brass doorknob spins.

Awkwardly, the door cracks open. An unshowered little girl is reaching her thin, tanned arms up. Her armpits are smooth. On tip toes, she uses her weight to pull the knob. It swings wide open. She stands alone in the doorway, with hands behind her back, looking up at Cub. Her top row of baby teeth bite her bottom lip in a mock smile, void of emotion, as if she's waiting for a photograph flash.

Remy leaps in front of Cub, who is trying his best to make his smile appear natural.

"Hi!" Remy says, extending her hand for a shake. "May we come in?" she asks with pressured speech. She bats her eyelashes. Her forehead itches. Her pulse reloads. Pressure beats in her eye sockets as sand passes through its chamber's neck. Red desert cracks *thump* her vision.

The little girl's blue irises watch Remy's mouth for a tell. They watch her outstretched hand give up looking for a shaker. She clenches her upper row harder. The little girl's head tilts and says, "Your hair is pretty."

"It's okay, dear," a voice calls from inside the black-eyed house. "You can let them in." The little one takes a final look at her new visitors before shuffling out of the way. Her tiny fingers writhe with each other against the door's frame. She watches long legs walk by and into the house before helping the door seal shut. She drags an old, wooden chair with cylinder dowel ribs and pushes it against the door. The blue-eyed girl pulls herself onto it and returns the brass slide-lock to its protective place.

The locking sound brings Remy relief, as if side-stepping peril. *But now, how do we justify our presence to Hen, whose relationship we've long neglected?*

Scent carries memories. To Remy, there is familiarity. The aromas of mold and hairdryer-warmed sweaty scalp mingles with stale, aging cigarette smoke and athlete's foot in a fog of body odor. Without consciously trying, clock arms spin back to the last time she was here. *The smell never left.* She clearly recalls the events but strangely, the colors have been lifted, leaving only soft grayscale moving pictures.

"It's okay. You can touch it."

Little Remy allows the plush rug's fibers to poke up between her toes. She doesn't want to, touch it, that is. *It is too unpredictable. It has teeth that don't fit in its mouth. It has claws too big for its paws.* It scares her without trying. Down casting her eyes, she shakes her head.

"You don't know what you're missing!" An older girl wearing a stone-gray dress flaunts as claws crawl up her wrist. She offers a hand as support in case it loses grip—arm training wheels. It makes its way across her forearm. The gray-dressed girl observes Little Remy's disgust. Timidly, Little Remy sneaks a glance at the rodent. Its tail always hovering, never dragging. A wood shaving from its transplanted home flutters from a claw down to the heavily stained flooring.

The gray-dressed girl's tongue hangs, hungry for Little Remy's reaction. Her caught stare returns to the plush rug. The room's scent reminds Remy of liquified shame with sprinkles of insecurity.

A pulled tooth never feels at home.

SCALING PAINT

The dense aroma doesn't strike Cub the same. To him, this place smells like an old shoe store filled with armpits. No pots of gold at the end of this colorful mirage. Mold befriends spiderwebs. His tongue samples the air.

Pupils widen. No one inside moves or speaks. The audience stand-off seems unintentionally stoic. Cub hears a steady water drip into what sounds like an empty pan, along with a soft hiss like a deflating bicycle tire. Coiling metallic boiler horns keep autumn uncomfortably warm. Anxiety doesn't help.

SHE IS A POOR MAN FROM WASECA'S ORACLE

Figures pop from the shadows as eyesight adjusts. Remy recognizes Hen. She was always big, but even more so today. She rocks in a chair the shade of putting greens. Her oily complexion sets the stage for a sprouting mustache beneath a nose shaped like a prairie falcon's beak. The eerie mix of light and shadows deepen wrinkles making her face resemble a mid-December jack-o-lantern. Her stained shirt stretches to completely cover her torso, but fans out near the bottom of her protruding belly. Sloppy appearances aside, she is the hen *and* the rooster here.

In a losing effort, she pulls the bottom of her shirt down before addressing her visitors. Hen scans Remy, from feet to upturned nose. Remy holds composure's hand. *I shouldn't be intimidated.* Fingers hide in pockets. *I've been here before and shouldn't have to explain why I'm here, right?* Hands unhide and dry themselves on denim flanks. Remy clears her throat and uncomfortably straightens her posture. Hen observes.

Remy looks around. Children, many of them, have stopped mid-play to gather as chicklings at Hen's feet. Some sit Indian-style. Most prop themselves on a pair of bent knees. Their mouths breathe.

Behind, Remy notes Cub's shuffling shoes.

She meant to say, "Hi," but all that came out was a single-handed wave while the other fingers bashfully stuff themselves back in her pocket.

This place continues to be a flop house because of Hen. She was boisterous, but funny. Loud, but understanding. Unfiltered, but protective.

"You were hardly a woman last time," says the hen. She leans back to peel apart the uneven blinds behind her chair as if she's lost interest in her guests. Dust motes weightlessly mingle in penetrating light shafts that spill across the walls and floor.

Remy wants to explain everything. She wants to tell someone who cares, but, "Hi, umm... Yeah. No, I wasn't," is all that dribbles out before she breaks down.

Hen allows her to momentarily sulk before turning to Cub. "What was all that racket?" Her tone goes from hysteric to stern. "You best not carry your troubles."

Her attention returns to Remy. Through darkness, Hen stares the way hungry predators stalk. Blush blooms across Remy's face. Her tiny, pointed nose itches.

"We are in danger, Missus—"

"You didn't answer me, young lady," Hen firmly interrupts. Her voice growls with impatience. "Did you?"

"No, Ma'am." Tear ducts clamp tight like used coffins. Taking a scolding after losing one's parents doesn't ease Remy's sorrow.

Stepping in front of her, Cub interjects, "Mom and Dad just got shot!" Half-moons well at Remy's bases, pecking at the slanted light. She hears Hen let out a sigh, vaguely resembling compassion. Remy disguises a tear wipe with a double eye scratch.

Hen's tribe watches their chieftain for direction. She parts the blinds again, this time, rubbing her forehead as if to massage out a tension headache. Her lower arms wobble like fat hammocks.

Still rubbing, Hen waves, "Come here."

Cub starts forward.

"Not you, Cubbie. Your sister."

He steps aside.

Remy's first shuffles are abbreviated. Ahead, the big chair rocks, releasing a handful of squeaks, thirsty for water displacement fluid. Back and forth and back, each bigger, until it vaults Hen to her feet.

When she opens her arms, Hen is only slightly taller than Remy's shoulders. Loose clothing conceals a lifetime of inactivity.

She perches a tiny head on Remy's bony shoulder while patting her back.

Cupping hands under Remy's jawline, Hen's eyes judge Remy. Even if Hen doesn't believe it, she confidently tells Remy, "You are ready."

Hen raises her heels. Wise lips whisper into a young ear. Breath lifts thin neck hairs. She loses her balance. Remy braces the rotund woman. As if interrupted, she perches in Remy's ear for an unfinished word. Remy nods as they separate. Bracing Remy's arms on each side, Hen looks up, as a dog does to his master. Instead of cleanly breaking, Hen drags her fingertips down Remy's arms as if she longs to hold on a bit longer.

"Thank you, Ma'am." Her tension abates.

Hen responds with an open-palmed gesture of mercy, before plopping back into her still-warm chair.

"A dog doesn't return to his own vomit," Hen calls out, shaking her head.

A wind gust blows a leafless branch, banging it against the black-eyed house. Cub is the only one to flinch.

"Things gonna' get worse before they get any better," she says pushing off the floor to rock in her putting-green chair. "I know, it doesn't seem like it, but..." she trails for a moment. "They is."

"You'll know and you'll know," she says pointing to each of her newest guests, "the real prices. 'Cause they were never stickers waiting for a store clerk."

It was getting hard to tell the seriousness of this old lady.

Biting her top lip, Hen produces a high-pitched whistle.

"Cassie, get your brother. You will join our nice, new friends," she says with a calm grin.

The one that must be Cassie stands up. Wavy black hair and a smooth brown complexion sit atop a dreadfully skinny frame. Each joint is punctuated in sharp, boney edges. She hasn't yet developed curves to fill the aqua-colored dress with ruffled lace sleeves.

Cassie softly walks to a small boy on the other side of the room. She extends a hand, "Sydney." His thick afro hair looks like black fiberglass insulation. His limbs have a little more meat on them, but not by much. She takes his hand and guides him to face Hen. The backs of his elbows have dimples. From behind, the kids look like black, pleated paper dolls linked at the fingers.

"That's it, now pick out a coat and your favorite toy from the playroom, each of you. I'll fix you a treat for the road."

They obediently dart toward the back of the house as if it is a race. Cassie casts an arm across her younger brother's chest to stay ahead of him. Hen playfully chuckles until they are safely out of earshot. The laugh drops into a cold, purse-lipped stare at Cub.

CHAPTER 8

A GRAPE THAT ALMOST ESCAPED

The tinkerer tinkers while the toilers toil because that is what they do. There is tragedy in staying busy under a sun that doesn't care about its beings appearing busy. Many grains of sand slip down the narrow neck, each faster than the next, like a desert avalanche. It is natural to resist the inevitable, but the inevitable is always changing. If only one could awaken before the reality of one's own demise.

CHAPTER 9

LANGUAGES OF UNDERSTANDING BETWEEN DAUGHTERS

Remy and Cub gulp in solidarity. *What have we learned? She's telling us to watch these kids? Maybe, it's not too late to avoid this situation.* Both eye the door before meeting nervous glances.

Rapid little muffled footsteps from darker rooms become clearer. The two run up to their guests' feet. Cassie's head reaches Remy's armpit and Sydney comes up to his sister's shoulders.

"Come ear, kids. Give ol' Corky a hug before you leave with this young man and nice lady. *They* are going to be in charge." Cassie and Sydney run toward Hen. She gives them a warm, but not hot, hug.

The black-eyed house's door slams shut.

A French rooster scampers across the home's anemic front lawn. Molting feathers leave bare patches. Its neck struts first, then the body follows.

Remy puffs her cheeks and turns to Cub. He shrugs her off. She reflects. *We came here looking for protection, but leave with—*

Behind them, the slide lock latches from inside with finality. *Responsibility.*

"So, you guys are our babysitters?" Sydney asks.

Remy checks her mobile phone, which reads, "No service."

"We have to go back," Cub says.

"No. You remember, the dog and the vomit."

"I don't care, Rem. I need to. *We* need to. And it's getting late," he snaps.

"Cub, I don't want to see Mom and Dad that way!" Her voice pops and cracks. Sydney and Cassie observe the older siblings while holding each other's hand.

Teachers come in all ages, whether they know it or not.

He bolts, waving the kids to follow. "Close your eyes then."

FOSTERING ICEBERGS

Feathers momentarily distract from the inevitable.

With lights off, some neighbors peer from upstairs windows. Necks made of rubber halt traffic.

The bravest few hold their mouths in a gathered congregation around the fresh massacre, attempting to contact help. A lady Remy does not recognize cries while shielding the gore from her view. Many pairs of crossed arms contemplate their own future. An interrogator's salutation would unlock watersheds of desperate secrets.

"Bring what you can! They may come back!" Cub announces. Remy watches Cub hurdle the porch steps, leaving black shoe prints while oxygen divorces Mom's hemoglobin. He says, "Give me five," but it will be closer to more. Sydney cautiously follows him inside.

She looks back at Cassie. "You want to come in?"

The skinny brown girl shrugs.

Remy observes the commotion collecting in their neighborhood. "Well, don't go far, okay? I won't be long."

Cassie nods before Remy darts upstairs.

I don't understand. Where are we going? How long will we be gone? Where is my other bag? I should probably bring food. There's my brush. Where did I leave my phone? I need to bring a charger, home and vehicle. I suppose. Oh, never mind. And toilet paper. Two rolls, just in case. Maybe two pairs of everything.

Remy's heartbeat matches her racing thoughts, stride for excruciating stride. She circles her room with the uncertainty of a hotel. She emerges from her home with a turquoise airport-rolling bag, two backpacks, and a purse—all stuffed.

Sucking her thumb, Cassie sits on the broken porch swinging her legs. She is staring down at Mom through the railing. "Please look away, Cassie." The skinny black girl stops sucking to wipe her mouth, blinks a couple times, then returns to looking at the delicate horror.

Seeing Remy struggle, a neighbor breaks away from the pack of rubbernecks. "Where are you going, young lady?" He towers a full head taller than her, obstructing the straight sunlight. Whiskey, nicotine, and ultraviolet have all weathered his face, leaving a wrinkled shell of sunbaked bronze skin. If she had to guess, maybe sixty, or ten processions, would be her flattering estimate of his age.

"Hey, Steve," she says with deflated enthusiasm.

Steve has been their neighbor her entire life. He had been a career fireman, now "happily retired," but he isn't one to idle and his physique thanks him. He only has one chin and it is proudly Indian-shaped. Wispy gray hairs flee his eyebrows. Slightly loose skin surrounds muscular arms and legs. His fingers are thick as broom handles. Only a small fat pad has ever settled in his belly.

His eyes soften. His mouth tightens. He places a gentle paw on her shoulder.

Steve has always been quiet, at least as long as she's known him. He continues to get more stoic in his older age. First, he lost his wife. Then a dog. Then another. Each paved his mouth over a little more.

A KOALA BEAR CLINGING TO A EUCALYPTUS BRANCH

Inside, Sydney gums the ear of his favorite plush teddy bear while watching Cub dart through the house. He studies Cub's appearance. *His hair is barely there, mostly scalp—like black whiskers. He's so tall and strong. I wonder which sports he plays.* Sydney's brow scrunches. *Wait, what is that?* He twists his little neck. *Is that a scratch?* Sydney hadn't noticed it in the shadows of the black-eyed house. A scar made of smooth skin runs from the corner of Cub's mouth to the base of his right cheekbone. Sydney grins. *I have a scar, too, but mine is on my knee.*

Outside, the trunk lock clicks open. Cub heaves carefully packed supplies inside, pushing them deep into the cabin. His trip back into the house is interrupted.

"How about we take my industrial," Steve suggests, seeming surprised those words fell from his tongue. Remy is hugging him with two arms. He is hugging her with one, like a bashful man who wants to escape being held—avoiding feelings. Bonded by loss, her heart tugs his in a way he hasn't felt in a long time. Cub freezes to look at Remy before answering the old man.

"I've already packed our vehicle, but thanks." Cub turns around only to be interrupted again.

"No big deal. I'll bring them over."

Cub appears reluctant. "I'd hate to redo all this."

"Full tank," Steve coaxes.

Cub rubs his chin, "I guess a long bed would have its advantages..."

Remy looks back and forth between the guys' expressions—a high-noon duel. Cub's ego yields. He nods.

Steve's lips part, revealing yellowed teeth and missing ones. "Four of you, right? Good." He points a straight finger at his vehicle next door, "I call her Lucy."

CHAPTER 10

SELF-MUTINY

The color of the fingers quietly tapping on a keyboard didn't matter. They will never be found red. The intention behind those strokes and their impact were as unpredictable as touch-up paint on the Mona Lisa. Money only yields power when enough people believe it has value. *It does until it doesn't* is a revolution.

Investors stop buying companies that have been split into millions of pieces. Mailmen stop deliveries. Truckers stop delivering fuel. The last milliliters of gasoline swirl into gasping vehicles of pre-abandoned families. Grocery stores stop receiving inventory. Police stop enforcing. Locked doors soon accommodate forced entry. Firefighters stop fighting. Hospitals stop serving. Planes stop departing. Janitors stop gathering filth that garbagemen stopped picking up. Electric companies halt service for energy they no longer have. Everything stands still for the same reason—greed. Communication goes into "face-to-face" mode. Churches become standing room only.

CHAPTER 11

WHITTLED WOOD AND LEAVING HOME

Two bear paws slam the tailgate shut. The scowl on Cub's face tugs at his fascial scar as he unbrokenly stares at their new helper.

"Thanks," Remy says squeezing Steve's forearm from the middle seat.

There is no turning back.

Steve's listened to half a lifetime of conspiracy programs. Cub notices an excitement in his neighbor as theory ignites into practice. "The freeze-dried food was still in date," he says. Lucy, the blue industrial with metallic flecks, rolls down his driveway for the last time. Steve softly pumps the brake to size up one final image of the house he called home for over forty revolutions. "I don't know why I locked the doors and secured the windows. Hope is an ironic fantasy."

Brake lights dim and the engine roars. Cub's freedom shrinks in mirrors. He has gone from the driver's seat to the passenger's on a metaphorical merry-go-round. White knuckles suppress truthful emotions for a little while.

"We have to leave town," Steve tells the windshield. With noses pressed against the glass, Cassie and Sydney watch their entire world get smaller from the backseat. Steve's windows greet tiny handprints for the first time. The back cushions have never experienced human weight.

"The city will run out of food inside of three rotations. Fuel is already gone." Cub listens to doom from the other side of Remy. It bothers him to believe Steve's words. Youth hung shadows over his outlook. Graduation broke shackles, freeing him to the opportunity of choice, his own trail. Liberation allowed the undesirables to be trimmed. Now, he finds himself ten calendars earlier in a prison built by big kids to detain little ones. Daycare and nightcare and life-care. Looking in the sideview mirror, he slides his hand around the door handle and tries to remember how to tuck and roll from a moving vehicle.

JEALOUS PAIRS EYE OTHER'S PILES

The highway is a parking lot. Ditches are a campsite. "We'll take side roads," Steve says leaning toward Remy, but keeping his eyes on traffic. *This isn't a closely guarded secret.* Warnings have been regularly broadcasted, along with weather and the time, for several sunrises leading up to the silence.

"It's like an evacuation," Remy tonelessly says. The inner city, while having vehicles, did not have many moving ones. Steve swerves around a red utility vehicle with its rear sticking out. He slow-rolls at intersections, lampless or otherwise. A startled driver squeals tires, depositing a long strip of black rubber on the pavement, to avoid the belly of Steve's ride. Cassie's grip tightens, then relaxes.

Approaching the major freeway pipeline, traffic thickens. Vehicles have long since given up, their doors swung wide open. Cub notices windowed trunks packed skin-to-skin with items. Bending birdcage bars and brown argyle blankets pin a statue of a bronzed man being thrown from a horse. A white dowel-swing oscillates in a birdless prison. Seed has scattered onto neighboring pillows.

Families have exited their vehicles. A mother bounces her child on a tilted hip while adjusting its pacifier and bonnet.

Steve aims directly over the dashing centerline to avoid the milling pedestrians on either shoulder. Many gather beneath an underpass seeking shade. Remy points out people talking, not only with their hands, but also with quick arm gestures. Words aren't enough.

"Busy both ways," Steve says after clearing his throat.

CHAPTER 12

THE DEVIL NEVER MADE ANYBODY DO ANYTHING, BUT THE DEVIL NEVER STOPPED ANYBODY FROM DOING ANYTHING

Evening sets in. Newly born oranges contrast the previously unlit, polluted black sky. Billions of billions of pale white photons from dead stars scatter as a ball of flames crawls up city hall.

Two cowardly steps away, onlookers film the revolt using unnetworked cameras. Wind stokes burning which resembles a snapping flag demanding new freedoms.

The cowards take a step back—the heroes, a step closer to heat their cheeks.

In the distance, glass smashes. Handheld lamps glow like upheld Zippos worshipping their favorite celebrity poet who happens to have an amazing voice.

Reels of footage never to be broadcasted, never to be leaked, never to be used as propaganda—most never to be viewed even once—will be shot tonight by protesters without a solution. Many don't realize the issues they are protesting or even know their enemy. To them, this is just an event they would be embarrassed to *not* be a part of.

And so, they point their glowing red buttons at screaming women chasing children under unlit streetlamps. Tonight, they will rest comfortably believing deadbolts will keep them from becoming victims from the hungry, violent, growing masses. Desperation flames lick at their heels, turning the pious into predators and ignoring flicked locks.

CHAPTER 13

INSECT CARAPACE

Cub hand-cranks the window down a crack. *Everything about Steve is old—vehicle included.* Air rushes in like an eager puppy or an angry flag. Poking his nostrils outside, he catches puffs of autumn's decay.

Cassie plugs her ears to block the bright white noise.

Many small backroads between city and suburbs allow for collateral traffic. "We'll take the third," Steve confidently announces.

Vehicles and their parasites line the ditches like vehicular cholesterol. The bubble compass above Remy's head spins north. The road opens into less traffic and more cracks.

On both sides, crops have been stripped for the season. A few lonely stalks escaped their annual holocaust to proudly protest.

"Let me know if you have to go to the bathroom, okay?" Steve asks, looking in the rearview mirror. Sydney and Cassie both exaggeratingly nod before returning to their window stare.

A PIRATE SHIP BUILT WITH FINGERS

The host spins its passengers.

Minor tributaries funnel back into major ones despite Steve's best efforts.

Remy isn't familiar with the route, having only driven a couple revolutions, but she can't tell the difference between these rural homes pre- and post-crisis. She tries to pick out memorable landmarks like a mouse memorizing a cheese maze but finds very little to go on.

Forced to choose left or right, Steve turns the setting sun toward their backs. Three children emerge from the bushes to chase their exhaust.

"We are being led back to the pipeline," Cub remarks. Steve didn't need to be told. He groans in agreement, sparking a lighter in his cupped hand. Knees stabilize the steering wheel. A smoke stream leaks and he cranks down his window a crack, blowing mouth air with manners.

Remy watches the cigarette dance between his sausage fingers, frosted in white calluses. The trail lingers, almost suspended. Rising slowly, the smoke's borders draw opaque and crisp until catching a current which stretches and thins the herd, rapidly disintegrating its form into a wispy, spiritual release.

Springs gently yield to their master, making for a comfortably smooth ride. *May the sun always set on our backs.* Western progress recesses.

CHAPTER 14

WINDS OF CHANGE REQUIRE INCENTIVES

The poorest of the poor were first to fall. They barely felt it—a love spanking. When the middle-class caved, the fat lady began her final verse. Domestic funds funneled to foreign banks spelled in letters unfamiliar to a native alphabet. Families scrambled to withdraw their savings. This worked until politics intervened.

Currency froze with temporarily-permanent government mandates. Vendors accepted credit until accounts became delinquent. Then, it was cash only.

Political promises hushed concerns. Federal reserves ran dry. Emergency greenbacks were pressed into circulation. Money was thrown at money problems. A match would have worked as well as the Federal Mint.

Middle-class employees stopped being employees. Why spend life at a job that rewards only with lost time? The government would save their unemployment, or so they hoped. Society's wheels squeal before falling off.

Clerks don't show up to sell goods that never got delivered.

Food disappears in riots, erupting from fear of shrinking stomachs.

Medications stop showing up to empty hospitals full of appointments. Professionals feel Earth move under their feet and the sky comes tumbling down. Professionals cannot perform professional jobs without the unprofessional.

Fuel deliveries halt. Stations run dry. The fuel one has is all they ever will. Scarcity becomes the old maid.

Then, electricity stops. A stork gently swoops down. Within its beak, among the swaddling cloth, hysteria is born.

CHAPTER 15

AMBUSH MEAT

It's been a while since they were traveling north. The clean road clutters. Remy squints to examine the obstruction. Two service vehicles are positioned perpendicular to the ditch, their broad sides facing traffic in both directions to form a wall. Four large men stand with fists perched on their hips as Steve pulls close. A bigger, taller man jumps down off one of the hoods. The vehicle wobbles to sleep. While removing a toothpick from his mouth, the tall man holds an outstretched palm toward Steve.

The tall man has closely cropped, black hair with a matching beard perched upon a Spanish jawline. His unabashed, suntanned complexion has hints of pink. A tight, red shirt shrink-wraps his broad shoulders. Loose, black, denim jeans stay stiff. The outfit reminds Remy of a bullfighter.

Brakes obey, squealing only at the very end. Steve rolls the window down halfway.

"Howdy, friends," says the matador as he approaches Steve's side. "I'm really sorry. This road is closed."

Silence evolves into a lawless climate. With his forearm draped loosely over the top of the steering wheel, Steve squints down the obstruction. *No authority closed this road unless these thugs constitute road-closers.* Ahead, two of the cross-armed men lean on tipped toes as if eavesdropping or awaiting commands.

The matador scratches his thick, foresting neck hair. "Sure wish there was something we could do to help," he says the way policemen hint that they need their palms greased. He sizes up the vehicle. Steve watches him, not breaking to blink. His stare could grind pulp.

"You folks on vacation? Heck of a time for it, with the world ending and all..." The matador's voice trails as he reaches into the bed to lift a backpack.

"He's a liar," Cub fumes, surprised by his own aggression.

"What's that, young man?" The matador puffs his chest. He seems to live for confrontation and just received an appetizer. His four henchmen step closer, two on each side. "Repeat yourself, boy," he shouts. Fingertips deepen red over the top of Steve's half-window.

Steve squares his shoulders, reaching for the belt buckle, slow and steady. He stares at the matador who stares at Cub who looks away. He wants to taste Cub's fear with an intimidating tongue.

Steve flinches when his sleeve gets tugged from behind. It's a little hand. Cassie says, "I have to go potty." He briefly turns to acknowledge her. His big paw scoops at the console in front of Remy.

"Alright. Everyone out!" The matador reaches inside, fumbling with the door handle. The four henchmen eagerly charge.

Cub hammers down the lock on his side. Steve's door swings open to play tug-of-war. Two thugs join the beard.

Cub reaches across Remy's lap. His stretching hands grab air, waiting for Steve's inward tug. The hand comes. He grips and leans back. The backseat kids watch with eyes that fear blinking more than bedtime. Fingers invade the light between the closing door. They writhe like angry worms.

Steve brings a closed fist over the seat. "Do me a favor, kids. Pick up these coins." The paw releases. It sounds like bullet shells. Cassie and Sydney obediently duck down to pluck them off the backseat's floor.

Fingers turn to groping hands around the open door's perimeter. Forearms on each side tense and flex, displaying their best slap-shot muscles. "Let... Go," an outsider grunts through barred teeth.

Behind the outstretching Cub, Remy unhooks her brother's seatbelt. She looks up. The thugs opposite Steve's side have made their way around back, one heaving his body into the vehicle's bed.

Steve shifts into gear. His door swings wide open and human claws pull at his clothing. His foot slams. Lucy jolts backward like a spurred horse. They accelerate in reverse. Clambering from behind sounds like books falling down stairs. *Someone's been struck.* Steve's door wrenches so far open, it looks as if it may bend from its hinge.

He releases to shift into drive. Four of five passenger necks snap backward in recoil. Remy turns around. Two legs wave in Lucy's rear bed. The front end rises like a boat gaining speed.

Hands flee the swinging door. Steve pulls tight before veering toward the unmowed grass around the road-closers' blockade. Anger and urgency thump the windowpanes. Yells rumble with the engine's roar like a room filled with snores. A stiff boot claims its territory in the rear quarter panel before the blue industrial rocks its way down the ravine, putting space between the herd.

Remy watches the tall, fist-waving men shrink and lose hope. The passenger window rolls down. Cub lets out a victory howl that must have spooked away his teenage angst, if even for a short while. She hasn't seen him this happy, this gratified, this fired up, since he wore much smaller clothes. A giggle foams up her throat in their shared victory.

The kids poke their heads over the seats. Each holds out a mittful of coins and an unabashed grin.

"Thank you, sweetheart," she tells Cassie. "And, thank you, too, Sydney." She accepts their coin offering. "Can you two buckle up for me?"

Motion behind them catches her attention. The barnacle man in the bed of their vehicle has managed to right himself into a crouch. Thinning brown hair whips across his face. With squinting eyes, he appears to be calculating his options.

The suspension's springs stretch, limiting side-to-side wobble, across Earth's uneven terrain.

Panic observes his spectators. The ground below blurs parallel to peril. His companions shrink. The matador stands tall, shielding his face. The others clutch their knees in exhaust and defeat.

Steve raises an eyebrow toward the rearview mirror—sizing up the barnacle. A smooth transition from ditch to road approaches near a tunnel drain.

Steve leads the wheels, swaying into the turn. Barnacle adjusts his grip. The vehicle ramps, then plateaus. Pink returns to Barnacle's knuckles.

Remy notices Cub noticing Steve eyeing the intruder and follows his stare. Steve wobbles the steering wheel tightly the way wet dogs shake off pool water.

Barnacle receives the message: he is not welcome.

Asphalt streaks beneath. Cub rolls down his window and launches a lump of spit that quickly disintegrates. He pounds the door with his palm as if to scare away scavengers. Steve accelerates.

"Out!" Cub pounds the door, harder this time. Wind currents tug at his cupping palm like a freed kite.

The engine purrs louder, shifts gears, and then angers further.

Barnacle's lower lip hangs, as if contemplating the best way to exit the roof of a burning building.

He straps on one of their backpacks. "Hey!" Cub screams from the gravel in his throat. "Drop it!"

A lightbulb appears to flicker in Barnacle's brain. He begins bailing all the bed's contents out the rear. A turquoise duffel bag tumbles and bursts, spilling white shirts, shorts, and wadded socks onto the road's shoulder.

"My bag!" Remy gasps. She motions. Brake pads clench tight to rotors. Friction generates poorly dissipating heat. The back end rears its hind legs, throwing Barnacle headlong. Safety seat-belts engage, preventing passengers from ejection. Everyone slides forward in their seats. Waistlines compress.

Cub grips the door handle before they come to a complete stop. He toggles it in a chagrin fit. Gears shift into park. A stereo *click* signals all doors have been unlocked.

Cub spills out only to find himself caught in the seatbelt. Embarrassed, but refusing to acknowledge it, he maintains eye contact with his target. He leans in, pops the latch, and then dashes toward his future victim, who is scaling the tailgate.

As he closes in on Barnacle, the man is far older than he visualized. Facial creases match their forehead's wrinkles. His cheeks are chubby and hold patches of sprouting white whiskers like a lawn attacked by carelessly sprayed herbicide. His black mustache is full of pride, acting like an awning to two large, white buckteeth.

There is deviance in attacking an opponent who doesn't physically compare. Cub would never consider himself athletic, but financial and emotional instability had kept him thin. He jumps up to grab the man by the lapels. Fiercely, he yanks. Cub imagined one snap would have dragged Barnacle down. Instead, Barnacle hunkers, straddling the tailgate. He ducks into Cub's next pull. The cheapest of threads stretch from his collar.

Cub climbs the rear to rein repeating right elbows to the

man's temple, most are blocked, but the ones that find a home cause Barnacle to see white flashes. Arms and legs waver.

The next pull feels all of Cub's weight. Cub's breathing labors. The man is whining. Deep-red trickles out from inside Barnacle's right ear. *He doesn't really look like a criminal anymore.* Cub takes a step away in a gentlemen's silent armistice. Terrorists and criminals don't match their profession while pleading for mercy. A trickle of blood escapes Barnacle's left nostril. Catching the closing rays of sunlight, it merges with a tear and accelerates down the man's cheek in diluted mischief.

"Up," Steve says with the firm authority of a fitness coach. Together they lift the man out, this time, he offers very little resistance.

Cub wriggles the arm straps, stripping him of his spoils. Splayed on the pavement, the defunct intruder kicks at Cub's calves like a pouting child sentenced to "timeout" for a crime he freely admits.

Still boiling, Cub pushes Barnacle's face into the road. He winds a right hand and thrusts it into Barnacle's back. Spit splatters his face. A slow bead finds its way into his ear canal.

Cub combs fingers over his own sweaty scalp while catching his breath. He steals a glance at the truck. Two young heads duck. A wave of embarrassment washes over him as he allowed emotions to steer his actions. Behind, Remy and Steve have already started down the road, gathering the bailed goods.

"Stay," Cub commands, standing above his victim. He takes a step away, the man motions to get up. "Stay!" This time, he does.

Doors clap shut. A key turns. Taillights illuminate, leaving a quivering man in its wake. Lucky for euphemisms, he is no longer a victim, but a survivor.

Inside, Steve responds to another tug from behind. Tucking chin to shoulder, he looks back. The children's expressions are painted in horror. "Oh yes, potty time." As if in defeat, Steve sighs, "I should have dropped the coins a second time."

DORMANT POLYPS, NAMED BENIGN, LIVING IN DAMP DARKNESS

The sky overhead reflects pale blue as if that was the last crayon in God's box. Black trees conceal the western horizon line. Tiny rays weave through bare branches to remind Earth of its insignificance.

Cassie finishes, wiping her hands on the grass. Everyone else tries. Hunching over his thoughts, Cub calms. He sits on the road's shoulder inhaling idle fumes. Sunglasses reaffirm his style rather than provide needed protection. *Was there anything I could have done to keep my parents? It doesn't even seem real to think they are gone. They will always stay gone.* His teeth clench. Tears stay in, barely. When he pictures his mom's smile, he feels her warm understanding—her unflinching love. He can't imagine those feelings existing in his own body.

Blinks bring black. Replacing the dark, images flash of her cooling corpse lying in their overgrown, green lawn. Deep red, as if burnt in a kiln, soaks and expands from her abdomen. A loose hand lays limp over her wound. Suds of escaping air build around her fingers on a sopping pool like forever-pain, thickening in autumn. *Imagine the scab.* Nobody needs to see what Cub wipes beneath the sunglasses' lens. He suppresses the hurt. Pain has no memory. He flexes his right hand, in and out, before shaking it into a twiddle.

Cassie skips, swinging Remy's held hand while returning to their vehicle. Sydney seems to be less chipper, more internally bothered. Dragging his feet, nose first, he kicks a stone down the road. Hands hide in pockets of the down. Thoughtful minds stir in their own silence.

A silver sedan slows as it approaches, then races by in the opposite direction. *Self-sacrifice is a better teacher than finely crafted words.*

TASK SUCCESSFULLY FAILED

The remaining golden pollen beads dangle from black barbed, mate-seeking legs during the season's last call.

From outside Lucy, Remy holds the seat, allowing Sydney to climb inside.

"Come sit by me, Sydney!" Cassie says tapping the spot beside her. Her positivity chases his gloom away and he leaps up and clicks the belt into its home. Cassie shuffles closer to him so they touch from hips to toes. *In five revolutions, he'll hate this, but today, he loves it.*

She can't help it. Remy's cheeks and heart blush with admiration. She releases the back seat and hops in. Cub, with his low hanging chin, slowly approaches from behind.

From her middle seat, Remy attempts to build up the confidence, or break down her insecurity, to imitate Cassie's excitement for her own brother. Remy watches herself in Cub's mirrored sunglasses. She cannot even believe the smile on her face. It looks like it was drawn by a Parkinson's hand.

Almost in, Cub looks up at her and asks, "What?"

Caught in her thought's trap, Remy's face pinks with embarrassment. "Nothing. Just waiting. Ready?"

Cub didn't believe her. *Paranoia is often accurate.* He concedes after attempting to translate her facial expressions. Flipping the glasses onto his forehead, he closes the door. She knows she watched strike three.

A brown finger taps Cub from behind. He turns. Sydney leans back in his seat, then points out the window asking Cub, "What is that tall guy's name?"

"Which tall guy?"

"Our driver."

As if realizing he'd neglected the introductions, Cub smirks, "*Indian* Steve."

Remy hammer-fists her brother's thigh. "Don't call him—"

The Indian approaches. A sharp smell of freshly burned menthol accompanies Steve's figure as he enters. The last door claps shut.

"Thank you for stopping, Indian Steve."

Steve looks in the rearview mirror.

"Yeah. Thanks, Indian Steve," Cassie chimes.

Remy has never seen a red man blush. *He wears his heritage like a sore spot—a nose zit.* He looks across at her and Cub. *We effortlessly embarrassed him.* Both shrug.

Dust puffs from under the rear tires and they are moving.

FROM ORDINARY PEOPLE TO THEIR OFFSPRING'S HERD WITHOUT A PHONE BOOTH

Her thrumming engine serenades children's yawns as Lucy returns toward the state's spinal column. The setting sun draws out the blue industrial's shadow only to be blanched by her headlights.

A frontage road runs parallel to its parent. This one is lined with vehicular carcasses on both sides. Headlights bounce off their bellies like shiny dead fish surrounding a poisoned river.

Colors dull as tall, slender silhouettes prance among the gray as if startled by synthetic photons. Nearby, a controlled fire spats orange foundation on palms and faces of its worshippers.

Steve allows Lucy to roll to a stop just short of the frontage's northbound left turn. Exhaust catches up and moves by like passing black clouds.

Inside is silent. Like conjoined twins, the little ones in back lean sleeping heads against one another. Their mouths loosely hang.

A very tall man with a receding hairline walks into Lucy's high beams from the adjacent field. His untoned body is draped in an oversized shirt containing cartoon campers roasting marshmallows with the caption: *Life is Good*. Shielding his eyes, he approaches. Another converges from the other side. This one is also losing his closely cropped hair. He is much shorter and heavier. His oversized dad-shirt reads: *Raskol*.

Exhaust haze washes over them. Both posture toward Lucy with open palms as if she was a mailman with their welfare check.

Lucy restlessly idles. Her gas gauge quivers under three-quarters. Steve kills the lights and swings his stead in the other direction. The dads give chase, but quickly break stride in a quagmire of sedentarism, breathing heavy and clutching their knees in a tripod stance.

Lucy's running lights close in the ditch, a long run from her aggressors. Keys click. Steve's large hand mutes their chimes. *She is meant to appear thirsty and abandoned to discourage passersby*—a Michigan possum.

Cub and Remy clear spots in the back of Lucy's bed to sleep. It passes for comfort, but not by much.

Steve chooses to lay across the front bench seats. His farmer's frame doesn't quite fit and needs to bend at the knee. Cassie and Sydney claim the backseat.

After seven-hundred and something, Remy gives up counting sheep in favor of watching stars twinkle. There seems to be an added richness in the blackness of space she has never taken time to appreciate. It is surprisingly easy to pick out dimmer stars, smears of them, in the spaces between the brilliant ones. The longer she keeps her eyes open, the more they pop from their hiding spots. She blinks. Some recede.

Rest doesn't come easily in a confetti of insects. Everyone closes their eyes, but no one sleeps well, and everyone thinks they're the only one.

Lucy expels a sequence of hissing sounds like a final, relaxing sigh before relinquishing to the Sandman.

FATE AND BLOOD DRY THE SAME

Cub pulls at areas of moist skin. He rubs the dirt and oils into little balls and brings them beneath his nostrils. The fragrance pleases him, but he recognizes others would describe it as disgusting.

Folding hands behind his head, Cub stretches on his back. A light, night breeze brings whispers through grooves in Lucy's curves.

Restless minds seldom tranquilize. Cub replays his confrontation with the matador. *He thought I was weak. He sized me up and thought he was stronger and smarter.* Cub visualizes his taunting expression, his dark facial features, his downcast eyebrows. *How dare he challenge me.* In the replay, fists and knees connect with Matador in a fit of revolting laughter. Cub's forearms tense as he pictures the moving pictures. *Next time, I mean, I'm not going to hold back. I'm stronger than they give me credit for—than anyone does.*

His teeth are clenched. His eyes are open, staring up, but not seeing. He is watching something that never happened. *I should have pushed dirt into his mouth for defying me—to teach him respect.* Cub listens to his own narration: *I'm the wrong one to pick on and he never knew it. I'm not going to let people push me around. My ideas are important, most important!*

The bullied writhe in fantasy, wishing they had sprung earlier. Clever comebacks arrive tardy. Anger loves to bask in hate's wake and refuses to listen to rationality. Hot, bright fuels ignite into bursting orange flames of remorse, only dissected by tools of leverage.

Soft whimpering interrupts Cub's internal monologue. His sister's body quivers as if cold, but not—at least on the outside. It pauses, then seems to pinch gutturally inward.

"Come on, what's wrong?" he asks Remy, already knowing what she's thinking. Immediately, he despises the syllables for making him look stupid.

"Hey, hey, hey," he says in a hushing tone. He wraps an arm behind her neck. She leans into his armpit. When she rolls toward him, moonlight reveals the eye rivers. Her cries become more audible as if embracing her audience.

While she has always been the kinder, more thoughtful of the two, she was also strong and independent in Cub's opinion. Witnessing her wilting feels strangely out of place. The weight of emotions overcrowds him.

"They're gone," she manages through pockets of whines. Her mouth is open and wet. Moisture penetrates his shirt, sticking to the skin. "And I..." she chokes as a breath and sobbing and words emerge through a pinch point. "Can't get Mom's image out of my head. The last one." *The violence. The shades of red. The life and then not.* Tonight's sleep chamber is full of blanks and all that remains is a funeral hug with a consoling, gentle, back-tap.

A hiss, like cool tears falling on a hot frying pan, stretches the open air as Lucy expels once more.

Her hair carries oils. In the awkward position, Cub fakes interest in watching tiny stars wink. His arm is falling asleep, but the rest of his body is not. *When will she stop? Does sadness defy death or alleviate grieving?* If it does, he doesn't want to get caught finding out.

"Everything's going to be okay," he lies to her earlobe. A photogenic smile flashes and fizzles like firecracker duds.

Her hand casually brushes below his equator on its path to his further hemisphere. The bottom ridge of his shirt flips up, exposing skin to the cool night's air. She squeezes his rib cage in a hot hug before weeping, again. Faint chemicals in girls' tears annoy boys.

Cub stretches his neck, tilting his head back. His Adam's apple jumps with each swallow. His mind hungers to unpack the rotation's events but feels the obligation to pacify his sibling.

Lies are paint and white rarely covers what's underneath.

"I'll be right back." Cub shrimps away from Remy's grip. She lifts her head like a feline awakened by creaky steps, only to bury it once again.

Lucy bounces on her rear suspension when Cub's feet clomp the plucked field. There isn't and hasn't been a tree around here since a man dreamed of feeding his family with long summer labor.

What's the difference? Night will obscure his toilet parts and walking around will calm him.

Silence always tails a symphony and fireworks. Then, an applause erupts with cheers and whistles. If it's really good, standing feet.

Cub pauses, sphincters relax, sensing danger has passed. Midstream, he scratches the back of his passively itchy arm. Upon closer inspection, fingernails bring clotted blood to his attention in the blue lunar light.

Thin, long lacerations pinstripe his right elbow as if he's crossed barbed wire. He picks and rubs the sticky, darkened material. A dull, pushing pain like long-boned, growth spurts hum over the wound. He massages the area with his palm. He can hear skin friction above the meddling night creatures. It feels good to bend, but growth pains return when he stretches it out.

On his backtrack to Lucy, Cub rubs the length of his arms to scare away gooseflesh that the crisp night left behind.

TRANSLATING THERAPY

Spreading his knees apart for a better view, Steve watches the young man return through ice chip eyes. *We both sleep light, perhaps one of us shouldn't at all,* the old man contemplates. *Things may be this way a while. Then again, collapsing economies have happened before. Insulating borders with water and loaded weapons have assured we don't witness suffering or allow it to infiltrate our happy little lives.*

Steve fills his lungs. His barreled abdomen expands to accommodate.

What fixed it before? What events took place to reset society—reset currencies—reset value? Nothing brings a fractured nation together like team mentality, a structured focus, but, most importantly, a common foe. This has happened before, and man has persevered and survived to hand-pick genetics. Maybe this will usher in a new wave of government and governing once things recover. Shed skin leaves its shedder nimbler, more adaptive, and more modern than ever before.

This may be a good thing, right? Why can't it be? Through struggle comes rebirth. Fire maple tree.

The hardiest will flourish, leaving a wake of weak corpses toward a cleansed dynasty. The past to be forgiven until it's forgotten under sediment. This could be great.

A small, new smile cracks a big, old face and Steve closes his ice chips.

IN SICKNESS AND IN WEALTH

Tonight, Cub watches the lone moon glide. There come moments when taught beliefs mature into fallacy. *Mom and Dad aren't superheroes with all the right answers. They are, and always were, just bigger versions of us with more confident answers—politicians "acting" on behalf of their constituents.*

Stewing in a cooling vat of his own thoughts without ink and paper to prove his madness, Cub drifts further with growing pains in his holster.

Time must have passed. He emerges from sleep to Steve's growling bark as a man scavenges Lucy's bed beside them.

Peril waterboards sleep and content, leaving puddles of dark eye circles.

With Steve's door open, a rear light above Cub and Remy's head illuminates the intruder. "Please. I'm hungry," pleads words from a mouth that tries its best not to whine. *He is familiar. This is the man from before. His shirt still reads: Life is Good.* The collar is still stretched.

"My family's stomachs hurt with hunger," he begs.

Everyone in Lucy is awake. Cub sits up, furrows his mouth as if to say: *Leave us alone—not my problem*. He kicks at the exploring arms of Mr. Goodlife. The arms reach toward the luggage, avoiding kicks as if the goods are tepid to the touch.

With him focusing on feet, Steve easily captures Mr. Goodlife from behind. His belly sticks out like an apprehended felon. Steve throws Mr. Goodlife to the ground a few paces back.

"Just go, Steve," Cub yells, "I've got him." No sooner does the man hit the ground before he pops back up. A giddiness sweeps through Cub.

Turning toward the truck, Mr. Goodlife leaps onto Steve as if to receive a piggyback ride. There is an obvious size and physical discrepancy between the two. Steve, although old enough to be Mr. Goodlife's parent, stands both taller and more fit than the shorter, chubby-armed man.

Steve fights the wrists that wrap around his neck like a scarf. Cub vaults out. The ground is closer than he thought and his hip twinges. From behind, Cub pulls at Mr. Goodlife's face. It is wet. Tears, perhaps, maybe sweat. The man stinks the smell of yeasty, folded skin.

Despite the Mr. Goodlife-backpack, Steve is still able to lumber toward his open door. He steals a glance in the backseat. Cub peers in. Both faces are scared in the lit cabin. Steve shakes his head with regret.

Cub twists Mr. Goodlife's face backward in torticollis. A finger finds an accidental tongue and that tongue's friends, the teeth, make an impression. Cub howls. Jaws tighten. Cub pulls. Then harder. The hand may very well give its digit up for adoption. The hand's friend, the fist, boxes the biter's ear. Repeatedly. Repeatedly. Jaws tense. Cub finds a socket. He pushes Mr. Goodlife's eyeball inward. Like a popped lock, the jaws release in tandem with its owner's scream.

Two chubby legs, crisscrossed at the feet, start slipping. Mr.

Goodlife's breath becomes gasping huffs. "I saw what you have! Please, share with my starving family!" Every beg should end in: *God bless*. He pants. "Just a little, please?"

Mr. Goodlife clings to Steve's shoulders, pulling them back. Steve narrowly loses his balance backward, before gripping the driver's side door.

"Please!" the chubby man pleads.

Cub punches the biter's flank where he thinks the kidneys reside. Arms drop to hug Steve's waist. Shots thump in the kidneys' neighborhood. The first few don't seem to faze him. The next few do. He crumples into a pile of gluttony, clinging now to Steve's feet like an infant. Wailing and trying to shield some of Cub's blows, Mr. Goodlife curls.

The key, already dangling in the ignition, turns with aid from an old hand.

"Please. No. Don't leave me."

Headlights *splish* and *splash* as Lucy wobbles around in the ditch. Mr. Goodlife's slumping pity party tucks under a blanket of taillights and distance.

"You okay, brother?" Cub doesn't realize he isn't until Remy rests a caring hand on his shoulder. Lucy's bed is hard and digs into his thinly padded hip.

Remy rubs smooth circles around Cub's back. He's leaning off the side, over the rear quarter panel, as if it was a toilet after sour sushi. Road noise leaves conversation to brief yells. Remy switches from palm rub to light fingernails.

I'D SEARCH FOR HEAVEN WITH A METAL DETECTOR IF GOD HAD BRACES

In Lucy's bed, Cub flexes his shoulder blades as if to shake away a bothersome insect. Remy recoils, momentarily waiting for him to turn around scowling—but he doesn't. Sunrise will bring a better time to speak. She wedges her small frame between their large bags. Her hands become a pillow, but her eyes don't close. She pictures purple and the vehicle gently bumps along.

CTHULHU'S FATHER

Steve doesn't like the idea of heading back to the highway but likes the other options worse. Trusting Lucy would handle the ride, completely bypassing the road system would be an alternative in this lawless state. Cool night air rushes through the open window, down his underarm gutter. The flapping white noise comes in waves. Steve watches the lit asphalt patterns go from blurry to clear and then back to blurry. *This doesn't feel like driving.* If an accident happened, he would scarcely recall details of the passing time as his mind chatters to itself about the situation for which he volunteered.

The kids are too short to spot in the rearview mirror without adjustments. Steve tilts it down. Exhaustion took them for a spell or else they are both good possums.

Predawn leaves a thin film of skin filth. The eastern horizon winks through the passenger window. Blueberry pie gives birth to apricot.

Steve uses limp arms to steer north on the highway's frontage road. Parked vehicles line either side, in some areas, double-parked like automotive plaque. Bubbles of condensation fog the windows' crust.

Activity is sparse at this hour. A fluffy, butterscotch dog bends his neck to the growing grass when it spots Lucy. Steve notices a dew-wetted snout and whiskers. He maintains eye contact after passing and notes how strange it is that animals seem to understand the functionality of eyes.

A lot of gas, too much, burned when they backtracked. The needle vibrates with the engine's purr, but hovers just above the half-tank mark.

Lucy slows to weave, hoping not to disturb the rest. Leaning out the window, he can see occupants stir as they pass. Some roll down windows. Others crack their door. They represent anchors to Steve's trip and he's already taking in water.

He nudges the rearview to see further back. His red gas tank rocks near Cub's feet. Moisture runs down the nozzle's black plastic seal. He may be forced to part with Lucy sooner than expected.

Remy pulls out her mobile phone. It turns on but she quickly flings it away. *The globe's network hibernates. Frozen communication has yet to thaw.*

TRAUMA'S APPETITE

At the morning's first pitstop, Cassie asks, "Are we running away, Remy?" Her brown eyes widen with concern, looking up for understanding. She scratches her hip while waiting for Remy to finish chewing a granola bar. "Cause, it feels like we are."

"It does? How so?" Remy asks back.

Cassie rubs her chin, looking down in careful thought, before readdressing Remy. "Cause it feels like we are doing something wrong—like we are not being nice." She briefly looks over at Cub, before leaning closer to Remy's ear, "with all the blood stuff."

"Oh, honey." She wraps an arm around Cassie and pulls her into a tender hug. *What is the best way to justify last night's violence to a small child? How does one impersonate an umbrella?* Cassie hugs back. Her body feels like fish bones. *We were only defending our stuff, but did things need to escalate?* Cassie slowly peels away to read Remy's body language. "You see," she swallows the last bit of granola debris, "we were trying—"

Sydney interrupts by leaping into Remy's hug fest. "I want one, too!" Remy lets out a short burst of air as he collides.

"How are you doing, Syd? Hungry?"

"Yeah!" he belts out with youthful excitement.

She grabs a trail bar, but before she unwraps it, he reaches both arms up toward it exclaiming, "I can do it!"

Remy and Cassie laugh. "Okay, I get it," Remy says handing him breakfast and ruffling his curly black hair. This interruption buys her time, but not a good answer. She'd have to explain. It is her responsibility to translate and articulate in kid's logic. Morality monitors the circus net below, without understanding it has no control over circus nets.

OUTSIDE, THE WIND COUGHS

He studies me like a fool's-gold-plated opportunity—the way a cat does a twitching tail sticking out of a mouse hole.

Scant paces away, but separated, the men sit in solitude. People gravitate to that which they aspire. A gentle heart satisfies the kids' appetite today.

Night-driving leaves bags under Steve's eyes that could smuggle drugs across stringent borders. Truth be told, no one slept with much depth, including him.

ATMOSPHERES DIGEST

Cassie and Sydney tumbling over Remy was a welcome distraction, but it did allow her to reconsider the ethics of abandonment. Worse yet, they left yesterday's beggars with new marks for their troubles.

Is this the new living? When will we go back to "normal?" The term carries a more ungrounded definition considering the recent events. A thousand compliments drown at the hands of one criticizing anchor.

She turns on her mobile phone. Her breath stays in a bit longer with hopeful expectation. *No signal.* Her shoulders deflate with heaviness.

"Did it work?" Cassie asks.

She shakes her head.

"Is something wrong?"

"Nope," Remy lies.

"Then why are you so sad?"

"I'm not," she lies again, straining her lips in a flash-awaiting grin. She grabs Cassie's ankles and drags her upside-down.

The girl squeals with laughter, holding her shirt to keep from exposing her big-girl parts.

Sydney jumps to his feet and pokes his sister's belly button yelling, "Placenta! Placenta!" Steve and Cub turn from their meals.

THE PRINCE AND THE SALAMANDER

Putting distance between them and the city has thinned the line of exhausted vehicles along the interstate. Occasionally, a stray will peek over the vanishing point and grow toward them. Most often, spotting Lucy, the occupants emerge from their vehicle or the local foliage.

Remy fights the urge to meet their pleading. She avoids confrontation the same way she did homeless beggars displaying cardboard signs. God blesses guilt dispensed in large pills.

Cassie and Sydney wave. *There's no way they understand what's happening,* Remy thinks. *I'm barely keeping up.*

Beggars shrink, kick dust, and then blend away in the rearview mirror.

"Are we almost there?" Cassie watches the backs of their heads for a response.

Steve briefly removes his eyes from the dashing white lines, attempting to meet Remy's without rotating his head. She notices. He returns to the dashing lines.

Less elegantly, Cub nudges Remy as if to encourage his sister. She turns around in her middle seat the way eggs spin in a carton. She rests her pointed chin on the headrest. Both kids address her with attention, looking for the right answer that she doesn't have.

She feels herself channeling her mom. She imagines the way her mom used to communicate with her—taking big, complex adult-problems and breaking them down into bite-sized kid pieces.

"Have you ever heard the story about the prince and the sala-mander?" she asks, emulating her mom.

"Yes. I'm not a little, *little* kid," Cassie says.

"I haven't!" Sydney exclaims.

"Okay, Cassie," Remy says, "you tell him."

"It's about this prince and he has a salamander... or he found a salamander and then these bad guys..." she struggles. "You just say it, Remy," she yields.

Sydney darts between his sister and Remy. Raising his hands to the vehicle's ceiling, he begs, "Somebody, just tell me!"

Cassie's attitude softens. Remy permits a smile and begins:

There once was a prince who was exceedingly wealthy. He had exotic furs crafted into clothing with the rarest blue and purple dyes, perilously gathered for his pleasure from places he could never pronounce by servants with names he would never bother to remember. He had giant chests spilling over with wonderful toys, but he wasn't happy. Wind through the chamber window was his only friend. He walked over. Below, in the courtyard, he watched happy subjects laughing and playing together while they worked, yet they had nothing compared to him. He contemplated, "What makes them so gleeful?"

One morning, the king chartered a boat ride for his mopey prince. Reluctantly, the prince obliged. All afternoon, the crew of servants paddled at sea until they came upon a giant rock, all by itself, with only water around it—as far as the eye could see.

The prince shouted, "What's that?" They rowed toward the rock and sitting on the very top was a little lizard.

A crewman whipped out a knife and explained that it was a magic salamander! "Prince, if you cut off its toes, they will magically grow back!"

The once mopey prince was now excited and directed them to get closer. He hopped off the boat and went to scoop up the salamander. When he did, it wiggled out of reach. The prince scratched his head and knelt to grab it again, but again, it wriggled out of reach.

He instructed the crew to wait while he pursued the salamander. Up and over the giant rock he went until he was out of the boat's sight.

At last, he captured it. It was much slipperier than he expected. When he looked up from his new pet, he noticed a beautiful mermaid watching him. Shocked by the female's attention, he slipped the salamander into his pocket and cautiously approached. She laughed and splashed with him. She listened to him. They enjoyed each other's company until, from behind the giant rock, a crewman yelled, "It's getting late, fair prince. We must go home!"

Saddened, he waved. She waved. He promised to return soon. She watched him disappear behind the giant rock.

On the ride home, he patted his slimy salamander, but all he could think about was the mermaid.

The next morning, he awoke, bright and early. Dressed in his best clothing and jewelry, he paddled out to the giant rock, but she wasn't there. He decided to leave his royal clothing and jewels there, so she knew he would come back, then he paddled home.

That night, he talked to his salamander. Remembering his crewman's tale, he took a knife and sliced off the salamander's toe.

The following morning, he woke up early and paddled out to the giant rock. This time, he brought his two giant chests filled with toys. When he arrived, the clothes and jewelry were gone and so was the mermaid. To let her know he'd come back, he left the toy-filled chests. Then he paddled home.

That night, he cried to his salamander and cut off another toe.

The next morning, he looked around his chamber. There were no pretty clothes, no beautiful jewelry, and no toys—just his slimy salamander and the crown his father told him never to wear outside the kingdom.

Betraying his father's advice, the prince paddled out to the rock wearing his crown. When he arrived, there were no clothes, no jewelry, no chest with toys, and no mermaid. He decided to leave his crown on the rock, so she'd know he was coming back.

That night at dinner, the king asked why he wasn't wearing his crown. Petting the salamander, the prince hung his head. "For what is a prince without a crown, but an ordinary boy?" the king bellowed and kicked the prince out of the kingdom.

Having nowhere to go, the prince paddled back out to the giant rock with his salamander and they slept under the moonlight.

Morning came, and he was awoken to weeping. Behold! It was the mermaid, his mermaid! She was surrounded by his toy chests and she was wearing his clothes and his jewelry and his crown—but she was crying.

He approached and asked why she was so sad. Drying her eyes, she saw the salamander. She held hands over her heart and then reached for it.

The prince pulled back saying, "You have my toys. You have my clothes. You have my jewels. You have my crown! This is all I have left, and it is mine!"

The mermaid, among all the prince's treasures, wept.

With guilt, the prince looked down at his salamander and noticed that the toes grew back!

He approached the mermaid, offering her the salamander, and they laughed and played together happily ever after.

"So, how old was the prince?" Sydney asks

"I don't know, not that old—" Remy hesitates.

"My age?"

"Well," she shrugs, "I guess he could be your age—"

"Wait, am I the salamander in that story or the prince?" Sydney prods.

"I thought there were some bad guys in that story..." Cassie says.

"Actually, the mermaid sounds more like an ex-wife than a fish," Steve grins.

Remy shakes her head, burying it in the seat with defeat. *Parenting takes practice.*

NEVER TWO ALPHAS

Above, the sun radiantly climbs. Below, the quiet vehicle cabin behaves like a dog pound forcing animals to play together. "Let me drive." Cub has been monitoring Steve's wilting attention. *He is seeing the glass world with eyes half-empty.*

Slumped over the wheel, hands dangling in front of the eco-air conditioning vent, Steve lifts his chin to nod. A dark red spot marks where it had been resting too long.

"Besides," Cub adds, "I have to visit a man about a horse."

The stop stays brief, but long enough for Steve to empty the last drop of fossilized fuel from his plastic red gas can. The kids watch from behind tinted sliding glass. The highway is officially orphaned. Steve leaves the can on the rear bumper's narrow ledge and hops in the passenger side. Remy sits between the little ones in back.

Midday passes. The blue digital clock's colon blinks. Lucy's key turns. Her engine coughs to life like an exhumed body. Cub flinches when the wipers squawk against the dry windshield.

"That's for the wipers," Steve points.

Unappreciative of the obvious commentary, Cub returns a flattened affect. Gears shift and pink cheeks fade.

Through the rearview, two kids with big heads perched on fragile necks lean against Remy. Surely to grow a kink, hers is precariously cranked back without a headrest.

Lucy groans with acceleration and the red gas can falls to its grave.

Cub flaps a wing out his window. The road-wind cools his forearm numb. He exhales. The outside waits. Something about this situation won't allow him to relax. *Is it the reluctant company? The unfamiliar vehicle? The decimation of technology and its impending uncertainty? Familial pillars tumbling into marble rubble? I am the magnet among iron filings.*

Traveling north, the cities get smaller and the distance between stretches like unfamiliar relatives. Across the bench seat, Cub notes his slumped copilot. His imposing hands have soaked in a lifetime of physical labor—fingers, swollen as a farmer, and hide tanned with hints of red. He's tall and slender, concealing only traces of metabolized beer. *He tucks in his tee shirt like a gentleman.*

Cub's eyes move upward to study the man's face. Deep smilelines frame his cracked mouth. Inside, tar and coffee left teethgraffiti.

Between brief glances at the empty asphalt road, Cub leans closer to his neighbor. Closer. Yellow dashed lines. Closer. White bordered shoulders. Closer.

"You asking for trouble?"

The comment spooks Cub—*caught staring.*

"I said, you asking for trouble," Steve repeats in a tone expecting a response.

Cub shrinks and shakes his head. "I was just..." There was no alibi—a cookie grabbing hand can only beg forgiveness. "...being annoying."

Cub tries his best not to balk. He feels Steve's stare. If it were the sun, one hemisphere would be white, the other, red. Straining, his lids flap. Stealing a peek through a shifting corner pocket, he notices Steve has lost interest and now surveys out the passenger pane. A cold horror of Dad shoots through his heart. Cub's shoulders slump as tension releases.

Cub turns, mouth primed to speak. Steve doesn't flinch. Blankets wrap the man's upper body, tucked close under the chin, like Christmas presents wrapped by a child. Cub's words never leave home. He re-glues to the road.

Growing up, Cub's classmates regarded him as dangerous, unpredictable. His collection of detentions and suspensions rivaled nearly everyone. Yet, he was an enigma. Grade-school teachers showered him with accommodations, marks far closer to the front of the alphabet than the rear. He kept them tucked away in spider-filled closets, away from schoolmates' memories, for it may tarnish his façade.

Somehow, they, the classmates he spent time tap dancing for, would always be surprised when he accompanied them to the next grade. He had constructed an image to obscure nature's flow. A small-scale dam. In doing, the snake's scales grew to like him more than a poindexter's protected pocket. The creeping Charlie persona out-weeded healthy, sprouting greens. Some may say the fingertip blood has already dried on Lucifer's contract.

Cub quickly, almost with mounting anger, boils a stare at Steve. His mouth tightens into a shorter line. Steve finally blinks and confronts his junior.

For a moment, Cub almost breaks. Held breaths swell with underwater pressure. Surely, Steve caught him bend.

"Why help us?" Cub asks through grinding molars. He holds the glare until Lucy's tires hop on the rumble track outside the bold, white lines.

Startled, Cub pulls the wheel to swerve back into his lane.

CONCENTRIC TRIANGLES

Steve speaks. "Son, you see life–"

"I'm not your son," Cub blurts.

Steve sharply raises a finger to Cub's lips. His own, zipped tight as a pulled purse string.

"Don't interrupt," he commands with an unbroken scowl and wide eyes, compared to their usual half-opened calm. He continues. "You see life as a retail store. Customers enter, browse, and then plunk down money for products they think they'll enjoy."

Steve pauses to roll up his window. Cub stares out the windshield like a scolded child.

Shielding with a cupped hand, he lights a new cigarette. Blue smoke coughs. Steve cracks his window to allow the fumes their escape.

"At some point," he says out the side of his mouth, "one realizes this is an immature way to approach relationships." Exhaust exits his lips in a narrow stream. "At some point, it is important to do things with the expectation of naught." He plucks the white stick in parallel fingers. "Only then, comes satisfaction and a life teeming with far less disappointment." He pregnantly pauses as if in quiet reflection. "Took me 'til my kids were born before I figured that one out." He taps ashes over the window's lip. "Another's joy doesn't have to occur at the expense of one's own." Raising his eyebrows, Steve leans toward Cub, "You'd be wise to remember that."

Steve addresses him directly, expecting some internalization. Cub maintains a frozen glare out the windshield as one does after a long night of alcohol, chasing one's spirit away. Steve observes crease marks where Cub grips the steering wheel. *He is tense— unwilling and uncomfortable.*

Fanning a dismissive hand toward the lad, Steve thinks, *It's a lost cause. He's a lost cause.* He returns to his cigarette. The extending ash column glows orange into pepper. Without raising his voice, Steve rolls up the window after silently discarding his butt.

HAWAIIAN PIZZA, HOLD THE EVERYTHING

Both men resemble sulking boys, each doing their best to show the other they are ignoring.

In back, Remy watches Cassie and Sydney play on her lap. Each place their hands, palms up, on her thighs. They take turns trying to slap one another's hand. If one of them misses, Remy gathers, the swatter loses. Sydney does more losing to his big sister's reflexes.

Cassie swats at Syd's hand, but this time, he quickly pulls his palm away. Sydney quietly covers his mouth with both hands, disguising a laugh. Cassie frowns. Remy winces to the sting of the open-clapped hand. Cassie's giggle can't hide any longer.

"How about a different game?" Remy asks, playfully clinking their heads together over her lap. This teases a laugh from each as they squirm away.

"No," Sydney cries before realizing it came out louder than he expected. "No," he whispers, holding an index finger. He leans over, "I win." He gestures to his sister and flexes his muscles.

Cassie shakes her head. "Again?"

"No."

"Again," she nips, pointing down at Remy's lap.

Sydney crosses his arms and exaggeratingly shakes his head.

"Again," she insists in her best big-kid impression, posturing up straight.

MANY WILL COME, DONNING THORNED CROWNS

Red and blue flash behind them. A siren whoops. Cub whirls to his copilot. *Sure. Now Cub seeks my advice,* Steve thinks.

The siren whoops a second time. Almost out of reflex, Cub heeds, easing Lucy onto the road's shoulder. No one in the vehicle objects, but everyone in the vehicle is frightened.

Strange lines of order are still obliged despite a collapse of the ruling body to enforce them. The squad-vehicle sits parked on the roadside directly behind Lucy. Soft, black smoke stutters from her tailpipe.

Remy turns to the sound of two doors clapping shut, almost in unison. The purring engine seems to be muted in anxiety.

Through the rearview, Cub tracks the approaching uniformed man. Gravel slides under black, imitated-leather shoes. Mirrored aviator sunglasses hide motives. The man's hair is almost clean shaven across his temples with gel glossing his slightly longer black military cut. A full, dark, bushy mustache rounds out the notable features.

Framing his fatherly physique, broad shoulders wave like an ape strutting through its territory. He casually lifts the tarp, exposing Lucy's bed.

Cub pays less attention to the gentleman approaching Steve's passenger side. That man seems to mimic his superior's actions in both look and swagger, right down to the aviators and admittedly thinner mustache. *He trails him by at least a decade.* A white patch dots his right temple in a field of otherwise slightly longer, brown hair.

The superior stops at Cub's up-rolled window. He looks off in either direction as if to cross traffic. He looks anywhere except at his subject as if avoiding eye contact with a movie camera. A metal badge, Cub fails to recognize as an officer, winks sunlight on his upper-left chest. Two pinstripes of polished silver buttons run in tandem down his torso with militaristic prestige. His subordinate reaches the front passenger door. The man observes his superior as if awaiting orders.

Cub steals a glance at Steve and notes him notch the door's

lock before gripping the door handle. Cub follows suit. When he turns back, the superior is peering inside, taking role of the vehicle's occupants. *We are butterflies pinned between the fingers of a curious child.*

Polarized aviator sunglasses pan the inside. A grin briefly parts one side of his lips—then closes. After an excruciatingly long moment, he shouts, "No ports, Charlie!" Three sharp knocks rap the window, expecting the pinned butterflies to acquiesce.

Steve forfeits a nod. Cub rolls the window down enough for a stuck-up nose to poke through.

The superior straightens his posture and pauses before asking, "You folks have a destination?" The man has a drawn accent.

"Yes," Cub poorly lies.

Superior clears his throat, avoiding the movie camera. He continues, "'Tis so, huh? Where?"

That's when Cub's brain stops working. Stunted growth, more in the moment than thinking after the moment's funeral. He defends, "We didn't do anything wrong. Now, would you–"

"Wait. What didn't you do?" Superior asks. "*I* never accused you of anything." He lays arms on top of Lucy and leans toward the window's opening. "We will not allow you to leave." Cub's mouth drops open, stopped in its tracks. "We have all done things wrong. You see, perfection writes fairy tales without smells and unresolved conflict. Fortunately, for you," Superior hikes up his belt and smooths down his fitted, black dress shirt, "we have your solution."

Remy uncomfortably shuffles the way a lab rat does as giant fingers unlatch its cage and reach in. Superior sharply bends over to monitor her as if she's attempting sudden defiance. She lifts her hands in the air as if at gunpoint's request.

"We don't have a problem," Cub nervously says. Confidence lost its automobile keys.

"You *do* have a problem." Superior straightens his back. "We *all* have a problem. Don't you understand what's happening to you? To us?"

Superior steps back, rubbing his chin and studying Cub as if carefully balancing a pound of flesh on Roman scales. Cub's security scatters under scrutiny like a startled kitten. Superior enjoys this soft waterboarding. The subordinate makes mental notes, studying Superior studying the kitten.

At last, satisfied, he concludes, "I'm willing to take a chance on you—all of you, rather." He clasps both hands behind. "You see," scuffing his feet for dramatic effect, "there are changes taking place. Some, you may be aware of, others, you undoubtedly are not."

Cub recognizes a confidence in the man before him. *He dresses and speaks in syllables of success. He articulates the way teachers do toward pupils. He pays attention, undividedly.*

"The world is changing, my friends. Adapting. Evolving. Do you honestly believe we are the first flea to be swatted by a deer's floppy ear? Does a snake's skin really believe, if shed, it will never grow back, and certainly not better than before?" Superior stands at militaristic attention, minus the salute. Cub swallows hard. Unconsciously, or maybe subconsciously, he nods in agreement.

"Lava coats villagers that don't move. Those who chose to live in danger without an exit strategy, well, they'll receive an unhappily ever after. Those unable to adapt to change will be doomed to plead at unmerciful feet." He raises an eyebrow over the aviator sunglasses.

"Then, the good news." A wispy breeze waves through the roadside's undisturbed grass. "Occasionally, and I do mean, occasionally, mercy touches those who never asked. I'm prepared to offer you hope among a growing litter of hopelessness. I'm prepared to offer you food among a symphony of growling stomachs. I'm prepared to offer answers to questions tangled on puzzled tongues. I'm prepared to offer salvation among amassing graves. I'm prepared to offer a fourth act, instead of a closing curtain. Join me and my friend here," he points toward his subordinate, "as we have been preparing for this for a long time."

Superior announces, "Call me Rex. And over there," he points, "my partner's name is Charlie." Rex leans toward the window's crack. Motioning up the road, "We have a re-appropriated silo that I personally renovated for this exact event. It's packed with plenty of food, two revolutions, in fact. And, an endless supply of renewable water and energy."

Rex straightens, this time extending a hand toward the window—waiting to be shook. "Join us."

In the vehicle, Steve reaches for Cub's arm, but it evades. Separated by the pane of glass, Rex's hand stalls in suspended motion. Cub is hypnotized. A figurehead, a role model, a confident leader, a reflection he wishes came back in the mirror. Snapping fingers are unlikely to break the spell.

SUNK BOBBER

He couldn't see it, but Steve imagines Cub's mouth hanging in awe with a silver drool-strand pouring out.

Steve has been around enough good things that have turned out not to be true. This may or may not be one of those, but it certainly carried a similar fragrance.

Rex cracks a smile that quickly fades back into a straight line. "Good. Follow me. It is not far."

Rex taps on the hood with a flat palm, "You made the right decision," he calls out while walking back to his squad vehicle. Charlie taps, too, just beats behind.

MARCHING TO THE BEAT OF AN OIL DRUM

Not far yawns into *further-than-expected*. Cub fixates on the tail-lights ahead. He counts the following distance: *one, two, three* heartbeats. Two is the minimum.

It irritates Cub to hear Steve say, "Be careful. Don't let your stuff outta' your sight." The fact that Remy agrees, only annoys him further.

With all windows up in a radioless Lucy, the gravel road noises sound like grape-nuts being divided by molars. Behind the wheel and tracking Rex's squad, Cub replays the conversation—the questionable motives, the banter, the promises. Second guesses scrape the insides of their coffin. Cub struggles to deny it: *Something about this feels like a trap—suffocating. We, the cattle, are led toward a white barn with red flooring. Many walk in, but none walk out. It must be crowded.*

Cub clicks off the autopilot. He refuses to make eye contact with Steve, afraid to welcome judgement or criticism. Offspring proudly defy their parents' best advice; the kernel of doubt lives in a colorless pit beneath motionless vocal cords. Some call it: intuition. Others call it: gut feelings. Defying it usually leaves one with a learned lesson and a cheekful of unswallowed pride.

Remy clears her throat. She begins to speak, but then bites her taste buds.

Steve breaks the silence. "I don't trust them." Ahead, the rear license plate rattles on two screws instead of four. "He wants something."

"It should be fine," Cub objects.

Steve lobbies to Remy, "You see, *should* leaves *him*," pointing to Cub, "responsible for *us*."

Cub erupts. "Steve, would you stop questioning me—my decisions?" He glares at Steve. "I don't see *you* offering up any answers! I mean, where were we even going and who were we running from?" He catches a quick glance at the road to straighten their course and then returns to Steve. "We can't just drive around here forever. Look, we'll go there for a little while—find out what they know. If we don't like it—we'll leave. Simple as that—promise."

"He wants ours to become his." Steve's arms cross as if he's lost in an ego-skirmish.

Steve may be right, but Cub will never admit it.

Each kid squeezes Remy's hand while watching harvested fields blur away. She kisses Cassie's head before realizing she may have broken a boundary.

AIRTIGHT SILO LINED IN LEAD

Lucy's left blinker rapidly flickers—broken relay switch. The squad's front wheels slowly ease down onto neither a road nor driveway, but a strip of grass separating two expansive, plucked crop beds. The grass between has matted tracks indicating vehicular traffic. The marks are subtle, and Cub wouldn't have thought it a path to anywhere.

Second guesses quarrel with ego inside Cub's head like neighboring sparrows. *This could be the fork in my life's road that defines all the other forks in all my other roads. Ahead, the highway is wide open. I could hammer the accelerator and roll the dice without being tied to these... officers.* Opportunity opens her loveless arms. *Besides, isn't all this secret bunker stuff overkill? The government wouldn't allow its country to free-fall for long, would it?*

Threats of government shutdowns had become more frequent. They never lasted more than a few news cycles and, even then, politicians, Cub was told, were still paid. Leverage at someone else's throat. Public workers and beneficiaries still received paychecks. Without a reporter, he would never have noticed.

Steve nervously taps his fingers.

The lead window rolls down. "This way." Rex points down the matted path that seems to extend to infinity's horizon. "Not far." He drops his hand and slaps the door. The tires ease into the matted grooves and move through. The window rolls up.

Out of autopilot, his foot thumbs the parking brake. Cub hesitates. His gut hesitates. His heart speeds.

Just ahead, the squad stops, watching, noting hesitation. The front window comes down, again.

Cub closes his eyes, takes a deep nose-breath, holds, then opens and releases.

Lucy obediently eases off the road. The squad's window rolls up. Smeared in Cub's periphery, he sees Steve shake his head with disappointment.

Distance passes underneath, leaving the road behind out of eyeshot. Squealing brakes announce their arrival, halting in front of a towering, metallic silo saddled on each side by steel-rung ladders that end at the top with a hatch. The body is lined with ruffled circumferential waves, like metal potato chips. A white dome, with a black painted triangle, caps the silver silo. A rooster weathervane spins in the breeze at its peak.

Everyone would agree with no one: *there is something impending about the structure—humbling.* A child lives in their parents' shadow and its mercy. It is the way a leg amputee sees his new wheelchair after white surgical bandages are pulled from his eyes for the first time—the sentence of home.

Rows of greenhouses stretch outward from the silo on both sides like military barracks. Steve looks back at the long-vanished road.

Rex and Charlie are already standing in front of Lucy before Cub and Steve exit. Aviators track Remy and the kids as they gather their gear from the back. Steve and Cub bend their seats forward to allow them out.

Clasping hands behind their back, the aviators watch with restrained impatience and passive pressure. Remy feels it, the discomfort of an automobile salesman watching her inspect his wares—her every move is being analyzed. If Cassie and Sydney were dogs, they'd have downturned ears trying to avoid punishment they've learned to avoid.

Cub stretches out of nervousness, not because he must. Steve stares back at Rex. His old muscles could use a stretch but won't offer satisfaction to his new leash.

Rex watches. He slowly turns to Charlie and briefly nods before returning his attention to the newcomers. Unclasping and now holding them out, palms up, like a preacher offering his congregation forgiveness hors d'oeuvres, Rex announces, "Welcome... to Delta."

CHAPTER 16

DELTA

Each foot-echo rings like a telephone-can swirling in circular fashion, disguising sound's third dimension. With Charlie leading the descent, the newcomers follow in chronological procession. Rex protects the rear, last in line.

The smell is immediate and musty—as if clove leaves floating atop sweat cultivated from eleven armpits filled a fluid potpourri dish. Rex explains the well outside and how to use it. He gets the feeling his new guests aren't paying attention—the way patients stare after receiving an unexpected cancer diagnosis.

A building hum resonates, scrambling in circles up the silo's ribcage and ending with a cymbalist's crash of the hatchway door. Rex spins the steering wheel which reminds Cub of an airtight lock he's seen in submarine footage. Its padlock hops until entropy loses interest.

Amidst the descent, Remy gets a feeling that she is passing beneath ground level. The air cools and a new odor mingles. This one, like freshly hose-watered soil. She imagines what it would be like if Delta's walls were invisible. *Worms burrowing holes, leaving behind crumbling caves of fertilizer. Finger-sized larvae with their shiny-black segmented bodies fleeing the sun like it was a bomb threat. White roots seeking flavor in shredded silk strands. The beings below forfeit their eyes for enhanced touch.*

Delta would have been pitch black without the scattered miner's lamps in their wrought-iron cases. Brown wire crawls like teenager's braces, knitting them together. Amber wall-light splatters at irregular intervals.

After Charlie, Sydney's toe reaches for flattened flooring like one feeling around in darkness.

"What smells like burritos?" Sydney asks.

Cassie shushes him.

The ladder broadens out into a wide living room area outlined in fainting couches. The centerpiece is a large, rectangular table made of dark wood. *How did they get that through the hatch?* From here, corridors branch out in two directions, from above, resembling an 'L.'

Knots of stained-glass color hatch in globes. Tiffany lamps are the invasive species, adding class to a chamber that would otherwise bear likeness to a boy's dormitory.

Three new faces obstruct Sydney's view, standing shoulder to shoulder, next to Charlie. He begins to open his mouth, but then closes it when Rex calls out from atop the ladder, "Wait for me, Chuck."

He does.

The crowded room segregates into two groups, old and new. Rex stands in the middle like a stiff-backed referee performing a coin toss. He looks down, admiring his shiny-black polished shoes, before calling out introductions. "This is the rest of my crew." He points at a squat, pear-shaped man with circular, gold-rimmed glasses. Remy would guess him to be slightly older than Rex. He wears an oversized solid-green shirt, pink skin, and buckteeth. Oily hair rounds out his low attractive number. "Hoagland. He is my second brain. My war strategist." Ironically, he sports arms similar to Hen. Hoagland acknowledges by pushing up the bridge of his glasses and then briefly flashing a bashful wave.

"Next to him is Trey." He's a short, pudgy Asian man wearing a white chef's apron. His gloss-black hair almost looks blue and a thin mustache provides an awning over his smile. "I've known him a long time." Rex holds out the 'o' in *long*.

Like a trained speaker, Trey's eye contact moves caringly between the guests. "Welcome!" His Asian accent is faint. "I look forward to learning more about you." He speaks with careful annunciation to mute it. He politely steps backward to make room for the spotlight.

"Lastly, there's Linus." Rex's voice sinks as if it's run out of air —mandatory obligation. Linus slithers forward, eyes downcast, fiddling with something resembling a Rubik's cube. Restless, fidgeting, occasionally stealing a glimpse at Cassie before being noticed and returning to his downcast shyness. Concave shoulders, narrow face, and pillow-wrestled red hair match freckles, spanning cheek to cheek. "He's pretty new, too." Linus creepily shuffles behind the body-shield of his peers. An aroma of cottage cheese dissipates.

Cassie gasps in surprise before covering her mouth.

Short, rapid movement behind Linus catches her attention. Upturned wet black nostrils pulse between white whiskers. She nudges her little brother. He gets excited and brings both fists to his ears.

The group follows Cassie's distraction. Rex, visibly annoyed, is the last to turn.

"Ah, yes. I should have mentioned our furry friend." He addresses the newcomers. "Hopefully, none of you have allergies." Without waiting for a 'yeah' or 'nah,' he continues. "Anyways, we have pills for that."

"Trey," Rex snaps his fingers at the Asian, "and I will unload your ride. Your quarters are down the hall." He waves a dismissive wrist at the pear-shaped man. "Hoagland, show them, if you would." The pear-shaped man in gold-rimmed glasses looks like he wouldn't dare not. "Dinner will be served at sun-fall. Any questions?" Without waiting for a response, he adds, "Very good. At ease, gentlemen." He begins to walk away and then stops, raising a finger as if struck by an idea. Making eye contact with Remy, he finishes, "...and ladies." The smile looks uncomfortably crooked, the way unfunny people end unfunny jokes. He nods an invisible top hat in her direction before ascending the ladder. Trey flashes a smile that looks more like an apology. He follows behind his commander.

Down one narrow arm of the L-shaped complex, the new guests follow Hoagland like buyers feigning interest in a realtor's property.

Hoagland swivels as he waddles, like a penguin nursing the wear and tear of joints bearing revolutions of obesity. He shuffles sideways to avoid an end table placed in the middle of the hallway. Two tall, narrow unlit candles rock in their holders when his rump bumps the rickety table. Remy lightly glides her fingers along the concrete walls. They emit a musty coolness that soothes her skin. It unmistakably smells like a basement fitting to take in flood water.

"This will be the kids' room." With erect fingertips, he pushes the first door on the left open. Inside, a lone twin bed sits against the side wall. Pink, crudely folded blankets cling to the end, opposite an uncased pillow. A lamp stretches its cord across the poured concrete floor. It smells uninhabited. "We'll throw down an air mattress from the closet." Cassie gulps before turning to Sydney —giving him a look, calling dibs on the bed.

Further down, the smell of soil intensifies. "Sorry there's no light." He brushes the next door open. "This one is for the girl," he pauses, then asks, "What's your name, again?"

"Remy."

"Okay, Remy. This is yours and across the hall here," he gestures, "is for the guys."

"Maybe Cub and I should share a room, so Steve gets his own?"

Cub shoots her a dirty look.

"No," Hoagland replies.

"Why not?"

"Because. Rex says."

CONCENTRATION HIDEOUTS

Steve's first impression is reassured. *These are our allies? They are not soldiers. They need us more than we need them.* He admits: *the bunker is nice, the supplies are convenient, but the company is abysmal.*

Steve and Cub plop down on their assigned beds while Hoagland enters, closing the door behind him. With hands behind his back, Hoagland's head twitches in silence, studying. He looks like a Santa Claus who traded his red suit for a green one—complete with an alcoholic's bulbous red nose. Feet drag across the cement floor when he spins a chair around to sit backwards, facing Cub. Arms drape over the chair's back in a mock-comfort pose. Cub's back straightens. Hoagland speaks.

"I know what you're thinking, 'this place is less inviting than a budget motel during the apocalypse.'"

"You don't know what I'm thinking," Cub grits.

Ignoring the comment, Hoagland persists. "You really *are* lucky to be here and not out *there*. You know that, don't you?" Cub almost squeezes a sound that doesn't seem lucky, before Hoagland goes on. "This has been a long time coming. The collapse. Prophesies have been telling us for lifetimes—giving us signs and clues. The tremors have been rumbling, had one only leaned down to listen." Hoagland creeps closer to whisper, "We aren't the first."

A loud knock interrupts. "You guys in there?" *It's Rex's voice.* "We eat now."

"Yes, sir."

Hoagland listens for decrescendo footsteps, then meets Cub's eyes. He points at him as if to say: *we'll finish this later*.

CHAPTER 17

PRESIDENTIAL INTRODUCTION

I n a distant palace in a capitol city, farther than farther used to be, he remembers watching his decision unfold. Advisors with strong accents and sweet cologne lobbied their ideas. *Their* nameless ideas became *his* final solution.

He remembers excitement. He remembers elation. As time closed, he remembers gripping the banister, vaulting himself up the velvet-red carpeted spiral staircase. At the top, he struggled with the heavy sliding glass door. *It always stuck.* Panic spurred his heart's hoofbeats.

"Vivian," he called out, fidgeting with the latch. Peering through the finely stitched lace veil of her sitting room across the hall, he pleaded, "Viv?"

It clicked. *Relief.* He remembers gliding it open. Fresh cool night air splashed across his face like new skin.

On the balcony of this distant, ivory-white mansion, a red tie knot tightened before straightening in picturesque symmetry. He smoothed his custom-tailored black suit with nervousness like a groom waiting for his bride to enter the chapel. A hand pocketed in exquisitely soft, lined fabric. Pride unpockets in the form of a smile.

"You might want to come and see this," he yelled through the balcony door.

He remembers thinking, *it's done. The reboot is underway—just as I'd imagined. Perfectly planned—perfectly executed.*

The setting sun looked as beautiful as he ever remembers. *When it sleeps, I am the tiny glow among darkness. The trusted watcher. Their beacon. Their hope.*

Sure, there will be some collateral damage. There is always collateral damage. But, those will be the undesirables, those that didn't contribute, he convinced himself.

He caught himself sneering at their misfortune. *They deserve it.*

He edged the balcony's lip, standing at the altar of himself. He observed his sprawling, manicured estate, paid for by nameless taxpayers.

Too many skeletons, too little closet space.

With a bit of bashfulness, he remembers snapping his fingers and proclaiming aloud, "Oh, I left the oven on!" A legitimate excuse for a more honest feeling: *I'd rather not be out here when it gets really dark.*

CHAPTER 18

WITNESS PROTECTION AVENUE

A scrawny finger taps Remy's shoulder.

"That's my chair," Linus slithers. A white foamy spit-bubble ejects, landing on his pink lower lip. He lathers it back with a sly tongue as if he did it without anyone noticing.

She noticed.

Remy barely has room to slide out her own chair to exchange spots without running into his pale, spindly legs. She scoots sideways. His eyes track her moves like a virgin. She senses his obsession. Lying in a thicket of wood ticks would make her skin crawl less.

"Assigned seating—got it," she says apologetically and to warn the others.

Off-white, folded tents instruct them where to sit. Cub's name is fully spelled out. Sydney's reads, 'Syd.' Rex sits at the head of the table. No one sits at the tail. The arrangement seems to be loosely caste-based. The kids sit furthest away—last to receive nourishment.

Rex waves Trey into the dining room. Drying his hands with a white terry cloth, Trey abides. "Bring in the peach bubbles." Trey raises a finger as if he was reminded and then disappears behind the kitchen counter. An emerald bottle peeks into view.

Rex squares to the table. His tandem silver buttons catch a spot of orange from the neighboring Tiffany lamp. "Before we eat, I'd like to toast our new guests." A cork pops. Rex pulls the edge of his mustache. "I'd like to dedicate this meal to them," he gestures toward his new silo-mates. Trey makes his way around the table, pouring carbonated pale-peach elixir into everyone's fluted glass. "May they share our home. May they share our abundance. May they thrive in our prosperity. We are fortunate to have found them and have them with us this evening."

He salutes his glass and everyone around the table raises theirs.

"To the future... *with* a future!"

Glasses clink and throats swallow.

The first course is devoured only to the irregular pangs of cutlery ringing on porcelain.

Remy dabs her mouth, "Salad's good." Everything is miniature: the lettuce, the tomatoes, the strawberries. They are surprisingly full of flavor. She can tell they are fresh by the deep green color in their attached stems and leaves.

Trey raises a fork in acknowledgement. For all Remy knew, he must be this place's chef. Cassie and Sydney pick out the berries, leaving the rest on their plates.

Between bites, Remy chases Linus' staring eyes away as if he were a dog eyeing her forbidden milk bone. *I wish he'd stop looking at me.* If the situation was different and she wasn't so dependent, he'd be wearing red rouge in the shape of her palm.

Trey circles the long rectangular table, dispensing a fist-sized piece of meat. Bubbles of oily juices roll down the sides, pooling at the base. Rising white steam brings a strangely unfamiliar scent.

"Venison. Deer," he says. With a knife in one hand and a fork in the other, Sydney leans over his piece and, closing both eyes, fills his nostrils with the aromatics.

"Yummy!"

Trey satisfyingly grins.

THE ISLAND OF MEXICO

Hoagland clears his throat and pads his mouth with a napkin before addressing Rex. "So, can you explain to our guests about the purge?" Hesitation attaches to his voice box like suffocating vines, sucking enthusiasm and confidence before the question mark.

Linus freezes. Trey stops chewing. A spoon falls from someone's fingers—clashing into their plate. Charlie turns to Rex. Everyone does. Rex's fork halts in mid-air—mouth still open. A lettuce leaf flutters from the fork's fingers. To Cub, it seems boundaries have been crossed. If only shoehorns removed feet from mouths.

"Sorry, sir, I—"

"They are our fellow patriots."

"I didn't mean—"

"You asked me a question. Let me speak."

Hoagland nods. Stern words chase cheerfulness away.

Rex straightens. Lower buttons lift over the tabletop. With elbows planted on the placemat, he folds his hands, taking a silent moment to compose his thoughts. If tension was smoke, it'd be difficult to see across the table. Then, he begins.

"Gentlemen," he nods toward Remy and Cassie, "...and ladies. I make it a habit not to discuss business at dinner." He flicks an accusatory glance at Hoagland. "Business is weighty and spoils digestion. That being said, briefly..." He pauses as if reconsidering if he should continue, "We have been attacked. Our country... has been attacked." He looks down at his plate.

His audience watches while he uses a fork to separate the food, leaving white space in between. Grooming the sustenance.

"Eat." His eyes get big—whites surround their iris. "And enjoy!" he bellows. In panic, each diner scrambles for their utensils and resumes shoveling until cheeks narrowly burst. "What we took for granted yesterday will be tomorrow's luxury." Cub pauses chewing to appreciate the commentary. "Charlie and Hoagland will finish that which you cannot." They nod in agreement, chins hanging over plates like gardens of wonder. "Linus," Rex snaps his fingers, "you are on clean up."

"Sir," he replies with a snake's lisp.

Cub watches Rex disappear down the corridor opposite his own quarters. Steve is first to excuse himself and the rest rapidly follow. Sydney's hands got sticky, so Charlie shows him the sink. "Don't drink from this one, but it is good for cleaning," he tells the boy. Charlie and Hoagland don't have much to finish in the way of table scraps. Linus quietly, but efficiently, cleans. Garbage goes into a wide-mouthed canister, flatware goes into white, plastic, air-raided cylinders that remind Cub of large hair-curlers. The dinner table is restored to a conference one in short order. The room circles around Cub.

A fresh bandage and plump tube of antibiotic ointment land on the cleaned table in front of him. Charlie notices him observing. "No gas, all electric, renewable." Charlie dries his hands and throws the rag in a tall, narrow, flip-top hamper. He pulls the edge of his thin mustache and claps once. "More reliable."

Rubbing ointment on his elbow, Cub marvels at the well-oiled engine around him.

"Did you notice the grid of panels out there?"

Cub didn't, so he shakes his head.

Pointing at his own eyes, Charlie says, "You should notice your surroundings."

The organization with which this place runs must have taken a lot of thought. "Thanks." Cub excuses himself from the table.

SUNSET ON SATURN

Back down the coffin-narrow hallway, away from the Tiffany-lit central area, Cub turns the knob to his room. The door fans open. Steve is silent. Musky armpits and sour sweat of decaying skin remind Cub of gray.

Steve sits on the bed's edge, his knees bouncing to fidgeting feet. Tonight, Cub has been left with more loose ends. Steve appears similar—restless minds. New inmates all feel the same once they sober. Plans and schemes crack like breakfast eggs. Regret and reflection occupy the moments before surface sleep. And then, the wheel turns, the planet spins, fear dangles carrots, threatening humanity's scrolling credits—but they never come.

Cub closes the door behind him, but then reaches back to open it a crack—a fallacy of fresh air. Someone parked luggage at the foot of their twin beds. *The turquoise bag is Remy's.* Cub finds comfort that they didn't thoroughly dig through his belongings. *Or did they?* One step ahead. False security.

He exits.

He enters.

"Thanks, Cub," she says as the bag kicks up a puff of fine floor powder. Remy motions to close the door. He obeys. "Why us?" she whispers, leaning in.

At first, he shrugs her off. As if struck with common sense, he unconsciously echoes Steve's words, "Because we have something they need."

CHAPTER 19

PRESIDENTIAL PRIDE

A balcony door at the ivory palace glides shut. Latches click. Alarm systems beep, signaling their protection.

His red silk tie pulls from its symmetric knot. He tosses it over the back of his ivory-accented easy chair. While unbuttoning his costume, he reflects.

I didn't want my future steered by a committee of elders. Let my experience navigate the unknown in all its insecurity, for security is a figment of someone else's imagination.

Let me howl. Let them beg. To this, I yawn. Fairy tales wrap themselves in watercolors. Tiny droplets of ink splatter and run in rivers of current. Blind men in a crowd riot over a fallen dictator at the hands of foreign riches—leaving the wealthy with more. Snapping emptied fingers of pristine white gloves leave printless faucet handles.

Rivulets swell and trickle down a steamy, smeared mirror. Textile workers line box seams on pined-resin wood planks in preparation for a feast. Bits of meat shed in tangled flecks of spun floss. Unfocus to refocus—images blur and sharpen. Spoons need a healthy landing. *Leave counting to those without the time.*

The air is only thin to those breathing the thick. The curvature is within view. Atmosphere hasn't colored this place in ages. Pebbles rain without meteorologists. Ironically, that's exactly what we need. Hot rocks generating dark friction in the absence of nothingness. Here, there is eternal peace. Here, we pray to others for conflict. We listen for conflict. We hunger for conflict. We hunger. We are the hungry. Eye-water falls slow, persuaded by less gravity. Our ears grow bigger as we listen to the whispers of you.

CHAPTER 20

CAPTURED SUNSHINE

Stern knuckles wrap the boys' bedroom door with a hollow echo. Cub is immediately alert. His first conscious, deep breath fills nostrils with bacon's aroma. Steve stares up at the cement ceiling. Trowel marks reveal the author's code. It is impossible to gauge time in this underground cell.

The skillet's sizzle and scent intensify as Cub's feet drag toward the main room. He concentrates on not spilling the sloshing chamber pot. He can hear a fan which must be attached to a ventilation system that's not strong enough to clear the thin white haze Trey cooks at the stovetop. He flashes Cub a welcoming grin before returning to his pan. His white apron contains a cartoon toad sticking out its tongue in a sickly sneer. The caption beneath reads: *I'm a Princess.*

Charlie approaches from the opposite hall. Tucking in his shirt, he already appears professionally assembled. "Bucket of well-water in the utility closet for you. Soap up the essentials."

The bacon is soy. The milk isn't milk. The eggs used to be powder. The vegetables are small, but surprisingly delicious.

Trey cooks. Linus cleans. The engine purrs. The cat hides. "Everybody gets to be a helper today." From behind their chairs, Charlie pats Steve and Cub on the back. "Rex is waiting above."

A BOATLESS WORLD MAY AS WELL BE PANGEA

Steve's head sprouts from the silo's hatch. *Lucy is gone. They took her. This was all a predicted trap.*

"Morning, men!" Rex's voice echoes everywhere. His high-pointing chin asks, "How'd you sleep?" as they climb down. "It sure will be nice with a couple extra hands around here, isn't that right, Chuck?"

"Yes, sir," Charlie replies, pushing out a mock laugh.

"With the extra bodies around comes extra waste. Charlie, show these boys to our landfill out back. We are going to need to double the width. Shovels are already out there."

Charlie studies the newcomers' reactions. "Yes, sir," he salutes. "I'll show them, sir." Wedging between, he leads both by the elbow.

Under a full mustache, teeth grin watching them walk away. "You're in charge, Chuck!" When they get further away, he adds, "Oh, if you boys finish that, we'll start on the sewer chute!" With his chest sticking out, Rex rubs his mouth until they disappear behind the greenhouse.

GYPSY HORSES WITH THEIR BELL-BOTTOM FUR

Cassie's bags are emptied before Sydney finishes breakfast.

"Get your stuff off my bed, Cass!"

"Sorry." She flicks crayons and a compact onto the nightstand. "It's *not* a bed, it's an *air mattress*."

"Whatever. It's mine." He pulls out a coloring book from the black-eyed house and lays on the air mattress. "Have any oranges?"

She picks up the cardboard carton, flips the top, and feathers through the dull crayons. "Yellow-orange or orange-yellow?"

He shoots her a clueless look. "Whichever looks more like a sun." It lands between his arms. "Thanks." He traces the outline and shades the middle while Cassie separates and folds her clothes on the bed.

"Do you want me to do yours next?"

"My what?" He shades.

"Your clothes. I can fold them next."

"Sure." He sets down the sun-color. "Any greens in there?" She tosses the box and colors scatter from the tray. He starts the grass. "Think we'll ever go back to that house?"

"Which one?" she asks.

"The one with all the kids—that Mom dropped us off at."

"Oh. I don't know."

"I really liked it there. That lady makes really good chicken nuggets!"

"Yeah." Cassie turns her dress outside-in. "She does *bake* really good nuggets." She folds. "But I don't think we can go there again."

He stops coloring to look at her back. *The way she moves her arms makes it look like she knows what she's doing.* He dejectedly frowns.

SERVE THE SERVANTS

He steps on the shovel's head to push it deeper into the ground, then pauses. Rex and Charlie have left them unattended. With whisker fuzz, sweat freely runs down his skull. Using a wrist, he swipes his forehead and leans on the handle.

"They are using us... for our youth."

Steve thrusts his shovel, scooping a clump of dirt. He carries it a couple steps to the growing mound. "You got the first part right." He adds to the mound and scoops again.

"Well, they are using us as slaves," Cub corrects himself.

Steve empties another shovelful on the mound. Cub watches. "They are..." he digs. "Using us for something..." He unloads. "That's for sure..."

The old man keeps working like a well-crafted watch. The earth quakes. Cub turns to check if their supervisors have returned. The earth stops quaking. Satisfied, he goes back to leaning on the shovel. Steve unloads, again.

"You know, I didn't call you 'Indian Steve.'" Mid-scoop, the old man pauses, wincing with insult, but doesn't look up from his labor. A bead of sweat runs down his chin. He subtly shakes his head and continues scooping.

Cub scratches the back of his neck and then scoops.

STALKING FISHNETS

Sitting alone on her bed, Remy's face warms, as if by a spotlight. Looking up, she catches a blur of red-motion through the crack in her open door. *Was someone just there?* She blinks, and there's no one. *Was that real?* Her face resists cooling off. *Violated.* She shudders and gets up to close the door.

COMPLEX FRACTIONS

Cassie and Sydney spend the long afternoon in their small room. "They don't even have colored pencils."

He's right. This isn't a fun house. This is an adult house with adult things.

Sydney stops shading his drawing of a werewolf, "Because the legs got too skinny." He asks his sister, "How will we get back home?"

Sitting on the cold flat floor, Cassie straightens her Indian-style. Without using shampoo, her hair carries a smooth, shiny curl. She feathers it from below. Thinking back to cartoons and televised programming, she tries to remember ways big sisters comforted and protected their siblings. She cannot pinpoint a line but, rather, a theme. They are the shield and the barrier and the book. *Little sister wants to be like big sister. In a way, they wear the same clothes and pretend to act like them—a model. A bodyguard model. A pretty bodyguard model, with light brown skin.*

Sydney catches her in dancing thoughts. "Well?"

"I'm your big sister. Do you trust me?"

He nods.

"Good. I'll help us back."

In poverty, like politics, all one has left to peddle is words.

AGE IS BUT A STATE OF MIND, TO THE PROPERLY CONVINCED

Cub spears his shovel into the growing pit. It stands up by itself in the dirt. Mid-shovel, Steve stops to acknowledge the young man's gesture before continuing his own labors. Cub swigs a mouthful of water from a Delta-provided bottle. In the distance, he spots Rex pointing between the solar farm and the silo. He looks to be lecturing Charlie, but it is impossible to hear what they are discussing. Cub watches Steve unload a heaping pile of unearthed soil.

"Where do you think they put Lucy?"

Steve uninterruptedly shovels.

"You know, our vehicle..."

Steve stops to scowl at Cub.

"*Your* vehicle."

He keeps shoveling.

Cub scratches his cheek and swats a pestering fly. "It isn't quite what I expected, but... it *is* safe. These guys know how to stay alive—how to sustain life."

"Life isn't *just* meant to be *sustained*."

"You know what I mean," Cub retaliates. Studying Steve's

body at work, it amazes him to believe the man doesn't fatigue. He glances over the old man's back to verify Rex and Charlie are still out of earshot. "Level with me. What was the purpose of taking us with you?"

He pauses in contemplation, then Steve mutters, "Purpose."

"Excuse me?"

Several beats of silence separate the response. "My life didn't need to be *sustained*. It was doing that fine enough. It needed *purpose*."

A questioning facial slur drags across Cub. He bends down, attempting to catch Steve's attention between scoops. It doesn't work.

"Life hasn't time for bluffing," he tells Cub. "If you don't show the people you care about *that* you care, you are missing the whole point."

Cub pulls back. "You *care* about us?"

With a helping of dirt crowning his shovel, Steve stops to meet Cub's eyes and says, "Keep shoveling."

BUTTERED BREAD

Chair legs drag across the floor. Delta's occupants turn to observe Rex rising. They keep chewing. He clears his throat. They swallow. He picks up the chair to push it in. Someone pats their mouth with a white handkerchief. Rex speaks.

"It's a cycle. It always was. No one ever gave it a reason to change—no excuse not to.

"It is bigger than us. The ultimate recycler. Humanity and its fancy conscience believe it can make a difference the same way a tiny pup reveals its fangs while ferociously yelping at a silverback gorilla." Rex paces slowly around the backs of his guests' chairs. The clap of his dress shoes sound like high heels.

"Man, in all its dynastic glory, dangerously underestimates its own vulnerability." He leans in to Cub's ear, "Rationality never works on crazy." He paces behind them. "The remote little earth moves amongst a brotherhood of rocks, forever clinging to its Mother Sun's ankle until she sheds in a spectacular bloat."

He grabs Trey's bicep, wiggling it, while the cook attempts to dry a rinsed pan. "Philosophers and prima donnas down through the ages have long predicted the end. Their motivations were similar. It was never to warn. It was always to shift power—to sway opinion."

He perches his hands on the back of his chair and sternly stares into his audience's apprehension as if to spook it away. "All of them were wrong and all of them were liars. More importantly, all of them vastly misunderstood the power of time."

Every light flickers off, leaving them in black, then they come back on. Unaffected by Rex's speech, Steve resumes shoveling food in. Cub and Cassie follow his lead. Remy sits with hands in her lap. "What's wrong with those?" Sydney timidly asks. Half the Tiffanys wink out again like emergency lights.

"No danger," Trey reassures him. "But, yeah, happens all the time. Batteries still have plenty of charge. It's like it's drawing too much at one time or—"

"Series," Steve mutters between bites.

"Pardon?"

"Series," he repeats. "Instead of parallel." He chews. "Demand outweighs load and power is lost." Steve wipes his mouth with the back of his paw. "Are they connected to the same circuit as the larger appliances?"

Trey shrugs and redirects to Rex who now takes interest. "I think they may be. Would you take a look?" Rex asks in more of a commanding tone.

Steve grunts. "After food."

BLINK TWICE

"May I come in?"

With a gasp, Remy stops crying and spins on her bed. The door cracks open and Rex's voice seeps in.

"Pardon my manners. I should have knocked." He enters her room.

She wipes, smudging eye-juice across her cheeks. "No, I'm sorry for... I should have—"

"I noticed you were troubled," he interrupts. "You are in a wonderful place. A safe place. Tell me what's wrong." Towering over her, Rex stands next to her bed with crossed arms.

With her back to Rex, she motionlessly sits in static silence, staring at the concrete wall. He observes her posture, her soft slouching shoulders and her bowed head. He scrunches his face, fuzzing the vision. His mustache rises. He tries to fit inside her, imagining himself in herself. Panning the area, he recognizes her new room as resembling a prison with its barren, impersonal walls. *This place feels blank and hollow to her.*

His focus returns to Remy. In a strange way, he finds a match. *Her life hasn't yet been written. She is empty and lost—a ship at sea, bobbing offshore, unsure of where to navigate, waiting for someone else to blow wind in her sails.* Without realizing it, he leans closer in quiet evaluation. *She doesn't believe in herself, so she imitates that which she wishes to become.*

With her back still toward me, she invites vulnerability and submission. She enjoys playing the victim to an audience of victims. She's the kind that embraces a leash... when finally coerced to wear one.

I can play the role...

"Alright," his voice loosens its authority. His arms uncross. He takes a deep, brave breath and tells Remy's back, "I've spent most of my life alone."

Her ears perk. She tries to peer around the corner of her face but then catches herself and just listens.

"I haven't always been right. In fact, my theories haven't been very popular. Who am I kidding, I accepted ridicule from people I loved for those ideas I believed to be true. This led me down a long path of solitude."

His voice lifts with confidence, "I never allowed their words to discourage me. I used them as motivation. Life doesn't hand its participants a blueprint or treasure map with a big juicy 'X.'" He raises a hand to his chin. "How is one to know where to end if they haven't been told how to begin?

"One is not born knowing everything." From behind, Rex briefly runs a pair of fingers over her forearm. "Your family elected against enhancing you as a child—and that turned out to be a good thing... especially now.

"We tend to teach the same way we were taught. In the beginning, mistakes taught life how to become life and, in turn, life teaches us with similar tools.

"How can *I* help *you*?" he asks. "Is there something I should know?"

Rex watches her waver.

His voice softens further. "I want to be open and honest with you, but I need you to be open and honest with me. What was your family running from out there?"

She straightens up in bed. Weight shifts from her shoulders. She turns to face Rex and unloads. "Well, it all happened so fast. We got home. Mom and Dad were murdered right in front of us by I-don't-know-who! We ran to the neighbors' house and they gave us Syd and Cassie to look after. Now we are on the run, but I don't know what we are running from or where we are going, except you came to help us—which is great because—"

"Wait. You aren't all related?"

"No, you see, Cub is my sister. I mean he, I'm *his* sister and Cassie and Sydney are brother and sister. Steve isn't related to—"

"Perfect." Rex leans over and brings Remy's hand up as if he were going to kiss it—but then doesn't. "I understand. I understand what you are going through." He looks directly into her eyes. "You lost a loving family. It won't be the same, but we will support you as part of *our* family."

Remy breaks eye contact to look at her unheld hand.

"Listen."

She does.

"Things will be... difficult in ways none of us imagined. The world was not ready, and it never will be. More spins and more revolutions only make us dizzy and more likely to point the scope at our own throat.

"Preparation is an illusion of the mind—a false comfort, but in what and what for? No one is prepared to lose their parents, just like no one is prepared to become a parent. No one is prepared. One can only become *more* prepared. Let me help you watch over the children." Rex studies her sadness.

She hesitates. "If you would have asked me how I felt right after Mom and Dad died... I thought I would have been sadder," she admits.

"Don't be ashamed. Take credit for your strength! Each moment provides an opportunity to alter one's script, one's preparation!" Confidence in his voice grows, "Are these illusions, too? Are these fingerprints of a sloppy creator? Philosophers fancy categorizing religion as a virus. Strumming it with vocal chords carries a certain panache. Others label religion as an antibiotic against bad people.

"Humans, despite popular belief, share more traits with wildlife than we care to admit. We are all stitched and sutured with primal instincts. We'll get through this... together."

Remy withdraws her hand to cover her nose.

She's getting emotional, again. He pats the top of her head. "We all have a *role* to play. Get some rest."

Walking backward, Rex disappears out her door. A moment later, his hand slips into view to pull her door shut.

IF HAPPINESS SPRINGS FROM HOPE, WHAT GROWS IN THE GARDEN OF CHAOS?

"That's it! Keep working, old man!" Charlie claps at Steve like a dog trainer.

Rex swoops in. He pries the shovel's handle away from Steve. Cub suspiciously steps back. Steve does, too. "It's for the greater good!" Rex encourages. Straightening the old man's posture, he pats Steve's back with gratitude. Passing the shovel to Charlie, Rex guides Steve away, toward the solar field.

One shovelful follows the next. More distance separates Rex's voice from Cub's ears, but with the animated expression, Cub assumes he is trying to sell Steve something too good to be true.

PLASTIC BLUE RAIN DRUMS OUTSIDE THE SILO

"This is going to blow over, just not quickly. Together, we can help each other, not only survive, but thrive!" Rex placates to Steve's skeptical hippo-eyes.

Steve stops.

Rex stops and cocks his head in puzzlement. This is the part a salesman lives for. Rex recognizes it. The part of the rollercoaster which presses the stomach toward the throat. The part where all faith, in each tiny component, gets tested and there is a chance, however small, that one may not make it out intact. This is the part that the salesman anticipates the entire time. This is where the intentionally inflated price goes dieting. The customer feels good, but that was the plan all along and he would have slimmed further if the customer played their cards better. Salesmen live for the bluff.

"Why us?" Steve asks in a tone expecting honesty.

Rex takes a deep-mouthed breath and plays the pitch.

CHANGING LANES

Tectonic plates shift. A sweat rivulet jiggles down Cub's nose only to swan dive from his nostril. The quaking stops. He heaves his shovel into the dirt hard enough to stand on its own.

Cub has been watching Steve and Rex pace back and forth through the solar field. Steve's once stiff body language has now massaged to a relaxed comfort.

Alcohol and Rohypnol are jealous.

Cub licks his dry lips. He had almost forgotten its power. His brain tricks his tongue into thinking a couple splashes of sweet cherry amaretto follow his throat's waterslide. Cub only had a few revolutions to witness the intoxicating chemical's ability of convincing. Three thousand beautiful arguments couldn't lure foreign fingers to say 'touch me' like three stiff elixirs. They don't turn 'no' into 'yes,' but rather, a seductive 'mmhmm' will do. Eyes roll upward between slow blinks. Smiles seem to be tacked up at the corners with finishing nails. Suggestion and attention tug the orange and yellow bobber, rippling waves in an otherwise still lake, in front of the hungry fisher of men.

Steve laughs for the first time since this adventure started. A slice of Cub's hope grows a dark spot like aging bread in humidity. Without chemicals or tricks, it becomes obvious, Rex is good.

TIME TRAVELING TOWARD TOMORROW, HEARTBEAT BY LOUSY HEARTBEAT

Outside, the afternoon winds down to the clangs of organized tools. Inside, Cassie and Sydney arrive at the big wooden table first. Trey busies himself in the back kitchen. He blends in as if he has no eyes or ears.

"I'm bored," Sydney tells her.

She nods in agreement as Hoagland emerges from the hallway.

"It's a trick," he tells the kids. He pulls out a chair across from them. "Media intentionally bombards your senses, attempting to separate you from your mind." He sits. "We are told, 'You can be anyone or anything!' We are encouraged to explore the world or space with chemicals and equations. Meanwhile, we don't understand our own minds. So many fundamental answers to our deepest questions, that actually matter, live alongside us, being ignored by us."

With a puzzled look, Sydney asks, "So, what's the trick?"

"The trick is," Hoagland points, "look over *there*."

The kids follow his finger toward the ceiling.

"Now look over *here*," he points again.

They trace the path of his outstretched arm but see nothing special.

He points toward the kitchen. Trey briefly looks up. "*Quick*, look right *there*!"

Frustration spray paints expressions on Cassie and Sydney's faces and both frown at Hoagland, unappreciative of his apparent teasing.

"Misdirection. The trick is simple—keep your subjects busy. No one ever says, 'Look here,'" Hoagland taps his head. "Listen to the plants," he tells them with a forced grin.

He reaches into his shirt's chest pocket. He slides a concealed fist across the table, toward Cassie and Sydney. Two heart-shaped boxes tumble out.

Rex files into the room, closely followed by Charlie.

Hoagland leans in, "Don't let it ruin your appetite." He flashes a genuine smile.

Cassie and Sydney quickly glance at one another before each snatching up a box and hiding their prize under the table.

Stained-glass lights don't wink.

"Hey, they're not blinking!" Sydney points.

Rex leans toward a lamp. Grinning with satisfaction, his face gathers the orange light. His posture and grin both quickly correct to a straight line. "We wait until *everyone* is here."

MEMORIES ARE MANMADE PRISONS WITH BROKEN LOCKS

Steve hasn't come down from Earth for supper. He is the last empty seat.

Turning toward the kitchen, Cub watches a frozen cylinder slide out of its cardboard sheath and land in a transparent serving pitcher. Trey tosses a slice of lemon inside and fills the container with water. The fluid pinks as he stirs. The lemon slice somersaults in the current.

Cub's lips pinch with anticipation as he imagines its tart flavor. He can't remember the last time he had pink lemonade, but he can remember a time.

Mom and Dad left the house to somewhere he's lucky to have convinced them he should avoid. He twists the ice cube container. All but two stubborn ones clang into the glass pitcher in simple luxury. He tears open a narrow paper packet. Parting the opening releases a complex plume of concentrated sour. His lips pucker and saliva leaks from each parotid. The powder falls from its tomb like pink funeral ashes, coating the top cubes. With her favorite turquoise blanket ruffling the skin under her nose, Young Remy watches her brother push a chair up to the kitchen counter. "Rem, can you hand me the cup, please?" She retrieves a plastic orange measuring cup, blows out the dust, taps it on her palm, and then hands it to Young Cub who looms over the double-lined bag of white granulated sugar.

"I think it's two," she tells him. He scoops, levels with a pointer finger, and then dumps. He doesn't do two or three or four.

The faucet squeaks. Young Cub stirs with Mom's wooden spoon while balancing on the chair. Some granules never dissolve in this dentist's nightmare. When he holds it up, among white particles, there are a couple black specks he cannot explain.

Melting ice cubes dump over the spout into Young Cub's glass first. Dried soap bubbles left by the dish washer dissolve in the supersaturated pink solution. Young Remy gets a smaller glass. He fills hers three-quarters-full before slipping. Her glass tilts. A small waterfall trickles and pools around the base of her cup on the outside.

"That's enough for now." Young Cub can't wait. He doesn't even take time to climb off the chair. Crisp and refreshing as it goes down, the aftertaste pulls his lips together in a drawstring. "This is the best lemonade I've ever had," he proclaims.

Memories highlight moods and often vice versa.

A final drop oscillates on the rim of Young Cub's cup. Underneath, Young Remy watches his tongue quiver like an octopus tentacle with its suction-cup taste ears. He shakes the cup, but the drop hesitates as if it doesn't know how to use a rip cord and, thus, refuses its jump instructor's command. Metaphorically lost.

A *clump* sounds above. A long deadbolt slips. Feet rattle ladder rungs. Steve smells of an electrical fire.

DISSOCIATIVE ANESTHETIC

Cassie watches Rex circle the table, dishing out the main course. He *always* dishes out the main course. Today, it's stuffing. Nobody touches their food until he sits down. Cassie spots a speck of her ice cream scoop-shaped food that looks like celery. *Eww, celery.* When Rex sits, she'll pick it out and put it on Sydney's plate even though he likes it less.

Rex puts two scoops, instead of one, on Indian Steve's plate. It seems like Rex wants a 'thank you' by the way he keeps hovering over Steve. Rex's friends look up with curiosity. Indian Steve doesn't. Trey doesn't either, but *he's busy cooking*.

Rex sits. Sydney punches Cassie's leg when she wipes off her celery. He makes a pouty face and then swallows it after a big gulp of water like Mom with her party pills.

Cassie feels a leg rub. She sets down her fork to pet the affectionate orange cat. She slowly chews with her mouth closed. *A strange part about this place is that the food doesn't smell right. Mom would say it's "processed."*

This place isn't that fun. The adults don't laugh. When me and Sydney and Remy laugh together, they look at us like we are zoo animals. Instead of joining in, they quietly wait for us to stop.

When I woke up this morning, our room smelled exactly like Syd's feet, so I waved the door open and closed to air it out. It was funny, he didn't even wake up.

It's hard to believe I like sharing a room with my little brother. He used to be so annoying, but now he is the only thing that seems normal. Last night, when all the adults went to sleep, we closed the door and whispered in the dark. All this stuff happening to us... he's worse off than me, but he isn't even scared. Maybe it's because of my girl genes. If I lose Sydney, life will be really hard. So hard, I hope I can fall asleep and not wake up as a person. Maybe I could wake up as a bird with white wings and a long beak and a pink body. That would be better than losing my brother.

Ringing the stem of his water glass with a fork, Rex stands.

THE ENIGMATIC AND INEVITABLE SOMEDAY

"I know some of you have questions. Well, you are in the right place. I," he corrects himself, "*we*, have some answers to those questions. Sadly, some might not be what you want to hear. But we are not in the business of lying." Cub notices Trey mouthing the words with Rex, the way proud parents do in a dark audience, watching their children on stage reciting memorized lines. "We are in the business of *living*!" Hoagland raises a pumping fist. Trey joins him in gesture.

"The ejection seat's wheels sat on the tarmac for a long time," Rex continues with presidential confidence. "Pieces positioned with haphazard progressivism." He paces behind their chairs. "Amendments to a constitution that no longer heeded the warning of its original authors. In principal, ideas presented with good intentions, but like Troy's horse, carried insidious motives." One hand is behind his back, the other swings an invisible conductor's baton. "Euphemistic names bannered promises of change and wealth and innovation, masking control and fear and oppression." Trey's mouth says invisible words like a bad ventriloquist. "Dissolution of lies and secrets ended personal privacy. Strange, how our new comfort in discomfort allows us to biblically shed our own fig leaves. Daily substances correct chemical imbalances created by people we trust. Remember, the privileged require the underprivileged to fill their pockets." Having fully circled the room, he returns to the back of his empty chair. "I truly thought it was over when their algorithms finally allowed them to sift through our collective data. Properly organized, our history will be recreated. Trips back in time can be taken in the simulation without altering the one true timeline. In fact, one can step into a re-creation of a re-creation, a department store's triple mirror, with endless facsimiles. This is not advised because our human minds are easily lost, tracking shell games. I digress, but these are the topics that excite me."

"Wait," Cub protests. "Are you saying this is some sort of simulation?"

Rex raises a hand, closing his eyes to interrupt.

"If you have to ask, you do not know. None, one, or all of us may be lost on a couch or bed, experiencing the senses this machine has to offer, while our muscles atrophy like space cadet's in a future world."

Cub starts to ask, "What's the chances——"

"High," Trey nods to Rex. "Very high."

The scar-faced young man had heard similar stories that seemed too far-fetched. This man spoke with calm confidence that now frightened Cub. *The idea seems more plausible.*

"I tell you this because it is a beautiful story—thought provoking. Not that anything can be done about it." Rex pushes his chair in with his kneecaps. "We have to focus on things we can do, not on things we cannot do. Steve did a tremendous job helping streamline our power source. Isn't that correct?"

As if caught in a daydream, Steve shakes his head before responding, "Agreed."

"Excellent. We should all be appreciative of that," Rex says without thanking him.

UTERINE FIBROIDS / WELCOME TO NINETEEN EIGHTY-WHATEVER

Candlelight's pulsing glow hypnotizes. Cub watches its tail wiggle. Steve's body creaks in the far bed.

Rotations feel like recess in Stockholm. Everything else tastes of prison.

Is this living? Is this life support? Maybe I should have opened the front door and fertilized the lawn with body fluids. Why did it happen this way—me left here? Am I supposed to feel lucky? Grateful?

Cub imagines similar questions rolling down the neural circuitry of cancer patients. Living death sentences with Doctor Guillotine's creation just out of focus.

With his back to Cub, Steve's spine aligns perfect as a mattress commercial. His aging body worked harder than anyone else's today. The fact that he passes out right after dinner isn't surprising.

Rex has assembled a competent team. Maybe, Cub thinks, *I don't give him enough credit—enough respect. Rex had the forethought to start Delta. He squirreled away supplies, including food and renewable resources, before there was ever a problem. He did it for more than just himself. I had been living in the moment, instead of in preparation for a revolutionary one.*

He turns the doorknob slowly so as not to make a sound. The seal smacks its lips open. The hinges briefly squeak like a warfarin-nibbling mouse.

Down the dark hall, Tiffany lamps never go out. They color

the main room in reds and oranges and golds. It is too early for Cub to fall asleep. He listens for motion, leaning on the door jam, but no one down there stirs. *Oh, what I would give for a glimpse of passion.*

Dejected, he pushes the door closed, but just as the woken may recall life's last few moments, Cub swears he hears his sister say, "No!"

He swings it back open. Steve rustles. Cub knocks twice on Remy's door and then opens it. Someone on the inside piled bags up, making it more difficult to enter. He flicks the light switch up in the pitch-black room. The cat leaps over baggage, out the door, down the hall.

Linus' pale, curved body lurches on the bed over Remy like a Lovecraftian cave dweller. There is an insect quality to the way he freezes, mid-clothes peel, over his prey.

Pupils dilate. Panic is obvious in his red-handed posture. His eyes dart as his brain calculates its host's escape.

Cub lunges at Linus. Angry fingers grasp Linus' shirt around the equator as he trips over the obstructive baggage. They don't let go. Stumbling. Scrambling like two free-range felines taking play seriously. Remy fetally recoils on her bed in the corner of the room, de-exposing her pretty pieces.

With his unclenched hand, Cub paws at Linus, catching only airspace. Linus' kneecaps smash against the bare concrete floor. Vibrations rattle the hallway table. *Everyone in Delta feels the vibrations.* He springs up, dodging another Cub-swipe. His shirt tears. Remy's bag catches his toe, spins, propping her door open and he whimpers off down the hall, leaving Cub with a fistful of purple cloth.

He glances at Remy as if to ask if she's okay. He takes her not crying as an upward thumb and bolts out the door.

"Cub?" she chirps. His clomping pauses. She knows he's there. "Careful, kay?" His clomping smooths. She knows he's hunting.

Rage has a tendency to start fires it cannot burn out.

Cub feels like a passenger in his own body—virtual reality. Drinking fuel of betrayal, he stomps down the hallway and then down the western wing. Similar to his own, closed doors line the dark hall's lumen. He realizes he hasn't been down this way before and doesn't know to whom each room belongs.

Rocking hives stirs bees.

He wouldn't want to wake Trey. He wants Trey to like him. *Hoagland is simply old, and bothering him, at whatever time this is, seems disrespectful.* If ego served as a logistical compass, Rex's room would be at the very end—intelligent money.

Cub hovers an ear next to the faux wooden door with faux wood grain like he's deciphering clicks of a popping vault lock. *No snoring or stirring or speaking on the other side.* Cub cocks his hand, then catches himself. *Is this the right thing to do? What am I going to say to this adult? Steve would do a better job. Rex has taken a fancy to him. Maybe he is still up. It's not too late to go back.* And then, it was. Cub's virtual reality knuckles the door. He listens. He expected an echo from the other side like his and Remy's rooms, but the sound quickly mutes.

Was it inaudible? His ear strains for movement. He looks back down the hallway from whence he came. Stained-glass orange patches splatter the walls. He gestures the way one does to a street beggar as if himself penniless.

He knocks again.

A voice from the other side, dipped in annoyance, bellows, "I said, come!"

Embarrassed, Cub's body radiates with a numbness as if struck with a sleep arrow. He swallows, blinks, and returns to the moment.

Now, even louder, Rex yells, "I said..."

The knob clicks in Cub's hand. Light spills from the room, across Cub's chest.

"In."

Cub slips through the narrow door crack as a teenager does

attempting to enter a classroom late without catching the teacher's notice.

The room is well furnished and more than double the size of the other bedrooms. The Tiffany lamp influence is apparent. One sits on the nightstand. Another larger, globe-shaped one attached to a thick chain dangles from the ceiling over Rex's walnut roll-top desk. He notices three half-empty liquor bottles and a bucket of melting ice—each on its own coaster. Plush faux fur massages Cub's rough feet.

The top of Rex's head pokes over the back of a shiny, studded-leather chair. Cub cranes his neck to get a cleaner view. The anger he felt moments earlier wilts to intimidation. Rex lifts his glass. An ice cube rattles. Using two hands, Cub quietly closes the door behind him.

The back of the chair speaks. "I know why you are here."

"It's just that—"

"Please. Don't interrupt me."

"I did, but—"

"Did you hear what I just said?" Rex interrupts. He sips, awaiting Cub's response.

Cub stays quiet.

"Good. Then I don't have to repeat myself." He clears his throat. "Sit."

The polished chair opposite Rex squeaks when Cub slides in.

"Cub. Is that your birth name?"

With hands on the armrest, Cub can tell the leather was freshly treated with a moisturizing chemical. It smells like imitated lemons.

"You are tense. Relax." The ice cube in Rex's glass is as big as a baby's fist wrapped around a xylophone mallet. The sticky brown elixir reminds Cub of simmering furniture stain.

Rex's nose pokes from the side of the chair. "Cub, most people wouldn't even recognize paradise." Proud of the prolific statement, Rex holds his glass at nose level and rattles it around like windless chimes. He raises an eyebrow.

Cub grows impatient. He is a held hostage to a rudderless conversation. He almost replies but is caught off guard.

"Ketamine?"

"Sir?"

"Not that I have it or even wish to, but, have you ever?"

"Nope, I can't say—"

Rex cuts him off as if only interested in a rhetorical sense. He swivels the chair around to face Cub. "We've all been young and experimental. Little scientists." He coughs out a phony chuckle. "It really is a brilliant excuse for poor decisions. Little, stupid, scientists." One end of Rex's lip pulls up as if snagged on a lure hook. "Anyways, it is or was an illegal substance with a curious aftertaste. Shortly after ingestion of smaller doses, the mind pulls, separating from its physical sleeve, spiritually hovering over its user. An out-of-body experience not dissimilar from haunting stories of death told by the revived."

Rex crosses one leg over the other at the knee. He points his glass with the big ice cube and the furniture stain at Cub. "While intriguing, that's not what excites me. You see, in stiff doses, the user falls into a hole. A rollercoaster with a broken steering wheel. To the outside observer, the user often appears to be intently staring at a nondescript wall. But, it's like Mother always told her bullied child, 'It is what's inside that counts!'" Rex leans forward. "Peering out an upper floor window from an empty skyscraper overlooking an empty city. For some—a nightmare. Wind blowing through your lonely hair, you desperately try to cover your inevitability. Terrors of a future you now actually have to control. But for us few, it is the opportunity. One man's seized moment is another's snapping trachea."

Rex drifts longingly at the ceiling in the afterglow of his own parade.

"Linus touched my sister."

Rex doesn't flinch. "It only surprises me that he waited. I won't beat around a barren bush. My cousin is a pervert. I know it and now you do. I make no excuses for his behavior. Rest assured, he will be dealt with accordingly."

Behind lips, Cub's teeth clench.

"I can see you are upset, but I am in *complete* control."

Cub stands. Tension tightens all extremities. He wishes there was something around sharper to throw at Rex than a tantrum. He shoves Rex's shoe from its crossed position. Rex braces himself in the shiny brown chair. The dark elixir sloshes and spots Rex's pants. Cub stomps away. Just before the door slams, a voice from inside the room calmly calls out, "Relax."

PULLED COLLAR NERVES

Her eyes blink away darkness. Rods open to dimness. She's disoriented. Exposed. Uncertain. Unsafe. She feels like a painting of a panic attack. In Führerbunker, toothpicks guard against the calm. Black blind spots blot in step with her racing pulse.

I should be mad. I deserve to be upset. Her mind races in a frozen body. The cringing yoga pose only becomes uncomfortable with thought. The words *retaliation, clenched fists, missing teeth,* and *strangulation* don't compete in her race. *Uneasy familiarity, quenching, guilt,* and *hushed pleasure* stand upon her podium. *I shouldn't feel this way. I know better.* She's been told she knows better. *Then why? Why do I welcome the pain and helplessness? And why should I feel ashamed to do so?* Scattering sand over the assailant's footprints. Already, the taste has left her tongue's tip and swan dove into lower pH. The tongue always wants more. Sticking out, it dries. How long does a waiting tongue take to dry? A hunger strike. Serial killers obtain their fix, but the fix, just like an appetite, always requires satiation. Always.

Shallow pants leak air. Like December mornings, she can almost see her breath. *Which part forgot the scream when his cool, bony finger slipped between my elastic waist band and my soft, pink flesh? Which part surrendered like prey, accepting its fate in powerful jaws?* A single ink droplet falling through a cold, clear, crisp glass of water. It twirls in invisible current. The denser blob passes, leaving a comet's tail in its wake. The same part hides its secret enjoyment. It doesn't take much to stain the column. Anyone born around B.C. would agree, purity is unattainable.

A knock.

Tingling re-freezes her body—expecting an encore.

The knock doesn't wait.

He pushes inside.

She only moves her eyes in a train of four.

"I don't like this place," her brother mumbles.

She thaws but feels as if she was caught doing forbidden things.

"Why isn't the light on?"

"I'm okay," she appreciates, but would rather be alone.

Cub steps forward into the dark room, stumbling over her bag. "I don't trust this..." He looks around, adjusting to black. "The whole place is probably bugged." Cub listens to the dark, waiting for a response. "You have clean socks?"

"I'm okay," she repeats in a voice Cub doesn't seem to believe. It sounds like she's speaking while still trying to hold her breath in. "Don't tell Steve. Please?"

Cub wedges the door open with her luggage. Then, he leaves.

IN CYGNUS, WE SLEEP

There are many different places one calls *home:* A nest, a hive, a house, a riverbed, a web, a reef, a den, a hole, a thicket, a cell. By design, they should give the occupant comfort and security—a sense of safety and belonging. That is the design, at least. Others promise the heart exists there. Many serve as nothing more than shelter with a good view or an escape route. Elegantly comfortable in tribal numbers. This assumes an ideal world. A world that ignores poverty, pain, bloodshed, and fear. A world that resists viewing the top part of the half-filled glass. The unprepared, unsharpened, well-manicured are first to sip their last. Most forgot the true feeling of starvation in their dusted and polished roost. They will thrive and then they will perish—with their things. Vultures will strip their bones.

Cub returns to his kennel.

It will be just as difficult to fall asleep tonight between snores.

LIGHT TRESPASSES

He wakes to a loud noise and arguing. Feet bang steel ladder rungs —blunted, the way carpet does footsteps.

Sydney squirms under the covers. Cassie doesn't move. A voice creatively screams bad words in tones that crack like a teenager or a trained whip. *It is Charlie.* Throwing the blanket off, Sydney hops toward the door—his bile-green tube socks dangling by the toes. He leans an ear as if trying to listen for reindeer hoofbeats. Using two hands, he quietly turns the knob. The hinge creaks the way heavy limbs do in stiff wind. His sister stretches. Noticing activity in the main room, he creeps down the narrow hallway. Cassie follows in frog pajamas.

Standing behind his chair in a perfectly pressed military outfit, Rex greets them, "How did you sleep?"

The chair's wooden feet drag across poured concrete when Rex offers a seat to his youngest guests.

"Good," they reply in unison.

"Did you dream?"

Sydney did, Cassie didn't. He nods. She doesn't.

"What of?" To Sydney, Rex doesn't look interested. He looks fake the way he leans in—waiting for answers—he blinks like Pepé Le Pew at pretty cats.

"You never had kids, did you, Mr. Rex?" Sydney asks. Rex

raises both eyebrows, creasing his smooth forehead. "Didn't think so."

Interest in himself interests Rex. "What makes you say that, young Sydney?"

The boy looks down at his plate, then back up at Rex. "Because. You talk more like a principal than a mom."

For once, Rex doesn't correct him.

SLEEP UNTIES RUMINATING MISCHIEF FROM THE ROTATION'S KNOTS—SOME ROTATIONS HAVE STRONGER HANDS

Remy is the next to appear from the hallway. Cub is a step behind. She longingly looks back at him, smiles, holding it intentionally long, waiting for a happy response. She doesn't appear to get what she wants. His mouth stays straight. They sit.

"Nice of you to join us. Steve and Charlie are already hard at work topside."

Slithering steps become more audible. The orange cat bursts into the main room, then slows to look back.

It's him.

Linus is a special kind of creepy. When shaking his hand, assume to be touching body fluids.

Cub anticipated emotions. He expected a soured affect from a disciplined cousin. Instead, the crescent figure calmly offers a finger. The cat reaches its nose up. It sniffs and then licks. Linus gives his best friend a grin and sits down. He closes his eyes while taking in a deep lungful of breakfast aroma. "Ah," looking up at Trey, Linus says, "I think today ith going to be a good today."

NEWTON'S CRADLE

Cub smells raised suspicion. Lucy has been gone since his feet tapped Delta's uppermost rung. *This is quicksand.* Elements haven't changed, but the game has—and he is losing.

Cub lost thirst for competition since his first puff. Strange how negative-reinforcement drives many but snuffs others. Some of its potency originates from respect toward the tongue shaping its criticism. Some, not. In this manner, humans appear less like machines.

It is not difficult to fight inevitability, but it is impossible to win. Some claim, *everything happens for a reason.* These *some* lack understanding and desire forgiveness without begging for it.

Mistakes drive evolution. They always have. Big or small, they shape tomorrow's progeny. The imagination that our entire known world forms primordial soup, slicking the brow of a gigantic being, or that we *are* that gigantic being is simply back-door reality. Metaphorical examples of a greater truth—that we are the crops to be harvested. Yet, the harvesters never realize, they are also crops.

Aboveground, Cub picks at his elbow scab. All morning, he and Charlie have been obeying orders while Trey and Rex praise Steve. *Steve is smart—old smart. There's no denying that annoying truth.*

Trey is always happy, like someone tattooed a smile between his thin mustache and chin stubble. Rex only laughs around Steve, and it sounds forced. Everything else is business. I look forward to hurting Linus.

Steve has this idea. It is a perspiration system for collecting water. "It's drinkable." A large clear-plastic sheet domes over a smaller black tarp. Water condenses on the clear plastic and rolls down the rim into a funnel. The collecting pipe runs in an undug trench below the frost line.

"That's where you come in," Rex says pointing to Charlie and Cub before handing them each a spaded shovel.

Dew droplets dry in the autumn sun. Tiny clear pearls of

perspiration desperately cling to Cub's tanning skin, trying not to be bucked off with each exhaustive load.

Steve explains plans to Trey and Rex's open ears on the far end of the solar farm.

TIME TRAVELERS, WHO DO YOU THINK CONTROLS FOSSIL FUELS?

Earth rumbles. This time, it is a long one. It stops.

"Wow. That was a big one," Cub mutters.

"Of course it is. The procession is coming," Charlie says.

Hunched over his shovel, Cub shoots Charlie a sneer. Charlie doesn't notice.

"I'm the vice president, you know," Charlie manages between heaves, interrupting a long episode of silence.

The trench gets longer, and the dirt mound grows taller.

Cub gives him a puzzled look, "You're *what?*"

"Vice president. Rex said so."

Sydney was right. Charlie does smell like burritos.

Cub points toward the three tall men in the distance. "Your vice president is over *there*." Jealousy peppers Charlie's resentment.

LINES MADE FOR WAITING

"Mister Hoagland likes to talk in hieroglyphics, doesn't he?"

Alone in their room, Cassie looks down at her brother. His eyes are fixated on a drawing. She drifts back, considering their conversation with him at the table about tricks and misdirection. "Yeah, he does." The conversation ends.

"Syd?" She interrupts his concentration. "Did you see the cat this morning?" He nods. "Me too." They both look at the door, then back at each other. "I'm going to find it!" she giggles, bolting for the door.

"Cass, wait for me!"

TRAUMA'S MENU

The circular center area which was their breakfast room has been transformed back to a living area. Tiffany bulbs spit out oranges and reds and golds.

A neck stretches to rub the back of its master's hand. Its eyes roll back before blissfully closing. The fur underneath vibrates while its master lays on the long, fainting couch.

Giggling gradually clears the hallway.

In one quick motion, the orange feline is at attention. It perches. Linus recognizes. He turns. Two snow globes sitting on separate doilies decorate the coffee table in front of the couch. He crinkles his body to get a cleaner view.

Spotting Linus and the cat, Sydney stops laughing and freezes. His sister crashes into him from behind.

"Hey! Why—"

He points. She follows his finger to understanding.

"Didn't your parenth teach you ith rude to point at people?" Linus lisps.

Sydney shrugs. Disarmed, he approaches. "Can we pet it?"

Linus sits up. A puff of red hair sits atop his head and tufts brush out from each temple. The cat accommodates and plants in his lap. Fur-coated muscles tense.

"Ith not an it. Ith a he. Hith name ith Archie."

Nystagmus jiggles Linus' eyeballs. He observes the black children across the coffee table. *Apprehension.*

"Ith okay." Linus strokes Archie, nose to haunches, giving the tail a gentle tug at the end. "He duthen't bite humanth." The cat rubs his face against Linus' belt.

DANGLING KARATS

Sydney looks at his big sister for consent. Her face doesn't discourage, so he approaches the couch.

Linus slides over. "You, too," he tells Cassie. She hesitates, checking the hallway behind for excuses. *Empty.*

Slowly, Sydney sits. Linus' smile looks villainous. He clasps Sydney's hand and moves it toward Archie. Sydney pulls away.

"I wath jutht helping."

Sydney hovers his hand over the cat's head. Instead of embracing it, the nose sniffs. Its nostrils pinch and flare. Body muscles relax. It levels its head and blinks with approval. Linus nudges Sydney.

The first stroke stutters. The second smooths. Sydney's mouth corners curl up.

Cassie whispers, "I want to try."

Linus makes room on his other side. She sits. His grin grows. He places her hand on Archie's head and strokes hers while she pets Archie—hand-on-hand contact.

She whispers, "Soft." Sydney nods, vision fixed on the cat. Linus' eyes move up Cassie's forearm. His touch follows. *Her skin is smooth.* His thumb swirls her tiny arm hair in circles. Under his breath, he chuckles. *She didn't stop me.* He inspects her arms. *No ports. Perfect. Good catch, Rex.*

"I bet your parenth were poor, right?"

Sydney shrugs, but Linus is fixed on Cassie. She shrugs, cocking her head away from him, maintaining stroke rhythm. Archie buries his head in Linus' lap.

"I can hear him purring," she says.

"He really liketh you."

"I really like him."

"I really like *you*."

KNOCKOUT MICE

Before dining, Rex aligns his utensils. "Let me tell you a story. A true story... about misunderstanding." Except for the kids, he captures their attention.

A smile can't hide. "Once upon a time, the world viewed mental illness as physical struggles. Constricted blood flow of humanity's carotid arteries. Shiny dark medicine balls attached to its anklets—preventing progression. Scientists manipulated molecules, concentrating chemicals drawn up and derived on shale-black boards using compressed shells. Tinctures were given to the detained, unwilling participants, to be observed. Some failed, but others succeeded! Multiple personalities lost their voices, trading them for stiff legs, dry mouths, and jingling keys to unlock their straight jacket. White men in white coats unhumbly accepted the glory of success, and blame fell to the feline. Great, right?" Rex rhetorically pauses. "Wrong. This, my friends, is misunderstanding. Confirmation bias sold us an alternative truth. It happens all the time. Throughout history, people have been exiled for discovering truths too early which violated the commonwealth's beliefs." Science stifles evolution like a catholic candle snuffer.

"Schizophrenia is a big, scary term for someone advanced enough to peer through the thin film between our world and its parallel. Their new sense allows them to see through the milky bubble in which we are trapped. Captives. And this... is freedom?" Rex cracks his knuckles.

DOWNPOUR AND CAUGHT IN THE NETTINGS OF NOW

It is quiet and alone. Remy lays on her full stomach amongst the Tiffany globes. She saw the kids drawing earlier and it reminded her of what she was told she used to enjoy.

Mom and Dad shepherded us, burdening life's responsibilities. They swept our mistakes under lumpy rugs without the expectation of apologies. They took pride in helping us learn and teaching us to become better people.

Did they embrace their roles right away or was it... unexpected? In a strange, unexpected way, I feel responsible for Cassie and Syd, but I don't think I'm ready yet. I miss Mom. I miss Dad. I want to cry. Remy looks around for voyeurs. *I should be able to cry, but then again, Mom and Dad are heroes until they are seen crying.*

I miss being a kid and its relief from responsibility. She sketches a short triangular dress on a crudely drawn girl with uneven eyes and a nose that looks more like a question mark. *I miss the freedom to make mistakes.*

"Salt."

Remy looks up from a woken, internal dialogue. Her thoughts have been chasing each other in a borderless game of tag across kerosene-slicked monkey bars of *what-ifs.*

"Excuse me?" she defensively asks. She wonders how the rotations have learned to stretch like Kayan necks. She wonders how long she has been motionlessly hunched over her hands, lining up the creases in her fingers in Feng Shui fashion, because it feels correct. She wonders even more how long this warden, with all the answers to survival but none of the answers to social etiquette, has been staring at a skinny, plain girl half his age. She pulls the lower trim of her shorts down to hide her golden-hair-sprouting thighs.

THIS... IS DELTA

He senses her discomfort, if only momentarily. *We wouldn't have let a neck of whiskey derail.*

"Sodium, more specifically. You see, it's a simple element, but oh, how vital." He approaches her brown fainting couch in the living room. She slinks to the far end, isolating on a single cushion. She pans the room, but they are the only ones around. He coughs a laugh as if to expel her passive aggressiveness.

"It is mental illness' counterbalance. Bowling's bumpers. It is the figurative mother of every child—cheering up when things are bad and calming in moments of omnipotence.

"Mental illness didn't start as a chemical imbalance, it ended as a chemical imbalance. It started as a kidney problem." He explains that kidneys have a simple job. Much like mail sorters, they observe, identify, and then file according to chemical and charge. When impulses slither down nerve tissue, they rely on the correct chemicals being filed in the correct zip code.

Rex watches confusion grow in Remy's expression and senses her attention planning an escape. "Let me put it another way," he regroups. "We evolved from the oceans—a giant saltwater bathtub. Our body and organs function better nearest their roots. And then, there's lithium..." He looks off in contemplation. "The problem is, lithium looks like sodium to a mail sorter." When his glance returns, his fishing pole bends.

HISTORIANS ARE KNOWN FOR LONG WIND

Lithium? Remy will never forget going to a friend's friend's house after sports practice. This second-hand friend had an older first-hand brother who glamorized drugs and bizarre music.

> "You have any money?" he'd asked, brushing away her golden bangs, caught between her eyelashes. She didn't. "Then, take this." He closed four large pale-pink capsules into her hand. His hands were cold as if he had been redecorating an ice box. "My sister will show you how." He dragged his fingernails along her legs. "Smooth."
>
> Giggling out of uncertainty and captured in the moment, the friends ran downstairs. The lights were off, and no one turned them on. Laughter bounced off the marble floor and faux marble

pillars into one another's ear holes. Poolside lamplight splashed through the French doors, allowing the group to find their way to an empty spare basement bedroom. Ponytails bounced with dog-treat excitement.

"Shut the door!" It slammed. "I meant quietly!" Girls infectiously giggled.

"Sorry," she said, but hardly was.

Someone pulled out a disposable lighter. Someone emptied a capsule and asked, "All of them?" Someone tapped each half of the single aught capsules. White micronized powder, lighter than flour, drifted down the cylinder's mouth into a holding bulb.

"I guess so," someone responded. This was the point Remy realized she was more scared than excited. She also realized that she was the youngest girl here. Her brain scrambled for excuses like a cornered convict.

Someone tapped the glass, so the reluctant powder unstuck from the sides and tumbled into the bulb.

The lighter sounded like dry heaves before it ignited. A bashful flame heated the base. Scorch marks grew. It clouded in yellow condensation. Curious cumulous nimbus in the shape of a straight-jacketed witch's face. Someone corked something and handed her the glass science experiment. Straw pointing in, a friend's friend told Remy, "You first."

"I remember inhaling coils of smoky white yarn. Swallowing rubber bands like thick, viral mucus," she tells Rex. "It felt like—"

"Stop!" he interrupts. "I'll tell you how you felt." Remy hides her frustration behind a gin rummy face. "Lithium wasn't formulated for inhalation, so I'm sure the powder caused you to cough and gag, unless you are a seasoned smoker." Remy neither confirms nor denies. Rex continues.

"The chalky powder expelled from your lungs, some landing on your tongue, confusing taste buds into a racial riot with one-quarter salt and three-quarters poison. Your lips looked like you just finished a powdered-sugar donut." Remy crosses her arms but remains attentive.

"We are now six heartbeats in. The tiny sacs in your lungs have been hard at work exchanging carbon dioxide for oxygen under pale yellow snowfall. The flakes melted when they landed, as the first ones of new winter always do. Dissolution. Transport. Smuggling. The drug entered circulation like an illegal immigrant. Five heartbeats are enough to spread the influence. No manmade wall ever successfully kept out all the unwanted. Your blood-brain barrier suffered the same fate."

Remy attempts to correct him, but he only speaks louder. "Then. Then. Then, you felt the absence of hopelessness. The absence of helplessness." Rex's eyes widen, and he points at Remy saying, "Free from restlessness, anxiety, and racing thoughts! It made you feel extra medium!"

"Nope," shaking her head. "It just gave me a headache and made it hard to think—kind of like someone flipped a giant wine glass upside-down and snuggly fit it around my entire body," she mocks. "Like, a pacifist capturing a cockroach—too afraid to kill it while God watches from above. I mean, from everywhere."

"Oh," Rex dismisses. "Well, you just didn't take enough."

SOMETHING FALLS APART

Nights have their means of scrubbing turmoil away. Thick bristles remove hard, caked-on grudges from almost any surface. There was never a problem that good old-fashioned elbow grease couldn't cleanse.

And that's the morning when everyone was surprised—almost everyone. Yesterday's trash needs garbagemen. The table bustles to a noisy clanging of flatware on flat plates. A soft, kitchen sizzle heats timeless meat and meat-like products.

Charlie never seems to eat breakfast. Without a mirror, he pictures himself as Rex. Standing, with one hand gripping his chair's backrest, he judges. There are two types of people: those that live for personal accomplishments and those that live for the praise of others. Charlie would rather have the newcomers believe he *had* power, than actually *earn* it.

Linus sits next to an empty chair across from Steve and Cub. All three men avoid eye contact unless it is with their plate. Remy breaks up a spat between the kids. Trey flips a powdered egg.

From down the hallway, a surprise momentarily halts chewing, clanging cutlery, and quarreling. It stops scolding and judging—everything but the flipping. In walks Rex. He's trying to ignore it, but with each step, he winces.

Growing up, siblings learn early never to hit one another in the face, otherwise Mom and Dad may find out, and that makes more trouble for both. This morning, everyone found out about a big brother. Marionette strings. Observed in the right light, make-up lines reveal flaws. Scripts behind actor's mouths. Software glitches.

HEIMLICH'S SWALLOWED PRIDE

The legs drag when Rex pulls out his chair. Eyes return to their own paper when the teacher comes back. *The room pretends not to see my new black-eye.* He studies them—around the table—assessing their reaction. Nobody is obvious enough. Rex clears his throat before tucking a napkin into his shirt's collar.

The shooting pain has dulled to a red pulse around his tender socket. Picking up a knife and fork, he attempts to challenge the eyes of his comrades. None offer. *They all know. They all see it.* Morning mucus and pride make it difficult to swallow.

"Eggs?" Over his shoulder, a spatula and a smile come into view. The scrambled eggs have a gentle bounce when landing in the center of his plate.

Rex surveys the audience of downcast eyes. The kids resume their squabble.

"There's more where that came from, boss," Trey playfully says from the kitchen. Rex dabs his darkened eye before letting the warm, shiny meal cool. No one needs to clean his utensils this morning. Behind the countertop, Trey ices his bruised knuckles.

MADE IN STOCKHOLM

"Every rotation is Saturday and I miss school."

Cassie agrees with her brother. Secretly, she misses fur through her fingers more than school. Linus' orange cat likes her. It arches its back to meet the pressure of her touch. When the door opens at night without a knock, the cat pushes its triangular snout through. Whiskers press against its cheeks as it wedges its way in. It always finds her first. She can't remember a time when she was ever a favorite. Linus likes her, too. *But he is cold and smells invisible. When I pet his cat, he pets me.*

"I love you and I'm glad you are home," he tells her. *He acts like Sydney isn't even there so Sydney gets a lot more drawing done.*

Sometimes, when Linus does bad touches, it makes me feel tingly. He whispers, "Ith okay to keep theecreth from adulth," *which is hard to understand because he is an adult.* His lips brush her earlobe, *"You're thpecial." I make the cat's fur so shiny with the brush. Clumps of hair come off. Thank goodness for fur having roots or Archie would be bald! Linus kisses the top of my head and takes a deep breath like he is sniffing me.*

It used to make me feel more weird than it does now. I like the attention. I am more important. He paws me like I paw his cat. "You make me happy," he tells me. Sydney rolls his eyes the same way he does when actors in films kiss. Archie is warm. The tuft behind his ears is the softest. His tail seems too thin, but that's okay.

TIME IS A HUMAN CONCEPT

Trey loads plates with pasta before anyone arrives at the dinner table. Humans file in. The warm aroma clings to the air. With everyone else seated, Rex seems to glide, instead of walk, to the back of his pushed in chair.

Ting, ting, ting.

He raises his glass and chin. Rex's black-eye arrogantly looks down his nose at his tablemates.

There is a flowing looseness to his movement that Cub doesn't recognize. *He's under the influence... of something.*

Placing elbows on the table, Steve folds his fingers and leans into them. He shakes his head as if to crack the tiny vertebrae in his neck.

Rex begins speaking.

"Time is a human concept. Time *was* a human concept. Down through history, self-important people filled their lungs with the smoke of burning libraries. Oranges bronzed their complexion. Yellows and blues added twinkle to their eyes' reflection as flames played tag from one stack to another. Did guilt or doubt ever crawl on eight legs in the back of their minds?" He rhetorically pauses. "No. Leaders would wise up, covering their faces with 0.22-micron filters as they watched electrical fires spew black waste-clouds up into a thinning ozone layer. Digital encoding saved rainforests for other indulgences. Slaughtered rainforests saved the planet from complex plastic wastelands. The elimination half-life of timber is far shorter than high-density poly-ethylene.

"The fantasy of a digital home over an analog, terrestrial one stinks of luxury and prestige. But, what happens when the code scrambles?" Rex looks around the table. "Ah, the connection fails, even after multiple attempts. Flicking a power switch doesn't fix anything. The ability to use technology should not dismiss the user's responsibility to understand how that technology works."

Ice cubes clink as Rex sips his water. The brow near his nose curves downward. He scowls at his tablemates as his voice grows.

"You actually think you are unique? Some, freak cosmic accident?

"You are simply recycled notes from an undying symphony by an orchestra that never tires. Never loses its breath. Its conductor never gets sore arms.

"You are sweat off the backs of past dictators. The blood of past slaves. Your new ideas are your ancestor's old, forgotten ones.

"You see, life is merely a costume party. We wear the consequences of our decisions until our shoulders cave. Atlas should have done more cardiovascular exercise.

"Even your finest accomplishment is a priceless ring slung off the stern of a boat into a deep, dark lake in a world full of countless deep, dark lakes. Maybe your impact on the world will send a couple lazy bubbles back to the surface. If you're lucky, a small ripple.

"That which separates the winners from the losers is the ability to identify and then correct one's own mistakes.

"Whether anyone likes it or not, the world belongs to a hidden dynasty of architects that communicate in a clacking cacophony of silver spoons.

"Civilizations have risen and burned. They will continue to do so. Technology advances and then accepts deep regressions into digital smithereens, leaving its survivors and predecessors to decipher the ashes. But, I'm fireproof! I'm not a piglet waiting for government-mother's trickling nipple! Green will reclaim the planet in abundance! I have not the desire nor the power to save everyone." Rex slams his fist into the table. Cutlery rattles. "I've resigned myself to become king of the cockroaches!"

A CONSTELLATION OF SYNDROMES

Rotations in a bunker never seem to begin until pupils touch the radiant sun. This morning hasn't begun yet. As usual, Steve and Rex have skipped breakfast and gone to the surface. Trey rotates the meals. This one consists of oatmeal, an egg, and tiny blueberries. Cub can't remember what real milk tastes like anymore. He splashes the runny white fluid over his cooked oats and passes the container toward Sydney.

An untrained *thunk* followed by something dragging repeats itself down the master's hallway. Cassie and Sydney crane their necks toward the sound's direction.

"Aren't you kids hungry?" Trey calls from the kitchen. Remy stops chewing and, under the table, squeezes Cub's thigh. She knows and now he knows—Rex took care of it.

Thunk and drag.

"Eat, you two," Remy adds.

Thunk and drag.

"It sounds like a zombie," Sydney tells her.

"Just eat."

The orange cat trots into the kitchen's light, emitted from diodes. He freezes and turns his head. The tail's tip twitches.

With crutches tucked under each arm, Linus appears, moving in swings. The rubber tips *thunk* in unison. His left leg drags, finding balance, while the bent right leg hovers just off the ground behind him. His foot is swaddled in a faded-blue towel, heavily peppered with rusty red stains.

In exhaustion, Linus collapses into his chair, slumping over his clean empty plate.

"Seconds, anyone?" Trey chirps. "Last call!" he says with cheer.

AN IDEAL CONCUSSION

Cassie's face warms. *I bet it is glowing red.* Hot histamine turns noisy faucet handles across millions of immature facial pores that know not how to pronounce *acne*. Misdirection is the only way to avoid the spotlight's heat. Ask any politician.

She reaches for the cat's tail as it passes under her chair. In the background, soft tapping on the skillet stops. She purses her lips and makes mouse whistles. The cat comes. Underneath the tablecloth's overhang, she observes Linus' limb. It looks terribly uncomfortable. *Did I do something wrong? Is this my fault? Did he fall?*

"Cass."

She lifts her ducked head right up into the table's belly. Silverware rattles above. Something tips over. A saltshaker, perhaps. She immediately covers her new bump with a rubbing hand to calm the throbs.

"Owey." Her head breaches the tabletop to find everyone's stare.

"Finish eating and then you can play," Trey says. Underneath, the cat licks her calf.

THE GREAT MAZE OF BIRTH

It has been three sunrises since her flesh produced natural melanin. Remy watches his every move without understanding—without even trying to understand because it is not necessary to enjoy the story—the way a creator studies his subjects.

She watches his large hands manipulate fray-tipped wires. Some, he twists and clamps, others, he snips and strips. Her eyes drift up to his thin gray hairs, sparsely covering his balding head. The dark aging spots remind her of lefsa.

Strange. No matter one's beauty, the eyes always draw back to the blemishes.

She feels uneasy in the silent static. "Can you tell me a story?"

He stops tying something black to another something black, judges her expression, and then returns to work.

"Please? Something real. About you." A laugh pops out like an engine misfiring. He shakes his head. "Anything?"

Continuing to work, he says, "When I was your age, I never expected forever to last this long..."

She sits in silence, watching his face crinkle and wince. The wrinkles pull apart his mouth like matinee curtains. She can tell he doesn't enjoy talking about himself, but she listens anyway.

He hesitates like a cat pawing a dead mouse. "My dad never thought much of me. Nothing like I thought of him." His hands slow. "I used to spend calendars watching him move around a dirty garage before he let me touch anything. And, when I finally did, he told me I was doing it wrong." Steve relives his story. She can tell.

"Gradually, he let me pass him tools. He taught with cursing. I imagine that's how he learned." His hands stop. He leans in. "We teach the way we were taught."

She scratches the back of her arm.

"When we would finally emerge from a garage-afternoon for supper, Ma' would be so proud. It was as if Dad and I worked *together*. I appreciated it, but looking back, it felt hollow—empty calories. I wanted *his* approval more.

"I remember the moment more clearly than my wedding. In soiled overalls, left side buttoned, right side hanging down, just like him, we were fixing the washing machine. 'Engine blowed out,' he said. I was seven and stupid-young. Monarchs fluttering in my belly. He hadn't cursed all morning. That rotation, I always handed him the right tools." Remy notices a twinkle in the gutter of Steve's eye before he blinks it away.

"With the rebuilt engine installed, we tested it out before putting it back together." Steve tells Remy an aside. "When fixing something, do one piece at a time, then test. Otherwise you'll never know what part's wrong when you think you're finished."

Remy nods.

"When he plugged it in, I waited for the smoke. I shielded my ears in case something exploded. But, it worked! He knew it would, I think. I got excited to hear it rumble to life. Over the noise of the machine, he yelled, 'Okay, shut it off!' I did. One after another, like an assistant passing surgical equipment to his superior, he began to reassemble the casing.

"Life has turning points—growth spurts. With the tub back together, he noticed me. Alive. He noticed the little him in me. I was waiting for him to ask for the spanner wrench, but instead he said, 'C'mere.' He pulled over a shop chair and said, 'Up.' I did. He pointed, I turned clockwise. I remember his powerful hand closing over mine, closing over the wrench for the final tightening. I didn't dare look into his eyes for fear of breaking the spell. I did without words. He clapped me on the shoulder when it was done.

"I'm pretty sure that was the first time Dad liked me—the first time he considered me a friend. My hands were dirty just like his and it felt good. Mom called us in for dinner that night like she always did—showering me with hollow praise. This time, I was already full."

Steve didn't cry telling his story, but he softened. "Thank you, Steve." He tinkers.

"He was never proud of me unless I did something he couldn't."

"I'm proud of you, Steve!" he hears her say with an unearned, hollow receipt.

GRAHAM CRACKERS AND ARTHRITIS

Maybe it was curiosity. Maybe it was fate. Maybe it was all the maybes that seemed to confine him to "Delta Island." Whatever the reason, Cub's feet propel his legs which propel his body down the master's hall. He wraps three times on the heavy fire-resistant door.

He waits. He slowly tests the knob. Latches move. *It isn't locked.* He knocks three times again, only louder. Amber light spills from under the door. Clouds of nag champa incense find olfactory glands when he bends down to peer beneath the door. A reflection of white cotton socks off the shined floor shuffles shadows. *The old man is dancing by himself with himself.*

Correcting his crumpled posture, Cub knocks again, this time breaking the door's seal. "Hello? Mister Hoagland?" He opens it further. Nag champa fumes spill out like an opened ice box in Haiti. The smell is pleasing to Cub, but the thickness gathers in the back of his throat like sawdust.

A white awninged eye obstructs the opening. Excitement displaces shock on the septuagenarian's face to greet Cub like an old friend.

"Hey, hey young fella'. Come on in!"

"I knocked a couple times, but..."

"Yeah, sorry about that," Hoagland interrupts. "My hearing isn't what it once was." The door springs open. Two streams of smoke spew from separate brown incense sticks on opposite sides of the room. Hoagland is wearing an almost-transparent white undershirt and equally clear boxer shorts, but the welcoming grin is inviting enough to disarm Cub's hesitation to bother the man, triple his age, this late in the evening.

"Don't worry. I wasn't in bed yet. In fact, I sleep very little. Has been that way for a while." He coughs out a short, abrupt chuckle. "Guess it comes with old age." Hoagland offers Cub a seat at the far end of the room, then holds out a Swarovski glass dish full of aged after-dinner mint pillows. "Take lots, take two!"

Cub waves them off and then he permits a grin. On the desk is a Fisher-Wallace Stimulator. Picking it up, Cub stretches the headband's elastic. "Doesn't this electrocute your brain?"

A blanket of seriousness crosses Hoagland. "Electrocute implies demise, but it shocks. It also saves my life." He places the candy dish down and Cub settles into the seat.

"So, Hoagland, what were you saying about us not being the first?"

CHARLIE AND THE VEGETABLE FACTORY

Waking in panic sets the morning's mood.

Charlie's screams echo down the barrel of Delta's entryway.

Vibrations carry urgency. "Thieves in the greenhouse!" Remy's entire body pulses once, like a sleeping limb—her heart galloping like clomping hoofbeats.

Chairs drag in high pitches. Silverware recklessly crashes to the floor like drum cymbals. Only those practiced in panicked-waters thrive under its wet pressure.

She inhales deeply as if her diaphragm is on lunch break, before whipping off the covers. More commotion stirs outside her cell. She cracks the door to catch Steve striding down the hall, stretching one arm into his black-and-white-flannel sweatshirt. Through her cracked door, through his, she sees her brother lacing up his boots. Thankful for old world chivalry, she pulls her blended-cotton pink robe over her shoulders.

Feet ring ladder rungs. The kids' door opens as if timid of boogeymen. Remy scurries to them, draping her robe around them like a cape.

When the silo's hatch opens above, she hears domestically-violent yells echoing images only seen by Fort Worth's finest or hostages in sandy places by brown men dressed in black beards. The hatch clatters shut, muffling trebles, but the bass in their voice transduces. Cassie and Sydney's narrow bones hug tighter.

SHE THROWS AWAY PRAYERS LIKE LOSING LOTTERY TICKETS

Curiosity is life's greatest tease. Energy fills the above-ground voices. The bass resonates with a terminal vibrating shrill reminiscent of fluted glasses having their rims rubbed.

Remy stands at the base of the ladder. Looking up plays bifurcating tricks on the two-eyed girl. The kids, a pace behind, shiver for her next move.

Remy's ears seem highly tuned to the upstairs activity, painting dirty pictures in her imagination. "You don't have to," she tells them before reintroducing her soles to the ladder.

The first two steps out the front door are a marathoner's most difficult. Courage builds. Her senses are dramatically heightened. Clarity reveals the language. She notices soot in the ribbing of the dimly lit silo walls. The smell is sharp with aluminum and mildew.

Morning sunlight coquettishly pushes through the flap's outline. Using a finger, she nudges it open as a swimmer tests water temperature, or a golfer judges wind.

Screams. A man's curdled and cracking in its highest breaking octave. To her, it sounds more porcine than person. It begs in pants and syllable-less pleas. And then stops. She listens, but only hears a high-pitched whine like a music-less stereo turned way up. A bird squawks for its mate.

Expecting murder, she wasn't surprised. "Don't shield them! Reality is gritty! They deserve to receive their burden of survival." *Rex is talking.* Pride fills his voice—a sense of accomplishment. A successful hunt. Rex would slaughter a flamboyance of flamingos if their feathers brought his cheeks a rosier glow.

She can't help it. She coddles them, and she knows it. "You coddle them, and you know it," Rex calls out. "You are an enabler. Step into the sun and taste its shape."

She passes through the hatch and bashfully descends the outer ladder. Cassie and Sydney stick to her shadow like it's raining eggs and Remy is the only one with an umbrella.

She still can't see him. She drags her feet around the closest greenhouse. Golden field-grass waves in frog heartbeats at the property's perimeter. Hazy green plexiglass has been removed from an upper greenhouse panel and haphazardly balances on the white frame.

She peers around the corner. A little hand squeezes and pulls on her hind leg. Rex comes into her long view amongst the matted grass at the far end of his greenhouse parade. He stands with a fist resting on each hip. His chest is out. His chin is up. He looks triumphant.

Below him, in a puddle of meat, is the assailant, she presumes.

He takes inventory of her timidity. "It's okay, my dear. This is over."

The walk doesn't seem necessary. At least a pirate's plank-walker never faces post-traumatic stress. She does it anyway. She encourages the kids but feels as if she is pushing them to approach a funeral wake-casket. When unsure how to express their emotions, children cry. They both do. She cradles the nape of their skinny necks.

Charlie emerges from the golden grass. Steve rubs his hands on the trimmed grass, looks at them, and rubs some more.

She can tell it *was* a man. His oily black hair clings in shiny black ribbons strewn across his forehead. His hands look like claws, frozen in time, immediately after touching an incredibly hot panhandle. His posture is fetal. One barefoot is exposed, growing thick yellow nails with dark deposits packed underneath them. One crumpled hand covers his mouth.

Rex watches Remy watching the brand-new corpse. He sees her lips recoil and stifles a laugh. Charlie soccer-ball kicks the meat pile.

"That's enough," Steve says.

Charlie seeks Rex's approval.

"That's enough," Rex agrees. "Boy, get the shovel."

PRODROMES

Tiny knuckles rap at her door. In some respect, it is better than roosters afraid of Earth's star.

Cassie is first. "Remy? You napping?" She wasn't before.

"Yeah, Remy, you asleep?" Sydney adds.

"Come in you two." She props herself up against the wall, legs still under the covers.

Fumbling at the knob, it finally turns the correct way, and both burst through. They leap, each to a side of her, mimicking her posture.

In the air, Sydney holds up a black piece of plastic. "Look what I found!"

"Look what *we* found," Cassie corrects him.

"No, *I* found it, look!"

Both are nearly out of breath with enthusiasm. It's hard to focus when the thing is practically touching her nose. She withdraws his hand.

"What is it?" She pries it from Sydney's fingers.

"Let her have it, Syd."

"I know. I am. Here."

Remy doesn't recognize it, but it seems like it could be a plastic shell for a ping pong ball. She straightens up. "Did you find it outside?"

"No!" Sydney yells, springing to his knees.

"Softer, Syd."

"No, we were asleep and then it—"

"It sounded like keys dropping on the—" she interrupts before being interrupted.

"No, Cass. Let me tell her. I want to tell her," he pouts.

"Fine, just tell," Cassie crosses her arms.

Remy motions as if to hurry along with his story. "So, this was in your room?"

"Yes!"

"Softer."

"Yes!" he whispers. "It sounded like dropped keys and it fell on the floor in the corner by our feet and I found it."

Sydney is a run-on away from breathless. She looks questioningly at him. "Show me where."

The kids scamper off the bed like a dog chasing a teeth-marked rubber ball.

"Wait." They turn back. "First let me put on socks." They race out of the room.

A SOCIOPATH'S PAIN-SARCOPHAGUS

Although different folds of fabric, tree limbs and dead bodies are both cumbersome and heavier than they appear.

The sun casts sharp shadow-borders over his chore. Cub holds hands with the previous him, but they are limp. The grass acts like Velcro. Tugging yields centimeters. Yanking yields a few more. *Maybe, when it stiffens, things will be... better.*

The older men have hidden their shadows like eager ground-hogs. This, they claim, is "for his own good." It will "make him stronger." He rubs a hand across his mending elbows with thoughts of brandishing them.

Digging joins mindless labors aimed at cultivating thoughts. Cub wishes for a better way. The handle slicks in his paws. Head-shaking frees sweat droplets from the tip of his nose. Earth grumbles. Bent knees steady him, lowering his center of gravity. Perspiration jiggles loose. Grumbles pass.

Leaning on the tool, he looks skyward for the culprit, but finds none amongst the blue. In the distance, his lifeless chore lays heavy. *Maybe softer earth would make this easier, maybe not.* A few scoops under, the soil behaves more like clay. It flakes instead of clumps. *No one will know if this is shallow.*

Time passes as it almost always does. Everyone seems to have gone underground, leaving him unsupervised—unchaperoned. Give a mortician enough anonymity, and digits will explore.

Breaking from the hole, Cub looms above. His head cocks like a dog trying to figure out a sudoku. He brushes hair off the body's forehead. The soul left this vehicle half-unopened.

Cub lifts the vehicle's shirt, exposing loose skin. He dangles the shovel over its pinkish flesh, then stops. He senses familiar eyes laundering him. Satisfied in his solitude, he scrapes the shovel's fingernail across the body's abdomen. A white line forms first, then black-cherry beads bubble up. He replaces the shirt. Cotton wicks up Cub's mess, as several paces away, the shovel plunges back into clay.

THE ONLY THING THIS MANSION DOESN'T HAVE IS SPACE

"I found it right here!"

"On the floor?" she asks. Sydney corroborates. She pats the bare bricks. Each groove, a signature, not unlike her own prints. Her eyes pan upward. Tuskegee strikes. Where the walls meet the ceiling, a piece of grout has been chiseled out and replaced with a voyeur's touch. The kids' black evidence is a lens collar.

"What is it?" Cassie asks.

How long have they been monitoring? Is there one in every room?

"Did we do good?" Sydney asks.

I've got to tell Steve, or does he already know? Does my brother know? Should I even tell him, or would that ignite our peril? This isn't something the kids need to know... yet.

"Or something wrong?" Concern crosses the little ones' faces.

She gathers herself, straightens her long sleeves and puts on her best Mom voice. "No. You two did absolutely the right thing. Thank you for telling me."

"Are we all in trouble, Remy?" Cassie asks.

"No," she lies. "Of course not," she lies, again. "Well, I'm not sure yet, but when I figure it out, I'll tell both of you. For now, please keep it our secret in case it is dangerous. Please?"

They both aggressively nod in understanding, but she knows kids and their porous mouths. The hourglass has been flipped and the whole bunker is full of eyes and ears.

DEATH SUPPORT

Like a family desperately trying to imitate one, everyone sits down for dinner together. Tiffany lights set the ambiance for a warm meal that resembles oatmeal.

"It's porridge," Trey says with a smile, ladling a steamy spoonful as he circles the table. "Like the three bears, I think."

Rex clears his throat and unfolds his napkin across his lap. Tension is palpable. Of the newcomers, everyone but Steve stares down at their bowls with arms at their sides. His old crew pays no attention. They already spoon mouthfuls into sloppy lips. The other side of the table sits motionless.

He wads a napkin and picks on the weakest. "Sydney, tell me about your rotation." The boy doesn't make eye contact—just shrugs. "Did you learn anything?" This time, Sydney doesn't even flinch.

"What about you, Cassandra? What did you do today?" She rapidly shakes her head like someone being force-fed locusts. Remy notices Rex picking up a scent.

"Why don't you tell him about the picture we—"

"Excuse me. But, I'm talking to Cassie," Rex raises his voice to Remy. This draws the attention of everyone.

Steve sets down his utensils. Without making eye contact, he calmly says, "Lower your voice. You are scaring the children."

SADLY, SOME KIDS KNOW ABOUT TUMOR LYSIS

For Cassie, the next few moments occur under a concussive halo. The wide world webbed around her own smaller one moves, but she doesn't take part. It is not uncommon for young molestation victims to curdle into a seizure-ball during times of extreme pain or stress—nature's nurturing mechanism.

Ushered in slow motion, Rex stands. His hips jolt the table. Cassie doesn't hear silver forks and spoons crash to the floor. To his immediate left, Steve jumps, bracing an arm across Rex's chest as if to break up a schoolyard fight. Cassie's eyelids rapidly flutter. She doesn't hear Rex's chair teeter on its hind legs and topple backward. Rex's pointed yells are politely muted by warm waves of gamma-aminobutyric acid kicking through the blood-brain barrier's batwing doors. Her spine buckles. Charlie lightly dabs his mouth with a red and yellow napkin after finishing his plate.

Reality wobbles with Vaseline-smeared eyesight. Cathode rays sputter into darkness. Her screen saver engages. The hard drive stops recording. She misses Remy clutching her sheik body before it slumps in the chair. She misses horror striking her little brother before an avalanche of dewy tears. She doesn't witness the grin on Trey's face drop.

A GENTLY BLOWN OUT MATCH

Like a slow hot bubble through honey, reality fades in. Her lap is warm. One hand is being cradled. With her free one, Cassie cups Archie's head. The cat exhales a vibration without moving.

FRUIT OF THE LUMINARY

Encouraged, Remy sits up in bed, hovering over Cassie. "Cass, you..." she recites Hen's secret, "we all came from a happy place to go to a sad one. Faith ushers its loved ones back to that happy place."

Why is it so much easier to express emotions to someone who lacks the ability to appreciate them?

Cassie's eyelids flicker reality away. Remy can't tell if her words sunk in. She rubs Cassie's little fingers in hers. "Be strong, for me."

Mercy is a lousy apologizer.

LAPPING TEAR PUDDLES WITH SANDPAPER TONGUES

Cassie oscillates with coherence over the next five thousand heartbeats. She emerges submerged under a prolactin spell. Her post-ictal mind boots in safe mode. Her sweet brother coils around her left arm in the small twin bed. A damp rag sleeps on her forehead. Remy sandwiches Cassie's hand in hers.

Burning pain gusts like wind through skyscrapers from Cassie's tongue. She mouths a cry but the rest of her refuses to cooperate.

Near her knees, the mattress sinks as if from a small, landing dumbbell. The volume knob on her ears turns clockwise. She sticks out her tongue the way an old man stretches before rising. Muffled mouth-sounds proclaim, "She'll be alright."

She feels finger pads on her thighs. They creep her lap. An eyebrow pulls its lower friend open to enjoy the view. Hot cement settles between her legs. A tail softly claps her thigh like a dropped jumping rope.

Cassie cranes her neck like a frail can opener. Bright lamplight floods her optics. Saturation accommodates. Down regulation of neural data reveals an orange feline. She recognizes the white whiskers and relaxes her head back with happiness. The cat stretches its chin over crisscrossed arms across her belly button. He doesn't seem to mind the rise and fall of her breathing.

CHIRAL REFLECTING POOL

Doctor Mohs carves ice cream scoops of time from Cassie's memory. She doesn't forget the lap warmth. Her stomach gets up before her—a dark black pit filled with emptiness. Smooth muscle rings her stomach like a bar rag draining only gastric juicy juices.

Bending at the waist in bed, she slips a hand under her shirt to palm her thin belly. The fur-ball perks—not quite looking at her directly but watching her. If cats had eyebrows, his would lift in questioning disposition.

"Sorry, boy," she pats his head. The eyes calm. The room is

empty. The door is cracked a feline-width. A glass of warm water sits undisturbed on the nightstand.

Since arriving, this is the first time she can remember not having Sydney at her side.

With the guilt of Damocles, she lifts her furry friend. He seems to not understand why one would ever move. Out the door, Cassie creeps, and the cat follows.

ENRICHMENT QUESTIONS ARE TOO DIFFICULT

No matter one's environment, spins become routine. For growing brains trying to make sense of a world around them, consistency forms scaffolding on which mistletoe hangs.

After supper, he waits because he always finishes before his big sister. He flips off stiff socks that used to be white. *An idea!* He closes the bedroom door. *I'll surprise Cass by hiding in her bed!*

Stripping off her covers teases up giggles. He hurries, carelessly tossing her blankets on his air mattress. He hunkers under his blankets on her bed. *Hers is nice and big!* Crouching under the covers, he hides. The room's light is on, but he is buried in black. He listens for her. He smells his own breath and the plaque-coated teeth. He scratches an incisor and sniffs the filth under his fingernail. He holds his breath to listen closer. He listens to nothingness.

After a short while that feels like a long while, a cool non-claustrophobic rush of air washes over him when he defeatedly whips off the blankets. He sits on his crossed feet in the center of her bed. A clump of her bedding rests tousled on his empty mattress on the other side of the room.

Sydney's shoulders slump. His head hangs, and his bottom lip pops out like a cash register drawer. Aloud, he mutters, "Oh, poop."

PILLARS OF CREATION

"I know this may sound strange," the old man begins. His face is a niacin head-rush, puffy and noticeably redder than the rest of his flesh. Under circular gold-rimmed glasses, his bulb nose looks like acne's homeless shelter. Hoagland's pale-blue eyes quiver, whether from intensity or neurodegeneration. The old man looks to either side like a paranoid drug dealer before leaning in close to his pupil. "We are not the first," he says raising a pointer finger between them. Cub hasn't noticed him blink. "We have naïveté like a budding relationship, but it's just not the case. Old documents clearly explain this."

"Dead sea scrolls, you mean?" Cub offers.

"Older. Much older. Older in a way we cannot comprehend. To us, it is just a big number. To *them*, it has meaning."

Cub watches the storyteller's expression sharpen. His tone limbers. The man has told this before—a singer's rebirth the moment microphones warm.

"Of course, we don't know or understand all the details." Hoagland admits as an aside, "Probably never will." Back to unblinking, "It's difficult to believe genetic material can be born of nothingness, an innocent primitive soup of free-range amino acids and electrical charge. That's because it is. It's almost impossible." He pauses. "Once the proverbial ball gets rolling, well, *they* do the rest. Welcome to the baptism of secrets!" he proudly smirks.

Cub squishes a confused face.

Mildly frustrated, Hoagland reaches into his side pocket for a handkerchief, dabs his pink brow, and perseveres.

"It was the beginning of artificial intelligence." He straightens with confidence. "If a race advances far enough without slitting its own throat, it will develop a partnership. On this planet, we call them: machines. You see, but that's not good enough. That's not effortless enough. There is an expectation of better—a *need* for automation."

Cub watches the picture focus, and this excites Hoagland.

"Yes, you see. We developed artificial intelligence. But, we weren't the first. This *always* happens." Words start merging on Hoagland's crowded mouth-highway in pressured speech. "You see. You see, the ancients, the very first, gave orders to their heartless ones: *improve our environment, replenish resources, and make abundant foods*. The machine's logic converges on a single, optimized solution—destruction of their creators." He wipes the handkerchief under his nose.

"Given a long enough timeline, every creation is encouraged to turn on its creator.

"Fuels and resources on *their* primitive planet eroded and logic pointed to the stars and neighboring spheres. Where *ours* is motivated by procreation, *theirs* is motivated by preservation. You see, time is a human concept."

"You sound like Rex," Cub says.

"Nah," Hoagland chuckles. "*He* sounds like *me*... in a Dunning-Kruger way."

A soft, bashful knock interrupts. "Who is it?"

"Me," Remy's muffled voice replies.

Upset to share his Cub-time, Hoagland doesn't deny her entry. "Come on in."

He drags a footstool next to Cub. She sits. Her hair looks as if built by bees.

"So, how were we made?" Cub asks.

FIAT-INSURED PONZI RETIREMENT ACCOUNTS

"Technologic epiphanies, the ones that hum with their simplicity... The ones that make you stand and ask, '*Why didn't I think of that?*' Innovation is local and not new, but often buds in desperation. Not little ones like new techniques for tattooing. I'm talking about the big ones. Fire. Oral communication. Mathematics. Religion. Money. These are the universals. They are our way of interpreting our surroundings.

"Yes. The ancients were enslaved by *their own* inventions. To these metaphorical golden calves, logic outweighed emotion. With *their* expansion came a new thirst for resources. Fragments of genetic material carved from our ancient ancestors were systematically launched into space toward prospective, fertile lands in an effort to seed the area for harvest. Genetic jump-starting—inherited terraforming.

"It's elegant to believe evolution flows along the curves of its surroundings. Sadly, for the poet, most begin and end roughly the same. Fate's blueprint."

"Wait. So, we are living because... The meaning of life is to be cultivated?" Cub pointedly asks.

"Well, that's part of it. The resources thing. They expect us to make the same mistakes. In fact, we will, eventually. If you bury a dandelion seed in dirt, don't expect to grow pink chrysanthemums."

"If we know this, we can stop it."

"Nope. It doesn't matter if *we* know this. Evolution is only missing a precursory 'R.'" He waits for them to understand, but they don't. "Evolution is actually revolution, and this is a momentum thing. What happens to a coastal man who stands on the shores with his hands outspread to stop the incoming tsunami?"

"Bubbles," Remy says.

"Bubbles," Hoagland agrees, "And then nothingness."

STUFFED TO THE GILLS WITH FISH STICKS

"How do you know all this? Where's the proof?" Cub questions.

Hoagland waits for Cub's words to settle to the floor.

"Proof." He stands. "Proof?" His eyes bug out above his

bulbous nose. Cub stares at the divots. "Proof only stretches to the edges of our own understanding—our own imaginations—and that's not far. Certainly not far enough!" Arms swing wildly in circles. "And *they* have a massive head start!" He composes himself, sitting back in his chair, "Look, many systems operate with only simple relics of proof, and this is no different. We call these, for lack of a better term, traditions. But, just beyond our grasp, are straws of truth."

Hoagland's concentration bounces between the siblings in front of him, trying to take their temperature of belief. He raises a hand as if to plead for silence. "An example: why do we bow our heads, close our eyes, and fold our hands before praying?"

Remy's shoulders roll. Cub's don't.

"We saw *them*! *They* visited us long ago and we observed *them* communicate! Nowadays, we call it telepathy, but *theirs* was far more sophisticated. In all our foolishness, we mimic out of fondness for understanding. Watch a small child observe their parent talking on a mobile communicator. Later, that child will pick up anything that resembles one and speak into it as if to have an actual conversation. Just—like—Mom."

"This is going to sound stupid, but when we learned that God is everywhere—"

Hoagland doesn't let her finish. "*They* are everywhere, or at least a lot of places around us—tricking our senses. Invisibility was so 'two-solar-system-revolutions ago' to *them*.

"The visible will always be our first threat." Hoagland rises, rubbing his hair with a slick palm as he paces in front of them. Nerves squirm.

He snatches a peek at his audience. Scales slide on a chemical brain imbalance. *Should I divulge this next piece of truth?* The words writhe on his tongue with anticipation the way a first 'I love you' does.

And then, they come out in projectile fashion.

"I've seen *them*. Beings with gas masks. Uncontrollable fires.

Demon-sneers watch us perish. Locusts gather our crops. Black boils sour our skin!" Hoagland's pacing ramps. He disconnects and now seems to be speed-reading incomplete sentences.

"A new Anne Frank of cleansing ethics. Chanting the sermon of tyrants. Streamlining the hive's mind. Unification of thoughts. Ignoring fear. In a facsimile of fraud. Many acting like one, as one lobbies for the greater good of one. Lisa Frank's rainbow-yolks bleach in color-blind depravity, hatching us from the new Anne Frank!"

Cub grabs Remy's arm and lunges for the door. Hoagland's hypnotic state breaks. "Wait! Too much?"

Cub drags his sister out. With the door still cracked open, Hoagland stands dejected, by himself. *Was it something I said?*

THE LAST TO FALL ASLEEP WAS MIDNIGHT

Perhaps, it was out of protection that Cub yanked her from that chair. Maybe it was out of brotherly love that he tugged her hand and led her back to her cell like a teenager, caught by Daddy, necking her crush. Maybe it just appeared to be less effort than coddling her through sleepless nightmares and interrogation. Little did he predict, by escorting her away, *his* tonight would be sleepless.

Remy places the lens cap in his hand and softly whispers, "They always watch us," before disappearing into her dark room.

Cub lays on his back in blackness he can't ever imagine getting used to. His eyes are open and dilated but that doesn't help sort out direction. Had it not been for the bed, he'd believe gravity to be a faerie's tale.

He restlessly tosses, listening to his roommate pass air through tar-stiffened windpipes, belching the occasional glottal snore.

New questions pulled from old soil swirl in his mind like fiber-clogged toilets. Hope seeks an answer the way televangelists' phones never cease. Burgundy can't find her way home.

Satisfied in dissatisfaction, he crawls out, keeping low, tapping his hands in front the way blind people use their outstretched cane. Locating the door jamb across the room, his hands walk upward to spin the handle.

To his surprise, light washes over his cones. He shields his face but unflinchingly walks in sideways humility toward the source.

He knows who it is, and he has been expected. A hook has been set in his cheek by a fisher of men.

Seated on the sofa, a single Tiffany illuminates a seemingly transformed Hoagland. Where once there was a nervous cocoon of bashful thoughts and downcast eyes, now hatches a confident man: shoulders back, arms akimbo like a Hindu god breathing the cleanest of oxygen through re-gifted incantations. He doesn't ask Cub to sit, he *commands* it.

CHAPTER 21

PRESIDENTIAL ADDRESS

P eeling back the sheer bathroom curtain, he gazes out his ivory castle. The night is shrouded in its finest dark blues. Behind him, he hears a drip.

Pajama bottoms embroidered with noble symbolism slink to the cold tile floor. He turns around to sit and think in solitude.

Faucets leak, but no one fixes. Alarms beep, but no one changes the batteries. Orange lamps tell us to check our engines, but we ignore them. It is far easier to purr than to stroke. Greed pushed the hypnotized back toward the caves. Artificial rewards measured in bank account numbers and cluttered homes supplanted life's simple pleasures. We had been blessed with entitlement, the gift that keeps on taking. We demanded respect instead of earned respect. We fought with lawyers instead of fists in a fantasy world of sophistication. We lived in fear of scars. We regularly gave to the charity of me.

It splashes. He tidies and flushes. After cleansing his royal hands, he dries them and shuffles off to bed. Behind him, he hears a drip.

CHAPTER 22

BRAIDED NARCOLEPTICS

Cub obeys. No wonder confidence resides atop a heap of attractive traits, not limited to humans. It is the timeless, intoxicating powder dusted into the unsuspecting sipper's cup beneath parasols of power.

He perches on the seat's edge with laced fingers, waiting to accept Hoagland's sermon, and eager to yell *Hallelujah* or *Amen* during every pause.

Hoagland is the storyteller sitting around the figurative campfire. His monsters aren't fixed with long claws and short tempers. They aren't dressed in shadows or eternity. They don't enjoy feeding on conjugated terror. They eat the finest flavors. They sip from fluted glasses. They dress with tailors' help from womb to tomb. They manipulate rules and industries to remain in veiled power using everyone beneath them as personal human resources.

Amazing how the directionless seek a compass. Primeval retinas turned to constellations to explain their origins—fixing an answer, wrong or almost-right, to a problem. Assigning a name makes hardships easier to digest—meat body tenderizer.

Cub sways in a trance, open to suggestion, like a charmed cobra sprung from a woven basket.

"I understand," he says before the young man explains anything. Tension dissipates.

Hoagland's face looks like it has undergone a chemical peel, stealing lines and wrinkles the way late night advertisements only promise. Cucumber smoothed sockets demand Cub's attention. The old man could be a reincarnated cult leader, for one.

"You protect her, and I admire that."

Hallelujah.

"You were brought here for a greater reason."

Hallelujah.

"You are being groomed for the new beginning."

Hallelujah.

"A brown leather rope slips through the government's curled hand and its best friend, tongue loosely hanging, races after a pretty white spouse perfumed in fertile hormones."

For his steadfast love endures forever.

"The first steps are always the most difficult."

Hallelujah.

"But we must not be paralyzed by fear."

Hallelujah.

"A domestic cat believes its whole world, *the* whole world, exists in its master's home. Is it so hard to believe we would think any different about *our* whole world?"

Cub realizes, then utters, "Hallelujah."

Pleased, Hoagland continues, "We define ourselves by our own perceived limitations. I'm here to tell you, those limitations do not exist!"

Amen.

UNDERSTANDING CHANGES EYESIGHT

He drifts away to a choir of angels plucking taut wires on ancient instruments. Their lyrics drown in harmony as if they've rehearsed this a little longer than forever.

Tonight, Cub never heard his roommate's snore. He doesn't remember slipping off dingy socks. He doesn't even remember leaving Hoagland's presence. Sleep digests life's conflict into bite-sized forgiveness, and relief surfaces in a way only it knows how.

Morning dark brings a tabula rasa of clarity and amnesia. Steve's empty bed is his rooster call. Pieces fit together to form a cascading Russian Tetris. Uncertainty has been alleviated by organized thought. If hypnosis worked this well, toilets would be full of pills that poorly balance neurochemicals.

He feels like a hero, *the* hero, chosen among many. He no longer fears mortality. He is not aboard a ride, sliding upon a spine of black ice. He *is* the ride. Axles spin with intent, moving treaded tires, gripping ground with complete control.

Today is the first today since arriving that Cub makes his bed and folds his clothes. Shoulders back, chest out, he struts to the main room for the last breakfast.

Sydney and Cassie hum together at the table, waving spoons above their unsuspecting heads. They clash silverware in imaginary explosions. Sydney's cheeks swell with food—bursting soggy whole grains on his chin's shelf. Linus quietly sits to their left with hands neatly folded in his lap. His plate is empty. He simply watches them as if memorizing. He subtly sways with their movements as one does watching boxing—avoiding punches. A crutch leans against the back of his chair. A fixture in the background, Trey scrubs the kitchen countertops. No one else is in Cub's sight.

The table greets him with a bowl of rolled oats. Skin has grown over the top while waiting for him. Raisins nest the crown. Interrupting play, the kids wave.

"Everyone else finished. They are waiting for you topside."

"Morning, Trey," Cub replies to the background.

"Good morning, sir. Enjoy your meal."

Cub leans over his raisin-speckled oatmeal, glaring at Linus, watching *his* kids. *He ignores, but still feels my stare.* Linus' larynx jumps to dampen a dry, intimidated throat. The puffy-haired redhead steals a glance at Cub before pretending to ignore.

"Enough," he raises his voice, still glaring. Everyone at the table turns to him. Scrubbing in the background stops. Cub stands. Walking to the other side of the table, he picks up Linus' dishes and brings them to the sink. Table eyes follow him. Returning and from behind, he thrusts hands in Linus' armpits and lifts the reluctant, but feeble, redhead. The protests aren't sentences or words, but merely whining sounds. His wounded gait *thunks*, disappearing down his corridor in a sulking slouch.

Cub returns to his seat. *The kids watch me.* He turns to them. They recoil with assumed guilt. "Eat. And enjoy." Behind, a rag resumes mopping the countertop. Cassie and Sydney glue their attention to their food. Cub's spoon breaks oatmeal skin and raisins climb aboard.

After eating, Cub emerges from the hatch atop Delta. Fresh wind brushes his skin. Its coolness rustles his short sleeves. *Where did they hide Steve's vehicle?* The surrounding topography is low and flat. *Elevation offers the best vantage point for spotting Lucy.* He swivels on the top ladder rung, scanning all directions. Greenhouses fan away from Delta in two opposite directions like a bowtie. Perpendicularly, the solar panel farm emits a low buzzing sound like overhead power lines. Track marks, like scars, conceal buried cables extending out from the silo. Digging the new landfill, Cub has spent most of his time beyond the solar farm.

He takes a moment to appreciate the beauty of Rex's compound. Even though Cub recognizes he is being abused for labor in completing the landfill, he basks in the gratification of finishing a project. The sense of accomplishment revs his confidence.

He recalls a conversation with Steve. He can't remember how many sunrises ago it happened although he remembers Steve's emphasis on the word "purpose." He reflects on the importance of life with purpose.

"Come on down, young man. We have a lot of work to do." *It's Rex.*

"I'm enjoying the view."

"I didn't ask what you were doing. Let's go."

Cub admires Rex's sprawling success, but realizes Delta as someone else's project, not his. He desires control. With a hand in his pocket, he fiddles with the lens cap he received from Remy. He contemplates Steve's mantra. *Purpose above sustainability paves a path toward freedom.*

"Now!" *This freedom suffocates.* Cub obeys. "Excellent." Rex aggressively squeezes Cub's trapezius, pulling their bodies close. Guiding him toward the solar farm, Rex's voice echoes in the emptiness, "Charlie will work with you on that sewer chute."

SYMPTOMS OF GOD

Trey exits, leaving Rex alone in his room with only an assignment. Breaking stern lips into happy ones, Trey disappears toward the kitchen.

Now alone, Rex reaches for a low-profile glass. He sloshes the melting ice cube in a sticky brown elixir. It beautifully rattles against the glass. *I love that sound.* He raises it to his lips, tilting his head back, but changes his mind. He doesn't drink. He sets it on a coaster. Clutching his temples, he winces, pleading the ether for an answer. *They don't appreciate my genius. How can I convince them into understanding? I have become the father that labored but never loved.*

His composure and tie straighten in an oval vanity mirror. He notes the handsome man's reflection. He studies the reflection's dimensions, realizing his is unbalanced—too manic. He pulls two handles, revealing a long, flat drawer just under the vanity's table.

Inside, a rectangular mirror with a small mound of pinkish powder looks up at him. He bows and sniffs.

Wind burns his septum. Senses flood as he erects. He feels a gentle breeze, that doesn't exist, brush through hair, that does. The air never felt so new, so soothing—fresh menthol lungs. Relaxed, yet not. Toes curl over the edge. They flex over an ending. "It could all be yours," says a disconnected voice. "The last punctuation."

Positive airway pressure peaks at the end. Arms stretch in a Christian torture-pose. Triceps wiggle. He senses warmth. He becomes the warmth. He is the glow. He feels candle wax running from its wick. Once-priceless vases shatter. *Some things aren't worth fixing. Some people aren't worth saving.* Calendars suddenly flash open. He attempts to stuff others' screams back in their cage. They are auditory victims on parole.

He turns up the tip of his pointy nose toward the oval vanity mirror, inspecting nose hairs for flakes. Satisfied, he slides the long drawer shut. Ego dissolves into numbness as a bubble finds the center of its leveler.

Between glorified statements, a buyer's feet shuffle closer to the door. He must deliver one last argument as the orator of chaos. He turns the knob and struts down the hallway.

Rex doesn't wait for the curtains to open, he rips them apart.

Rex doesn't wait for the Tiffany lamps to cast his shadow before speaking.

"Good evening, everyone," he calls from the hallway. Table conversations hush when he appears. He approaches the back of his chair like a podium. Wisps of white steam waft up from each heaping plateful of food. With hands behind, his back proudly pushes his chest forward. His navy military outfit is perfect down to those shiny silver buttons. His mustache hair flows together. He is Delta. *I am Delta.*

"As some of you may or may not know... I have not been completely honest with you... about our situation." Around the table, faces exchange puzzled glances. "For this, I beg forgiveness." Trey dries his hands while hips swivel around the granite counter to enter the main room. He stops behind Rex's left shoulder.

"While our location appears to be secluded, it is not. New evidence has come to my attention that our coordinates have been compromised." His eyes pierce and walk around the table. Hoagland is visibly the most distraught.

"The attack on the greenhouse, *our* greenhouse, was only the first of many. Intelligence admits there are more to come... many more." Charlie scratches the white patch on his temple and then nods with understanding. "The next wave will be more ambitious... more violent. We are being targeted by those that don't have, because of the things we do have."

Rex slowly walks, heel-first steps, around the table. "Then, the good news." He pats Cassie's shoulder as he passes. "The good news... I was ready for this. I will not let them steal that which they do not deserve. I will not let them take that which they did not earn. I will protect you from them. I know exactly how to keep you safe. You know I have proven my ability to overcome adversity against shrinking odds. I have demonstrated forethought and preparation." He raises his arms out, offering the prepared bunker as proof. "I have provided for each and every one of you the luxury of not starving."

Rex catches the Asian's expression curious, rather than cheerful. *No matter.*

Slightly irritated, his volume grows. Emphatically, he points toward the ladder, "Out there is trying to drag you down. Well, I'm not going to let that happen to my friends. I... *we,* will not cower in fear. *We* are the rabbit's egg that was meant to be found!

"*Out there* is poverty, while in here is abundance.

"*Out there* is desperation, while in here is thriving.

"*Out there* is greed, while in here is camaraderie.

"*Out there* is chaos, while in here is hope.

"*Out there* is a purge, while in here is a renewal."

Hoagland pumps his fist after each proclamation. At the end, Trey does, too.

"The world dry heaves and we are all that's left in its belly! We are life's stubborn survivors!"

He expected rallied applause. He expected a standing ovation, but Trey and Hoagland were the only ones to oblige. Their clapping rapidly peters out. Sydney raises a nervous hand to speak, but Rex shoots him an icy bug-eyed glare. The boy lowers his hand and Rex's face relaxes.

"I am truly honored to have you all with me through this turbulence. I am comforted knowing this..." he raises a finger. "Progress always saves room for dessert."

Trey attempts to pat Rex's back but swipes at dead air as, heel-walking away, Rex disappears down his hallway, leaving a plateful of untouched food.

Everyone but Sydney bends their neck to watch him vanish. The boy asks, "Remy, where did you leave the bathroom jug?"

LOPERAMIDE COULDN'T STOP THIS SOCIAL MOVEMENT

With the evening meal filling their bellies, Delta's occupants gradually disperse. Last to leave the table, Cub scowls, watching Linus clean dishes. *I make him uncomfortable—ashamed of himself—the way it should be.* He catches Linus glancing his direction. Linus' movement becomes clumsy like one who is aware he is being scrutinized. Cub withholds a grin. Linus flashes a quick wave before *thunk*-ing and dragging to his room.

Cub pulls out the chairs and folds up the table, converting the dining room back into a living space. Leaning on the exit ladder's bottom rungs, he stares up the silo's throat. *I should be nervous.* He superimposes his future on his lack of freedom. He visualizes liberation. His eyes begin to cross. The ruffled metal above creates a spiraling optical illusion which appears to pull the ladder into an event horizon. Bothered by the vertigo, he flicks the light switch, extinguishing the miner's lamps lining the silo's neck. Eyes adjust. He double-takes. *Odd?* At the domed top, moonlight sneaks around the borders of the hatch's door. *It isn't even locked?*

IF THE BATON ISN'T SWEATY, YOU ARE OFF THE TEAM!

He knocks once. Without waiting for a response, he opens Remy's door.

"We leave tonight. Make sure the kids are ready," he tells her. She nods. She shuts her door.

The light is off when he enters his room. The pitch-black snores. Instead of flipping the light on, he crawls toward the glottal noise. He feels for the bedposts and shuffles in between them. *Snores loudly rumble tonight.* He reaches into his pocket and pulls out a closed hand. Dragging fingers along the mattress, he locates where it sags most. He lowers his fist on the body. It lands above Steve's waist. *He's sleeping on his back.* Using gentle pressure, he agitates Steve's stomach with the fist. Snoring punctuates with a sound that reminds Cub of a surprised hiccup.

"Take it," Cub whispers to the darkness. Large hands close around his. "They've been spying on us." Cub places the lens cap into large hands. Hoping for a more encouraging reaction, Cub reveals his vulnerability. "At night, they touch my sister."

Anger tinges Steve's audible sigh.

"If you are coming, pack with the lights off." Crawling toward the door, Cub tells the dark, "We're leaving shortly."

A blade of light escapes beneath the children's door. Cub turns the knob without knocking. Poking his head in, the giggling stops. Two guilty faces, surrounded by a perimeter of toys and unfolded clothes, stare back at him. Insulted by the messy room, his lips purse. Eyebrows lash like angry check marks.

"Didn't my sister tell you to bundle your things?" he growls. In unison, they nervously shrug.

"I'm not telling you again," he threatens before abruptly slamming their door. *Manners are stomped flowers beneath a tyrant's march.*

INDIGENOUS TRIBE ENCOUNTERS CIVILITY

Before knocking, he listens. He doesn't hear music. He doesn't hear dancing, but someone's feet shuffle inside. *He's pacing.* Cub knocks. Hoagland opens. The door quietly closes them in. "Let me tell you a story about two tribes." Hoagland's tale begins with a tribesman confiding in another about a recent encounter with a foreign tribe.

> "He brought another one back. I don't know why. They are careless. They have soft hands and feet. They smell like flowers. They talk too much with their *mouth*. They ask too many questions.
>
> "This is not a good time for us. Our shaman fell ill and seeks healing from our brother tribe. We trust them. Chief seems unconfident. His people sense it and he knows this. We rely on our shaman and, without him, we are weak.
>
> "We have agreements with neighbors. Much blood sealed the pact a long time ago on both sides. We live in calmed tension. Controlled anger. Unspoken fear.
>
> "But now, that fear is spoken and exposed!
>
> "Their shaman is a wise man. In our weakness, he casts curses on us and our crops. Air bends our arrows and straightens our fishhooks. Things crawl underground, consuming the roots of our harvest.
>
> "This is not the time to bring a new one in. His tongue speaks in soft clicks. He blinks too much. His clothes twinkle and shine.
>
> "He uses telepathy to communicate with his relatives. Where we may only speak to our ancestors during rituals, he straps eyes

atop his own for enhanced vision. I don't like him or his voodoo."

Hoagland's glossy stare breaks to meet Cub's attention. He quietly waits for the moral.

"Through translation, he finds out that the tribesmen didn't even know there was a massacre of his own only two generations prior. Indigenous' grasp on history is loose. Today is more important."

Cub twinges with under-understanding. He pans the room one last time, appreciating the relics of an old world with which Hoagland currently lives. "Well, we leave tonight," Cub says.

Sighing, Hoagland nods the way a man does receiving news that his best friend must move away because of separating parents. "Focusing only on the box before him, Skinner missed the box *around* him... May you be blessed in the treasure of darkness."

WHAT LAWYERS DESCRIBE AS *TEMPORARY INSANITY,* PARENTS DESCRIBE AS A *TEMPER TANTRUM*

Cub lies in ways he'd never admit. He embellishes to shock, not to dictate history. Some events require fewer bent lilies.

He doesn't need to break oath on re-telling the hysteric act with which he commanded the kids to pack or the way wind whistled by his ears while dashing toward the escape ladder.

He doesn't have to invent a new shade of nervous red colors overwhelming Steve's cheeks as he waves the crew from atop the silo. He would have made a good third base coach of a dying pastime.

He doesn't need to compose ear-splitting pitchy notes to describe Cassie's screams belted out of tune. The way she squats in anchor, kicking her feet in a desperate tantrum, refusing to

SCOTT LUTHER LARSON

leave under the veil of night. Ear drums rupture and awaken Delta's sleeping occupants.

He doesn't have to exaggerate a story about tugging her hand so hard he could feel the elbow slip from her little joint. He yanked only to have her settle back into the same position.

He doesn't ever remember hearing her beg but his memory imagines his sister's pleas before watching her feet disappear out the hatch ahead of him.

Bodies flood the entryway in equal palettes of half panic, half curiosity, and half anger.

"I want to stay!" were the last words he remembers her saying before being swallowed by his former comrades.

"I'm getting my gun," was the last thing he heard before scampering up the silo's ladder, shaking off desperate middle-aged hands.

"Over there!" echoed off the stars before he heard a rifle slot loading ammunition. His bag bounces off his back with each sprinting step. The nitrogen-filled air burns his lungs the way hydrochloric acid stains.

He passes his sister right before he hears the first bullet whizzing dangerously close. When it passes, it sounds like it is sizzling its surrounding air, ripping molecules from their companions in a celebrity divorce.

Another shot rings out. They don't outrun gun smoke's cologne. Sulfur bonds with concubine oxygens that wed on the very back of their retreating tonsils.

He catches up to Steve. The old man is fading with Sydney in his arms. The field has grown since they first rode Lucy, slurping her last gasoline sips.

Cub's legs feel red with lactic acid as he takes first place in a checkered flagless race. Behind him, he hears Steve ask, "You see that big tree over there?"

Sydney says, "No."

"Good. Run to it," he pants between deep belly breaths. "We'll catch up."

The last thing Cub saw before bracing hands upon each knee in desperate recovery was that little dark boy sprinting toward a darker nothingness in a hungry world of vanishing points.

SUDDEN LOSS OF CABIN SOCIAL-PRESSURE

Tonight would be historically referred to as: *the first*—fireless, cold, and scary. No one under the tall dark tree in this unfriendly thicket-of-unknown admits this with any shame.

The farmland around them grows without barbers. Once separate, now wants and needs grow together the way vines seek to suffocate their surroundings.

We are the weeds.

"They weren't aiming for us," Steve says pulling Sydney toward him. Steve strokes the boy's goose-bumped narrow arms to generate friction. Sydney stiffens and relaxes before approving, the way sheep submit to their shearer.

Eyes adjust but nerves don't.

The group sits in a silence of restless insect noise. Black tree-tentacles spread toward space above them. With backs supported by its large trunk, everyone sits in a circle surrounding the base. Cards are held close to vests with cautious gratitude. No one speaks.

Steve rubs his old knees and clears his throat before lighting a cigarette. It's impossible not to watch the glowing tip. Remy tracks it like a magician's wand—orange dot in a blue ocean. It sounds like an old painting by a forgotten artist.

In a strange way, she invites the smoke into her clean lungs. The wand loosely dangles between two thick fingers. A thin stream disintegrates while it integrates with its new atmosphere. *It's free—liberated. Was it better off before the flame? Do those robbed of sight feel the same way after morning awakens them?*

Unknown is the only certainty, no matter how Mother Nature dresses the crib.

Thoughts and questions chase one another up Escher's spiral staircase. Inside, Remy's skull feels like a carved pumpkin filled with hot bright candles of *what ifs*.

She is too frightened to cry, too frightened to sleep, and too frightened to show courage. She wants to ask what comes next but fears its answer. She wants to ask if it was a mistake to leave a bunker filled with food and warmth. She wants to ask how they will survive. She wants to know why they chose tonight. She wants to ask about Cassie, but before she can, Steve tells Sydney, "I'm sorry."

CHAPTER 23

PRESIDENTIAL SECOND THOUGHTS

Fruit prunes and sweet sours.

Presidential guilt awakens him from thin sleep. Toes quietly slip into plush slippers stitched in a foreign land.

Strange how his bed companion always complained of his snoring, but somehow can sleep through the noisy power generators.

He paws the dimly lit matte wall next to his nightstand to appreciate the rumbling. It continuously speaks in the same forked tongue a right-shouldered demon does to convince its host that the left-shouldered angel doesn't exist.

Floorboards creak when making his way to the window. The pane vibrates in sine waves of second guesses. He attempts to steady them with his fingertips only to find the pane chilly and resilient.

Having been upright for a few moments, presidential post-nasal mucus slides down the back of his throat. He swallows, but it seems stuck in a drain trap like a buoyed wishbone.

Maybe, I had no choice. He scratches a fingernail at a small spot of white paint that happened upon the window instead of the pane by an imperfect painter. *I came in with good intentions—not like my predecessors—but upon arrival to this respected position, I quickly realized it was a shackled seat in an archaic system controlled by outside powers with primitive leverage. I was David and slingshots weren't in our unbalanced budget.* Momentum and denial are smooth pills designed to easily slide down pacifists' throats.

CHAPTER 24

THE MORNING AFTER

The solitary sun stretches its bright arms through stiff morning clouds, fingerprinting black skies pale-blue. Cub's eyes sting in sleeplessness. Bringing them shut calms the strain but doesn't hum lullabies.

They snap open with a panic as an earthquake smiles. Shifting shoulder blades slide beneath. Thinking back, he doesn't remember any earthquakes while hanging their hats in Delta. Nature has plenty of tectonic reminders. They are Kennedy's moon, and Earth stuck a flag in their cratered spine.

Beside Cub, Remy stares with vacant eyes across unplowed fields. Plump wheat heads barely sway on their skyscraper stems. Their cracked-brown fuzz dryly clings, waiting for a beast or breeze to bring them to a suitor.

The planet spends a lot of life waiting. Pulled from a rich, entertaining habitat of sports, girls, hormones, and drama, Cub had never noticed the waiting. Patience would be a new trick for these old dogs.

The sun's rays yawn across the horizon but fail to bring their warmth. Cub runs fingers around the curves of his nose to discover a greasy film of oily sweat. He's cold. He's dirty. He's hungry. Still bundled in stolen blankets, he paces the length of the stray fence to generate body heat. In some respect, it is a walk of shame not dissimilar to a morning following a sin-filled evening of indulgence. *Last night deserved it.*

After walking the length, he returns to stand above Steve as if, in body language, to ask: *what's next?* The stoic old man sits, leaning against the fence, staring out. To Cub, he looks like a cigar store Indian statue.

A young man stares down at an old man staring out at eternity. Age stretches patience. Youth breaks first.

Stuccoing his question, "Now what?"

Remy turns as if she wouldn't mind hearing the answer as well.

Steve doesn't flinch.

"I said, now what?" he repeats with a healthy dash of frustration.

Steve looks up at impatience, only to be met by a scowl. "We sit."

"We sit? What's that supposed to mean?" His voice pops out, on the verge of yelling. At this point, it would be pleasing to see some emotion from the calm statue.

Remy sits up in case she needs to separate two hot heads.

"We sit. Then, we eat."

Ignoring the fact that he initiated the escape, Cub leverages burden on Steve. "We left a warm home with food and water and beds and shelter and safety and a plan... For what, this?" He opens his arms as if to display his surroundings to Steve. "We have nothing, and you say, 'sit and eat,' like it's so simple."

Stirring awake, Sydney's head pops off the pillow.

Staring back at the horizon, Steve replies, "We escaped a cage. And, life *is* that simple. We only complicate it with our own expectations." He flings a zippered knapsack at Cub's feet. "Share with your sister."

GIRLS ARE SELDOM WRONG UNLESS IT IS ABOUT SOMETHING THAT MATTERS

Breakfast forbids dessert without silver spoons.

The morning wanes with long strides of dissatisfaction. This is the feeling every ex-convict experiences when he first discovers his newly naked wrists.

The quartet walks alone together in single file, spaced apart in order of leg length. Everybody watches their own boots navigating unfamiliarity overcrowded by uncertainty.

Remy has questions she promises herself to ask. She shouldn't be shy. Equality saw its shadow. Ego and disrespect need a medicine ball. She crosses her heart, but her mind has its fingers crossed. *Tonight, I'll get answers.* She could guess but wants to hear —*needs* to hear—*wants* to hear.

She watches Sydney stumble behind her and extends a hand. He smiles big and runs toward it. He is a bouncing warm ball of glow. Histamine leaks through biologic pressure valves.

The world around her, with all its question marks and caution signs, melts away into a clear assignment. She shares invisible feelings with someone willing to unconditionally share. She looks down at his pink tongue framed in ivory teeth and can't believe life's black ice cast her in this direction after the collapse. Dust settles enough to see her purpose.

Led by Steve, they walk along the hypotenuse. Few find solidarity in loneliness, most find unwant.

Steve parts tall dry field-grass the way swimmers cut currents. Like deep steps in sparsely travelled snow, the rest follow in his footsteps.

He sees what most don't. The sun ticks its second hand, and he observes. Catching his breath atop an old utility road delineating property or possibly crop types, he stands on the raised ground, waiting for the others to catch up.

SHOWERING IN FIREWORKS OF BONE SPLINTERS

From Sydney's perspective, the man is omnipresent. *If Mom knows all the right answers, Mom's mom is way smarter.* Steve could be a hero waiting for a sculptor. His slender frame and tall stature commands respect. Sydney watches the icon cup hands around his mouth. Closer, Sydney moves. Slower become the steps toward greatness. He is at eye level with Steve's large black boots.

Cub climbs up next to Steve. *Cub is admirable but thinks second. That's okay.* When Sydney pictures himself, he moves in skin shaped like Cub, and that makes him happy.

A quick puff of white smoke jettisons Steve's paws and disintegrates into nature. He winces and blows a stream from the corner of his mouth like someone who's spent a millennium practicing. Catching Cub's attention, he points the cigarette toward distance.

Remy offers an outstretched hand to help Sydney up the elevated shelf. He clasps both hands around hers. His weight is more than she expected. Her knees buckle forward as he leans his butt out. He gives up trying, expecting her to do the lifting. She is his amusement ride.

Cub steps out of his interaction with Steve to support Remy. He grabs the boy's wrist. The squeeze surprises Sydney like a snake's bite and he peddles up the incline.

When Cub lets go, Sydney watches the handprint on his wrist unblanch from white to brown. *His touch is special. I disappointed him.* He swallows a nervous smile while Remy wraps an arm around his shoulders, bringing him in. *Her arms are nothing like his.* He watches Cub with Steve.

"I want to get there by nightfall." Steve motions. Cub shades his eyes toward their destination. Sydney recognizes the crop on the new side of the road.

Cub shrugs. Steve's eyes widen at the young man that thinks second. Shrugs turn into affirmative nods and they descend the road's backside.

Steps come quick. At the base, Sydney asks Remy, "Can we eat the corn?"

Granted wishes quench thirst like salt water.

Wealth narrows the line between want and need. Poverty is a bouncer with an impressive physique.

Always taller than it appears, thick corn stalks with yellow spears shoot up the way bamboo grazes. Traversing proves more difficult. Perhaps the "forest and trees" analogy should be rewritten in cobs.

Daylight smears to richer blues and Steve doesn't get what he wanted. Curtains of clouds close out the afternoon to an applause of hunting arthropods playing their mating songs with violin legs.

Steve uses a striker on Cub's gathered tinder before Remy and Sydney reach them. Brief orange sparks ignite the undeveloped darkness. Pockets of camera bulbs pop under dry shadows. Anemic twigs ember and burst. Sydney breathes in a lungful of pyrogenic pollution. Hints of tobacco tattle on Steve.

BROKE OUR MIRRORS

Their tonight's-home is another utility road between another unplowed field. Had any of them been green thumbs, their stomachs wouldn't groan in a choir of rearview mirrors. Instead, they pass freeze-dried astronaut food in vacuum-sealed pouches. The taste of water begins to sicken Sydney, but it is undoubtedly refreshing.

Walls of corn claustrophobically border them to the north and south. Occasional gusts catch through the road's throat, but otherwise, there is a cozy warmth to their sheltered wilderness.

Tonight, Cub and Remy's appetite is for more than just food. They watch Steve chew a dried brown jerky stick. Campfire light draws deep shadows in all the facial grooves time left behind.

They watch him the way dogs beg their master for table scraps. Steve tries his best to ignore them. It's obvious. Elephants play a rotten game of hide-and-seek.

Steve shoots the brother and sister an annoyed glare. They sit together undeterred.

"We knew, but how did you know it was time to leave?" Remy gently asks.

Staring into the fire, Steve contemplates unplayed cards. Orange waves pulse his figure. Shadows dance behind him in tandem. He rubs his thighs. He feels their anticipation. Sydney half-pays attention to the one-sided conversation while quietly playing with his food. He studies it. The corner of Steve's eye verifies they are still watching. He finds comfort in this. He shuffles his butt toward the begging dogs. Tonight, they get their bone.

He leans in. Excitement grows in the listeners. While staring into the flames, he asks, "Do you know why they chose us? In the beginning. You know why?"

"They didn't even lock the escape door. They were inviting us to leave," Cub mumbles.

"We had something they wanted?" Remy finally offers.

Turning, he winks at her.

SIMMERING POT OF OILS AND PHEROMONES AND SHARED CHROMOSOMES OF SELF

Steve glorifies lung cancer. After a few more puffs and begs, Steve admits secrets. "There were two fundamental differences between the man who raided Rex's greenhouse and us."

Remy's hands moisten but she doesn't know where to wipe them.

"He was traceable, and we weren't all men."

Remy passively rubs her smooth forearm and reflects. *They needed a portless Eve—free from infiltration. An unmodified Punnett square. She and Cassie were the unadulterated wild-type nucleic acid puddles in this place's new primordial gene pool. She was to become a docile queen bee without a diving board. Dividing hers were intended to relearn gravity.* Remy finds the thought hauntingly romantic. Desire, no matter its twisted roots, crafts a potent aphrodisiac.

CHAPTER 25

SPIDERS MUST BELIEVE IN GODS

Witches don't exist anymore, or at least not at this time, but the potions of today are miraculously better and taste more like chalk and third-world fingers than fungus-filled dirt and frog legs.

A bottled "yelp" and muffled sadness serenade an eternity of bloomless springs.

Cassie awakens as if emerging from the submerged. Flashing images, unsafe for epileptics, meddle her memory. On her back, she tugs the restraints. Wrists are attached to long white bedposts. The background is black. She remembers wailing. *Flash.* Eye-light saturates and then she's blinded. She remembers abdominal pain. *Flash.* She remembers bleeding. *Flash.* She remembers powerlessness. *Flash.* She remembers punishment. *Flash.* She remembers zipper-mouth. *Flash.* Asphyxiation. *Flash.* She finds herself bound in a eugenic web.

Spiders superstitiously stitch their homes with vandalism. They need not swell waterless tear ducts over their beloved. Fortune for one is failure for the other—competing at life with siblings and kin. They are hardened to screams of a living meal and filth never settles on their dessert.

A nest is the hook, a vibration is the bobber. They will always choose a moving van over a feather duster.

Chance remains a youthful belief. Stories aren't passed down. Ancestors live as forgotten skeletons.

Timelines breathe a single lifespan. Natural selection is the only means to evolve. Music distracts dinner.

Dream-memories are helium balloons. In summer light, without focus, they climb the atmosphere out of sight and mind. Recall is terribly inaccurate, and, in many ways, that is probably a blessing.

CHAPTER 26

HAUNTED BY FRIENDLY GHOSTS

"Cassie!" Moving mind-images of unwashed grown men groping an unripe body in helplessly primal ways disgusts Remy. She spits out her tongue with a gag. Her body tenses with anger.

She jumps to her feet with clenching fists akimbo. Sydney reels. Neither man flinches.

"Persephone in a bottle," Steve mutters to the fire. He motions for her to sit. She doesn't.

"She's gone, Rem," Cub says. There is a tender sprig of sorrow and understanding in his tone. She can't remember hearing those notes from him since they were each other's only friends. She sits, joining them in silence.

PARSED LIFE ALWAYS APPEARS MORE PROFOUND

Shame thrives in isolation. Hours pass in syllables of steps. When mouth-voices hush, head-voices chase each other like unchaperoned teenagers.

Time became a marathon runner's mile-nine hum. Tense mental knots tighten and loosen in non-verbal agony. The sun licks up sadness' evidence.

They tug together. The crust aches. "Again?" Sydney rhetorically asks. The earthquake is his punctuation.

Strange to consider, some never stopped living like this. Technology passed them by, the way vehicles do homeless men hunched over park benches. Neither seem to mind.

They still believe powers, greater than them, guide fate, based on their deity's mood. Anger leads to unavoidable misfortune. Sacrifice keeps anger at bay.

Then again, maybe this is just a test. A fire drill. A false alarm. An imagined mock setup in preparation for the real one. Scriptures mention believers being put to the test.

God plays chess with Satan, and both cheat.

WILLING AND CONDESCENDING ADULTS

Sleep can't hold its spell. Their star stretches its eye open once more. The first blink clears a cloudy film. He always wakes before them. Dawn doesn't mind seeing its highest primates return to the trees.

"Possession" has become a foreign term with ancient rules. Civility gave the world possessions. A lion does not collect items or coins and compare his pile to his neighbor's pile. Biblical texts don't separate a kangaroo's food from the hippopotamus'.

Power maintains civility. It has for a very long time. Control has evolved but the role it plays has largely remained unchanged. Gradually, the flavor progressed from survival, to strength, to salt, to weapons, to fossilized fuels, to skin color, to currency, to information. The chronologic chain decrescendos. It is intuitive to respect the strongest ape or the one with all the food, but as generations turn, the governing bodies' grip slips.

Civility gave the world laws. Civility gave the world slavery.

Civility drew invisible lines on stones the world called, "home," and civility gave the world slaughter to those that refused to respect invisible lines.

This morning, civility didn't wake up.

A spool of toilet paper only lasts until one is left wiping with the core.

We were told that is how this, which has no name, happened. The illusion was strong, but there really were only a few threads left. "I guess we shouldn't have spent so much time worrying about our national debt," Cub mockingly shrugs. His beard grows patchy and thin.

After breakfast, they tightly tidy their belongings. Predictable collectivism amongst victims carries positivity in the morning air.

"*Where* is the end? *Why* are we here?" Steve zips his backpack. "Conflict forces us to make decisions based only on the tools of our own history, but," he leans toward Sydney's ear, "this is the important part..." His posture straightens to include Remy and Cub. "*Where* is as important as *why* and both are ages old."

"Yeah," says Sydney.

"What is the result of all these seemingly minor decisions within the grander picture?"

"Yeah."

Steve pauses to make eye contact with each listener, hoping they don't answer, because these are all rhetorical. They don't answer.

"Well, I'll tell you. Don't expect a checkered flag or cheering crowds." Looping the big backpack over his shoulder, "Don't expect confetti and marching bands. I guarantee there isn't a block of our Creator's cheese at the end of this maze. If it were, the moldy stench would have been easier to follow." Steve swigs from his canteen. The leather strap inelegantly lays across his face as he swallows a couple healthy gulps. He felt his dad channeling through the storytelling, right up until the flapping strap.

"North," Cub says. "We are going North."

SINCE WE ARE INMATES, WE MAY AS WELL NOT BURY THE HATCHET IN EACH OTHER'S BACK

Remy wraps an arm around Sydney. *It's easy to trust this little guy. Cub doesn't. Sydney looks up to us like a puppy pleading for attention. His head half-cocks when he stares back. He appears tranquil as he sleeps. Peace doesn't really come around here much anymore now that greed moved in next door.*

Steve thinks we should stay within sight of water. Cub is more interested in not being wrong.

Skin drinks what the mouth does not. Vigor races through the running water despite it being numbingly cold. After cleansing their morning faces, they leave the river.

Remy asks Cub, "Do you remember key lime pie?"

When you've lost culture for a week, all conversation circles back to food.

Smell becomes primal again. The first few rotations after fleeing, both of us got dirty and stinky. The choking stench of body odor surrounded Cub like a hen does her egg. After about four sunsets, the odor turned into 'Cub's aroma.' I can smell him approaching like silent footsteps. Last night, we found a pink cosmetic handbag that had been ripped apart. I could smell all the beautiful herbs its owner must have rubbed in her hair. With eyes closed, I pictured each scent like sheet-music notes. The soap was overpoweringly strong, almost distracting. I wanted to sneeze out the floral bouquet. I bet our ancestors would say the same about our night sky.

CAMPFIRE STORIES

"His choice of hat tells a great deal about a man's character," Steve begins. He has their attention. Instead of a guardian or a neighbor or a babysitter, he holds them as almost-equals. "The lighter the tan, the richer the man—or so he *wants* you to believe." Sydney observes Remy for a response the way a kid does when he doesn't understand an adult joke. "The stiffer the hat, the more he cares about the way *others* see him. Floppy is the lazy man's hat—one that doesn't have regard for his own appearance—or smell for that matter."

Sydney giggles and steals another glance at Remy's cheeks which have picked up yellow highlights from the flames. His mouth unrequitedly straightens to catch Steve's next words.

"And then, there's those that choose black..." Steve needles the fire to compose his thoughts, but more so for dramatic effect. "In the great war, black-soaked soldiers patrolled enemy lines. Fueled by sulfur. Death. Void. Finality." In midair, embers dangle like marionettes before blinking away.

"Some choose to be marked—to have a label. They wouldn't have it any other way. It is permission to intimidate their surroundings. This, they enjoy. They are the self-made demons and have the regalia to prove it."

DSM-IV

Moons and stomachs turn over spoiled dinner. Defeat and despair do-si-do to the sound of: *I can't take this anymore!*

Tears separate me from loneliness and sleep. I remember when, standing perfectly still, you could hear a buzz in the air, like subsonic traffic. Now, silence is chilling. Without distractions, hearing-senses have sharpened. Swaying branches clumsily clank together like quarreling moose.

It's my turn to stay awake. Instead of twiddling thumbs, Remy pokes the dying fire. Back and forth, the ashes turn. Very little light emits but heat still lives beneath.

Self-control is a slippery snake. It is a steering wheel with too much play. It is an illusion that becomes an obsession. *None of us asked for this with closed eyes and crisscrossed fingers. We deal decks of Uno in Bethlehem colors.* The ride never cared much for its passengers.

Eyes accommodate the light's absence. Her stick turns over

the ashes. A coil of smoke pirouettes to heaven. Encounters play-back scenes between fast forwards. *Why did he say we should avoid the river? Steve knows better, right? Is Cub sabotaging our journey? Why doesn't he ask my opinion?* Internal dialogues, like skipping stones on a lake, don't intend to return.

She's looking, but not seeing. Ashes turn. Fear feeds paranoia minty girl scout cookies. More ashes turn. Paranoia feeds anger a bottle of bacon bits. Ashes sit. Anger feeds hopelessness a sertraline.

Rustling grass startles Remy. *I drifted off!* Memory records two instants before awakening. She recalls what sounded like legs pushing through tall grass. Turning left and right, nothing catches her attention. Pupils dilate in the company of darkness and sympathetic tone.

She looks over at her fast-asleep brother. *If he's disappointed in me...* She turns back to the night. Nothingness. *Was it real? Was it human? Is it watching helpless me?*

Remy pulls her stiff blanket up and over both shoulders. Wind keeps her exposed skin cold. There are no sounds, but the air around her tenses. A silent bass drum is in crescendo. She wishes this was over. She wishes the sounds would return. She clicks her heels.

Over her left shoulder, the rustling approaches. A washing panic strikes her in the chest like a rock coated with snow. White radiates from the impact site. She breathes in and turns like she's sitting on a pottery wheel.

Sydney is wiping his hands across his pants. He gestures to her that he is shivering. She closes her eyes. Quiet, shallow exhale. Safe in an open safe. As he passes by, she backhands him in the arm. He snaps, "What? You seemed peaceful."

Nervously, she laughs. *Why should I be upset with my own negligence? Big events overshadow smaller ones. Real stress mutes the fake everyday stuff that people complain about when they think they should be complaining but can't think of anything to complain about.* She shakes her head in mock-disgust but feels relief inside.

In a way, Sydney is our lucky prisoner. This seems a rather silly thought to the world that recently forgot the meaning of possessions.

Is this how couples feel in the dark hours of parenting?

She observes. Sydney burrows beneath blankets, exposing only his face to the chilled air. Her face relaxes. Tonight may pass without conflict and she won't complain. She spins Steve's large watch around her narrow wrist. Soon, she'll wake him, so she may escape into sleep's shallow water.

She brings a folded hand to her face for a closer look at her fingernails. They are dark from ignoring soap. She scratches dirt from beneath the white tips with her thumbnail. Rolling it up into a little, filthy ball, she brings it under her nose. It smells like oily clay which reminds her of peanut butter cups served at the school's cafeteria. *I miss them.* She used to peel away the wax paper sides and pop the entire ball onto her tongue. Peanut butter mixed with generic chocolate candies that melted in the mouth, not in hands. She loved to close her lips over it the way whales feed. She wouldn't chew. Not yet. She pictures her younger self and smiles. Reminded by its weight, she looks at Steve's watch. The moon's reflection tells her to keep night-dreaming.

Time drags its cloven hooves. Breezes bring startling sounds. Remy rises with a stretch. Her quadriceps and lower back thank her. She paces quiet circles around their campsite, pretending to be interested in kicking the growing brown grass.

Am I lucky? How many others are out there walking around at this very moment? She lifts her shirt, tucking it under her chin for a better view of her tummy. She was never overweight, but now fat has shrunk to reveal abdominal muscles, six of them. She rapidly taps her newly protruding hip bone with her right middle finger. It produces a hollow *thud* that reminds her of deer antlers. With satisfaction, she smiles.

Dropping her shirt, she follows a part in neighboring shrubs.

She wishes for water, even just to look at. Disappointment creeps into her foggy head. *My brother is an idiot.* Her stomach growls in agreement.

The dating moon scratches enough light to cast its host in deep blue hues. Remy climbs away from camp, up to a nearby mound. Crisp wind unexpectedly gusts against her exposed arms. She clutches them in a shivering pose as she breaches the top. She crouches. Something about cold air tells her to pee. She should probably be more discreet in the company of men, but none desire her—at least not in *that* way—*and that's okay.* Their revolt is her disgusting permit.

After emptying her bladder on the prettiest dandelion, she turns toward camp. Everyone remains motionless. No one watched her reveal her skin. *No one cares.* A small part of her wilts. *Attention would be welcome. Somebody interested in my thoughts or feelings or opinions would make the corners of my lips curl upward. At least the widest web provided simple bursts of synthetic affection. This is a fate, my fate. Instead, I will have to grow accustom to becoming the silent Fabergé egg.*

When atheists run out of friends, they check God's hearing.

Is that a vehicle? Remy turns in its direction. On her left, the glow of headlamps highlights a break between ground and sky. *People still have fuel?*

Steve warned about the dangers of foot travel at night. Direction is already tricky without global position services. Vehicles may cruise roads and that's about it. A map would keep course. Everybody with ears or photon-detecting eyes would be alerted, but feet could never compete with motorized speed.

The pair of high beams peek over the horizon. Remy freezes like a guilty raccoon. Doppler shares engine growls. Her head tracks like a turret across a two-point perspective.

Her shoulders relax as the taillights disappear. *The boys are going to ask questions that I've already forgotten the answers to. But, at least they will ask.*

A CHAIR NEVER ROCKS ITSELF

The shoulder-tap he's been anticipating happens. Sleep stayed light. He doesn't even stretch. "Everything okay?" he asks in hushed tones. She nods. "Get some rest, then."

He folds up the sleeping blanket but watches her out the side of his left eye. He hopes she doesn't get hurt. He thinks she will get hurt.

Crouching near the fire in twenty-year-old jeans, he places his hands, palms down, just over the ashes. The heat is almost gone. He stands and scratches the back of his head where hair used to grow. *Nothing needs to be fixed. Nobody is awake to listen to.*

There are two types of people: those who can grow ideas from boredom seeds and those who cannot.

Steve neatly packs away his belongings. Grabbing a full, clear water bottle, he begins to pace tomorrow's steps. *Cub would not agree with abandoning helpless sleepers, but he is in no state to object.* Dry tongues love room temperature water, well, room temperature was a luxury they used to know. Air temperature became a more appropriate term.

Porgy and Bess play in his head to the beat of two size-thir-teens. Steve squints. He pauses to listen. *Insects could not be bothered with complete economic collapse.* He pauses to look. Black treetops, like paper cutouts, gently sway. He continues. He has spent most of his time looking down. Old dogs never learn arithmetic. Every five steps, he looks up and fixes his location. The terrain is light, but untraveled. Grassy patches dot dry barren ones like cancer's head after a second chemotherapy cycle. Smooth gray stones, mostly small, scatter the landscape. None are big enough to make him stumble. More bland land extends over dying hope. Looking back toward their campsite, it is impossible to tell if anyone woke up, but he squints anyway.

Reaching into his left breast pocket, he pulls out a crumpled paper pack of cigarettes. Inside is a big lighter. He flicks with the muscle memory of a Western duelist. The tip glows. It is the only thing out here glowing. Deep indrawn breaths calm, even when filled with unpronounceable chemicals. He sits down with bent arms over bent knees and enjoys.

Lucky. I hope nobody describes me that way, Steve thinks. He exhales. *My life has been the result of good and bad decisions. Then again, there are always a few things the Almighty doesn't allow me to control.* He inhales, slowly. Deeply. *Since when did a farmer measure success in the currency of sunsets? This is a test. This is the test. All those tornado drills should be ashamed of themselves.* He taps the tip of his cigarette on a nearby stone and thinks of old men with old habits. *The Legend of Saint Milton Berle.* He exhales.

Everything up until now, equals now. *I am a widower because I chose to accept the title of widower. It is the part of my story I chose to carry.* Werner Eberhardt begins sweating. *I can look back or move forward.* One more deep, La Brea breath. Ultraviolet and dehydration tanned his arms almond. Under his breath, he recites his father's words, "We carry the weather."

Holding in smoke, a fleck of color catches his attention. He breaks to rotate. Blowing carcinogens out the crook of his mouth, he crawls over to what appears to be a narrow piece of plastic. On all fours, he pulls it into focus. Bite marks line the yellow stem. Night makes life dark, but not invisible. *A toothbrush?* Like his own head, it is missing a few bristles. He rolls onto his butt. His face wrinkles in a way that resembles found happiness. A smile refuses its cage. He twirls it between his thumb and pointer finger. He will make room for his new friend. Steve stares at his tired toothbrush and can't wait until right after breakfast.

ANGER AIMED AT THE PETTY IS PROOF OF A LIFE WITH FAR TOO LITTLE TRAGEDY

It doesn't take much to get warm coals blazing. The good news is, their packs are getting lighter. The bad news is, food is fleeting.

Like many yesterdays, breakfast feeds them canned beans and spinach. The luster of a campfire is gone. The awakening flames of new fire used to excite Remy. Now, they are tedious. The smell of smoky clothing used to cradle her to sleep. Now, the stench shakes hands with body odor as a peace offering to rot.

Remy's eyes scan to meet another's pair as they all quietly eat around the pit. Nobody embraces her. *Maybe last night's experience won't impress them.* Sydney finishes first. Licking his lips like a stray alley cat, he sets his bowl near Remy. She tilts her own over his and slides a spoonful of beans into his. Little eyes grow. He snatches the bowl with both hands. "Thanks, Remy!" Gratitude costs a growling stomach this someday.

Cub looks upset. Lately, Cub always looks upset. He stares with furrowed brows into the flames. Slowly chewing. *Is he captured in thought or porcupine-ing to be left alone?*

Remy catches Steve's attention with her goodwill gesture. "How was your watch, Rem?"

She didn't want to jackrabbit-start her response, but that's exactly how it blurted out. "There was this vehicle..." The men's jaws stop chewing to loosely hang. Their lower teeth reveal themselves.

"What color?"

"Did they see you?"

"Which way did it go?"

The excited boy bobs.

Remy's cheeks imitate blushing roses. She doesn't know all the answers, so she points north. "They didn't see us."

Cub lets his bowl and spoon clang on the earth in front of his lap. He stands, turns, and walks away toward his blanket pile. *He is making mountains from atom hills.* Steve's head follows. It's clear he doesn't approve of Cub's mountains. The camel carries another piece of straw.

Steve and Sydney square toward Remy. She raises her hands in innocence. Steve waves a dismissive hand at her brother. He lightly slaps her knee with the back of his hand. "Look what I found."

ARM-WRESTLING ANGST

Light pulses, like watching life through boiling water.

They don't understand the big picture. Violently, blankets stuff their way into a canvas camouflage duffle bag the way sour-smelling men do into crowded subway cars. Sweat trickles from one temple in the cool morning air. "Cloudy, again."

From his chore, Cub turns his head toward his crew like a tiger being disturbed from its meal. *They are weak, but I can make them stronger. They are slow, but I can make them faster. They are prey, but I can turn them into survivors.*

He hears Remy softly approach. Without turning, he says, "You should have told me *immediately*." Kindling innocents into co-dependents can be frustrating. *She has no good excuses and they all rhyme with "I'm sorry.* "Pack up. Now." *I would have raised strong children that burn participation ribbons in the bathtub.*

She watches her brother selfishly pout with his things. "Nobody was made great by others," she tells him.

He pauses.

Her head droops, and she walks away.

GOOD PEOPLE CARRY BAD MEMORIES

Dawn doesn't hold a grudge like a curmudgeon. Cloudy gray blankets separate the sun from a crime scene called, "home." They haven't spat rain in three spins. Clothing hasn't forgotten its master's musk.

Leading the silent group, Cub would never admit to being directionless. He avoids the river and maintains the power struggle, that is, the power struggle only he tries to win.

Without clocks and odometers, everything is measured in

spins. Data transferred from tangible to intangible. Albums and books and pictures and relationships all enter digital whirlpools. Vortexes of beautiful fragility. Without keys to unlock the clouds they float in; memories will be forgotten. Egypt's secrets hang in musty, digital coat-closets waiting for their owners to turn in the return stub. It is happening, again.

There is freedom in feeling powerless. Remy rakes a hand through Sydney's greasy black hair. "Thanks for following me." Syd responds with an impartial smirk before drifting a few strides behind her.

The overdrawn silence tenses Remy. She speeds her steps to catch up with Steve who follows fifteen paces behind her brother. She watches his cowlick bob.

"Steve, how long does it hurt?" He stops but doesn't turn. She closes distance between his back but doesn't catch his puzzled expression. "You know, after losing somebody you love, when does it get better?" She doesn't see his lips tighten. She doesn't see the stirred ocean bed of flashbacks. A disturbed crustacean doesn't realize the gravity of a finless air-breather. She stops behind him, watching his back muscles flex toward her.

Silent beats fill space like a candle taking advice from a lit match-head. He hides each hand in side pockets of worn denim. She listens to air pass through coarse nose fur to fill his alveoli. "It felt like the bottom of my heart broke off into nothingness when I learned she was sick." The back of his head tilts. Darkened, poorly drawn circles on his crown document sun damage. It reminds her of a turtle's shell. "It felt like the bottom of my lungs disappeared the first night I slept next to cold sheets." One hand escapes to scratch his turtle shell. A strand of grass blows into view. His long-sleeved, flannel shirt catches it in a ruga near his lower back. "My best friend slipping into helpless hopelessness stole more from me than these old cigarettes ever did." She doesn't see the unpocketed hand clamp his temples. Sydney almost catches up. "Helplessness and hopelessness are only fears

of the living. When her heart stilled, a part of me did, too."
Sydney catches up. He reads body language. Amazing how children pick up the queues of their parenting figures.

Remy notices pensiveness relax Steve's tongue, the way a stutterer's does while singing. She and Sydney listen.

"As they lowered her coffin, I looked up from my folded hands. I was surrounded by a semi-circle of her friends and people I'd paid to be there. Before parting, I shook hands with them. They said all the correct words, but the *meaning* wasn't there. *They* lacked connection.

"Beautifully manicured grass parted a path between the headstones. With hands in my pockets, I walked back to my old vehicle. I tried to think of friends to confide the burden of my misery. I tried to think of a family member, not already in the ground, with which to share these new terrible feelings.

"That's why.

"I'd narrowed my life down to just her, my one and only. Friendships and family drifted because I allowed them to float away. It wasn't a conscious decision. It just seemed to happen out of convenience, I guess, like unwatered flowers.

"That's when I bought Lucy," he smiles. "Because all I had left was my things.

"You see, the people at her funeral didn't lack connection, *I* did.

"Relationships take effort to grow. When I saw what happened to your parents, I figured you might feel the same way I did. I'm not full of many 'correct' words, but I hope the *meaning* was there. It seemed like a good opportunity to water some new flowers.

"That's why."

Young rhythmic footsteps are his speechless ovation.

"I suppose that doesn't answer your question about 'how long,' but..."

A bit embarrassed by the way he confessed, Remy shuffles.

Picking the grass strand and tugging on his flannel below the left elbow, she whispers, "I understand."

She doesn't see his brief, forced smile. It would have looked the way one man greets another at his mother's funeral. Steve's long legs move again. Sydney and Remy follow. Steve watches internal memories while they watch his back bear the weight.

ANOREXIA PROMISES CONTROL OVER ONLY ONE THING

Lunch in the cool shadow of a thin evergreen valley leaves them with three empty cans of fruit cocktail and four almost-empty stomachs. After relieving himself behind a buffalo bush, Sydney asks if bright yellow urine is normal. "It practically glows, like neon!"

"You're fine," Cub says with apathetic enthusiasm.

Fluffy clouds tuck their promises away in the siesta sun. Everybody agrees rain will be a blessing. Primitive peoples praying to minor gods for major rain doesn't seem nearly as foolish. For now, they wait under gray skies.

"Roads leave us vulnerable—unless that's what we are going for." Cub doesn't appreciate Steve's commentary, but realizes its logic. *Vehicles still breathe ancient fossils. Remy saw one. There are definitely more.*

Cub spots a distant hill to the north. The group makes a habit of camping on raised land for better visibility. Tonight will be no different.

Hearing a gasp behind him, Cub turns to see Sydney dashing toward a line of dark, full shrubs. The three watch his gallop, then look at each other. After shrugging, they follow.

Sydney darts from one limb to the next like a hungry hummingbird. Plucking shiny red berries, he rolls them between thumb and pointer finger. If they don't pop, he places them in his cupped hand.

By the time Remy approaches, berries spill at his feet. She smiles. She smiles wide. She shows teeth.

Steve picks one from a high branch. Adjusting his glasses like a microscope lens, he calculates the danger.

"So, what do you think?" she asks.

Steve and Cub exchange looks. It is difficult to restrain a child from opening presents on Christmas Eve.

"I think it will be alright," Steve says with a wink to Remy. An elated gasp escapes Sydney's uvula before he stuffs the handful of juicy red berries into his mouth. With newly empty hands, he gets back to plucking. Excitement is contagious. Cub's scowl loosens. The old feed off youthful enthusiasm—social security vampires. Today, they all feed on berries.

Everyone has grown mentally tougher, but the giggling and smiling this afternoon reminds them of muscles they have neglected. Insulin spikes. Sticky stains remain despite Remy's attempt to brush them away in the grass. Sydney's face has blotches like a Soviet leader's birthmark. Rainfall will rob them of guilty hands if, and when, it arrives. Filled stomachs leave the party a bit tired. Cautious eyes become lazy ones.

Each fills a bountiful pouch before bidding farewell to the clump of freshly picked bushes. The mood and the sky are light, but neither would last.

He points. "Before nightfall, let's get to the hilltop," Cub commands instead of suggests.

"It looks like the alphabet," Sydney adds.

Without direction, foot travel is painfully slow. To climb the hill, each must lean forward with flexing calves on tipped toes. Sydney readjusts his arm straps. They all bear what's left of their life on concave shoulders. Sunlight fades to twilight. There are no monsters to fear. No foreign terrorists. No archenemies. The game is simple. The players are few. Survival in a bottle of one's own landscape.

A head start is more than their ancestors could have wished

for. Sure, civilization was a brace. Their atrophic muscles must regrow. Today's simple man would have been yesterday's genius. Technology wrote the blueprints published on information super-toll-roads.

The steeper the climb, the more reluctant the salad. Cub's reward for reaching the peak is soft footsteps on fertile soil. The top's grass never met a barber, even before the end. Blades brush above his waist. Behind, the others almost reach the peak, encouraged by dying light. To uncover his path, Cub swims arms as if separating beaded doors. *No trees chose to live here.* The hill is cozier than he expected.

At the edge, a panoramic view opens. *We are getting too close to the road.* A chilling pulse concentrically spreads from his zyphoid process as he locks eyes with a farmhouse driveway below.

Instinctively, he crouches, scanning across Mother Nature's stage. He can't tell if he has already been spotted. Still crouching, he approaches the last of his "disciples," breaching Alphabet Hill. Using his left pointer finger, he gestures over his lips. He doesn't say, "shhh," but he means it. Remy throws back a puzzled demeanor. Sydney pulls himself to the top. Staying silent, Remy quickly clasps her hand over his mouth to stop the story about dinosaurs from coming out. His eyes widen as if he just dropped a tall glass of milk.

They collectively squat. Cub violently motions toward the hill's eastern edge. Steve puts his big hand on Remy's shoulder. She releases the little one's mouth. Yodeling teaches them: tonight, is for whispers.

There is no clearing amongst the unkept peak. There will be no fire. Dinner will be cold. Joy settles like dirt in a recently disturbed river.

Sydney quietly indicates to come hither. He cups his hands around Cub's ear. "Can I try guarding tonight?" There is a little giving up when yielding power to someone half one's age—sharing trust with one you don't yet. Extra rest wins. The balance tilts.

"You take the first little bit, then wake me up."

NO ONE EVER GOT A TICKET FOR JAY RUNNING

Responsibility! Sydney springs a Christmas morning expression. It is unrequited. He sharpens his disposition and purses his lips. He does his best to act like a serious adult and nods at Cub. This response is requited.

Night looms. The adults hide themselves in covers. He hears somebody uncomfortably turning over among the tall grass. *Maybe it is Indian Steve. Probably not.* Sydney sits on the other side of their hill. He monitors the farmhouse.

I am Alphabet Hill's protector!

He feels brave but, like one's first job after graduation, he can't believe *he* is in charge. Responsibility cradled in a doubter's arms feels a little less *noble* and a little more *please don't screw up.*

Wind gusts pull foliage tight like slick guido hair. Sydney's greasy bangs sway like stuffed bananas hanging from a convertible's rearview mirror. *Are my friends asleep?*

Surrounding sounds call out like distant voices traveling fathoms through tin can telephones. *Is it people language? Is it monsters?* Disorders of attention claim the best of the young hero this evening.

His arms stretch. He greets his fuzzy shadow. Looking up, the solitary moon is not full and the stars lose his interest. Between gusts, he stands and wraps a blanket tightly around his shoulders. Out his eye corner, the blanket reminds him of a cape. *A superhero's cape!* He puffs his chest. *I will protect this land from evil because I am strong, and I am brave, and I am smart, and they are dummies!*

Another strong gust blows him off balance. He stumbles. *Embarrassing.* No one moves. *No one saw.* Red face fades. He sits. *It feels like Tuesday before a sleepover weekend.*

GLORY LOCKS HERSELF IN A BOX

Sydney's thoughts nibble history. Glory *used* to have a name. Glory *used* to have a favorite color. Glory *used* to have a big brother. Whenever he came home to her, two excited arms threw a confetti parade filled with brass instruments. *Them* was he and she. Him and her. The kids. Two stood as one against the high-waisted adults.

We obeyed rules ending in, "Because, we said so."

Time spent being too young or too short sketched the boundaries around us. Shoulder to shoulder, she knew what we went through. Cub still has his. I miss Glory. Guilt corrects him. *I miss both of my sisters.* Sydney's stomach groans like an old recliner.

Mom said Glory was named that way because her shiny yellow hair reminded her of angel hair pasta. Cassie said, "Dad said it was because Mom said so."

Lying on his stomach, Sydney rests his chin on his palms' heels. From Alphabet Hill's edge, he stares through parted grass at the tiny white farmhouse. No lights. No shadows. No villains. *Cartoons make a hero's job more exciting than real life. Glory would have helped me feel important. Now she gets to wear long white robes and a halo to match her pretty hair. I hope she has been eating carrots, so she can watch me be brave.*

DESERTS DREAM OF MIRAGES

With eyes shut, Cub realizes that he's awake. He slowly opens them, as if opening them makes noise. Sydney isn't nearby. *How long have I been out?* The wind has not given up yet. He crawls through tall grass toward the northern lookout.

He spots Sydney watching his approach. *Reliable.* Cub grins on the inside. The kid signals his thumb up. Cub gets uncomfortably close to him. Below the hill is extra black. Primal insects play mating songs as if their race depends on it.

EXOTIC CATS VIOLENTLY PLAY

Looking up, Sydney attempts to decipher body language in the moon's light. No words. Shadows look back.

Cub locks his bicep around Sydney's skull and rubs a bony knuckle into greasy black hair. Struggling and giggling, Sydney attempts to break free as if a honey jar is stuck atop his head.

Why is he so rough? Is he upset? Is he kidding? Sydney breathes sweaty odor. Musk mixes with semi-sweet cinnamon butter. He feels Cub's heat. The grip tightens. Firm knuckles bury deep. Sydney winces. Panic squeezes out eye water. Gasping for air, he mouth-breathes, and a whine audibly exits.

Cub releases his prey. With a hand on each shoulder, he holds Sydney at arm's length. The whimpering pauses. Sydney fixates on the facial scar. Cub presses each hand together like paintings of Jesus praying and brings them up to his right ear. He closes his lids as if he were faking sleep. Sydney understands—tonight's watch has ended.

Crawling toward Steve and Remy, his butt gets swatted. When he turns, Cub's shadow is giving him an upward thumb of approval.

Feeling like an armadillo, Sydney settles near Remy. His sore eyes quickly sweep reality away.

HOLLY BERRIES STAIN

Cold air rides wind chariots. *Our survival rests on me.* Cub ducks near the perch where Sydney watched, overlooking the home below. A row of evergreen trees block wind on three of four sides. The exposed side permits a long gravel driveway's entry.

From his vantage point, the front door can't be seen. The second story window is unlit. It is more of a half-story than a full one. The main floor windows are also black. To his surprise, the lawn is relatively manicured. *A lack of recent rainfall certainly can stifle growth.*

Judging distance, he could jog there without breaking a sweat. *I want a closer look. If someone lives there, I will find out. I will watch. They will not even know they are going to make the first move. Patience may hand us a bounty.*

From behind, whimpering interrupts Cub's strategy. Noises permeate near the sleepers. Crouching, he crawls closer. Echoes fill hollowness on all sides. A tiny shadow leaps and dashes. *Sydney is missing!*

Remy and Steve stir as Cub passes. Each lift their head, then panic lifts their body. Wind blows dried sweat eastward.

Ducking, Cub chases the little black figure's path. Alphabet Hill steepens in starlight. An echoing whine is the stick's carrot.

It turns to its pursuer, holding hands up as if trying to stop traffic. Cub's traffic stops.

"Get away! I have to go!"

It's Sydney. Cub's pursuit halts on unsteady stones, six paces from his target. Darkness fails to disguise shame.

"Please."

He's on the brink of crying. Mercifully, Cub responds by holding both hands above his head. Sydney edges a bit further downhill with one hand holding his rear and the other counterbalancing his weight. He disappears behind a meager black tree among meager black trees. They fail to conceal the crying.

"Oh God!"

The sounds that follow resemble fishermen dumping chum buckets into the ocean. More crying. More echoes.

Above, Steve and Remy's black shadows grow against a deep blue canvas of light revolutions. Cub gestures them back but, himself, quietly disobeys Sydney's wishes.

More chum. More whining. More echoes. Signs of weakness feed prey to predators every moment. Hopefully, today will not be every moment.

Colons don't always wait for denim.

He's just a boy living out of captivity. No one will witness Cub's chuckle and grin at the circumstances. Nobody needs a sun to see a child breaking in a pool of shame.

"Hey, bud. Everything's going to be okay, you hear?" Racing below Sydney, Cub unbuttons and peels Sydney's pants down as if a bomb were attached. "Lean on me, kiddo." He spins the boy around and holds him up by the armpits. From slightly uphill, Sydney leans into his hero. Cramps wring his little tummy. He looks like he is squatting on an invisible chair. Waste passes under Cub's spread legs to slither downhill. Pulsatile gurgles expel runny shadows that look and splash like egg yolk.

Cub turns his head to avoid sight and stench. Muffled cries seek strange ears. Cub feels Sydney's body wilt. His forearms tense and strain to support the boy's weight.

Massaging, Sydney presses on his left lower quadrant. More dirty egg yolk splatters. More clean sobs.

"It's okay. Be strong. I'm here for you." Cub is tonight's chamomile.

"It was the berries. I know it," Sydney sniffles.

"Don't worry about that now. Get it all out." Tenderness is toughness' substitute teacher.

"I think it's over." The limp body lightens in his arms.

"May the earth rise to meet you, bud."

Shadows shaped like Remy and Steve, with hands on their knees, curiously loom from above. Hiking his pants, Sydney staggers back up Alphabet Hill like a child learning to walk, from one parent to another, for the second time.

Birds yawn. Their morning voices signal Mother Nature to cross off another box on her calendar.

"Anything I can do for you, Syd?" The boy shakes his head and parts the adults. His groan is not a word or an answer. There are plenty of moments before dawn. Steve forfeits sleep while the others rest.

Remy doesn't. Seeds of motherhood have broken soil. She watches Sydney before she can see. The morning sky is cranberry sauce with a dollop of whipped cream. Kilowatts of sun peek at Earth's passengers.

Crust from dead tears have gathered in the corners of his sunken orbitals. Cheekbones prominently frame his open-mouth breathing. She tenderly runs fingers through his hair.

CHAPTER 27

PRESIDENTIAL DENIAL AND JUSTIFICATION

Gold links on his oversized bracelet clang as he vigorously shakes an executive fist before setting the globe down on his gopher wood desk. He watches dandruff flakes swirl around the simulacrum of his estate and then gently flutter to the globe's flooring.

Loneliness falls like snow.

"This extinction event was a close call."

No extinction event is ever a close call.

"When my career started, I wanted to be remembered as a hero, not the lynchpin of my people's next mass genocide." His words vibrate in the empty, regal room.

"It needed to be done. It was a common solution to a common problem."

If we did our job, they will not be remembered.

Cultural shaping. Biologic cleansing. A fresh new start. These are beautiful, poetic euphemisms for destruction. Sanding the Statue of Liberty down to a perfectly polished copper-iron coin.

Hybrids are tagged with non-modifiable coding, a genetic

backdoor, left swaying on its hinges—flapping in the breeze. *We smell the changing wind as we do a spraying skunk—pungent and traceable.*

It's always the same. Don't think it isn't. The first million was cause for celebration—a monument, proof of tireless, hard work. But, by the sixtieth million, it was difficult to even crack a smile.

CHAPTER 28

GINGER BEER AND CLOVE CIGARETTES

They open. Pupils shrink to accommodate. His tongue plays with the roof of his mouth like peanut butter were stuck on top. Remy pets his hair. Sorrow only wears size black.

"He's dehydrated. Today, we replenish our water supply." Steve doesn't wait for the inevitable rebuttal. He wouldn't have gotten one anyways.

Old people say, "the first is the worst," and then extrapolate the cliché out to any situation that seems to fit. If one speaks largely in clichés, no one will visit their brain's mausoleum.

Sydney stumbles on his first step, clutches Remy, and tries harder. When he seems to have his feet beneath him, she lets go. He walks like Bambi on ice. "I'm dizzy." His face pinches as if it is sucking on something sour. Then, he widens. The cobwebs are still there. "Really dizzy." He braces himself on all fours.

Remy approaches, but is passed by Cub who picks the boy up across his arms. Sydney's joints swing limply like a stuffed animal. "Today, you are going to be my helper." Sydney slings his right arm around Cub's neck as they clomp down Alphabet Hill. "Remember pancakes?"

Punctuation interrupts life's run-on sentence.

The farmhouse may happen. A different today. By the time Cub reaches level ground, his calves burn. The added weight is a hero's crown. Sydney mouth-breathes. His plump, full lips are chapping and carry white flakes. Morning breath has become just breath.

This way of travel is clearly unsustainable. *I must develop a plan.* The river was about a half a spin back and runs roughly north to south. *Should I hide the boy and go after water myself?* Humility swallows like Adam's dry apple.

Everyone gathers at the hill's base. "Let Remy and Sydney recover in the shade," Steve says. Cub reluctantly agrees. Sydney's hopes of being a helper fall. Alphabet Hill will divide them from the farmhouse. "Start a fire down here at dusk. Please."

Sydney waves to the men as they disappear south. He would like to go, but instead, he'll spend today being too young.

SILENCE BREAKS LIKE UNSHARED TWIX

Scents of pollen hang thick in the morning air like stagnant waters. Birds and insects without names scream as if their feet are aflame. Power balances shift. Until now, modern western civilizations have never experienced the Tower of Babel. Earth's greatest villain has fallen to one knee.

Two men take high footsteps across unmowed fields. Both look at their feet while listening to one another not speak.

Cub's fist clenches. *Control slides beneath him like a pulled rug.*

Ego-threatened lips finally break the silence.

"We could use some rain."

The soil cracks and curls, resembling Sydney's lips. It crunches under human weight before turning to powder. Thirsty tongues seek desperation's reward.

Steve grunts in agreement. He follows a half-pace behind his young neighbor who wishes he was a man. He lets Cub's leash out, just to the point before self-destruction. Studying the whiskers growing on the back of Cub's head, he thinks: *He must learn. He doesn't want others to know he is learning from them, especially, it seems, from me. What's the use in fighting to steer a rollercoaster?*

BEHIND ADAMS' HILL, BUT WE ARE NOT RABBITS

Sydney swills the last bit of water from his royal blue tankard. Laying his head back into Remy's lap, he says, "I want to be a strong grown-up like Cub!"

She tightly covers the mouth of their last water jug with a brown towel. Flipping it upside-down, then back again, the stiff towel softens. She brushes hair off Sydney's brow with it. Trickles run down his temples. They tickle. He giggles. She smiles and looks at the sky. The last moon fades in overexposed sunlight like drying bird droppings on Earth's windshield. "You will, honey. You will."

The craft of parenting is difficult to teach. It is also difficult to learn. One sunrise, a body moves inside. The next, a body moves outside. In that time, answers to questions never thought of require immediate solutions. A call for help is dialed when the new parent is ready to listen. Otherwise, it is just pretend-parenting.

"Do you think they will bring us back a deer?"

Kids don't always understand that parents don't have all the answers. *Mom and Dad are heroes until they are seen crying.* Faith becomes hope, which implies doubt, which reveals vulnerability. Parents melt into microwaved plastic army men.

"We'll see." She moistens the towel. "Are you still thirsty?"

Earth tremors build. Remy stabilizes Sydney's body in her arms from behind. Shaking gradually calms. He pulls away, searching her face for an answer.

She points. "They are lining up."

DOGS AND CATS GO TOGETHER IN A BIG BLENDER

Cupped hands splash refreshing river against Steve's sunken cheeks. Breath held. Eyelids closed. Imposter tears stream down, gather at the chin, and then return home.

It doesn't run deep. Steve can touch the riverbed and still have dry elbows. It is difficult to tell where his tan ends and where the caked-filth stains of survival begin. *What a luxury to rub away darkness from one's arms.* After finishing, there is a certain susceptibility in the cleansed areas, like removal of a leather coating—armor. Cuts and scratches without a story reveal themselves. He thinks back for a moment but cannot remember a *when*. Flicking the cap off an empty milk jug, he lowers the mouth against the running stream.

Cub mimics, filling his containers. He reluctantly shows enthusiasm or playfulness in the river. He knows the river route is safest. He knows *he* knows the river route is safest. He knows *he* knows that *he* knows the river route is the safest. Unfortunately, razorblades lace pride's Halloween candy.

With jugs full and faces clean, the men cinch their packs to take their first steps back. The sun already passed its sky's fulcrum. *Hopefully only a few of our steps will be taken in the dark.*

SEPARATION ANXIETY

Remy looks over Sydney's head toward the men's vanishing point. Overgrowing fields with a forested backdrop unpredictably twitch. Under-understood physics turn calculable math into random movement.

She sways, massaging his back. No animals. No brother. No friend. Today ages. The last drop slithers down a favor's dry throat. Anxiety makes for an uncomfortable roommate. She pretends to relax in front of the boy. Concern rots from the inside out. *How can I relate to this kid without raising suspicion? Them not returning is a real possibility. Lost or worse.* She curls hair around his ears. *I trusted them, and they took almost all the water jugs and I don't know how to hunt. How will we eat?* She adjusts his weight against her chest. *I haven't been paying attention and I've left our survival in their hands and I should have been paying more attention and I should take a more active role—I mean, I will take a more active role.*

"Remy, what are you thinking about?"

"How excited I am to see the boys again."

"Yeah, me too. But wait, I'm a boy?"

"Yes. You are."

COLD WINDS HUNT IN ARTHRITIC JOINTS

Crispy grass snaps under snug boots. Blades stiffen and split in the center. The grassland has goldened. Trees here are thinly filled out. If this was junior high school, Sady Hawkins was full of shy girls.

Steve touches nature the closest. He knows this pace will keep them late.

Puffy clouds pull themselves across the pale blue sky like irradiated marshmallows. The sun plays more peek-a than boo. Silently, they walk four shoulder-widths apart.

He doesn't resent Steve. In fact, he respects the man's opinions. *He has better common sense than me. How does he see the big picture more clearly than I, or me? Even with those big, stupid glasses.*

Mental tension butters dry toast. *He is the older one. He should carry the conversation.* Footsteps sound like bubbling water. *Why isn't he asking me anything about me or my interests? Doesn't he care?*

Nodding at the setting sun, Steve mutters, "We are running late."

He thinks he's so intelligent because he barely speaks and when he does, he spouts out obvious information. He's not special. All sheep do is disagree. Shepherds take risks. Risks yield rewards. Rewards belong to heroes. He straightens his back amidst a long stride. A dog barks in the distance.

Both stop. They turn an ear. Facial colors fade, making ghosts look like they wear rouge.

"Farmhouse."

"Yep." *Again, obvious. He is a modern-day genius.*

Keeping heads low, their pace and pulse race toward fear.

IF I FEARED EVERYTHING THAT MIGHT HAPPEN, I'D LEARN TO WAVE WHITE FLAGS

She quickly pulls his head into her chest before the first throaty barks can even stop echoing. *Maybe he didn't hear it.* His smooshed cheeks make fish lips. *Maybe he did.*

Another series of three warning-calls scream. They sound slightly louder. It is difficult to tell which direction brings the sound waves, but invitation doesn't need to buy a vowel. If it's true that animals can smell fear, their olfactories will not go hungry this evening.

The sun rubber-necks around a full cloud. Sydney wedges an elbow between his head and her sternum. *He didn't mean to touch my chest, but this is an emergency, right?* Prying his neck free, she acquiesces. Both stumble backward as they stand like stag deer pulling apart tangled antlers.

Three more graveled barks. *Louder.* Filled with primal hate. The boy pauses. "Now! Come on!" she screams in a whisper.

Without technology, it is amazing how quickly animals scamper up the food chain.

She waves him behind a darkening set of evergreens. The barks are coming with regularity like a church bell stuck on twelve o'clock. *Should we hide up a tree?* She seems to remember hunting dogs treeing prey in old stories in musty library books. She wonders if hunters are following their man's best friend.

Besides water bottles, all their possessions reside atop

Alphabet Hill or with the men. "Up you go!" She lifts Sydney by the waist. Grabbing the lowest branch, he pulls up. It snaps. She flinches. Bits of shattered bark powder her face and hair. Closing an eye, she tightens around his waist to catch his falling weight. Winking, she says, "Try again, hun."

Spinning to a thicker branch, he pulls up. "Grip close to the trunk and don't stop climbing." Underdeveloped, thready branches snap in his pursuit upward. Hands become sticky. Green pine needles cling and poke. Amidst dark green cover, he can only see the outside world beneath his feet. The air tastes thinner.

Underneath the tree, Remy sees more. Parting, overgrown grass approaches. *The barks are directed toward me.* She hides, pressing her back to the sticky tree. Looking up, she sees white soles. Helplessness with impending-doom-sauce and a side of tachycardia.

BLACK GUMS AND BARBARIC BREAKS

Breath in. She hears galloping paws against hardened dirt. Breath out. The dog takes deep gulps of air between shouts. Breath in. The pounding paw steps slow to a trot as it cautiously approaches. Breath out. Barks twist into angry growls which crescendo into howls. Breath in. It maintains distance from her, pacing an arc around the trunk.

It stalks me. She stares straight forward. Sometimes bullying is just too loud to ignore. *It doesn't know why, but it hates me. I wish I had food. I wish I had Cub. I wish I had a weapon. I am lost.*

Surrender. A calmness of accepted fate chills her body like drying sweat.

She slowly turns to face the beast. Bits of bark and sap attached to her back make movement less elegant. The dog doesn't stop. *Laryngitis, where are you?* Sounds seem to approach her from a far-off tunnel.

It is hardly a beast. The top of its head barely reaches her waist. Its limbs posture out like the Eiffel Tower. Each bark starts as a growl behind barred teeth. Originating from its hips, a thrust violently pukes across frayed vocal cords through presented incisors before culminating in a procession of coughing pollution aimed upward. Eye contact locks with prey.

SURRENDER THE RESPONSIBILITY OF YOUR OWN LEGACY

Dirty honey blends with pale lavender in the western sky. The breeze is light enough to not wick sweat. Steve drops his hands to his knees in a pulmonary tripod. Age taxes attrition.

"C'mon, old man!"

The dog's vocal ballistics have changed. Pursuit swells into confrontation. Disappointed and scowling, Cub looks back at Steve looking up at the distant hilltop through a darkening forest.

"They've been found. We can't reach them until sunset." Sticky lungs reluctantly trade carbon dioxide for oxygen.

"Of course it is going to be too late if we stand around—"

"It already *is* too late." With sunken cheeks and sun-marked skin, the only thing Steve is missing is a headdress. "Take a water tank and my pocketknife. I'll carry your large pack."

Barking echoes a tense background. Upset at weakness, Cub sees reason in the plan. He unfolds crossed arms. He throws the pack at a beaten man's feet, slightly out of reach from both Steve and maturity. Children sometimes want adults to believe they are upset—the power struggles people play for heroic nonsense.

The pocketknife appears minuscule in Steve's large, labor-ridden hand. He places it in Cub's. "Be ruthless."

A ONE-NIGHT EVENT HORIZON

The dog snaps and barks and howls and growls only an arm's length away, but the sounds seem to flow over her in sheets, waving at her ears. Its fur pattern looks like a light brown dog that had black paint dumped on its back. The coat shines as if slicked with cod liver oil. *Healthy. It eats well. A balanced diet.*

The snout is long and narrow, somewhere between greyhound and a door wedge. Its thin short tail looks like a garter snake metronome trapped between the gravity of two giant planets. Sixteenth notes.

Remy spreads arms out toward the dog as if she is prepared to catch a human-sized rubber ball. One step forward. The dog backs up, maintaining distance. She hops once, quickly circling the trunk. The dog pursues, staying almost within reach. A lone bishop checks the lone king.

There is anger in its bark. Black gums sag over the sides of its jawline. Remy notices it's a *he.* A rope of saliva escapes and is flung over the bridge of his nose. Four legs outpace her two.

Arms still out, she positions her back westward. Her shadow crosses the animal's face and cuts the glassy reflection from his eyeballs. *He looks a bit less crazy this way.*

Remy no longer has to imagine what a nine-year-old boy falling out of a tree looks like. The unsuspecting dog without a name grunts when Sydney lands on the dog's back, mostly toward the hind legs. A swallowed bark squeezes into a yelp. His snout whips around and catches lower teeth in the boy's upper-right orbital, just under the eyebrow. Uneven top teeth sink into his straight hairline.

The dog's bite pulls. Legs brace. Pupils dilate. The dog lashes and twists, leaning his weight toward the rear, squirming as if to challenge his master for a chew toy. Exhales are riddled in growls. Hind legs plant. The boy winces. He outweighs the dog by double, but the jaws are impressively powerful. Blood trickles from both puncture sites.

"Syd!" She attempts to pry the heads apart. Success always comes with a cost. The dog releases a face and, without sheathing, bites her left arm. The nameless dog swallows and jaws tighten.

Front paws suspended in midair, yellowed teeth impregnate her tan forearm.

Her gasp startles Sydney. Eyes unsquint. He realizes how hot his own blood is as it runs under his lower eyelid, between nose and smile line.

Grabbing a hind leg in each hand, Sydney stands. The dog's legs wriggle, begging gravity to reclaim them. He holds the dog's rear driver-side leg high above his head and releases the other to bend down. Growls. Twisting body lashes.

Using her unbitten one, she muzzles the jaws to her arm and pulls backward, stretching the dog.

"Pull him apart!" The canine's belly sags. Legs scramble. Sydney takes a step back. It reminds Remy of the parachute exercise in elementary gym class.

And then, it doesn't. A small, white, fist-sized stone covered in a courageous black boy's hand finds a home in the doggy's cervical spine.

Bully realizes his own victimization.

Furry, downcast inner eyebrows turn upward. The little black arm reels back. Another strike doesn't miss. Neck fur peels in a clump.

The dog's throat makes a noise resembling a yawning parrot. The next blow lands at the base of his skull. Only chiropractors would appreciate these adjustments. Skeletal muscles relax. Anger downshifts to a whimper like impatient streetlights.

Remy lets the head go in favor of the throat. The dog's teeth unsheathe. If he had an Adam's apple, it didn't pass the squeezing-hand test. A failed swallowing attempt follows a squirm that should be ashamed of itself. The dog's mouth drops open like a crocodile while shallow breaths support life.

She grabs his, which grabs it. Teeth nip and her arm reels back with his. Syd lets her carry his clenching hand. Together, their fists crack his skull, above the right eye.

Whimpers.

Re-reeling.

She holds her breath. The next crushes the other socket. Skull bones slip and shift in places they shouldn't.

Crying.

Re-reel.

Sydney refuses to watch, and precociousness withdraws. The next hits like the first, only this time, flesh and fur tear apart. Skull relinquishes custody of gray matter. Speckles of blood spot tightened hands in a spritz of subdural hematemesis. The final vocal transmission sounds like an airplane's landing gear chirping.

Sydney's vision gaussian blurs. He attempts to wriggle his hand from hers but the grip is too strong. The next blow strikes the top of his skull. All paws go limp. Sydney remorsefully drops the dog. Remy catches and lowers him to the ground. She peels the murder weapon from his hand. Kneeling, she grips the stone with both hands. With overhead swings, she repeatedly smashes what's left of the head.

Youth sometimes lack accurate communication tools to convey their emotions, so they cry.

Her face blooms. She doesn't realize she has been holding her breath. She only blinks to avoid the splatters. His mutilated corpse peacefully stills.

Shrouded in shadows, Remy exhales an exhausted cry. Her mouth looks like tragedy's Janus mask. Her arms limply hang. The newly stained rock falls from shivering fingers. He stops weeping.

"Remy?"

"What."

"Is he in heaven now?"

YELLOWING SKY LIKE OLD NEWSPAPER OR TEETH THAT ENJOY WINE

Twilight peeks through black tree silhouettes. Specks of pollen weightlessly float among the living. Insects stir everywhere, and

Cub swears a frog's moan is following him. Barking ceases. Cub's jog slows to a hustle.

Breaking the tree line, he trails through waist-high wheat fields. Seeds fall off their stem when he brushes by. Adam's down sits thumb-sized in the distance. Its balding sides shimmer.

Cub pulls the pocketknife from his pocket. Using thumb and pointer finger, he exercises the blade back and forth across the locking latch. *Click* in the ready position, *click* in the folded position. He doesn't close it completely, just enough to pass over the latch into the downward dog. *Click, click. Click, click.* The sound is just a little slow to match the pace of his steps. *Click, click. Click, click.*

He consciously takes longer, slower steps. *Click, click. Click, click.* Something harmonious about having both in rhythm. *Click, click. Click, click.* Like a musician's tapping foot. *Click, click. Click, click.* Lower back pain fades. *Click, click. Click, click.* Brain siesta. *Click, click. Click, click.*

What is that song they play on a trumpet to fallen soldiers, chops? Something like that... I guess. He nose-laughs to the stalking frog. *Click, click. Click, click.*

TO HIM, WHOSE EARS ARE ALWAYS OPEN

The Bible spends many words discussing dead, unclean bodies. Until nightfall, those who touch dead bodies become unclean. Timing couldn't get much better. How is one person or even one group of people expected to provide so many sacrifices? A burnt offering, a sin offering, a drink offering, all without blemish, or else it will be an affront to Him who is called, "I am." Technology improved lives making them more convenient. Yet, some still utter ancient words in the company of a justified offering with folded hands, a bowed head, and closed eyes. Prayer is the inconvenience in a technology-filled world. It is no wonder technology keeps broken promises.

Remy scrapes the flint. *Media makes it look so easy.* Sydney scavenges for loose twigs and needles amongst the tree line. It is not difficult to find skinny sticks that snap. Everything is dry. Two handfuls at a time pile next to the unborn fire. *Thhtick, thhtick, thhtick*, like dragging a rock across cement. Occasionally, a spark lands on the dead brush pile. She would prefer to save the lighter for an emergency. *Maybe each moment is.*

With frustration, she inspects her fingernails the way she used to after applying fresh polish. Wrists rotate. Adrenaline hides pain like naughty secrets. Small cuts litter her dark, dirty fingers. The nail-beds on her left hand are sunken and bruising. The middle fingernail must have snagged—part has torn off, into the pink. The tips used to be white. Now they carry hard-pressed filth.

Thhtick, thhtick, thhtick. Two separate sparks leap, glow orange, dim, and then fade. No smoke. No smell of smoke. It has been two rotations since their last fire. Remy's stomach feels black with hunger. She flicks Steve's lighter.

AFTER COUNTLESS ROTATIONS OF THE SUN BULLYING THE LANDSCAPE...

Deep purple and black paint the evening sky with a thick, horse-hair brush as the final coals of daylight dim. Orange glows flicker to highlight the survivors' mugshots. Today's events weigh heavy. Death looms in the air like black smoke spat from burning plastic. Trapped spirits are unhealthy to inhale.

An ember pops and catches a feeble blade of yellowing grass, born too close. It burns down the stem in a lazy hurry. Coiling blackness crawls behind the muted flame, casting dull shadows of neighbors before extinguishing.

Sydney sits Indian-style ninety degrees from Remy around the shallow fire pit. He stares down, resting cheek on palm. With his other hand, he traces an arc, resembling a smiley face's mouth, in the dirt using a finger-length twig. Back and forth. Each pass grooves deeper in the dry soil, pushing dirt from the path. Repetitive motion. Forth and back. *He isn't thinking about digging.* Back and forth.

Something bothers him, which bothers her. *It should. It's obvious. It should be obvious. It should bother him.* Forth and back. *His mind is replaying.* Back and forth. For a little while, it was called post-traumatic stress. A little while later, softer words would be used to describe the everlasting haunt of emotional scars.

CIRCADIAN RHYMES

Click, click.
　　Back and forth.
　　Tidal locked in a trance.
　　Forth and back.
　　Click, click.
　　Mind treadmills.

His young calves tense in a poverty of hydration. Mouth breaths inhale the cooling air through parched, soft palettes. Stream water is unsafe until boiled. Without a mirror, man cannot see his own ear.

Light trespasses in a small pocket of lumens at the base of the hill. Relief washes down his body like a man on one knee, presenting jewelry, hearing, "I do." Steps quicken and clicking stops.

SIAMESE HERETICS

There is a stagnancy in the night. Maybe it is the relative lack of wind compared to last night. Maybe it is the uncertain reunion. Maybe it is the unstable silence with Sydney. Maybe it is a homicidal hangover.

Insects sing and flirt and play their legs in a mocking jury. Remy runs a finger over the puncture wounds on her forearm.

They are tender to the touch. *They would have ruined my port, if I had one.* Everything looks dark at night so she can't tell if the wound is changing color. Earth hasn't been this dark in her lifetime. Planet-wide blindness wouldn't solve racism.

Sydney's eyes are sunken like bird eggs in a black-eye nest. A dry dark trail starts under his eyebrow and ends adjacent to his nostril.

Poor little kiddo. He shouldn't have to see these... things. Age delivers sorrow to young people who have been dealt absolutely brutal cards.

"Hey."

He doesn't respond.

"How about you get some shut eye, bud?" *Is he ignoring?* "Hey! Did you hear me?"

Justifiably annoyed, "I don't want to. I should be awake when Steve and Cub get back."

Defiance. Bending boundaries. Growing up.

Rearview mirrors tell how far pendulums *should* have swung. Spirits devour the silence and belch up awkward tension in Icelandic fashion.

"You promise to wake me if there is a problem, okay?"

He nods.

"Okay."

The pendulum creaks. The twig grooves. The boy trances. The girl will only be able to pretend to sleep.

ENTERTAIN FELLOW INMATES BY RECOUNTING THEIR UNRECORDED MEMORIES

"Psst."

Cardiac-pause holds hands with blood draining from a face attached to a paralyzed body. The campfire meekly flickers.

"Psst."

Sydney turns as if his head, neck, and torso are all cut from the same block of wood.

"Cub!" he erupts before both hands do their best to muzzle. One of Remy's eyelids slides open, then closed. "Where's Indian Steve?"

"Coming. It's good to see you again, pal." He hugs Sydney with one arm. "Did you have any action here?"

The boy lights up and nods aggressively. He looks like a can of shaken soda. "I jumped out of a tree onto a dog!"

"Really?"

Sydney bounds with excitement, the kind that adults are too ashamed to share. "We hit it with a rock really, really hard until it stopped talking!"

"What's this?" Cub asks, thumbing the boy's eyebrow next to the puncture wound.

"Oh." He looks down. "It bit me and Remy... But we are okay!" He hides his hands and looks up at Cub.

"Where is it now?"

Sydney points away from the fire.

"How about you fetch some wood so we can get this water going and then you show me."

SHADOWS ON THE SUN

The unwatched pot bubbles in a freshly stoked fire. Cub follows Sydney following their long shadows in blind, uneven steps.

Walking an unstraight line, they approach a smell not unlike roadkill learning to go bad. With a hind leg in each hand, Cub picks up the victim. Fluid leaks from the vocal cords' old home. All that remains of its head appears to be the skullcap and a few tufts of attached fur.

"Hold this."

Sydney does.

Click. The first belly incision looks like a dull knife tore through a fluffy jacket. Flesh snags the jagged teeth nearest the handle.

Cub turns, avoiding casting shadows on his subject. Pupils widen. The ripping abdomen gives birth to previously-internal organs. Camp is too distant to provide sight. Even if it did, Cub has no names for what spills out. He would have imagined more blood.

Some pieces still seem stuck. *It must be bad to eat what it couldn't finish eating.* Sydney's arms are getting sore from unnaturally stretching out the ex-dog. Shadows portray the illusion of a hundred flies. Suction-cup mouths jab their supper. Sydney waves away their tiny copper bodies.

Neck to sphincter drops out after a couple violent incisions. What remains is a headless canine-tent of ribcage supporting four limbs.

Click.

"Up there." He points the boy to a tree. Puzzled, Sydney looks for clarification. He tilts his head a little. "Put it up there." The boy lifts one leg over the branch, but the other gets stuck. His arms struggle, and he flusters.

Cub helps drape the carcass cleanly over the low-hanging evergreen limb. It sags, but doesn't break, carrying the weight.

The slippery pocketknife passes from a big hand to smaller ones.

"When you skin him tomorrow morning, do your best to keep it in one piece."

I DIDN'T PLAN TO LIVE THIS LONG

The way old rocking chairs creak, so do old joints. Steve's broad frame unshoulders the heavy pack. Inside, water sloshes. The bag jiggles after hitting the ground.

Steve sighs in relief before dropping to a knee. He pats unempty pockets to locate cigarettes.

The wind is but a zephyr. Tonight, he shields the lighter out of habit and inhales. Nicotine and its accomplices cross petrified forests of cilia to traverse bronchiolar canals. He holds his breath as if it were a dream yet come true and, if held a little longer, it just may. Down his nose are two images of the glowing lux. Relief washes weathered cheeks. There is no cough. *Not anymore.* He blows smoke out the corner of his lips in a narrow stream. Fingers tap ash off Morris' dynasty.

The escape door has been left ajar. He doesn't *have* to catch up. He doesn't *have* to return. He doesn't *have* to deliver. He could retreat, guilt-free. Well, almost. Custom tailored guilt.

Why go back to this ka-tet? Everyone I ever loved is gone. Everyone I ever will love is gone. The end glows. *The oldest disrespects me. He believes my stoicism needs more practice. He sees weakness in caution and age.* Tar paints another coat. *The little black kid, well, he doesn't know me, and I don't know him. He looks up to me, but that may just be because I'm taller. And Remy... oh Remy.* It brightly glows. *She is a sweetheart unfit for this planet's new axis.* Traces of benzyls fist-bump alveoli. *Her heart is too warm for a world that isn't.*

Brown teeth release a stunted laugh and cough up held prisoners. The congruency surprises Steve. *In a world gone black, her heart is the glow, not unlike the end of this cigarette.* Ashes break off without a tap. *Maybe it makes sense to follow the pack, until it's done. Maybe not. But then again, maybe not, someday.*

CHAPTER 29

SOMEWHERE NEAR

Two mud-splattered black boots stop on a crooked rectangle of green faux grass with a fake sunflower. Thick fingers growing from the same hand carry filth in the grooves of their fingerprints. They push the screen door ajar enough for a lumpy, square face to fit. The screen door squeals like most do. Two fingers hold it open. Ears listen, but don't hear. *He would hear. His are better.* Eyes look, but don't see.

A cool, mild breeze splashes waves of unfreshness that flutter the brown hair escaping from the bottom of a red, mesh "Suds" ball-cap. A pair of exophoric eyes, deviating outward from his nose, narrow with caution of incoming air. Oxygen rushes through a broad nose pinned between chubby cheeks. No one would call the face "symmetrical." *Something is burning.*

Tightening jaws trigger a little muscle on his temple to bulge. Nostrils flare to a deep, audible breath. Spiders would be impressed by the things caught in his coarse nose hairs. Hold, hold, release. Two fingers allow the screen door to squeal shut. White flecks of paint flutter off the farmhouse's doorframe.

CHAPTER 30

IT'S HARD TO BELIEVE I'LL BE TURNING FORTY IN TWENTY-ONE REVOLUTIONS

T*ap, tap, tap.*

Consciousness reemerges. Cub rolls over from side to back.

"Do you think I could lay next to you tonight?"

Truthfully, he'd rather not. The boy stands in nervous anticipation. His blanket is tightly bunched in fists just below his nose. Eyes wide, unblinking. Eyebrows upturned. *It took courage to ask.* Cub respects that. His heart softens. His lips muster up a smile he hopes is believable.

Exhilaration and relief sculpt unsuccessful chameleons. Sydney's cheeks shine in the plumpness of a lip-stretching grin.

Remy opens an eye the way a disturbed cat would. She watches. Sydney spreads his blanket very straight, making sure some of it covers Cub, too. Sitting down, he pokes his toes beneath. Legs follow. He delicately scoots his butt as to not disturb a resting beast. She closes her eye. She smiles. She can now stop pretending to sleep.

Privilege, acceptance, and responsibility pass around a peace pipe. Clenched in his right fist like a favorite stuffed animal, the pocketknife rests. Young happiness swims in shallow pools. Old happiness dives in shallow pools.

COMPLIMENTS HOLD THE INSECURE'S TEARS HOSTAGE

The longer things stay this way, the narrower the gap of evil between primality and mankind.

Today's capital letter is sunrise punctuated in stars. Diurnal cycles weigh Cub's eyelids, but instinct leaves his conscience unsettled.

He sits up and runs fingers through his peach-fuzzed hair. It hasn't been this long since school.

> After graduation, I discovered the real world *feared* a man willing to shave a still-growing head of hair. I was young, but the public called me, "Sir." I liked that. Nobody picks fights with a facially scarred man.
>
> Mom and Dad ponied up money to send me to optional school. Half a term in, I discovered that girls and parties are better than passing marks—a lot better.

A mosquito lands on Cub's forearm. The mosquito is sentenced to death by hand-slap and finger-flick.

> Advisors called me in for an emergency meeting. "Probation," they said. "Shape up," they said. "Is there something you should tell us?" they asked. "If you keep this up, how do you see your future?" they asked. They were taught to use open-ended questions. They were taught to express tough love. Avoid negative terminology. Good cop, less good cop. Authority and I

don't mix well, no matter the alignment. This collegiate wake-up call went unanswered.

Looking back, it would have been fun to stay in school until I was officially sanitized. Sanity has nothing to do with cleaning. Endless pantries of blondes and brunettes that, "have never tried this before," enjoyed rubbing my shaved head. Hearts recycle when the alarm clock goes off.

By daylight, they try changing the world. By night, they are thumbing for a ride away from it. People live in a depravity of genuine compliments for fear they will be taken the wrong way. Simply listening to a date between sips and nods, often persuades them into saying, "Yes," to advances they would ordinarily avoid. If compliments were food, starving would be another ignored epidemic, overruled in favor of wars for which we were not invited.

The holidays came. Students were strongly advised to go home. Those that didn't were put on suicide watch. Statisticians don't place ugly bets. Ex-students were told not to return.

Less than half a revolution of sleepless sleeping-withs and testing intoxicating limits shrank my home. My old room had been re-appropriated as a workout area. Closets that used to harbor my style were now overrun with sweaters from Mom's experimental period.

Remy was thriving. She was earning excellent marks in school and playing tennis like she was on meldonium. My new independence gave her some in return, like plants that outgrow their potted cellmate.

"How is your new school, Cub?" asked Mom, Dad, grandparents, uncles, aunts, cousins, neighbors, and everybody.

Disappointment, regret, failure, sibling jealousy, anger, annoyance, but not necessarily in that order. In a word describing a hair transplant's before-picture and conveying one's own self-disinterest, I responded, "Fine."

Something feels like it is crawling on Cub's thigh. Nothing is. Nothing was. He brushes the area anyway. It feels better.

The tree was dressed the way it always was. Carols are sung. Snowmen are built and destroyed. Photographs are taken despite their reluctant subjects. Everybody wore red and green. Feasts are eaten. Indulgence. Warmth. Family. Cheer. Late mornings and evenings. Presents are opened. I purposely kept my mouth shut.

Would it be a true lie? A false truth? A half-truth? A white lie? A fib? Perhaps a lie by omission is the best euphemism for my sin.

I left family and holidays without a plan. Another partial truth. I had a hope, but then again, hope is just a long john that's been jelly-filled with doubt.

When I returned to campus, my soon-to-be-ex-friend, Miguel, an out-of-state Southern boy with Latin skin and lips like tightrope, felt sorry enough to let me stay on the couch of his dimly lit, upstairs one-bedroom apartment.

"Thirty spins, I promise," turned into "sixty spins, please," which turned into "I'm trying my best, stop bothering me." Borrowing money and sharing a home are two strike-anywhere matches specifically designed for bridge burning.

When Miguel left for morning class, I was there. When he stopped back between school and work, I was there. When he came home late from his job, I was there. The smell of my skin reigned thick in the apartment's air. Crooked blinds kept my pale complexion like uncooked turkey.

Being taken advantage of and frustration lived in the background of Miguel's mind while I lived in the background of his home. Tension was obvious. Conversation was brief. Tolerance was invisible.

I waited for the sound of the sliding lock preceded by the door being slammed shut every morning. "Today is the today," I said aloud. As much as people really believe yesterday is connected to today which is connected to tomorrow, it isn't. People voluntarily accept yesterday's burden, carrying it as one's own personal history book that no one will ever read. A colorless military badge. Titles like "cancer survivor" or "rape victim" define the way society would like to categorize and judge its population, throwing money at problems, instead of solutions. Tear up their charity checks. Let the past be just that. Today is only today.

The name is misleading because nobody is good at goodbyes. Before shutting the door for the last time, I ripped the corner from a white unpaid electric bill. I left the slip of paper on his kitchen table. In blue ink, it read, "I'm sorry."

PRODUCING IMPERFECTION RIVALS RECEIVING PRAISES OF PERFECTION

Hair rooted in oily soil bends back into place as Cub rubs his head. His palms have aged like circus peanuts removed from their package. Each passing sunset grows stiffer skin. Old black plastic hoses.

Sydney peacefully rests using his hands as a pillow. Remy is bundled in blankets. Faint snores occasionally escape through chapped lips. Steve is absent. Cub squints south for approaching shadows, but it is as futile as reading books submerged in flowing murky river water.

Darkness lives. Wild has reclaimed its wilderness. Insects celebrate. Grass stretches out into places lawn mower blades have not allowed. Humanity's flame struggles for oxygen in the lesser light.

A couple more prolonged moments and the sun will awaken. Cub doesn't wait. Lucky is the anxious life. Anxiety is a problem born from the womb of a problemless mother. Worrying about worrying. Rocking chairs and twiddling thumbs never won any races.

The second hand takes longer between ticks. Worn feet take longer between strides. Tongues conduct longer syllables.

Cub snaps off a couple almost-dying branches and casts them into the fire pit before hiking the hilltop. He strains ascending the pitch. With each step, he pushes palm to knee making the climb easier. It feels like skipping until it doesn't.

Cub peeks over the crest. He can feel heartbeats thump in his head like they want to burst out his ears. Respirations shift from nose to mouth without his brain's permission.

He takes a knee to observe. *No Steve. No movement by the camp-fire. No sun.* He can't quite see the farmhouse from this far side.

He checks his feet and, to his relief, he didn't step in Sydney's accident. *Poor kid.*

Cub remembers learning that air thins at higher altitudes which should labor breathing, but he finds this thin stuff more refreshing. *Perhaps the elevation wasn't enough to make a difference.*

Except for his, the gear and bags are scattered as if by rapture. Something breaks beneath his boot's heel when crossing between the packs. *A lesson for someone. Hopefully, not mine.*

Photons whisper, "Good morning, honey," like an automaton lover. *It seemed like that watched horizon would never boil.*

Still dim by the time Cub returns down the hill, Sydney is not in bed. He rocks Remy's hip. She stirs while taking a deep breath of morning air. Her face looks like it is yawning, but her mouth doesn't.

Cub makes his way to the tree line, pushing branches from his face. Wind rustles leaves which sound like applause. *It comes in cool waves—rain's prodrome.*

Sydney has his back to Cub and his front to his work. Cub approaches. Death's stench is egg-shaped around the former canine. Sydney seems unbothered. *His attention is fixed.*

His tongue sticks up and out the corner of his closed lips. Delicately separating skin from corpse in a single large piece prevents him from noticing Cub.

Without disturbing the boy, Cub turns around. He scavenges tree bases for larger sticks in preparation for a sterilizing fire.

EXOTHERMIC PRIDE

Short, frantic footsteps draw attention from fire stoking.

"Cub, look!" Sydney's voice cracks. The boy's cheeks pucker. Texture can be seen on his tongue. Last night's eye matter rests as yellow pebbles in the corners of his eyes. The puncture wound's blood has turned dark black. Oxidized. Dirty. Forgotten.

A blanket trails behind him like a bride without a bridesmaid. He presents it from behind his waist in a hairpin loop, revealing his handiwork on a blanket platter.

"The paws were kinda' tricky." Bated breath waits for compliments. With bottled excitement, Sydney searches Cub's face.

His eyes spread open. Eyebrows sharpen in an unblinking stare. He grabs the stained blanket and studies it with disbelief. *The lifespan of objects. Privileged athletes with tiny sponges won't be able to clean this massacre.*

"Why did you do this?" he growls. Nostrils flare. Jaw clenches.

"I... I don't know." Sydney's expression collapses like an umbrella beneath a waterfall.

"How are we supposed to *clean* this?" Cub snatches the blood-saturated blanket, one end heavier in afterlife than the other.

Remy whisks her covers off and scrambles toward the confrontation. "Whoa!" She slips a hand between them like a referee separating two boxers. "Stop yelling! What's the matter?" Her concern bounces between the boys. She doesn't hear a crow squawk.

Cub bats her hand away, stands, and pushes her crouching body with domestic violence. "Stay out of this." Her cowering figure houses a handful of tachycardic beats. Fists clenching and shoulders broad in imposing peacock fashion, he sneers before moving to the opposite side of the fire pit.

WE ARE RAINING ON RAIN'S PARADE

"I was just trying to—" is all Sydney chirps before tears drown out the rest. Embarrassment and confusion wring rags of sadness.

"Oh, come here, my darling." Remy offers outstretching arms in a kneeling, hugger's pose. Through wiperless windshields, Sydney sees his mom. He covers his face with blood-seasoned hands. Short, awkward steps dock him in waiting arms.

The boy's body jerks as he catches his breath amidst weeps. A lost tuft of fur rides a newly running river down his forearm.

"It's okay." Anger toward Cub disguises itself as compassion for Sydney. A yin and yak yo-yo. "He's not mad at you." She pats his back. More full body jerks. Skin on the backs of his arms is ashy and dry. Her blurry peripheral vision witnesses a sulking brother.

Especially to a growing boy, seldom disappoints more than discovering one's hero is just a plain old person.

Hope permits denial of flaws.

Dog juice slicks him from fingertips to forearms. The odor mixes with his musky dark skin which triggers Remy's hunger.

"Honey? Can you show *me* what you did?" Crying slows. Jerking stops. As they dry, his fingers stick together. He spreads them apart, holding up the dog pelt by its front legs. Besides a small tear in the white underbelly fur and the fraying front legs he tucks away, it is impressively all in one piece. "That's great, Sydney!" She hugs and pats his butt. A participation ribbon.

She casts a brief glance across the fire pit. Cub stares at the flames. *He never even looked at Sydney's pelt.* She caresses the boy's head. *Our voices carry, making it impossible to not overhear our exchange.*

"Thanks, Remy," he says with fleeting enthusiasm.

Attention returning to Sydney, "Now, why don't you go out and play while I clean this up."

"Alright," he says with a flattened affect. Head and chin slung low, he slowly mopes away.

She swats his butt, "Go!"

He covers the spot. When he looks back at her, she is smiling. His mouth-corners curl up.

CHAPTER 31

THIRD RESPONDERS

Lush clouds with deep blue bases slowly pull their way across the sky like hanging diapers.

A hinge door squeaks open and a screen door slams shut.

CHAPTER 32

OUR OWN HANDS AT OUR OWN THROATS

Still kneeling, Remy closes her eyes to inhale a controlled breath and exhale out her mouth like she's seen yogis do on film. It brings very little relief with only a dash of composure. Actors fake stuff.

Cub sits Indian-style, poking at the campfire with a long stick. She stands above him.

"Cub."

He pretends to ignore. He pokes. Actors.

"Cub!"

She notices a flinch, but he doesn't respond. Bad actors.

Her hands perch atop her hips. "So, you are going to ignore me?"

Cub suppresses his annoyance.

"Fine. What you did to Sydney was pretty..." She'd rather not curse. "Rude!" Divided parents are weak parents. "He worked hard to impress us, but you had to make it all about your..." She chokes down unsavory language. "Stuff."

He looks up at her through eyebrows. Cub's poker face struggles to hide two aces. His teeth tighten behind pursing lips like a child that doesn't want to take medicine.

"You didn't have many friends because you don't even know how to talk to people. You should be ashamed of not being ashamed of yourself."

"I'm not."

"You should be! You are too old to have to learn how to behave from your little sister! It's *one* stain on one *stupid* blanket!"

"Trade me, then."

"What?"

"Trade your blanket for mine—if it's such a not-big-deal."

"I don't want..." Her final nerve wiggles underneath the shadow of his shoe like a blind maggot.

He stops poking.

If I finish my sentence, he proves his point, she thinks. "Fine. Trade." Those that fret over the petty don't have enough tragedy in their life.

He raises one eyebrow with mild surprise as he pushes a twig into the white inner heat. She leaves.

INTERNAL DIALECTS

Bodyguards won't let the sun into the breakfast club. A low, cool breeze brushes Cub's arm hair.

Steve should be back by now. The other two left to clear brain traffic. "I do best on my own anyways," he says to alone.

A stoking fire's warmth trumps today's cool air. A Y-shaped stick sits on either side of the campfire. A wet stick bridges the Ys. Bones stuck to tendons stuck to muscle wrap around the spit. One side slipped off after a rotation, but it was too hot to correct the dangling meat.

HOW TO FALL MADLY IN LOVE IN NINE-THOUSAND EASY STEPS

Remy catches up to Sydney. He is squatting over a clearing with his back to her.

"Syd? What are you doing?"

The cheer in her voice sounds as phony as wigs pretending to be hair. He pushes dirt mounds together and stuffs them into his pocket. Some spills through his fingers. "Playing."

She crouches. He smells her, ripe and comfortable. She feathers his thick, curly black hair. He bashfully smiles, backing his head from her reach.

"You are a really thoughtful young man, you know that?"

Batting loose dirt on his pants, his head rises, looking back and forth between her right and left eye. He deciphers braille facial expressions as sincerity. It has been a long time since Sydney has felt the warmth of a true compliment. He doesn't know how to respond, so he doesn't.

"Can I ask you something?" Coyness coats her voice.

He nods.

She leans into his face and whispers, "Will you be my *best* friend?"

Expression pops like broken lightbulbs as he squeezes a hug around her neck.

"Is that a no?"

He giggles.

She laughs.

Then, he whispers into her ear, "Only if you will be mine."

She can tell by his voice, he is smiling.

Over her shoulder, Sydney spots a distant figure ambling to become less distant. He pulls the hug apart, but still grips her shoulder blades.

Pumping his fist, Sydney calls out, "Indian Steve!"

She turns. Her oily, dishwater blonde ponytail brushes his lips.

He pouts, feigning annoyance. He's not. She apologetically covers her own mouth. He combs his tongue in mock disgust. She playfully paws the side of his face. "Deal with it, *friend*."

His cheeks bloom in a meadow of his own bluff. *God, she is pretty. I like it when she touches me. I like it when she smiles at me. I like it when she talks to me or thinks about me.* She jogs back toward camp. *Her nose is perfect. I like the freckle under her eye. It goes well with her golden-tanned skin.* She waves him to follow. *She makes me feel like a grown-up instead of a little kid. I wonder what she looks like in a swimsuit.* "C'mon, lets surprise Steve!" *I wonder what it feels like to kiss her.*

"Wait up!" Sydney jumps to his feet, matching two strides for her one.

She slows, extending her arm backward. He carefully docks, weaving his small fingers between her bigger ones. "It is going to take him a while to get here but let's get ready!" They trot together, swinging laced hands.

HEALING WHIP-MARKS

Clear, liquified fat droplets hang from once-functional striated muscle like tears from a grieving widow—vaporizing in their sizzling demise.

Cub watches them return. Sydney releases hands and runs full speed toward this morning's disappointed.

"Cub!" It sounds more like a chirp from vocal cords not yet wading their toes in puberty. "We saw him. We saw Indian Steve!" His little chest heaves to regain its host's breath. "He is coming!" His hands rest on his hips. "What are you doing?" He looks at the spit with a cocking head, but he knows where it came from and he knows where it is going.

Should I lie or tell the kid the truth? Which would require less explaining? Drifting left and right like a quarantined bubble in a picture leveler on a boat at sea, he keeps it vague, "Lunch." A fat-tear sizzles. He rotates the center spit. Rivulets baste before welling back into droplets.

Remy arrives, but doesn't acknowledge the boys besides a passing grin toward Sydney. *She'll avoid eye contact until forgiven.*

A rusty brown autopsy blanket has replaced her thickest blue one—the one with lots of little white hearts. Cotton fibers have stiffened like gelled hair. Her posture droops. She sighs.

Cub sees her shamefully fold his old blanket. From behind, her bony elbows move like an orchestra conductor.

"Let's surprise Indian Steve!" Sydney jumps up and down in front of a distracted Cub, snapping him from captivity's guilty thoughts.

"Yeah. Let's surprise him." The smile looks phonier than foreign currency. Some kids choose to ignore what they see. Therapy will unlock tomorrow's vision of yesterday.

FOLDING MEMORIES OF MOM

When reality tightens its grip, drift into the blurry background. With a turned back, no one sees a red face.

She neatly folds her new blanket. His skin oils disgust her worse than the sour odor of decay. She drops to her knees.

Something about that last fold reminds her of Mom. Only Dad called her "Samantha." *We didn't dare or care to.*

"Take one corner in one hand," she would instruct. "Take the other corner in the other, the long way, like this." I sat on my hands on the aging white couch with black speckles—the edges fraying under the crooks of my knees. A white plastic tube protruded the stitching. My feet dangled, too short to touch the light brown carpet. "Fold it across your body like this." I brushed my hair from my eyes and curled it around each ear. I think Mom forgot I needed a haircut. I wasn't in a hurry to remind her. I slid a hand under each thigh. "Fold it over one last time and you are done!" She made it look easy. She had a way of making difficult things seem easy. She taught in a way that did not belittle and, when you succeeded, she made you feel it—impactful. She'd clap, and stomach butterflies would chase away like chalk dust from blackboard erasers. They'd flutter out my mouth in happiness. I hope heaven had room for her.

She kept religion close, but never forced it upon us or anyone. She led by example and we barely followed.

Remy's chin tucks. She looks over her shoulder. The boys prepare food. They aren't paying attention to her. She relaxes and straightens her neck. Her eyes close as she bows her head with folded hands.

"Dear God. Forgive me for not keeping in touch. Please don't think it is because I don't believe. Please don't think it is because I am too busy. The truth is, every excuse I have is not good enough. I am sorry for letting the cares of the living distract me from you. Please, forgive me."

Her face breathes. Vision glosses. Embarrassment. She hopes the boys aren't watching her, but she feels like she is being watched. Faith should not be viewed as a weakness or flaw. It isn't a crutch to support a character deformity. It isn't wax on a new car. It is the engine and should be celebrated with pale faces, not red ones.

She feels a cleanliness—a shedding—the way hands feel after soap suds run off, right after leaving the underside of a wet faucet, but right before they tuck themselves into a dry, warm towel. Remy unfolds her hands. She drags fingers over the bitten arm. The site has scabbed. Locating the sore, she circles the perimeter before pushing on it.

There is a pain, but not discomfort. *It feels good. It feels... therapeutic.* She keeps pushing. An eye peeks under a ruffled forehead. Redness around the scab blanches with pressure. Pain and pleasure distract.

She quickly re-closes the eye and refolds her hands like a child trying to fake obedience. Parents know better.

"Please help us find a safe place to live. Please help Cub understand how to be a better person. Please help Sydney forgive us for not being better providers. Please help keep our mouths wet and our bellies full.

Oh, and thank you for watching over us all these rotations. Thank you for giving us the strength to not give up—to persevere. Thank you for protecting us against the dog. Thank you for listening to me and being my friend."

Wireless communication persists.

"Please forgive our sins. Please watch over the family members we have already lost. Please give them a better life than they had here."

She feels a tap on the neck. Her eyes are still shut but her train of thought derails.

"Are you okay?"

In pressured internal speech, she recites to the Almighty, *"Thank you, Lord. Amen."*

She blinks open. "Yes, honey. I am."

Sydney stands taller than Remy kneels. He sticks out his stomach at her like a pulled bow. He puzzlingly stares down at her.

"Were you praying?"

She nods.

"My cousin says God is not real." He waits for her denial. Innocent eyes seek answers.

How does one teach a belief when, in one's own mind, the belief has a small dark roommate of doubt? "What do you think?" she asks.

The boy breaks eye contact. Synapses spark, attempting to piece experiences together. "Well, I don't know," he finally admits. "I've never seen him before."

Remy brushes a dark lock off his forehead with the back of her hand. "Do you only believe in things you can *see?*"

He shrugs.

"Do you think germs exist?"

He nods. Ideas rearrange their jigsaw pieces.

"But you've never seen them, right?"

He shakes his head.

"How about air or gravity, can you see them?"

He slowly shakes his head again.

"But those exist, right?"

He nods. Logic fuses half-truths.

"I think there are too many amazing things in this world that we don't understand to not be explained by a higher power."

"Like God?"

"Like God." She pinches his nose. He bashfully shows teeth and wriggles with arms straight at his side. "You know what my mom told me?"

He refocuses on her and shakes his head.

"She said, 'Religion can be a slippery thought that slides in and out of your life. Sometimes it's your best friend, sometimes it's a pen pal you haven't talked to for a long time, but always make sure to keep it in your life.'

"It's like blowing bubbles with a wand. Faith keeps the bubbles together. Some people blow too hard and they pop right away. Some blow too softly, and they never leave the ring. Still others form bubbles, but they only float a little while. You want your bubble to float all the way up."

He softly nods. He doesn't realize his mouth is open. Remy nudges his chin, closing his mouth.

She winks.

He blushes.

She hugs him.

He squeezes her.

She separates. "So, are you boys done cooking me dinner, yet?" she asks, slapping him on the butt.

He giggles. Holding his rear end and watching his feet, Sydney walks on tippy toes back to the fire, ahead of her.

THE SUN CHASES DARKNESS AWAY TO THE BEAT OF SQUINTING EYES AND STRETCHING ARMS

Three bright-white plates sit dressed in charred dog muscles. Cub scrapes the last bits off the makeshift skewer. He taps the tip on a fourth plate and juices splatter in all directions. Clear fat blobs collect like landlocked countries surrounded by heat-shocked proteins. Tossing it aside, he sucks his shiny thumb clean.

Ribbons of pale white smoke rise from each platter. He wipes both hands like snow angels on the grass, looks at them, and wipes again.

"Smells good. Is it all done?"

Cub nods at Sydney and slides the plate with the smallest, but still substantial, portion his direction. "This one's yours, bud."

"Thanks, Cub."

No response.

"Hey, Cub? Sorry about your blanket." The boy's eyes stay downcast and his feet nervously shuffle.

Cub takes a deep breath through his nose and holds it as if he is suppressing a violent outburst—a torn scab. He exhales. "Don't mention it." He playfully rocks Sydney's kneecap. Cub musters up what feels like a smile but looks more like a straight line.

COQUETTISHLY

"Smells good, boys. Did you save some for me?" Remy asks with three-quarters excitement and one-quarter anxiety. Cub withholds emotion from her. Tension clings to his disposition like a camel to a life preserver.

"Yeah. Which is hers, Cub?"

Three beats of silence follow.

"Give her the biggest one."

Sydney's eyes bulge. Children shouldn't play poker. Interactions would be kinder if adults followed kids' lead. Sydney fetches the overfilled plates one-by-one. Carrying hers with both hands underneath, he presents the platter. "Here you go, *friend*."

"Thank you, fellas." She casts for Cub's attention but only reels in a subtle nod. Beautiful moments spoil easily.

Cub reaches for his plate. The fork with bent teeth rattles on its ceramic bed while he drags it across the ground. Four plates for three appetites.

Most pieces are black and warm to the touch. Cub leans his neck over the meal as he chews.

Sydney's first bite burns the roof of his mouth. He spits it out and feverishly pants. His tongue wags like a happy dog's tail as he fans his mouth with an open palm.

Remy's eyes are closed. Smoke rises around her neatly laced fingers. Her mouth moves, but he can't hear any words. His tongue stops wagging and retracts. Cub's food receives Cub's attention. The boy folds his hands, closes his eyes, and bows his head. He moves his lips as if he whispers fake words to fake people.

One eye opens. He sees Remy carefully picking at her food. He re-closes the eye and says, "Amen," before snatching a piece of meat with his fingers.

Limbs chatter in the west wind's gust like audience members to an applause sign.

While chewing, Sydney asks, "What about Indian Steve?"

Remy watches Cub not responding. "We saw Steve coming on our way back."

He nods at her, still chewing with his mouth open.

A new gust thrusts through the party. Remy's sun-drenched hair blows back to front. This time, the wind punctuates with drizzle.

Cub perks up as if startled from a dream. He can't help but grin. Sydney sets down his plate to clap. He opens his mouth to catch raindrops. Remy smiles at the scene. *Communal happiness... finally.*

Light rain becomes heavier and the rich clouds promise more. Droplets hit the soil and disappear as if they are falling into sawdust. Vaporizing splashes hiss in the fire. Tall grass around them sways. Embers roll off and harmlessly threaten brushfires.

The sound is unpredictably consistent. It reminds Cub of listening to rain gutters when he would sit out in the garage. Bird voices and insect music wash away.

He turns over a cup and pan to catch some rainwater.

Sydney drops a long piece of meat in like a sword swallower and then stands up to dance in circles. He waves his arms as if with invisible pom-poms.

Remy has trouble holding in a laugh. A small chunk of fat ejects from her mouth and she quickly raises a hand to cover herself.

She backfists Cub in the bicep. He stops chewing. He looks over at her. Their eyes meet. She stops chewing. She stops breathing. Waiting. He inaudibly chuckles. She continues breathing and chewing and laughing. She'll take it as a non-verbal peace offering.

While chewing, Sydney hums and spins around—then he doesn't. He freezes, motionless. His body looks like pterodactyl fossils—a lowercase 't' whose arms got crinkled. It takes a couple moments, but both Cub and Remy look up from their dish—first at a scared Sydney, then at that which the boy has fixated.

LISTENING TO LIGHTNING

Rain falls unbothered on the still life. Droplets sound like little clumps of mayonnaise clapping on a cold kitchen floor.

Blood runs out of Remy's face, or so it would appear by the changing color. Cub's back stiffens, and his hunching posture corrects.

Twelve arm-lengths away stands a tall, well-fed large man wearing a faded red ball-cap with a beer logo which reads: *"Suds."* It has an obnoxious crease in the center of the bill. Droopy eyes sit atop two pudgy, pink cheeks, pinning a broad, flat nose in between. His mouth hangs open, displaying large gums and small teeth. His big square head effortlessly transitions into chins, cascading down to a sloppy, collared black-and-red-checked shirt tucked behind wet jean suspenders which, no doubt, hide an impressively smooth, round belly. His untied black rubber boots look two sizes too big and are speckled with brown dirt.

His short, chubby arms point a rain-slicked, shiny rifle at the little boy. Droopy eyes slowly move from one party member to the next between labored blinks. When getting to Cub, he re-fixes his gunsight on the alpha. Sheer numbers can level the playing field with even the most dangerous predator.

Driblets fall from the brim, across his vision. The left eye twitches. He squints. It stops. When he stops squinting, it twitches. The barrel looks like it is perspiring in the foreground.

He hasn't found what he sought.

Remy frowns and suppresses a frightened whimper. Cub raises his hands up with a gesture, somewhere between surrender and the beginning of an Egyptian bow. Sydney follows suit but raises his hands as if he is stretching to touch Earth's ceiling. Tippy toes.

"It doesn't have to be like this." Cub notices a chubby pointer finger curl around the trigger.

The giant grunts. His lips don't move.

The rain picks up. Soil darkens. Sydney's socks dampen. He rocks back onto his heels. Flat footing is more comfortable. He spreads his toes within the shoes.

"What do you want from us?" Cub asks in a louder, more annoyed than submissive, tone. *He hears us.* If only old MacDonald had a fat wife.

The large, egg-shaped man in the Suds hat unlocks his stare with Cub. *Why is he looking at the boy's shoes?* Suds shakes his right elbow, the one attached to the trigger finger. *Arm fatigue?* He shuffles toward Sydney but squares up with Cub.

Suds steps with the left and the right slides to catch up.

Sydney reaches for the sky on tippy toes, again. His back stiffens. *Step and slide.* The boy pretends to lose his balance backward, but really wants to escape the ambling figure. *Step and slide.* Sydney cracks. The bottom of his sight blurs. *Step and slide.*

"Leave him alone, please?" What starts as a scream, Remy ends as a plea. *Step and slide.* Cub adjusts himself to a crouch. His hands drop to nose level. *Step and slide.* The fire's glow reflects off the lower third of his rifle.

If Sydney reached out, he could touch the man who scares him. The business end of the barrel drops. The large man reaches down and grabs a chunk of the blackened meat from Sydney's plate.

IT MUST HAVE BEEN SOMETHING YOU DIDN'T EAT

Messy smacks of tongue and lips and teeth can easily be heard through the downpour's white noise.

"Sssgood," burps out between chomps. When food slinks back to his molars, his chins jiggle like birds on a power line. Kneeling, he rests the rifle across a bent leg. Bloated fingers plop another hunk on a thick, pink tongue.

The boy takes a couple baby steps away. Collectively, shoulders relax. Collectively, young eyes watch a bear consume.

Cub sneaks a tiny lump from his own plate. Slow mastication, but adrenals have stolen his appetite. Teeth shred, but throat refuses to swallow a parched palate. Never use a dry waterslide.

White smoke billows as water beats fire in a game of paper, rock, scissors. Cub's eyes sting from the emitting clouds.

"Kinda' gamey," the chewing monster says. "But, sssgood." He turns to the drenched kid. "What's your name?"

The little spine stiffens. His hands go up, but arms grow weaker. Unblinking, he looks at the giant. His walleyed stare is chilling, like two weighted-dice pupils pointing away from his nose. He wonders if the big man realizes he is staring at his anomaly. *Would he be offended? Will he become angry?* These questions trap his brain and paralyze his vocabulary.

"Sydney! His name is Sydney." Cub shoots Remy a cold glance as if she were not supposed to reveal his real name.

"Snydney," says the giant in a low voice as he nods his head. Another piece of meat hops in his mouth like popcorn. "Hi, Snydney."

Sydney's raised right hand waves.

"What do you want from us?" she asks. Suds keeps his attention glued to Sydney.

"Friend."

"We can be your friends—"

"No! Friend!" he interrupts. His eyebrows briefly furrow. He studies the boy's face, the boy's nose, the boy's thin neck, the boy's scabs.

Another piece disappears into his mouth. The plate is nearly empty. It rests on unlevel earth. Rainwater pools with grease and blackened specks. He rubs the last big chunk in the milieu before plopping it onto his tongue.

"Lost friend."

Becoming annoyed without a declaration of conflict, Cub pipes up through gritting teeth, "We haven't seen anyone."

A moment of discouragement, and then back to studying Sydney's face.

"Do you live around here, Mister?"

"No!" the man defensively says to Cub while looking at Sydney. He speaks as if his brain wrestles with a reluctant tongue to produce language.

The last piece of muscle dangling from a long, yellow tendon vanishes. He empties the remaining fluid and spins the plate. Splatters spray in a spiral circle. He stands still, giving the boy all his attention.

"Sir?"

Suds looks down at the feeble voice.

"Will you be my friend?"

The large mouth shrinks as if pulled shut by a drawstring. After careful thought, the giant mouth responds, "Kay."

The facial expression strikes Sydney more as a handshake than a hug. His socks are soaked. His meal is gone. His new friend turns him into a used friend. His posture slumps. He doesn't see it coming toward him. To Sydney, it feels like a bratwurst pushing against his forehead. Giant fingers trace the puncture site above the boy's eyebrow. Sydney can feel an unkept and chipped fingernail crease his skin. Suds traces the scab's border with the delicate stroke of a child writing his name in beach sand. Friendly unmixed human contact nourishes the heart.

"Get better." Instead of yanking his hand away, the giant drags fingers down Sydney's cheek and neck and chest. Ever lighter. Butterfly pirouettes. Two people pulled apart, each desperately and naïvely thinking, *I never want to forget this feeling because it may never happen to me again.*

Love's first tooth.

The large man leaves without addressing Remy or Cub. With rifle barrel slung over his right shoulder, he descends toward the western evergreens.

"Wait!" Sydney screams. His voice cracks above the beating rain. He dashes after the man who doesn't slow down. With his left fist pumping, the right digs into his pants pocket. He runs in front of his used friend, who continues the same pace. The boy walks backward to match. He pulls out a long white tooth. Wet brown sand speckles the broader face.

"Take this—for good luck."

They both stop. The man reaches out. Sydney places the tiny incisor into the giant's palm. Suds brings it up for a closer look. Stretching his neck up, Sydney can't tell which eye is actually inspecting the item. Both fisheyes appear as if they wouldn't be in a good position. It twirls between his thumb and index finger. The arm lowers. He breathes out exhaust. The loosest of water shakes from his hand and he stuffs the tooth into a small, stitched pocket on the chest of his suspenders.

"Thank you," Suds mumbles and then disappears into the trees.

WEAVING STORIES ACCELERATE THE PACE OF PAGE-TURNERS

He seemed to appear out of thick air.

"Get your biggest bag. We go now."

"Indian Steve! We've been—" is all Sydney could squeal before Steve presses a perpendicular finger across his lips. The company quiets. His demeanor truncates their hesitation. The company obeys.

"Now." He motions them to hurry. Many of the supplies still sat on the hilltop, but each manages to find a pack, in most cases, emptying its contents first.

Ducking, Steve hustles toward the road, waving them on. He is not known for being nimble, but the others break out into a jog to catch up, like a trench-running platoon.

The rain and wind lighten. A sun sliver peeks out from behind thick curtains. Each runs with his or her shadow for a short while, heat on their wet backs.

It came down faster than the planet could gulp. Shoes sink, causing a ring of mud to silhouette their past, leaving sloppy kissing noises in their wake.

The sand-colored gravel road opens to a sand-colored driveway lined on either side by aging evergreens.

"To block the wind," Steve says as more of a narrative than to anyone in particular.

"How do we know this is safe?"

Without looking back at her, "We don't, but I followed him into our camp."

The driveway is long. Cub feels vulnerable as they approach

the door. Orphan wind chimes sing like late-night dogs howl, to any ears willing to listen.

The driveway continues back toward a large closed barn. Its red paint is chipped and cracking. It doesn't appear as if there are any vehicles around to "borrow."

A crooked doormat that used to be green has two brown smears across the word, "Welcome." Toward the back of the house, a broken corner gutter allows a waterfall of roof run-off.

Steve wipes each eye as if shampoo got in them. Standing on the cement slab of the little white farmhouse's threshold, he briefly glances back at his posse to do a courage-check. Satisfied, he prepares for the slow rollercoaster clicks to become fast. Wiping each foot, he opens the screen door.

A PISCES EYES

Earth's west always beats east in tug-o-war games with the sun. It was winning again today as the flimsy screen door squawks open. The warped inner door is closed but unlatched due to ambivalent wood maintenance.

Steve pushes enough to fit two fingers between the jam, then waits. Stillness and silence beckon. His neck pulls back as his nose is struck with a choking stuffiness that only two large, sweaty bodies trapped overnight in close quarters produce. Fornication fossils. Notes of mildew and dried urine hang in tannins of the two-story home.

The living room furniture has seen a lot of living. A pair of windows with translucent brown curtains hang like coffee-stained teeth. Across from the doorway sits a boxy, three-cushion red couch. Its right armrest is separated, revealing yellow stuffing. The adjacent cushion sags like it was someone's favorite seat.

Nothing matches except the decade in which they were purchased. Broken cracker crumbs populate a gray recliner-chair with its back to the trespassers. Shaggy brown carpeting is browner in some spots than others. Cigarette tar darkens the low-hanging popcorn ceiling.

The living room opens into a kitchen, only interrupted by a gold band of stripping, marking the end of carpet and the beginning of peeling linoleum.

A smoke detector chirps.

CHAPTER 33

RELUCTANT TONGUES AND MUSCULAR DYSTROPHY

The sky falls west. Shadows grow. Sunlight twinkles through the dark side of evergreens. Photons are exhausted after traveling 150 million miles only to wink at a simple man. Black boots stop. Chins rotate around a hidden neck. Clumsy pigeon toes turn home.

CHAPTER 34

MOBILE FINGERS

From behind, she hears, "Tools and food." The group enters and spreads like a tactical team. Each footstep is greeted by the whine of an old man complaining about how bad everything has become. *Operation: illegal search and seizure.*

The shutting door catches the nose of its tiny brass latch. It clangs and chimes in its fisheye hook until it tires.

The kitchen doesn't echo. She pans the wooden cabinets. Flakes of white paint hang on longer than their warranty. Drawers dangle half-open, derailed and crooked. Remy swings cabinet doors open like a hurrying someone who doesn't know what she wants. One stubbornly slides open. It lost its track. Inside, she finds countless rubber bands of varying sizes and widths. She leans over. *It smells like kindergarten.* She grabs a handful and moves on.

CHAPTER 35

CONDIMENT ANALOGIES IN A WORLD OF PLAIN HAMBURGERS

Suds' mouth pops open like a cash register. Without manners, he reaches in and removes a wad of pink rubber bands, covered in tooth impressions, the size of a newborn's fist. He holds it up to his unlazy eye, shakes off some saliva, and returns it to his molars.

CHAPTER 36

THEIRS BECAME OURS

The kitchen sink is filled with pots, pans, a cookie sheet, and silverware. The drain is plugged or has been plugged. The top of the dishes that stick out of the water are dry and so is the food stuck to them. Beneath the waterline in stagnant dishwater, food bits loosely cling.

Something moving in the dishwater catches her attention. She looks but doesn't see. Leaning over the harvest-yellow countertop, she watches the skim on top. A clear tube-like worm, the length of her forearm, glides on the surface, twitching like a paramecium. Colliding into the sides, it redirects. *Segmented tapeworms?* She shudders.

The smoke detector chirps.

Two rooms branch off the living area, separated by a switch-back staircase. Steve opens the far door. He flicks the light switch out of habit. He is reminded that electricity has passed.

A single path carved from the door to the bed to the window is bordered by dirty, unfolded clothes. Steve shuffles his way down the strait.

Blinds hang crooked and split across the window. He parts them. The tall, red barn in back is still all closed up.

The smoke detector chirps, again.

A faux oak nightstand carries a visible layer of hazy dust. A cylinder aluminum cup sits nearest the bed along with a book lying face down. Steve flips it over. It doesn't have dust on it. Children's Illustrated Bible. He returns it upside-down and takes the cup.

He hears his name called from outside the room. *Sydney? Or is it Remy?* Presbycusis in a body-bag. He places the cup in his pack and pulls off the bedspread. Startled, clear silverfish freeze in panic like children who believe if they do not move, they won't be seen. He shakes out the bedspread and bundles it before exiting the room.

COLLECTING TIRES

Sydney makes his way to the back of the house. The bottom corner of a wood-chipped door drags along a well-worn arc in the carpet. He cautiously enters this northernmost room. Following his slow, short steps, Steve peers in. A sharp scent of brand-new basketballs widens his curiosity before his eyes adjust to the unlit room.

It chirps, again.

There is a window with drawn curtains opposite the doorway. The dark room contains no furniture. To his right, the closet door has been removed. Tires of various sizes and wears have been stacked into piles throughout the room.

Steve runs his finger along balding treads. He lifts one up. The one underneath has '*Uniroyal*' printed in white along its walls.

Setting it down, Steve moves to the next pile. His nose has adjusted, and he can no longer smell the rubber room.

'Bridgestone' embosses this one. Underneath, is another 'Bridgestone.'

And, again.

Sydney separates the curtains. Blue, rain-refracted light spills into the room. Two neatly stacked pillars of tires flank the window. He reaches for the top but can't touch. He looks back.

"Is he collecting these?"

Steve shakes his head with disbelief, not disagreement. He waves Sydney to leave the room.

POKER IS A SINNER'S GAME

Refrigerator lips smack when Remy opens its door. The hinge squeals like a whining child.

There is no rhythmic hum to the machine. Electricity left. A choking, claustrophobic belch waves across her face. It is strong enough to close her eyes. Aging plastic and spoiled milk host a fertile bacterial habitat. Things crawling on things in the dark. Evolution spared them sight and mirrors in favor of legs and asexual desires.

Remy pulls the top of her shirt up and breathes through the fabric like an apocalyptic Dracula. Plastic condiment bottles expand beyond their natural shape. Mayonnaise burped up its contents through a half-opened lid.

She pushes aside a bulging tin of baked beans with cellophane draped over the top. Seven boxes of film are stacked in the far back.

Chirp.

Beneath the white, caged shelves is a produce bin. She slides it out. Heavier than anticipated, Remy uses both hands. *Treasure.* Individually wrapped bags of beef jerky crown in a giant pile. Excitement mugs her vocal cords. The shirt drops to reveal happiness. She flips through the baggies in disbelief. Recently, good news seems to only land on leap revolutions.

Chirp.

GOD BLESSES THE MAGGOTS AND THE MILLIONAIRES

Each footstep comes with a creaking duet as Cub scales the hardwood stairs. The temperature gradually rises, and the air gets noticeably stuffier with every couple steps. They go up, stop at a landing, and then switchback.

There is only one upper room. Its low-hanging, slanted ceiling matches the tapered roof, split north to south. Cub would later describe the stuffy, thick air as 'evil,' but in the moment, it reminds him of a vegetarian's garbage can that should have been taken out before the flies showed up.

Each wall is flat, primer white. Black scuff marks and smears speckle the room as if moved furniture carelessly rubbed against the walls. A lone, four-squared window sits across from the stairwell. It doesn't look like it opens, except with a hammer. Below the window sits a large red dog dish surrounded by scattered brown gumballs. A stainless-steel water saucer with strands of fur clinging to the rim rests on the placemat nearby.

Cub finds it difficult to avoid the room's centerpieces: two long aluminum pig troughs lay in parallel. Floor scratches reveal the paths with which they were dragged. Each trough has been wound tightly with clear, freshness wrap. A narrow orange funnel has been poked in each of the plastics' far ends. After lightly kicking one of the troughs, the hum tells him it is about half-filled with fluid.

He stands over the kicked trough. Palms appreciate how tightly the wrap has been pulled. He can't see exactly what is inside but, through the beads of condensate, it looks like bread dough. He taps and the droplets release, clearing the view. He presses the object through its package. It isn't a bloated, arm-long piece of rising bread. It *is* a bloated arm.

His head cocks. He pokes the wrist through the clear plastic.

It doesn't seem real. It carries the pale color of a honeydew but fills with the pressure of a water balloon.

His face loses color. Gripping the railings, he leans over to where the head should be. Moisture obscures his view. He taps. The stalactite droplets fall back to their pool. White strands of thinning hair are suspended in the water like fly corpses in a spiderweb. *It is an old man.* One eye is open, the other is submerged. The tongue has swollen to prop his lips apart. Dark brown lesions spot his skull.

Cub wraps twice on the trough with a knuckle. The vibration echoes a low octave.

The other basin is similar. He peers in. This one is an old lady. She has a sundress with pale-orange pineapples splashed across a white background. The dress could compete in a wet T-shirt contest with tepees. She floats on her back. Her thin brown hair looks like it was pressed against her face when wet, but now curls upward upon drying. Her puffy face has the same swollen tongue. Eyes remain on, but pupils have rolled up to get a better view of her eyebrows.

Cub brings a palm to his chest as if presented a flag. He can't feel his heart beating. He closes his eyes to concentrate. *Strangely, still nothing.* He opens them.

Childish excitement builds in him. *This will gross-out Remy! I can't wait to show her!* His long, cold frown pivots to an open-mouthed grin in the company of nobody. Like a bathtub fart-bubble weaving its way to the almost-audible surface, so is his chuckle.

Unbending his posture, his back sorely wants to lean over. With a hand on each hip, he stretches backward. It hurts before it feels better.

His eyes square on the bright orange funnel at the foot of the lady's coffin. He walks to it. He wonders if it is tightly lodged and wonders about its purpose.

As his arm reaches out, his face passes through a spider's

home. Hands flail. His mouth was open. Cub's other hand paws most of the web from his head. He senses a fiber sticking to his cheek. He peels it away, holding it up to the window's light. The damaged webbing drifts upward as if thumbing through a current of air.

Relief comes.

His focus shifts to the window. White bird droppings smear diagonally, ending in a dry black clump. "Broken?" he asks the bloated bodies. The lower right corner of the window has pulled out of its frame. He wipes the web onto his pants. Crouching, he places a palm over the opening. *Cool air. It must be fresher than what I am breathing.*

Relief goes.

Eyes sharpen their corners. *Something moved.* A long shadow shares its feet with a large man. Starting up the driveway, he walks as slow as he thinks. Cub realizes his problem of feeling a racing heart has been solved.

TAMPERED EVIDENCE

His head hangs over his slumping shoulders. Each stride appears labored by mud. And then he stops. In the middle of the very long driveway, he stops. Light patterns of rain splatter the broken window.

Chins rise. Cub withdraws so his eyes barely peek over the sill. His brain pleads: *Please, don't see me.* Threats prioritize to manage stress. *Please, don't see me. Please, don't see me.*

The brim of the hat turns up. It looks back at that old upstairs farmhouse window. Telepathy exists in an under-understood way. Tension, static, and thoughts transmit at the speed of life and death and every beautiful thing in between.

Cub's eyes fear *his* eyes. He fixates on the bent bill. The dopey fisheyes. The feeling of food moving across his tongue in reverse.

Respiratory rate falls to zero. Cub realizes he is holding his breath. And then, the bill levels.

Resume respiratory rate. The hat rotates north. Satisfied, it slumps over to watch its owner's feet slowly shuffle up the rest of the driveway, toward home.

WITH THE SWIFTNESS OF DORMITORY ATHLETE'S FEET

No matter the depth of fear and regardless the pitch of screams, Cub's voice abandons him. A nightmare filmed in silence. If only legs could keep pace with his heart. One word manages to escape from the sympathetic gauntlet as he scrambles toward the top of the switchback stairwell.

Remy shovels another fistful of jerky into her pack. She raises the backpack by its arm straps to gauge the weight and consolidate. Baggies settle into nooks and corners. Her fortune packing is interrupted by a frightening warning, preceded by clomping footsteps.

"Fire!"

He reaches the bottom steps. He sees the screen door. *Clear.* Steve and Sydney stand in the doorway of the tire room. Upper extremities provoke Cub, "*What's the matter?*"

He fixes on the screen door while waving his arms like he's scaring pigeons.

CHAPTER 37

CHICKENS ROOST

Wet wind carries faint, dragging footsteps. Gravel slides under slow, rhythmic rubber. Grape-nuts grind under molar pressure.

CHAPTER 38

RED HANDS WITHOUT TOWELS

Remy, Sydney, and Steve follow Cub's stare.

There was no bolt of lightning—no thunderclap to add to the effect. This isn't a movie to focus on character development. Often the threat against one's own life, the glimpse of one's own rope's end, is enough. He wasn't there. Then, he was. A tall, dark stranger.

The tip of a shadow shuffles into view. Remy scrambles to shut the refrigerator. It catches her knee. She becomes frantic. She can't find the zipper-tassel on her pack.

Chirp.

Sydney looks up at Steve. The boy stands on a ledge of crying. His face looks like it's squeezing a lime without salt or tequila.

Steve pushes the boy back. Sydney smells tires. The shadow grows slumping shoulders.

She locates the zipper. Trembling hands snag the rail on blue fabric. The zipper goes crooked and stops. She squeals. She checks the entryway.

A large black silhouette peers in. His drinker's nose and

cap's bill smoosh against the mesh screen door. She can hear him smacking his gums. The rifle's barrel rests on his left shoulder.

Chirp.

Obstructing the front door, he looks left and right at the intruders. Steve steps forward. Cub doesn't stop him. Remy slowly stands as if in the audience of wildlife. She doesn't want to spook the deer or bear. She doesn't want to be the little blonde yarn-ball mountain lions chase. *No sudden movements.*

People say animals sense fear, but that's because they don't have a more accurate way to describe it. Predators watch fear rise in the air like slow moving rivers of smoke expelled from skin pores. It smells like satisfaction-prodromes.

Chirp.

INSTINCT SELDOM FIBS

The refrigerator door closes in a reverse kiss.

Suds responds. *They are not friends. They are not even pretending to be friends. They are stealing. They are naughty. They should be punished!*

HABITS OF CONTROL

Their world un-pauses.

He yanks the screen open. Steve steps in front of Sydney. Remy slings the pack over her shoulder and vaults her way through the living room, pursuing her brother... until she sees white. It sounds like a new rope's noose hanging in a stiff wind.

Suds has a fistful of dishwater blonde hair attached to a girl coiling in pain. He snaps his catch. Her face winces. Unharnessed agony disturbs the air like slowly tearing paper. She rolls to her side and breathes a lungful of spoiled-milk body odor. Suds winds his wrist, wrapping more hair behind his knuckles. She drops the duffle bag and reaches behind to alleviate the pull. Pain compliments the fear of being trapped. A mouse gets caught with guilt of hunger.

Fresh tears freely flow, encouraged by doom and being pinched for a crime. Martin Luther highlights number seven.

Cub weighs the loss of his sister against personal escape. Each option sits in a silver Roman saucer across from the balance—staring at one another. Waiting to flinch. It is close. At eye level, the meniscus always jiggles. The odds of escaping with his blood on the inside seems dismal. In precious heartbeats, eyes dart back and forth, comparing weights and odds. History attempts pattern recognition for future calculations. Abacus beads slide on vinyl wire. Deer go through similar calculations in front of high beams.

The sound is turned way down. Remy clutches at imprisoning hands. She winces. She looks at the backs of her eyelids and pictures air spiraling into her deep lungs. She clicks the heels of her un-red boots together. Nothing happens.

Like waiting at a green light for pedestrian toes to reach the curb, Cub seizes the opportunity to avoid sisterly guilt. Eyes closed, greener light. He breaks for the tire room. Avoiding Steve, Cub runs into a silently whimpering Sydney. The boy's knees are bent inward.

"Come on, bud."

Cub separates the curtains. The eastern window splashes fading light, fractured by cloud cover. Double pane windows were installed by the builder. More paint flicks off when Cub frantically pops the latches. They don't. *Circular sliding locks?* He turns the knob and tries lifting the heavy window. *Must be the other way.*

Chirp.

Screams from the living room jump on nerves in Cub's hands, but he doesn't flinch. He rotates the latch the opposite way. The window doesn't move.

Steve says something in a firm voice that sounds underwater. Followed closely, there is a stomp. *Maybe it was right before.* Sydney whines and sniffs up snot streams.

Chirp.

"Let's try it again, the other way," Cub mutters to himself. He slides the latch back. "I'm going to push as hard as I can..." Wedging the heel of his palm under the middle, horizontal check rail, he does. He can feel his face getting hot. Pressure in his head builds. He realizes he is holding his breath.

It gives. Then catches. Sydney pushes up on the lower sill. Tears take a backseat to focus. Together, they slide up the heavy pane. Cub punches out the screen behind it.

"You first."

Sydney is you. Cub is second.

IN LIFE'S STORY, EVERYONE IMAGINES THEMSELVES AS THE PROTAGONIST

Steve briefly looks over his shoulder to witness a man prove he is still a boy. Awareness heightens. Pupils dilate. Emotion hatches from stoic eggs.

"Why are you taking ma, ma, my food?" Suds reaches over the girl toward her partially opened pack. He tugs her hair like a horse collar. Howling, she slides from a crouch onto her butt.

To see a girl cry feels like injustice, but to hear the notes of a girl cry spills out a man's heart juice.

Chirp.

Steve kicks the outstretched arm before it grasps the jerky bag's handles. Suds must have forgotten his surroundings to tunnel vision. His balance slips. Her follicles tighten. Some roots give up like tornado-ed timbers. She inhales more spoiled milk.

Is it right for him to be taking away her bag? Is it fair he has to fight to keep his own food? Is it fair he has to defend his own property? Is a battle pitting four against one fair? Is it okay for a grown man to aggressively attack a fragile young woman?

Steve would never answer 'yes' to any of them. Often in learning, the easiest to remember is the first and last—so he pursues. He imagines his ancestors would approve.

Giant hands open toward Steve as if pleading for mercy. *What man with a fistful of woman's locks deserves mercy? Perhaps one with cake and a mouthful of it...*

Steve's teeth clench when he lunges for the man's face. His legs bump into the crouching girl. She whines. Fingers become claws. Faces become scratching posts. Suds loses his cap when arching his back to elude the Indian. Shoulder blades scrape the wall beside the front door.

Remy takes a deep breath of spoiled milk with a dash of ground cumin. She tries to ignore pain. She tries to flip her caring-switch off and pull loose of his grip. Her body unnaturally writhes. Fingers stretch for invisible ladder rungs until she wails out in neuropathic pain.

Chirp.

Steve's fingers find eye sockets. He presses and is surprised how easily they depress. Two knuckles deep. Eyeballs slide medially. Steve's fingertips curl around the backside.

Suds' face howls like a dying buffalo. Steve realizes this man fights more like a referee than a wrestler.

ICE SCREAM SCOOPS

Why are they attacking me? They are bad people. They break into my home. They steal my food. They want to hurt me. Bad. They are not my friends.

Chirp.

Steve grips the face like a bowling ball and pulls it toward his knee for contact: orbital, mandible, and nostril.

The world flashes white with each impact like pictures without smiles or cheese. The world comes back just to flicker black, maroon, and then white again. A warm trickle touches his top lip. In between flashes, he licks the salty, metallic fluid. He tries to shield the facial blows only to find his own arms crashing against his own shattering face.

A DEMONIC PACT WRITTEN WITH INVISIBLE INK

Losing count after eight strikes, the moment gets away from him. Steve senses the beast's muscles loosening. First, the knees buckle, then the back collapses.

Steve releases the sockets to brace himself as he rides the slumping mammal to the ground. Suspender clasps come undone. The rifle falls from grip and leans sideways against the door's frame. His right hand rises to cradle a throbbing face. Long gold hairs woven in finger creases are no longer attached to their head. Steve realizes the girl got free.

Chirp.

JACK OF ALL TRADES AND MASTER OF NUMB

The sides of her mouth ache from the stretches of wailing. The perimeter of her vision blurs with un-spilt tears. Remy hoists the bag over her shoulder. The front door is obstructed by man-meat. She staggers to the tire room, guided through wet windshields and new hope.

Pulses of orange light dance in the bedroom. Her brother waves ignited curtains on the end of a stick through the window.

"Hey!" The stick stops. The flames continue to lick precious oxygen. Black smoke emits a sharp odor that reminds Remy of poison. "I'm coming out!"

Cub aims the lit curtain at the base of a tire stack.

"Hurry!"

She throws the jerky bag out the window. Sydney steps forward to pull it out of the way.

Fumes choke. One leg out, then the other.

Cub returns to his fuse.

"Don't do that! Steve is still in there!"

Cub ignores his annoying sister. The tires aren't catching. The curtains turn ashy.

Remy steps in-between the house and Cub to push him away. He easily bats her down. She finds herself aggressively spun to the surrounding stones.

He coaxes the tires with the torch. She springs up. Grabbing the window screen, she blocks Cub out like a phalanx. Sydney takes a step away, hiding his hands behind his back and turning toward the red barn.

I WROTE THIS WITH EVERY INTENTION OF FAILURE

Between chews, Suds breathes heavy. His black-and-red-checkered flannel pulls up, exposing his bowling ball abdomen with its hairy belly button. *It looks like it has black eyelashes.*

Steve's expression hides answers to simple questions. *This is only a violent man in size, not intent.* When the world unravels, nobody stays to balance justice's seesaw.

A respectful smile creases Steve's cheek. *It's amazing this man has survived so long.* Steve admires the man's ingenuity in isolation. *Then again, the man may not understand the gravity of his situation.*

Chirp.

Suds' smooth, chubby cheeks shine as he mouths air the way fish do out of water. Steve wishes to be clean-shaven, too. Long, thin Indian facial fur was never an image he pursued. Luckily, mirrors no longer look his direction.

Shallow crescentic pools well in Suds' lids. The look in his lookers is serene. Strange how some mammals do not understand how eyes work, but they do understand their vulnerability—poorly hidden boiler rooms of emotions.

Steve apologetically pats the side of Suds' pot belly and begins to get back to his feet. "Old men dream of young knees."

Chirp.

He swings his leg off the heaving belly like a horse dismount. In the absence of sound, a quick flash disappears below him. *Pressure.* Fat fingers wrap tightly near Steve's inner thigh. Hearts keep beating. Something smells of melting plastic. Something feels foreign, like when a nurse pushes in a plunger and softly suggests, "There you go. It's almost done."

The fat fist twists. Red fibers separate against their will in a harmony of agony like a thick, bloody steak. The fat man bites his lower lip. Steve can't move his leg anymore and he rethinks about the word: *survivor.*

Chirp.

Warm spoons effortlessly move through cold ice cream. Steve's limb is on strike. Urgency burns in the Indian's panic as he stares into his assailant.

Steve's large calloused hands pry at the single fat one. Using his functional knee, he pins Suds' other arm from helping. One at a time, dirty fingers uncurl from the hilt.

Suds is scared. He should have been scared sunrises ago when the world turned off. He should have been scared when his dog didn't return, but he is slow.

From the size and triple rivet, Steve recognizes the bloody, wooden handle as a carving knife. The blade resists its exit like a bee's stinger. Twin barbs serrate Steve's meat in both directions.

Suds crab-walks away on elbows, fixating on his work. The man looks like a boy, guilty and unblinking.

Steve's teeth clench so tightly they threaten to loosen from their gummy roots. Whining alleviates a bit of the horror in removing a foreign body from a non-foreign one. Pain feels like helplessness in the shape of a broken violin.

Chirp.

The final third exits most easily through his new gash. Breath exhales relief. The knife's tip is bent at a right angle. Nestled snug in the angle's pocket is a small white lump Steve assumes to be leg bone.

He cocks the knife and flings it into the kitchen. Various-sized droplets of red blood cells tattoo wide arcs on the beige cabinets. The largest globs streak downward before coagulating.

Dark red blood pulses in gurgles from Steve's thigh. He pinches the edges. Rolling onto his back, he lifts the dying limb above his chest. *It may as well be lumber.* Blood thickens like Valentine's paint.

Audible air passes through coarse nose hairs. He focuses on breathing the way he used to holding in vomit after a night of imbibing. The throbbing heartbeat in his wound slows. His thumbs whiten from pressing the makeshift tourniquet.

Taken from the moment, Steve remembers the first time he timidly boarded a school bus.

I looked back and forth between my new shoes and Mom's face. She flicked her wrists and flapped her hands with encouragement. "It's okay, Stevie."

When she said my name, it sounded like the most beautiful harp. I'd have traded my new school shoes for the comfort of her arms.

I wanted to be Mom's brave little soldier. I remember the strong, black diesel fumes. The side railing was built for big kids and I was small. My bright, white toe touched the first step. The bus driver-lady's patience thinned watching my hesitation. She reminded me of a performer trapped between genders and singing dated music—too much blue eyeshadow.

In kid-fear, I turned to leave. She pulled a lever. The door shut. Between two, tall, narrow, scratched windowpanes, Mom's mouth blew kisses and she waved, "goodbye."

A clear, plastic cup crosses his field of vision and disturbs his daydream. Perspiration beads line the outside, above the water's fill-line. Big, fat hands make an offer.

"Drink. It helpth."

ALL-NATURAL SYNTHETICS

"You don't get it, Rem! You just don't!" Cub is now yelling. "This is not some fantasy world where everybody gets along and helps each other out!" Spittle ejects when he pronounces the "f." Continuing his tirade, "Times changed! *People* changed!" His arms violently swing like politicians emphasizing their one redeeming quality in a shell game of bad ones. "Those that didn't change aren't *here* anymore!"

Remy crumbles in quiet sadness. Sydney pretends to ignore the charged exchange. Cub feels remorse but holds back from consolation. He wants her to change. He *needs* her to change. He needs a stronger companion—a stronger soldier in a world of stacked chips.

"It's... we have to be greedy. Because there's not much left." He can hear his voice echo off the outbuilding and the emptiness. *Maybe my tone was too strong. Maybe my honesty was too much. Tomorrow will be thirsty for apologies.*

Cub rips down the other curtain. A couple lighter-flicks and polyester blends roar to life. Leaning through the window sill, he tucks the unburnt curtain and its Siamese flame into the tire stack. The first tire smooths and coughs out wisps of black smoke. He repositions the mounting flame until its heat becomes unbearable. The tire catches.

Searing white flickers dash up the tire column and skyward out the window. Yellows and oranges epileptically lash at oxygen the way frog tongues hunt flies. It sounds like crackles of sizzling bacon. The room quickly fills with black powder clouds. Soot crowds out clean air.

"Let's go," Cub says.

"I'm not leaving—"

"I said, time to go!" Cub interrupts while grabbing her arm in a way that leaves marks.

"I'm not leaving him!" she screams in an octave that would

straighten curved spines.

"Now!" He commands, dragging her away from the wilting window. In a much more controlled tone, he gestures, "Come on, Sydney."

The boy follows but finds it hard not to watch the flames devour the farmhouse.

THE LITTLE WHITE FARMHOUSE BECAME A GRILL COOKING TENNIS SHOES

Black smoke claws its way through the half-open bedroom door and spills across the living room ceiling. A drafting heat follows.

Each breath feels tainted in talc. Incinerated rubber coats Steve's tongue. Coughing fails to alleviate. He swishes and spits a mouthful of water. This doesn't help.

In a quick glance, Suds is breathing through the neck-hole fabric of his shirt like a bank bandit. Coughing fits interrupt his beautiful view of destruction.

Paparazzi camera-flashes strobe the bedroom. A heat wave nudges the door open further.

Steve spins to a crawl, dragging his dying limb toward the door. Exhaustion welcomes beads of brow sweat as he clutches the handle. Among the new popping and crackling, Steve can hear Suds moving behind him. *Would he drag me back into this coughing coffin? Will he refuse to go single file during this fire non-drill?*

The screen door effortlessly opens, splashing cool, refreshing air across his face. Upper body tugs lower body. He sympathizes with the snail. Freedom feels close and almost too easy as he rests on the wet doorstep.

Passing black strands obscure his vision, but he makes out Suds' shadow adjusting its cap. The simple man pulls the neck of his shirt over his nose and slowly walks up the stairs. The screen door slams shut.

CRYING INTO ONE'S OWN FLAG

The sky softens blue while its sun hides behind fluffy, pregnant clouds as if its face is full of acne. Rain pauses, leaving the crushed gravel driveway wet and darkened.

Steve's jeans carry an entry slit soaked in port wine stains. Shifting to his back, he elevates the dying leg above his heart. Adrenaline stitches tight vessels.

The tiny, white two-story farmhouse belches a steady black stream out its eastern flank like a lidded charcoal grill. Splatters of powdered soot cake the rotted siding. Steve watches a white flame whip the deepening skyline. With a lash, the ground brightens in living shadows before fading.

Where did the kids go? Perhaps this is the easiest way to part with them. Honorable discharge of child custody. Guilt and responsibility blanche.

Even more odd, why didn't Suds flee? He showed no fear or urgency. Could he really be that... simple? Steve listens to no coughing, no gasping, and no screaming. Even those who believe they desire a side of pain with their death plate, inevitably change their tune before bussing their dishes. Searing flesh dots Steve's vision like sun spots.

"Steve!" *It's Remy.* "This isn't safe. We have to leave!" Fingers wedge under his armpits. Safety ran away with Dr. Alzheimer.

She doesn't know I'm hurt. She doesn't know I'm a liability. She doesn't know I've become dead weight. She doesn't know I'm going home.

EVERYONE WISHES THEIR HOURGLASS DREW FROM THE DESERT

Steve's red scalp shines underneath thinly watered gray hairs. His body slumps. Heaving strains.

Cub takes the other side. The old man reminds Remy of a scarecrow. With an arm over their shoulder, they drag him down the long driveway like an injured athlete. The scarecrow clutches his expanding red stains.

Short shuffling steps work best for moving dead bodies and furniture. She listens to his abbreviated breaths passing through long, clenching teeth. She wishes she could bear part of his suffering.

IRON SHARPENS IRONY

The weight of his paralyzed limb gives him the notion that it is no longer his. The sharp, shocking nerve pain remembers his responsibility. Steve watches the world move away. It's as if he is perched on the tail of a boat and watching the shoreline vanish. He presses on the cut with kissing thumbs. *Good pain. Relieving pain.* It's bloody but has stopped bleeding. Pressing on the sides, the wound gapes open like a mouth with nothing to say.

"Enough." His voice sounds like gravel.

"We aren't leaving you here," she says.

"That's enough, Remy."

"She said, 'We are not leaving you here,'" Cub reiterates.

Sibling camaraderie. Steve can't remember these two agreeing on much since things began to end.

FROM GREAT DISTANCE, WE HOLD

This must be the last moments a shot fawn remembers. His butt numbs. Fingertips fall asleep on tingling pillows. *May it be as easy to give in to death as it is to give in to sleep.* Consciousness disengages.

Acute pain evolves into chronic pain.

Sydney wraps his hand around Steve's swollen, bloody pointer finger. "It's going to be okay, Indian Steve," he says with a forced smile.

Steve winces. He appreciates the boy's attempt—warm, honest parenting emulation. *It is easy to believe God lives closer to young people. Less self-editing. Less ego. Less fear of being wrong. Why would God want to live with an old soul that's been hand-dipped in black sin?*

Driveway smudges to grass under Steve and he stops them. He collapses at the base of Alphabet Hill. Steve clenches his fist to encourage blood flow. Sydney lets go.

"We'll come back for you in the morning. Food. Water and stuff," Cub says.

Steve nods.

Remy blows a kiss. "Goodnight, Steve."

"Goodnight, Indian Steve."

Footsteps leave him alone. Peace serenades in scents of burning wood.

PREVENTIVE DETENTION

Sydney squeezes Remy's hand and looks back. With each growing-boy step, Steve's figure gets smaller and meeker. *I didn't want to say 'goodbye.'* The old man slumps over his own belly like a jumbo shrimp. *Maybe he will pet the dog.*

A FIELD TRIP WITH ALBERT HOFMANN

Teeth chatter out of sync with his shivering body. He's not kidding himself. *It is coming. It took plenty long, but now, it is coming.* He has been sitting in Death's waiting room pretending to read magazines while younger, healthier people got their names called. The seats are uncomfortable. The thermostat is set too high. Two boys, probably brothers, hide from each other behind the bathroom door while their mother ignores them. It's okay. No one uses bathrooms here.

When he thinks about it, he can feel his heart race—a sprint toward the finish line. He wishes his tongue was wetter. He wishes he was cooler until he is, then he wishes the opposite. *If only this place had an Arabian lamp.*

Something about death alleviates guilt and responsibility. It feels like the last shift of a career. The final hour of realization sets in: *this place no longer welcomes me.*

Except for him, the lobby has emptied. The small knob on a thin, hollow door opens. A professionally dressed woman in brilliant white looks down at her clipboard and calls his name, punctuated by a question. He places the children's magazine back in the rack with all the other torn periodicals.

Excitement, anticipation, and fear all hold hands and chant: *This is supposed to happen! It is a routine. Every relative I've ever known passed through this same... process.*

Attempting to pull himself from the lucid place, Steve reclines against Alphabet Hill's base and plants a palm in each eye socket.

A light rain on broad, thirsty leaves sounds like midnight static. With open palms, Steve rubs his eyes. Stretching them wide, blackness slowly fades into washed-out color. Veiny silhouettes blot in beat with his heart. Steve sees visual pulses. Dim to clear. Rinse and repetition. Flip to side B. Thinking about his heart rate only quickens the pace.

Inevitability snatches him back.

The hallway to his pearly elevator smells like a freshly opened bag of black licorice. His pineal gland splinters, leaking fluid like a loose faucet.

The lady in brilliant white points to a door on the left at the end of the narrow hallway. His shoulders almost touch the walls on either side. The dull, bronze doorknob turns.

"Death will be with you shortly," she says without speaking.

Steve hops onto the exam table. Thin sheets of spooled, dull-white paper crinkle beneath him. Despite his height, his feet still helplessly dangle above the short-trimmed maroon carpet.

Steve unsuccessfully blinks away a fallen raindrop. Bubble-making solution wraps a tourniquet around his retina. Ribbons of blues and yellows, like oil-slicked lakes, provide a filter between reality and perception.

Dying with unforgiven sins leaves souls with an eternity of cold feet. He folds his fingers and prays to Our Father. After saying the memorized words, he feels unchanged.

As if awoken from a daydream, Steve frantically pats his chest and pants-pocket. He feels a lump in his back left. The large, tan cigar found water in patches and one side broke, revealing brown tobacco flakes. A thin collar of white paper reading, "Covered Wagon," decorates its throat, just off-center, like an adolescent's necktie.

With coaxing, the tip lights. Thick, white smoke clouds the glowing-embered edges. One puff provides anxiolysis. When he was a boy, Steve remembers his teacher proclaiming, "Each cigarette smoked takes six moments off your life!" *I'd gladly welcome six less moments of this.*

He balances the cigar on a small, neighboring stone—business end up. It falls. He props it up. It falls, again. He frustratingly stuffs it into the crook of his grin while fingering his wound.

Blood crusts. *It looks bad, but the bleeding stopped. Perhaps this was a false alarm. Why waste these grains of sand?* He suddenly feels better. Tapping ashes from a glowing tip, everything seems to be... okay. Folding fingers behind his head, Steve lays back and relinquishes.

BEAUTIFUL LITTLE LINES WITHOUT PARENTS

A narrow-boned finger taps his shoulder. Dim eyes open to a dimmer view. He whirls around. No one is behind him. He whirls back. No one is in front. Orange, balletic pulses cross the road, pulling back before reaching his retina like an angry, chained pet. Smoke fills black lungs. Brilliant brimstone flourishes.

We are God's slowly burning masterpiece.

Steve's visual field is poisoned by dark patches. Blind spots grew where they don't belong—blind spots and their babies.

He props up on uneven legs. Darkness closes toward the middle of his sight. His first steps up the hill wobble his head. Lips match his humor: dry and cracked.

He drops to a knee. Vision returns after a couple hard blinks. Baby blind spots still stipple his eyesight.

Maybe a different moment will be kinder.

He can't remember being so weak. In his youth, he could bear down and overcome seemingly impossible physical limitations. He stands, again. Visual edges close black. Gritting his teeth, he marches—until he doesn't. An observer would say his legs collapsed like an abandoned marionette. Limbs don't always bend correctly while their master is away.

It is dark. He looks up and it is she. Her body is surrounded in a soft white shell of glowing numbers endlessly flickering from 1 to 0 and back again in unpredictable patterns.

She shouldn't be here. She shouldn't be doing this. She owes nothing.

Rain gently falls.

Remy holds his ankles. Steve feels like a folded beach chair that couldn't outrun Pamplonian cattle. She washes his feet with her hair.

"No," he moans with a thick tongue. He attempts to shake her off. Only one leg responds.

"Be still. I want to do this, for tomorrow may not let me."

At first, it feels like a paintbrush. After careful thought, it feels more like threads of seaweed flossing their abstract way. Mucus settles on his voice box. It coats as he swallows, making it feel like his hoarse voice may temporarily produce mouth sounds.

He shivers in uncontrolled turbulence. Flattening his back on nature's floor—knees bent and feet flat, his head throbs. It spins as if trapped inside a clothing dryer. The planet rotates and for once, it doesn't feel normal. Closed eyes refuse to ease his sickness.

Blonde hair flosses his toes. Rain petals dot his face—cooling and evaporating. His forehead smolders as does the brain it shelters. He imagines monthly calendars tearing from page to page with increasing speed. "Time ticks swiftest with the finish line in focus," Steve mutters.

WRINGING THE RAG

"Did your mother ever tell Cubbie how he got that scar on his cheek? The *real* reason?"

She hadn't. Remy listens until his voice trails.

Heroism only appears when it's needed. In between mopping swaths, the clouds lift. Fog clears, if only for a moment of heroism. Deep effort provides a burst of coherence.

"They got what they wanted!" Steve exclaims.

The words startle Remy. She whips her greasy bangs over her head to ask, "Huh?"

His mouth hangs open like an anvil has been tied to the lower lip. His blinks don't even reach the lower lid to moisten his glaucoma-clouded eyeballs. He responds as one does with broken ears.

"What, Steve? Who?" she asks, grabbing an aging knee in each palm and shaking it like a vending machine that owes her snacks. She watches pain ripple from his wound to his face. Invisible fishhook fingers seem to invade his mouth corners from behind, stretching it wide open.

With one hand, he clutches his leg above the darkened gash. In panic, she releases, watching her martyr fade. His final transmission isn't audible. Clouds set. Fog rolls into his periphery. Using an outstretched, quivering finger, he draws a triangle in the air while mouthing the shape's Greek letter.

WITH DEATH COMES THE LOSS OF INFORMATION

Looking around the sterile exam room, he realizes he's alone. He scrunches and stretches his dangling, naked toes. He senses the coda's wiggle. *This is the time to reflect on the good things—to remember the highlights.*

Reaching in, he remembers his wife, but no video comes to mind. Thirty revolutions of laughing and loving, but all he remembers are sun-faded photographs sitting in frames at the old, lonely home.

And then, the jingle of a mattress commercial intrudes. *Why is this the time for a trapped song? He tightly locks his eyelids. Focus. Please, God.* An epileptic flash of her image. Hope. Then, back to: *The low, low prices of bedding.*

"No. I beg. It's all I have left," Steve moans in mumbles of marbled sleep.

"Rest with the best as we best the rest..."

Two hollow knocks before the knob turns. Wicks glow and fade. Dense chalkboard-black soot sweeps around the door, rapidly consuming the exam room. Steve battles to think of his beloved's smile. He digs for the happiness. Flickers of her like cheap lighters in a wind-tunnel spot his memory. Despite tightly sealed eyelids, in the lower right field, he watches an expanding white pinpoint of light, like moonlight rippling off a black ocean. He resists but feels like a horse drawn carriage. Someone calls his name with the voice of a harp. The smell of freshly opened black licorice intensifies. Hallucinogenic optic filters bleach reality. He hears his mom softly whisper. He feels her breath fogging his ear. "We sure had fun, didn't we, Stevie?"

WET HANDS GUARANTEE RESTLESS SLEEP

"Where do you think *you're* going?" A firm grip stops Sydney from leaving. His arm aches.

"Following Remy. She is seeing—"

"No, you are not," Cub interrupts.

"But, I want to—"

"You don't know what you want," he interrupts, again. Sydney's arm hurts more. "Come sit next to me, bud."

Hesitantly, he sits next to Cub. Circulation returns to his upper extremity. He can feel wetness penetrate his pants. "It's wet and I'm starting to hate rainy rotations."

"Don't ever plan on getting clean." Breathing fills the silence. The blazing house is unavoidable. Lapping flames, like forest minstrels, draw the eye in a panorama of darkness. Insects commune around outdoor lighting. Icarus and the moth have more in common. The sun would fill with bug ashes had they the strength to fly that high.

Smoke comforts. The stuff in that home was somebody else's in a world without possessions. A hand claps Sydney's shoulder. Cub is still staring at the farmhouse fire.

"Syd. You started off this whole thing as a little boy. But now, you are a little man."

Bashfully, the boy looks down and shuffles his boots. He swallows before clearing his throat. "Can I have a musta?" His little voice trails.

"Hmm?" Cub breaks from the fire.

"Can I have a musta?" Confidence cowers near the end of his question.

"What are you saying?"

"Can. I. Have. A. *Mustache?*"

It has been a while since Cub's last genuine smile, but it happens tonight. "Why would you want a mustache?"

"Because, I'm a *man* now."

Cub scrambles Sydney's greasy hair before playfully pushing his neck downward. The little man grins between red cheeks. "We'll see about getting you that mustache."

They both return to watching the flames... until he passes out... and Cub stands.

LATE NIGHT AFTER THE FIRE

Evil is new shoes that haven't yet been broken in.

She eases down next to Sydney so as not to coax him awake. She should be asleep, but she's not. Every time she tightens her eyes, footage of the house replays in all their vibrant colors. A flip book of scenarios re-imagined into the worst of fates, post-traumatically living out their future in her present.

She needs the sleep. She knows better. Each snapping branch transforms into a predator. Shadows take shape as revenge. Howls articulate as her hero's death rattle.

Why do terrible things happen to the kindest of hearts? Perhaps because theirs are the plumpest, juiciest, heaviest of fruits which prefer hanging low.

She squeezes Sydney beside her. A little juice runs down her cheek. *Thankfully, the rotation exhausted him, so his sweet brain can unpack and organize the events that make life less bleak.*

Remy closes her eyes and fights the nasty images. She fights the pulled hair. She pushes aside the puncture wound. She blows away the waving heat of processed lumber.

She pictures a page. A blank page. As if scribing with a disembodied hand, she crafts a Santa's list, of sorts, with India ink in beautiful calligraphy.

CHAPTER 39

PRESIDENTIAL ACCEPTANCE

Clomping footsteps startle his solid ivory palace. *They've come for me. Did the alarms go off?* Footsteps grow deeper volume. *Did they slip by my security?* Reaching for his First Lady, he knocks over his stiff, elephant-tusk-white cowboy hat. *She's gone. She must have been in on it, too. I should have suspected it! I deserve this.*

"Grandpa?"

Relief rushes in. He spins a dial to turn his heart rate down. It beeps at him. His neck cranes to see his grandson standing in the bedroom doorway.

"Yes?" He sits up in bed. Covers slip to his waist. A stuffed animal dangles from the small boy's hand.

"Grandpa, can I sleep with you and Grandma?"

He hears his First Lady flick the bathroom lights. As she crosses the sprawling bedroom, she pats her grandson's head and smiles through drowsiness.

"Come here, young man." The boy approaches on his side of the bed. "Tell Grandpa what's wrong."

He scrunches his little fists under his chin and says, "I miss my toys and my friends. I want things to go back to the way they used to be."

"We still have this big house," his wife crows as she slides into bed on the other side.

He can see her response doesn't satisfy his grandson. "Oh, I want it to go back to normal, too, but this was... unavoidable."

"Grandpa, what does that mean?"

"Well, it means that *we* did this... so *you* could have a brighter future. You understand?"

The boy shrugs.

"You will someday. Now go back in your room and get some rest."

"I can't."

"You can't? Why not?"

"Because I'm scared of monsters and they are in there."

He thinks for a moment, then asks his grandson, "Are you afraid of me?"

CHAPTER 40

ANTS

Morning comes. Sydney does push-ups—eleven good ones and three that are more of a hip-swivel.

A tiny shoulder tap awakens Cub long after the sun has yawned. "C'mere. I wanna show you somethin'." Sydney curls a beckoning finger.

Smoke took shelter in his clothing, making sleep all the more inviting. Grumbling, Cub's head separates from the pillow. *It was a late night... a very late night.* Remy is buried in covers. He kicks off the blankets and, rubbing the insensitive Sandman's dust from his eye-corners, follows Sydney to the edge of their hilltop.

The little hand points toward the old farmhouse's remains, scorched and collapsed. Two nearby trees caught fire, but the elements preserved the rest.

"See?"

Cub doesn't.

"Over *there*!"

Cub follows the little man's finger and squints. He sees. Chewing, Suds casually walks out of the old, red barn toward the wreck-age, disappearing from voyeurs' sight. *He's alive. He's rebuilding.*

"Ants."

Sydney's brow frowns with misunderstanding.

Cub loses interest in his own metaphor. "Never mind."

Back and forth and back, Suds hauls armfuls. From this perspective, he emotionlessly rebuilds his life.

"I wonder if he lost his cap," Sydney says.

Earth quakes, this time, a big one.

LIFE ISN'T THE SAME WITHOUT WAITING TO HEAR HIS SILENT RESPONSE

Thready clouds cross pale blue sky above a head that sits in a perch of his own palms.

Cub gathers his belongings and picks through his elder's gear. They won't be able to carry it all unless they grow more sore backs. At least food will disappear more slowly, in a glass half-un-empty way.

Pinned between a pair of sleeping-blankets, he notices some-thing resembling smashed eggshells. He fits the fragments together. *Broken plastic eyes? That was what I stepped on—Syd's favorite teddy bear.*

Cub rubs his chin with thought. In doing so, skin stains scream for attention. Browning red splatters dot his arms. He notices the evidence of dismantled training wheels. Cheeks blush. Cub frantically rubs his hands on his pants until friction warms them. Upon inspection, he spots a smooth lump of tissue, resem-bling chicken fat, clinging to the back of his hand. He flicks it. Dried rusty bits crack and scale like old fence paint, but much of the color remains—*tomorrow's problems.*

Standing with his back to Cub, Sydney watches Suds rebuild. Cub reels, throwing guilt and plush evidence in the opposite direction. Sydney doesn't seem to notice. *Men don't need toys or broken hearts.*

HEALING NEEDED

"You didn't come back until I fell asleep. What were you doing with Indian Steve, Remy?" Sydney asks.

"Saying, 'Goodbye.'"

"Oh," he pauses. "Can I say, 'Goodbye,' too?"

She nestles a finger under his chin and lifts it up. "You can *always* say, 'Goodbye.'"

"You can?"

"Sure. It's just that sometimes, that person will only be able to *feel* it, and not *hear* it."

"Did Indian Steve feel it or hear it?"

"Both."

Sydney swallows. "Is he gone?"

"He's going. Now let's help pack up."

ONE LESS

This and that were largely done. Seams on every bag begging for mercy, there was still too much. It's been a while since they ran into a good problem.

Leaning back on their heels, the quartet (minus one) slinks down Alphabet Hill for the last time. Cub leads. Sydney follows Remy.

They can always come back for the rest of *his* stuff or the stuff on top. Part of Cub feels like he is giving the unbrought to a thankless charity.

Timelines only move in one direction. Left homes, left relationships, and left jobs never feel right, and when they do, they shouldn't. Time forgets promises-to-visit by filling the space with newer, pettier excuses. A shoe left in the garage over winter seldom fits the same in spring.

"Cub, are you bleeding? You have a whole bunch of new—"

Pretending to ignore the boy's question, Cub drowns Sydney's voice out with a quick change of subject, "We'll keep the river and road in view. Sound okay?"

Remy and Sydney nod to the back of Cub's head.

Unkept grass grows long. It sounds like cheerleading pom-poms against denim. The song that doesn't end plays circles in Cub's head as he dreams of warm lasagna without onions.

MORE POETIC NONSENSE

Remy hikes her plump backpack higher on the shoulders.

You. You were supposed to help me. You. You were supposed to make my life easier—my job easier. You lied. You broke your promise, technology.

Technology's nose grew when it promised to free up lives. Technology severs human contact. Instead, it distracts from connections we do have, with those we do not—distracting livers from living. Friendly socialites twist into cave dwelling hermits huddling alone around glowing screens. Fast hands turn gears that drag slower ones. It tricks us into believing that time is not painfully slow. "June rushes through summer," Mom said. It doesn't. June stops to watch stems stretch toward the sun in photosynthetic brilliance. June breathes warm pollen-filled air above bronze fields, instead of trapping it in still life with broken keys and promises of experiencing them later across a glowing monitor at 60 hertz.

Nature is an unloved mother. It didn't used to be that way. Her hands wither and grow nodules in delicate joints while sons and daughters tap keys covered in unalphabetized letters. If Mother Nature claimed a name, it may as well be June.

Ironically or not, the joke is not on June. She moves slow but is still fertile. Children don't often inherit their parent's best traits and timeless-ness is one of them. She will live when offspring will not. Parents shouldn't have to witness their children's demise, but this won't be her first time.

It should not surprise anyone to find she'll have a new litter. One that starts with respect and ends the same as all the rest. A new litter born with congenital defects—perfect little imperfections.

SISYPHUS TIRES

Heat boils away the river's demons. Remy takes the opportunity to splash water on her hair and face. Oils cling to fingers.

"Drink until you pee clear." Sydney and Remy salute. Cub only hears their voices in whispers amongst each other. A tier system has formed, and he sits on top—alone.

Would they ever abandon me? Do they disapprove of my past actions? Do they think I am better than them? They versus me. They wouldn't survive. Leaders never intend themselves to be evil. History begs to differ.

They don't like me. They don't respect me. They should respect me. They will choose they over me when given an ultimatum. Drops coalesce on the tips of Remy's hair before falling. Two bent eyebrows overhang Cub's scowl.

"Taste okay?" he asks.

"Mmhmm," they respond through closed mouths.

"Good." He tips the canteen back, gulping warm water, looking slyly at them while doing so. After topping off the fluid, he spins the lid back on. "Good."

WE, THE WATERMILFOIL

Stiff clothes don't grip skin well. Mud paints in shades of age. With how quickly humanity unraveled, Remy wonders if the pain continues. *It must. We should consider ourselves lucky to escape greed's first attack only to be painted in age.*

With the rain came a coolness in the wind's kisses. Fall threatens to turn into its drunken uncle.

"Remember bean hot-dish?" she asks her brother. He does.

Its smell preceded its warmth. He used to close his eyes, crane his neck over the pan, and inhale the vapors. Some droplets would be confident enough to condense under his chin. Mom, with her mitted hands, would push him aside. He'd giggle. They'd giggle. He playfully fought to keep his nose over the dish until Mom swatted him with a kitchen rag.

Remy's arms would hang over the back of her chair watching the action. She laughed until Mom told her, "Remington, sit down in your chair the *right* way and don't encourage your brother." This would give Cub the opportunity for one more good sniff.

"Of course I remember bean hot-dish." Cub recognizes an olive branch.

REMY, I WISH I COULD MARRY YOU

Earth's sun plays tag with noon and runs away. Remy swears she hears a whimper. Behind her, Sydney wouldn't admit it. There it is, again.

"You alright, pal?" she asks.

I'd rather be called, 'sweetheart.' He nods.

She waits three bradycardic beats. "You sure?"

How do adults always know when kids are hiding things—especially the truth? "Um."

She slips out the arm holes and sets her bag down. Crouching beside him, Remy places a palm over his head like the brim of a ball-cap. His hair is sweaty. "Seriously, what's wrong?"

"It's just. The straps are cutting into my shoulders." Everybody's load became heavier after splitting Steve's belongings, Sydney's bag included.

"You two want a break?" Cub calls out from up ahead. The echo in his voice deserves an answer.

She studies Sydney, then replies, "Yeah, *I* could use one." She winks at the little man. His mouth-corners curl up, mouthing the words, 'thank you.'

Truth be told, her back ached, too. Often, it is easier to help others than to help oneself. "Let me get that for you," she says pulling off Sydney's pack. "Whoa! This *is* heavy. You are strong, you know that?"

Sydney bashfully looks away. "I don't know," he shrugs. *Her eyes and cheeks and nose are irresistible. They all match her tan skin and ever-highlighting hair. Kids at school would carry her books to class for her.*

He avoids prolonged eye contact because she might uncover his secret. Not a bad one, but certainly embarrassing. Adults have their ways of seeing through kids despite how clever kids think they are. *She, the sun, too pretty to stare.*

Remy hands him a jerky stick. It's tough. Two handed, he tugs against his teeth until the dried meat yields. His head snaps back. It tastes like metal—iron and satisfaction. A check found its box.

"Thanks, babe." The cat tumbles out of its bag. The horse escapes its barn. "Oops!" Red patches stipple Sydney's cheeks. *I was thinking 'babe,' but didn't mean to say it out loud! Maybe if I hide my eyes, she'll let it go.*

She punches his arm. He topples over onto his side like a domino. "Watch your mouth!" He groans. They both laugh the nervous energy away.

She is perfect.

BROTHERLY LIKE

It could have gone one of two ways and it went one. *Cub seems nicer, maybe not happier, but less bossy—even agreeable.* One alpha falls and the other postures less. For that, Remy is thankful. He hums while picking up twigs, gently shaking off wetness. It's still early, but she has learned to choose her battles.

"Where are we going?" Sydney asks Remy.

"Away," the eavesdropping man calls out.

Sydney and Remy look up, but he doesn't turn back to check for their approval. He continues scavenging for kindling.

She rests her hands on his knees. "Syd, there are good people, bad people, and good people that act like bad people. Right now, scared people are acting like bad people and we've got to get away from them for a while."

"How long?"

"How long and how far, we don't know," she says.

"When will we know for sure?"

"We won't. For sure. The future is never certain. It is normal to be scared of it. Security is not real. It felt like it was before, but it never was. Does that scare you?"

Sydney emphatically shakes his head, 'no,' like an angry cartoon character—her little man.

"You're a good kid."

"Man!"

"Hmm?"

"A good *man*!"

Remy lets go of his knees and holds up her hands as if at gunpoint. "Oh, I forgot. *Man*."

EMPTY HEARTS AND HIGHWAYS

Solitude slicks sanity's grip. Tonight's campsite was today's compromise. The river is within bathroom-distance. The road is within sprinting-distance. They will lay down in the ditch's suburbs between crackling fire and dribbling river. Together, they will cradle him asleep and that is already inviting.

"I wonder if," Cub mutters to himself. Steve left them with plenty of blankets—more than enough. He props up a downed tree branch. The brittle, wet bark peels in his hands. Holding it upright, he drapes a blanket over the top. *Placed a little off-center, it looks more like a lean-to than a tent, but this might be fun. Fun for Sydney.*

Remy claps while Cub observes his construction. He scratches the back of his neck's hairline, forgetting how to accept praise.

"I like it! This will be fun!" she says.

"That's what I was thinking," Cub replies as he flaps the blanket.

SHADES OF SEPIA

This is, by far, the earliest they had ever set down for the night. Cub calls it, "wasted daylight."

"But where are we going anyways?" Sydney asks.

It takes Cub a moment to respond. "Away... to nowhere."

PLUCKED VOCAL CHORDS

I've been nervous lately. Scrambling birds across twig beds make me flinch. Every night's noise haunts and threatens. I have a twitching left eyelid that won't leave me still. I'd rub a porcupine lamp for cradling arms and a soothing voice to tell me everything's going to be okay.

Cub approaches from behind. She startles. He sits beside her. Cub looks back to see Sydney scavenging in the blurry distance, before reaching into his pocket.

"In honor of Steve," he proffers her a crumpled, half-empty pack of cigarettes with the top flap open.

She scrunches her forehead. "Are those reds?"

He nods and, from the bottom, uses a finger to push one cigarette above the others.

"Are those Steve's?"

"Don't worry about it."

"Where did you get them?"

"I said, 'Don't worry about it.'"

"Did he give them to you?"

"Yes," Cub lies.

"When?"

"You sure ask a lot of questions, don't you?" He leans back, holding up an innocent hand. "I thought we could celebrate together, for a change."

Searching her brother's eyes, she reluctantly withdraws the raised cigarette and pokes it between her lips. "How do you even... I mean, I don't even know how to do this."

He plucks it out of her mouth and spins it around. "Open." She opens. He sticks the darker end in. "Close." She puckers it. "Good. Now breathe through it, like a straw." Her cheeks dimple as he raises Steve's old lighter. The flame fans to either side before torching the paper tip.

It glows and is almost immediately followed by a gagging cough that sounds more like a bothered goose. Faint white smoke streams out both nostrils and her mouth. The cigarette tumbles to the grass as she goose-coughs into her fist. Cub laughs.

"That's awful!"

"We have to light it again."

"I don't want to."

He settles his laugh. "For Steve."

She gives him a reluctant smirk before popping the filtered end between her tight lips. The lighter sparks. Her next goose-cough sounds more like a buried hatchet.

EASTER ISLAND CONNECTION

It was Steve's night. Remy volunteers to take his place, but Cub insists on watching tonight. Wealthy families quarrel over who gets to pay the restaurant bill—these and other wonderful problems of privilege.

"Cub, what was the first thing you thought of when you met me?"

"You are supposed to be in bed," he tells the little man.

"I *am*," he insists.

"You are supposed to be *asleep*."

Sydney pulls the stiff blanket up to cover his mouth.

Cub needles the fire, turning one branch over another in the fashion of twiddling thumbs. He could never admit it. Upon meeting, the first thing he noticed was the color of Sydney's skin. Dark-skinned people in Cub's life were athletes and musicians, not classmates or friends. He twiddles the fire.

Does recognition confer racism or prejudice? Is this something I should keep from the little guy while our new world molts in its cocoon?

Sydney rolls onto his side. Remy eavesdrops. Temptation to comfort the boy pounds at the gates of her tongue. She holds it in.

Why lie? "Your skin color." *Reality stirs a more interesting pot.* Sydney sits up. He scans his arms, observing the color, then shuffles his butt toward Cub.

"Back at the silo, Cassie talked about my Dad. She said, 'He's our *real* Dad but he's not Mom's husband.' I thought that was a funny thing—it didn't really make much sense." He scratches his chin. "That was, until she told me about our little sister, Glory." Cub's eyebrow rises. "You see, Glory is our sister, but *her* Dad is not the same. *Her* Dad is *your* color."

"Really?" Cub's demeanor crinkles into curiosity. "What was his name?"

Sydney shrugs. "Cassie said Mom asked her at the fair, this one time, if she would mind if she married Glory's dad."

Cub discovers how new pieces fit into his small world.

Sydney thumbs the scabbed brown spot above his eye. "Mom must have *really* loved Glory's dad."

Resisting the urge to reveal their connection, he plainly says, "I've never had a dark friend before."

"I am *your* friend?" Sydney fills with warmth.

"Go to sleep!" Cub playfully shouts.

Covers go from over his mouth to over his head so Cub can't hear his excitement above the hisses of their wet fire.

POSTAL SEGREGATION

Fall tells the sky to go to bed without a snack. The last long stick lands on a crumble of white glowing branches, casting embers toward their new homes.

Blackness hasn't fully set in, but a wind has. Cub shifts a step closer. Through the blankets, he feels cold nipping his knees. They ache. He is not an old man. They shouldn't. Steve used to say, "Old men dream of young knees." *I shouldn't have to.* Rubbing them against each other, as if they were flint, seems to help a little. More wood would more.

Cub throws the covers aside. His companions don't stir. *There is plenty more out there to burn.* Under the dark blues of moonlight, he hunts the area that was most fruitful, snapping big branches over his knee. Most break half-way until he finishes them with a stomp. Diminished visibility forces him to lean over for a better look. Hunched over, his face is almost on the ground.

He hears laughter. He freezes. A fine glitter of panic fills his accelerating heart, locking him into a position like he was pleading for Rapunzel's lock.

Voices carry in echoes through empty ravines. *They are men.* Flattening down on his stomach, he looks back at the fire. From this vantage point, he can't see his companions, but the flames are an unwanted beacon. Voices approach from all directions in a vestibular holiday. Cub hears gravel beneath their feet. *The road.*

He breathes in. Echoing distorts words. A hush settles over the insect community as they bow to their superiors. He exhales. The laughter and footsteps stop. Voices hush to listen.

Something crawls on Cub's arm, but he has not the time to be bothered. The road he wanted to avoid sits above a ditch and subsequent tall, grassy lowlands further out.

They saw. He knows they saw. Impending doom precedes acceptance of one's fate. Broken glass disturbs an entire home's sleep. Some confront insurmountable conflict with anger. Others help the executioner cinch the noose's knot.

People allow medical problems, social status, and victimization to define themselves, setting a narrative hook in their life's bait.

"Shhh." Gravel footsteps move to the sound of waist-high grass flirting with excited denim. Cub closes his eyes, but the world doesn't get darker. It sounds like three pairs of legs, maybe four, and he's tired of fighting. Tired of surviving.

Tonight, Cub powerlessly submits. Courage assuages to cowardice in the only way it knows how.

"I am going to die," Cub says under a soft breath to no ears but his own. This isn't a revolutionary thought, but it so often pushes its way to the surface in front of: *let me merge into traffic* and *her hair smells like warm hibiscus.* Everything has a lifespan, not just Steve, Remy, and Sydney, but all the way down to the shoes and socks that will eventually wear out. *This will not get any easier.*

Why does it seem that niceties are rewarded with punishment?

Cub strokes his skull from nose-bridge to crown. *Why keep doing this?* Another unrevolutionary thought with countless poor answers. *Heaven must think earthlings only repeat their mistakes. Heaven must think earthlings do not realize life's preciousness. Heaven must like to watch reruns. Heaven must be out of life vests so, instead, it tosses us anchors.*

Never the conformist. *Then again, why not keep doing this? Anything is better than giving up, right?* Why did anybody slip a coin into a Tetris machine? Not for visuals. Not for fame. Not to feel like a failure when the screen crowds with disorganization. They wanted to see how far they could get. Everybody is born, and everybody dies. It's the things in between that deserve celebration. Cub concludes: *I won't die with coins in my pocket.*

READING TEA LEAVES IN SATURN'S STRIPES

Voices grumble but pass by. They now appear to be between him and his campfire. He waits for the crying. He listens for the scream. He anticipates a violent exchange. Styles of death tend to eclipse the deceased's accomplishments.

Lying belly-down, he cups a hand around each ear—and hears nothing.

Could they possibly be friendly? Like us? Hitler would disagree with the way history remembers heroes. Suds would not portray Cub as a 'good guy' either.

History awaits its first friendly dictator.

Cub listens for his sister. Compassion lugs around a backpack stuffed with heavy emotions. Voices echo. He only hears men.

Alone, Cub commando-crawls toward the road. Insects bite. Thicker brush breaks at the ditch. His nose peeks out into the clearing.

A satchel and lit flashlight rest in the middle of the road. The beam points overhead toward his things, his camp, and his friends —or what's left of each.

Dust motes dance in the shaft of light. Convenience and loving relatives are taken for granted. *If the men have a camp of their own, it must be close for them to be traveling this late. They will return. He will follow. This is new living.*

BEAUTY MAKES THE WORLD MOVE AROUND YOU

"It's okay," Remy whispers to her little man. The 's' sound soothes him. If he were a cat, he'd purr.

Vultures descend. They watch from afar as the dying fire casts shadows outward. Strangers rifle through *their* possessions. She feels vulnerable and violated as someone picks up her pack. Stuff spills out. The zipper must have been left relaxed. A shadow leans down to pass a hand over the damp soil. Maybe he found what he was looking for, maybe not.

Another shadow collects the makeshift tent. It looks around like its hands were caked in red, then tucks the blankets under an armpit.

Remy hopes for the best and expects the worst. Sydney watches scary shadows but thinks about the girl's arm around him. He catches a reflection in the well of her eyes. Tears bud. He closes his own and nuzzles against her, burying his head in her warmth. He feels the weight of her right breast against his left cheek and the world flows.

MOLLUSCUM CONTAGIOSUM

It took a while—a long while. Insects gather their instruments. These rotations, it feels more like nature trying to outgrow humans.

First one, then more shadows break the road's crest, laboring new luggage. A hefty sack slides off a tired shoulder. One shadow pirouettes while another extends wings in confusion. A third's hands perch themselves atop its owner's head.

Cub hears inaudible grumbling. The tallest drops his pack and shoves a shorter one in the chest. The shorty almost loses balance. Great camaraderie doesn't dissolve in the face of adversity.

The tall one shields his eyebrows to consider the night. "Hello?" he calls. Cub shivers. A deep, richness in his baritone voice echoes in a telephonic chant, "We know you are out there." Thousands of insects stop playing. Violin bows screech.

"We know you can hear us." He stands and lifts his wide-rimmed, black hat to scratch the top of his head. Cub blinks. The hat returns.

"Come back with us. We can help you." He listens. "We *want* to help you."

Shorty leans toward the speaker. The tall one points to a backpack. Shorty hangs his head before bending down to pick it up.

Cub's stomach growls. Blood drains from his face. In his head, the growls echo.

"It's not right to take a man's things, you know?" says the tall shadow with his new loot. All the packs jump on backs and danger walks the road north.

CHAPTER 41

PRESIDENTIAL REGRET

O*h, to live with no regrets...*
Age teaches its listeners the preposterous nature of such thoughts. To live without regrets is selfish and short-sighted. It is to live without careful reflection. It is to repeat mistakes. It is the naïveté that every brushstroke is perfection.

The lights are closed but his eyes are not. Dark-blue drinks moonlight through slats in the blinds, casting the bedroom with simple shapes and silhouettes. Above him, a bald bird spreads across a field of red and white in the shadow of stars. He rolls toward his beloved and greatest confidant. Her breaths are audible and regular with hints of salivary strands spanning her airway.

Gathering courage, he whispers, "I regretted it immediately after authorizing the orders. I can't believe it came to this." *When did good intent get swept up into mandatory slaughter?* He studies her for signs of consciousness but is left with empty hands.

I did the right thing. I mean, I think I did the right thing. History, not the present, colors villains.

A rumble builds from the generator. The air conditioner winds. A fan circulates. He peels the covers away. Water in his clear glass on the nightstand vibrates, coating the surface with concentric circles. The ice cubes melted before he was supposed to be asleep. He gulps it down. The first mouthful is still cool, the rest, room temperature.

Live life like no one is watching. He is not positioned to do that. Well, maybe he is, now more than ever. *May history accept apologies.* His lower lip, shoulders, and self-esteem all drop. Cupped hands catch his face.

Infamy leaves a more pristine fossil than philanthropy.

A lifetime of effort won me a gigantic prison with open doors and closed freedom.

He wears more than his age.

When reminiscing, even God wears remorse over forty flooded rotations.

CHAPTER 42

WET HANDS SCARE SAND MEN

Wee hours chill uncovered bone.

The reluctant zipper finally gives in. His new camouflage pack is stuffed. The world is still coated in deep blues. At light-speed, other suns whisper to foreign lands. He will wait until dawn to inspect the cache.

Maybe they escaped. Maybe they acquiesced. Maybe they did neither, but they weren't with strangers. Undoubtedly, shadows will be back. Racing thoughts waterboard sleep. He will start earlier. Cub rubs the flashlight's handle—*textured aluminum.* Its switch tempts his thumb. He holds it facing down, cupping the lens in this sweatshirt.

Cub's thumb gets what it wants. He tilts the rim. Soft, yellow light stretches oblong up his abdomen. He quiets the lens. A metallic click reassures him the light went out.

A naughty smile breaks Cub's lips. Morning-breath-film cracks. His tongue tastes warm and heavy. He will search for his and theirs and them before the visitors return.

NOW THAT LIFE IS LIKE THIS, HOW DO WE CHANGE IT?

"They're coming back, aren't they?" Sydney asks, already knowing the answer.

"Yes, dear. They will, but I'll protect you."

"Are we supposed to just let them... Why can they take our stuff?"

"Possessions are a funny thing," she says. "Don't you think?"

The boy considers her odd question. "I guess. You mean, because, we took them from that man and his dog?"

Remy softly snaps her fingers with inspiration. "Remember the story about the prince and his salamander?"

"Yeah, and the mermaid?"

"She nods. "Our stuff is like the salamander's toes!"

"So, we'll grow it back?"

She pinches his nose. "Exactly." He turns away. He doesn't see her body tire, one pulled petal at a time. "Can you try to fall asleep for me?"

For her, he will try. He will do more than try. He wouldn't want to disappoint her. Moonshine touches her cheeks in two little white circles. After a couple short moments, Sydney's body powerlessly collapses into her lap. Today won't break into tomorrow. Hunger, fear, insomnia, and child-rearing labor shoulders and ruin posture.

The yelling men sounded angry on the road. Hiding will be safest. This area is too big for them to find us. It may also be too big to find my brother. Lacing her fingers, she prays: *Cub, please find us.*

Smoke billows in the distance. Birth and death punctuate in white smoke.

She forces lips through curly black hair. A kiss lands on his brown scalp. She wraps the blanket around them both, sharing body heat.

BRINK OF DISCOMFORT

Cub peers through the tall grass like vertical Venetian blinds. Any prey knows traps disguise themselves as wide open areas. The empty road reflects Kennedy's moon.

He closes his eyes, holding his breath and listening for predators. *This is as safe as it gets.* The road repeats his footsteps. Moist gravel keeps evidence. He steals a quick northern glance while crossing the road. Its vanishing point sharpens black without traces of life.

Descending the ditch on the campsite-side provides a familiarity—welcoming and homely—like a bedfellow's stench. Strange how children and even some adults tremble in the dark. Animals, and now Cub, find security in it.

The flashlight tempts him. Insect cacophony intensifies with expanding separation from the road. It's difficult to distinguish what brings him more warmth: excitement to recover possessions or physical activity.

The tall field carves unintelligible paths. *There is no fire. There is no Remy. There is no Sydney.* India ink shadows drenched in indigo. He waits for the sun to reveal what's left.

He waits longer.

Sleep attempts to hypnotize.

He resists.

From behind, he hears footsteps. Sunlight folds over the horizon without an obstructive cloud. There's an imbalance between the cool, crisp morning air and the sun's sharp, eye-stinging photons. *This morning, I'll cast a shadow for my trackers.*

Staying low, Cub squat-jogs. His hands paw the ground ahead of his feet. Ape's would sympathize.

Looking back for pursuers gives him an opportunity to break from squinting. Sprinkled sun spots dot his vision. He doesn't remember feeling more primal. If he had a reflection, he would agree that he never *looked* more primal.

He pauses to listen. Birds scream as if they had pulled tail feathers. Something resembling a frog who swallowed a whistle accompanies the wind's current.

I should be getting close but don't recognize the terrain. His heartbeat bounds as if begging to be released from his temples. Dehydrated blood attempts to quench vital organs. He hasn't urinated since last sunrise. Desperation creeps up his neck with jugular venous distention. Before bothering to analyze or calculate its risks, he releases a dove for all nature to repeat, yelling, "Cub!" He hopes it returns clutching an olive leaf.

OURS BECAME THEIRS

Her flinch spooks sleep from Sydney. He wipes his eyes the way mothers tell their children not to. Remy's dilate with hope. Voices seem to ricochet from everywhere with strange familiarity.

Sydney slides from her cradling arms as Remy stands. Craning her neck like a streetlamp, she perches a hand upon each hip. Throughout the night, she kept her toes in the direction of their campground. She fixes on the spot.

Sydney begins to speak, but she quickly snuffs him out with a raised hand and cupped ear—audible satellite dishes.

Time ticks swiftest with the finish line in focus.

She waits for movement. She isn't foolish enough to give away her position in case it's the last trap she gets to touch. *Or, is it a last chance?* Picked three-leafed clovers await judgement in one Roman balance, the four-leafed variety in the other. Sunlight and stress heat her back. Sweat buds her forehead.

Insulated living leaves chance's stakes low.

Sydney tucks his legs under his chin with the posture of a paperclip. The tips of his black, curly hair measure just above the grass line. He picks a stalk that reminds him of wheat. The grass has gone to seed. He pops the grounded end into the corner of his mouth. Its end waves smoothly up and down in the gentle breeze.

Remy is their lookout. The protector. His protector. He wraps an arm around her pant-leg. She acknowledges his leg-hug, then returns to searching.

He pulls out the stalk and spins it between a finger and thumb. He taps the end as if knocking ashes from a cigarette. Loosened seeds flutter to new homes. Puckering one side, he blows an invisible smoke stream away from Remy—to be polite. The chewed-up end parks itself back in the corner of his mouth. He squeezes her leg.

Bubbles move inside. Remy places a hand over her stomach. A perched blackbird flinches. They'll have to flee with peristaltic urgency.

She realizes her mouth has been hanging open. Grandpa would have said she's, "Trying to catch flies. Anyone who wants to be taken seriously should close their mouth while not speaking." It closes. She swallows sandpaper.

Life is Death's dress rehearsal and those blessed with birth only receive one opportunity.

Sydney's grip slips with her first forward steps. He scrambles to his feet to return to her side. Remy tiptoes in the damp soil as if to get a glimpse of the forager's remains over a fence of golden grass. Sydney briskly trots behind with a knuckle up his nose and a tongue sticking out. His two steps match her one. Creeping an invisible tightrope, she focuses. *It's coming.* The layout opens to a thinned area. From above, it could pass for drunken crop circles. *It's almost here...*

Sydney falls back. She stops, grabs his hand, and tows him behind her. Little feet patter underneath a whiplashing neck. Remy smells a strong campfire odor. There is no rising smoke. She brushes a passage of tall grass aside to reveal the leftovers.

Clothing and blankets with familiar scents are strewn like a washing machine exploded. Shirts pressed into soft soil by big, dirty feet. Pant-legs doing gymnastics.

Emotions gush. Tears well at the bases. Remy pulls her

emptied water bottle from the mud. Cleaning the nozzle with her thumb still leaves a dirty, brown pinstripe.

Her backpack is gone.

The food pack is gone.

How should we get our stuff back?

This is their new life. A new game. A clean, hungry slate.

It's impossible to bring possessions from life to the after.

"We worked so hard, for this... to happen."

Even names don't follow to the after.

A small, growing hand finds her's and squeezes, "I love you, Remy."

INDISPENSABILITY EMPOWERS

Across the campsite, a young scarecrow stands. His scarred face gives him away. Remy springs to taut legs. Two hands abort a birthing scream. Her feet blur. They could sprint to him across an ocean.

Each shuddering stride shakes joyful tears loose from their sentenced ducts. Five paces away, she would have appreciated wiper blades.

Her chest impacts his chest without fat's comfort. Remy tightens her hug. He wears her like a straitjacket. She wears him like a life preserver. They almost fall. His armpits stink. He feels uncomfortable with each arm pinned at the sides. The pose is off-balanced like the first, "I love you," lingering in the air between a young couple.

Hesitantly, his arms bend at the elbows. He pats her flank on either side, avoiding her rump. Untaught affection is baptism by fire outside the nest.

A littler one comes crashing into his right leg. Sydney squeezes. His grip pressurizes Cub's manhood. Discomfort doesn't describe the white flash of pain.

Cub uses the opportunity to break apart from his sister. He pries the boy off with a sheepish smile.

Remy alternates between Cub's left and right eye, attempting to decipher his emotions. She can't understand him and his absent happiness.

Sydney watches the reunion spoil.

"Pick up everything you can," Cub says. "We have to leave... now."

BOT FLIES AND PARASITES

Tension vibrates them like anger's heart jockey. Shadows hide as much as dawn shows. Tankards and blankets unstick from Earth's clay with a goodbye smooch.

Remy finds a small food knapsack she packed and has carried from home this entire trip. More frightened than helpful, Sydney nervously scurries around the site picking up small twigs.

Cub spots a brushed bronze buckle several paces away. His amygdala squirts a few droplets of its favorite fluid into his consciousness. *My backpack!* He turns away for a moment, then looks, again. *No mirage. No hallucination. No figment of someone else's imagination.* He can't believe it was passed over. His lips almost forget how to turn upward. Almost.

He jogs to it. Flipping it over, the contents still plump out the camouflage canvas. An untampered zipper.

Young, spoiled selfishness told him to take food for himself when he instructed them to keep food all in the same bag. He'll discover how selfishness gets to exercise selflessness to his only friends' hungry stomachs.

Slipping his arms through its worn holes, he calls out, "We all ready?" Cub heroically stands tall above his sunken-eyed comrades with their curved spines and beaten nerves.

They don't realize the urgency. They bask in an afterglow of reunion and sleep deprivation. Their survival pilot-light strikes without sparking.

"Now is not negotiable."

"Ouch, Cub. You are hurting me!" Remy squeals after he firmly squeezes her elbow. His other cups Sydney's armpit. "Wait!"

Cub looks like he is dragging two whiny children from a movie theatre. They resist, Remy worse than Sydney. She works to pry his grip.

With a swift yank, he pulls her face to his. Morning breath accompanies ketones. Violence color-coordinates with his lined eyebrows.

"We can't wait," forces its way between barred teeth. He motions toward Sydney. Parents keep secrets from their young in open gestures.

He lets her go. Before she can decipher his body language, he whisks Sydney away from her—away from the road.

Sydney stumbles, missing steps completely from time to time, before regaining stride. He can't feel his left wing caught in a Cub-tourniquet.

She gets the idea. Remy gives chase. When she does, a vibrating voice cracks out. Remy can't tell what he said but figures the worst.

Cub hears it, too. His pace quickens. Wind wheezes by his ears dangerously fast like overclocked processors—unsustainable. His left arm pumps while the right one is anchored.

Sydney goes from stumbling and missing an occasional step to double gripping and tucking his feet above the blurry surface. Cub's digits turn from red to purple. He tries to swing Sydney in some sort of rhythm. The weight is hourglass sand. His shoulder joint feels like it's loosening. Cub feels like there is a trapped bubble lodged in it, if only he could release the pressure.

Sweat pools in Sydney's palms. He is impressed by Cub's strength. He wishes he was big like Cub. He wishes Cub was his big brother. He re-grips at the pendulum's dead phase. His little fingers dig into Cub's wrist. He feels the cables that manipulate Cub's fingers.

Sydney senses his idol slowing. Cub's open-mouthed exhales accompany a faint goose honk. Sydney lets down his legs and scampers by Cub's side. Batman has Robin. Two little legs wish for more, like dogs.

SKINNY DIPS IN SHALLOW STREAMS

Remy keeps the boys' shadows obstructing the rising sun. Her tongue laps its dry roof. The roof pulls back. Now needs to wait, the way predators won't. Traveling without heavy packs seems easy. Survival will be quite the opposite. The moment must wait. There is only one threat. Life gets easy when it's simplified.

She is catching up to an eclipse. *This is bad. What should we do with Sydney?*

Lactic acid accumulates in large leg muscles. Blood seems to scarcely flow, like a strawberry clump stuck in a malt's straw. Her run turns into a limp. She could reach out and touch Sydney's floundering limbs. Small legs lack kinetics.

From behind, calling and cursing choke on panting, but safety doesn't come to mind. She learned from Lot's wife.

The river peeks. Its surface twinkles where ripples interrupt. *This was Steve's river, or at least his compass.* The closer she gets; the broader depth deceives. She guesses it to be waist-high on her, maybe deeper.

At their latitude, it now runs north-south. A glacial phlebotomy.

Cub pops out his canteen at the shore. Heavy breaths disturb deep chugs. Before tipping it completely vertical, he hands it down to Sydney.

"Finish."

The little man takes it in both hands. Remy catches up.

"You okay?"

Sydney nods to her. His unblinking, beady eyes remind her of a puppy. She waves him off when he offers her a sip.

Cub hands his shoes and socks to Sydney in exchange for the empty canteen. He dunks it under the cool water. Bubbles *glug* out.

Remy pulls off her shoes and socks. Cub stops Sydney from doing the same.

"You ever heard of piggyback rides?" he asks the little man.

AROUND MY EQUATOR

Sydney sees small, sprouting hairs push their way through Cub's tanned scalp. *The light hairs almost look gray.*

Each step *clumps*. Sydney's loose jaw snaps down. He wraps around Cub's neck, resting a cheek on his crown. *Cub smells like old laundry, warm and dirty. He smells like air trapped under blankets in Mom's room—mildly offensive in a naughty way, but comforting —secure.*

The water is smooth and refreshing. Remy's legs sip as she wades across. It's difficult to tell the more dangerous enemy, the callers or her growling tummy.

She places a hand over her stomach. It feels like it is making noise. It twists and writhes in pleading agony, unaccustomed to uneasy pickens. It feels like it's shaped like a bar rag. She massages it with a thumb, but it doesn't stop whining.

"One step in front of the other." Warm lactic acid icicles stiffen her lower extremities. She fixates on Cub's belt ahead of her. His brushed nickel canteen dangles off of his hip, bouncing in stride. She saw him fill it. One step follows the next.

ROTATIONS RUMBLE ALONG LIKE EMPTY SIAMESE STOMACHS

The river is wet. The shore is inviting. A recital with missed notes only embarrasses the performer and composer.

How many seasons must change to learn that the success of one does not necessarily come at the misfortune of another? Rusty flakes don't gather on those always prepared. Survival misses every holiday.

Cub extends a hand. *Remy is losing weight.* He can tell when she's drenched. Her fingers are little more than plump French fries.

She offers a smile after his tug. Her eyes belong to raccoons. Cub recognizes remorse. He pushes her. He has been pushing her beyond her body. He expects hers to match his. *Why would women ever want to be equivalent to men? In doing so, they surrender the beautiful qualities exclusive to themselves. The same goes for children wishing to be big kids.*

REHABILITATION

Sydney drops the shoes at his feet, but Cub waves him off. Digging into his own pack, he pulls out a pair of boots. *Those are Indian Steve's—were Indian Steve's.* He watches Cub trying them on. *They don't look like they fit.* Cub presses a thumb near the toe, indicating empty space at the tip. "Too roomy," he tells Sydney and slips on the shoes instead. "Keep riding, piggy?"

Remy shakes her pant-legs like a street mutt. "One foot in front of the other..."

Cub doesn't flinch. His arm drapes over her shoulder. He leans in. His lower lip incidentally feathers her ear lobe. She hears a *clack* in his dry whisper, "I'm sorry."

She wraps an arm around his waist and pats. *Her face looks like it just ate a lemon, but she isn't crying.* Tears want to come out but lack the fuel. Sydney briefly ruffles Remy's hair before Cub jogs off with the little-man-backpack.

DEATH ASYNCHRONY

Remy's four chambers boil. The boys' backs shrink further into the distance. *One foot in front of the next* becomes nothing more than a hollow mantra—an overplayed song.

She arches her painfully sore lower back. A trickle of sweat finds its way around her ear. She hears her own labored breathing swirl through eustachian tubes to flutter across her tongue in large, open-mouthed gasps.

I'm barely alive. Each blink causes the world to tumble back into focus like an unlatched dryer.

Machines have been carrying life's problems upon their shoulders, leaving Remy's relatively feeble—Atlas with a qwerty keyboard and carpal tunnel.

Time rubs man's signature from a death pact with each apocalyptic turn of the hourglass. The future doesn't keep promises. In fact, it seldom makes them at all.

One should hope to live long enough to not fit in anymore. Eternity doesn't need a new publicist. The one it has is doing just fine.

Her once wet pants have gone from floppy to stiff. She can see a silhouette stop. Its backpack points at her. The backpack crawls down. Remy puts one foot in front of the other to make the stationary silhouettes grow.

SOFT, WET PUPPY NOSE

Cub taps Sydney, motioning behind them. The boy lights up and runs with outstretched arms toward Remy. His excitement spooks away a small kernel of her exhaustion.

He climbs her arm for a better hug-angle. Surprisingly, she nearly caves in to him. It startles him the way a tipped glass of milk crashes on ceramic tile. She smirks. He squeezes. Her ribs remind him of fish bones.

Cub offers Remy a handful of peanuts and milk chocolate

coated candies. Sydney picks out a yellow before she dumps the lot into her mouth. Cub licks the salt grains off his hand.

"Time we head north, again. I want to get some fluid in you. You look... not good," he tells his sister.

She knows he is not lying.

"Do I look good?" Sydney asks.

"Of course you do, champ," Cub says.

CHASING THINGS

Bending blades begin to crisp. Stringy clouds against cornflower-blue frame a single blackbird. Sydney tracks it across. The wings barely beat before straightening in an effortless float. Sydney stumbles. When he goes back to the bird, it is gone. It isn't left. It isn't right. It was and now it isn't.

He more carefully watches his steps and the backs of his friends, but his mind returns to the blackbird. A quick glance reminds him it is gone. Next time he sees one, he won't let it escape.

DRAGGING STORYLINE FEET

Without reference, travels seem slow as boredom. Their shadows walk in the grass alongside of them. Soft, black soil was tilled crops not long ago. Trace corn stalks, snapped at the waist, remember the holocaust.

"This is us," Cub says pointing at the solitary stalk. He hears Remy's panting. *Another lost metaphor...* No one else talks. Both watch the tops of their own shoes.

He deeply inhales through his nose and holds. Lungs trade oxygen for their used-up carbon-laced brethren. Beautiful thoughts, jokes, and ideas will go underappreciated. An author must lead the audience and not be deterred when they struggle to follow breadcrumbs.

Cub points. "We'll set down up ahead, there."

UNHAPPY VALENTINE

She has gotten used to the sound. Her mouth would water with anticipation, if it could. First, tiny bubbles appear in a watched pot. Yesterday's meal crisps and flakes around the edges. Second, bigger bubbles emerge in streams. They rise to the surface. Had bubbles been memories, they needn't try to escape. Next, more violent bubbles dominate and obscure the once clear fluid, reflecting light away. Burying memories only rejuvenates its owner of the contents in revived technicolor.

Remy stirs. For a moment, violence ceases in dissipating heat before rumbling once more. Invisible germs shrivel in her imagination. She waves an open hand over the involuntary streams of steam.

What if we wake with placed memories? Each sunrise, we are born a new person in someone else's timeline, while a higher power judges how we deal with conflict. We allow memories to lead our decision-making. We believe we control our destiny, but this is simply an illusion created by sorcery, for lack of better understanding.

She pinches herself, but nothing else happens. She yawns.

We are not batteries so why would we need to recharge overnight? Dreams unwind the time's unresolved chaos into neat little digestible compromises. This is not dissimilar to forgiveness—true forgiveness. Not the kind that parents force their children to say.

Tomorrow, I may wake as the same soul in a new body with new situations and new memories. May that not be as bad as this for it will be a new dawn.

Our creator holds powers we could never imagine.

What I would do to hear the rattle of an ice cube at the bottom of a clean glass... She tips the canteen back.

Estranged we become on things we no longer rely, including one another and nature. Remy softly weeps behind a hand like a mouse protecting its last bite of cheese.

Sydney approaches from behind. She doesn't turn away in time. "What's the matter, Rem?" His unbelievably caring expression only waters her guilt.

She shakes her head. Strands of hair, like a wet corn broom, sway in large stuck-together blonde ribbons. She swallows the reluctant sadness and clears her throat.

"Nothing, honey. Did you get enough to eat?"

For all his naïveté, he still doesn't believe her. "Mom used to tell us it's not good to bottle your feelings. Otherwise, after a while, they will explode like a shaken can of seltzer."

"Seizure?"

"No, *seltzer.*"

"Seltzer?"

He nods.

Cub disappears into their makeshift tent.

CHAPTER 43

PRESIDENTIAL PUNISHMENT

When time was slower, law men and women dusted crime scenes for evidence. The most unscrupulous pre-criminals would singe their fingers smooth, erasing fingerprints in the event they were ever caught.

He's sticky. The fire still crackles. His gray hair smells like wood smoke. His skin isn't as oily as it once was. Doctors call it *turgor*, people call it old age. He needs to be recharged.

Toes neatly slip through slippers. He hates waiting for his veins, but it beats the alternative, light-headedness punctuated by a loss of consciousness and compound wrist fractures. He has his First Lady to thank for covering up his... mistake. *Sick people earn sympathy but rarely earn votes.*

Bed coils spring. He flexes his calves and toes. He beeps and then rises.

He spins an uncomfortable, faded-red chair toward the fire, opening his robe and exposing himself to the heat. Behind, shadows blink as if coaxed by paparazzi with phosphorescent camera flashes. He stiffly rubs both hands along the arm rests that once carried more cushion. *How many difficult decisions were made in this very room and this very chair?* One's own country typically views its leaders in kinder lighting. Less popular decisions trickle through creeks, eroding with forgiveness, forgetfulness, and excuses. This doesn't ease his nerves at night—during shutdown mode.

A hibiscus leaf floats in his half-empty water glass. One petal has separated and bobs by itself. The ice melted long ago.

He slides a coaster closer because his First Lady hates water spots. He looks back at her. Soft, Egyptian-cotton blankets coat the motionless lump.

She is clean. She forgives. How often has a First Lady forgiven a Second? She must know there were more. She is the one that picks up the pieces of a fallen man. She does it in front of pointed questions and accusations—in front of warm lights and microphones.

"Macrophone," he whispers.

A tone jiggles his skull behind the ear. Vibrations translate into sounds from the past. "Continue previous," he whispers. Reporters' voices escalate to cover up the background's hysteria. Protests and screaming voices crack like bottle rockets of lost freedom.

I am the orator of chaos.

Good people carry bad memories, internalizing vibrations like invited punishment. His eyes gloss. With a hand, Mister President leans over to grab the black iron rungs in front of the fireplace.

Searing flesh. Melting fingerprints. Inflamed tissue. First, then second, then third degrees of burning. Teeth clench as if biting a wallet. A single tear splashes out when he clamps his eyes. Gathering courage, he grips the other side, as if strangling the iron gate, squeezing until his knuckles whiten.

CHAPTER 44

THE EMPEROR'S NEW HEAD

Cub inspects the tent's canvas ceiling. Patterns crosshatch in the center, then fan out toward the edges. Almost all the small squares have caught debris in their corners. A solitary tear on the sidewall freely flaps, allowing starlight to play pat-a-cake in rhythm with fall's gusts. *The rip was probably from carelessness.* Finesse lost to muscle. Boxers relate. Artists cannot.

Cub's thumb flicks, exposing Steve's old blade. He folds it back in place with one hand. *It's calming.* Nervous movement calms nervous minds. At first, he tries to withdraw the blade in sync with the wind. Unpredictable and inconsistent, he falls behind. Instead, he patterns it after his breathing. Breathe in, knife comes out. Exhale, knife sheaths with an audible *click*. Breathe in, knife out. Breathe out, *click*.

He notices his breathing-transmission switch from automatic to manual. The brain knows what the body needs. His exhale claws its way toward dead space. He forces as much air out as he can. He feels his diaphragm resist. The coiling spring struggles to replenish. Air rapidly rushes in, carrying an exasperating wheeze. He slides onto his back. He'd rather think about other things.

PLACATE

"You're right, Syd. I wasn't telling the whole truth. Actually, I was thinking about my Dad and how I miss him." She recalls overhearing his earlier conversation with Cub. "Can you tell me about your Dad?"

Sydney bites his nether lip and uncomfortably shuffles his feet. "I'll only tell you what I remember," which is all Remy asked.

GROWN-UP GAMES

Freshly starched and pressed French uniforms, red with fashion, wrap themselves around young skin. White feathers bounce in unison atop black felt caps. A copy of a copy of a copy. Soldiers try on weapons in department store mirrors. Staying in single-file waves while uprooting trees and leaving a wake of animal parts. Black muskets draw. Soldiers' doll eyes wait for commands. Without a sound, split-shot smoke dry heaves freedom. White sulfur clouds hang thick as if condemned to a windless igloo.

Why do ocean waves endlessly play? Old husbands have difficulty pronouncing "compromise." Tug boats have all sunk. Cue the black background and up-scrolling words. His mechanical pencil ran out of lead, and paper never took handwriting class.

SUBTOTAL RECALL

Sydney wipes snot rivulets across his forearm and sniffles up the rest.

"I only remember his face from pictures at Mom's house. I remember his thin smile." *It struggled to hide thick anger.* "There was this one time when I was really small, maybe, um, four? I was sitting on his lap looking adorable." He bats his eyelashes at her.

Remy playfully slaps his elbow.

Sydney giggles before getting more serious. "His arm was folded over me, but his hand was me-sized. His fingers were as wide as my wrist. The picture reminds me of safety. A seatbelt against strangers." Violence often inherits the role of love's bodyguard. Sydney scratches an arm that doesn't itch. "Most of what I remember of him is from my sister, Cassie. She is older by two. *Was* older by two, I mean."

Remy shoots him a look. "Don't say that. We don't know."

Sydney's head wobbles with indecision. "Yeah, I guess. So, Cass said his voice used to rumble the whole house, even when he wasn't mad. She would do this when he spoke." Sydney shrinks back, pretending to be scared. "She told me to just get out of the way and hope he's not coming for you.

"But then there were the good times, when you got to be Daddy's little boy or girl. He would make you the center of his world. At first, the fear would have to melt like pain from a hot tub. When you knew he was okay, then you could enjoy. He'd cradle me. His warmth felt like welcoming blankets. His black beard looked like frozen lava, brittle black with curly gray accents. I remember it tickling the top of my head."

OXYGEN MASKS WILL DEPLOY

Eyes blink like camera shutters. The treadmill misses its 'off' switch. Cub senses sweating hands hungry to tug a closing-curtain rope. The orchestra's pause before a finale. A scarcity of resources. Too many straws and too few camel backs.

A WELL-HIDDEN BUNNY'S EGG

Sydney stares with unbroken concentration at absolutely nothing uninteresting as if receiving a skillet of history. Tiny embers enjoy a reflection on the lower third of real estate on his lenses.

"I don't remember the bad, but I'm told there was. I was probably too little."

In a beautiful harem, the ugly one stands out. The same can be said of a beautiful one in an ugly harem.

The throne passes to crown others. "Mom knows how to turn ordinary men into new Dads."

"Did you like any of them?" she asks.

Sydney makes a face as if he's holding in his cheeks before admitting, "Well... Glory's dad was amazing! Mom made him her husband. But even *he* left, for some reason." He considers, then admits, "All the other ones... they just didn't smell right."

"Glory's your sister?" *Odd... my cousin's name is Glory...* Remy feels temptation to share an experience about her past relationships, few as they were. Details clamber to the inside of her lips, begging to escape like excited dogs or juicy secrets. Her tongue swipes them aside. Limelight fades to sidelines. *This is Sydney's moment to feel special and important.* Nobody gets rewards for not stomping their neighbor's flowers. *Maybe parents deserve more than silent credit.*

SAFETY VALVE DISENGAGED

Above, the primed blade waves. The caring-switch gets bypassed. Multiple blank checks and balances fail.

IT NEVER FEELS GOOD TO BE THE BASKET FILLED WITH ALL OF SOMEONE ELSE'S EGGS

Stiff winds fill silence. A golden strand falls, dangling along Remy's peripheral vision. She tucks it behind her ear and says, "Well, I hope you find one that smells like a real—"

"New Dads pretend!" Sydney blurts. "They don't realize I don't want to be their 'buddy!' They are going to be there a while and then not."

Remy can tell he is getting aggravated.

"They don't know me! They buy me stuff I don't want. Everyone but Mom knows those stupid gifts are more to impress her." Evidence to convince the jury of caring. "I'd look at my feet and slur a 'thank you.'

"It won't be exciting to have a sleepover at *Tom's* house just the same as it wasn't exciting at *Derrick's* or *Travis'* or *Jason's!*" Sydney nasal salutes. "After a while, I was down to one shirt and one pair of shorts! All my clothes were left at Mom's extinct friends' houses!" He wipes the film on his dirty pants. "I don't think I'll ever have anybody to call..."

Tectonic shoulder blades glide on a magma bedspread. Rumbling friction shatters the fantasy that earthlings don't live atop the back of an ornery giant. A noise from within the tent punctuates the settling quake.

"Dad!" he chirps. The whites of his eyes frame brown irises all the way around.

Remy turns to follow his surprise.

From inside, it wasn't a scream or cursory word. It wasn't a grunt or a cry that interrupts Sydney, but rather, a smooth groan similar to overcoming constipation. Remy and Sydney break from their train of thought and turn toward the tent before returning confusing faces back at one another.

"Everything okay in there, Cub?" she asks the tent.

Wading through the silence, Sydney shrugs.

"Cub?"

A FOOL BELIEVES IN EMPTY PHILOSOPHY

Life isn't a game or a race or a play, but a ride. One with a beginning, middle, and end. To live for fame or wealth requires misguided discipline. Too many fear losing. *We, the people,* is becoming: *good at holding on.* New terms must be invented to quantify larger quantities of stored information. Images, video, contacts, best friend's names, colleagues, acquaintances, former flames, hidden crushes, and beautiful moments captured and locked away at a faster pace than lived life. Encryption locks forgotten images in a personalized prison. The reassurance of never losing a moment will rob those from ever experiencing one.

But, encryption requires a key, an algorithm, a series of codes to relieve its sentence. A time will come when a hand, led by blind eyes in one's own home, will lose those jingling keys. Comfort sells its home to distress. Security drops in a cableless elevator. This always ends the same. If only reincarnation didn't come with a helping of amnesia. Figments of thought, never intended as memories, are carried away by the west wind that never forgets how to blow.

Height markings on door frames were never carved, but digitally captured. The world will burn along with the paper inside it. Emboss moments that stand out in the company of imagination.

T'would be better to influence a candle carver before the match strikes. T'would be better to influence a sandcastle architect at low tide. T'would be better to influence an ice sculptor in winter than to sit behind a glowing terminal constructing a masterpiece of clicks.

FOREVER ALTERED

An anemic figure brushes the canvas flap to one side. The other hand clutches his eye socket. Clenching teeth release a *hiss* as if someone accidentally touched a hot pan. Sydney hops to his feet in one swift motion.

Thickening blood pools under a cradling hand until a single trickle runs into the corner of Cub's mouth.

Remy turns in time to gasp. "What happened?" she asks. "Why?"

Steve's pocket blade falls from Cub's grip, kicking up a puff of dirt. Earth-powder clings to the red-soaked tip. Curiosity had its way with the cat. He no longer wonders what *it* sounds like.

"I only have worse mistakes left," Cub mumbles, before falling to one knee.

Sydney gasps at the sky.

Cub turns to watch the Skinner Box within a Skinner Box. High above, a flying machine leaves white condensation trails. On its tail wing, hidden in plain sight, is the outline of a black triangle.

EIGHT YEARS WORTH OF ACKNOWLEDGMENTS

As a person learning to write, I never realized what a tremendous favor it was to ask someone to read and review a crudely written manuscript until most of them never found their way home.

Therein lies my greatest thanks to Linda and Jeanne Larson for reading revision after revision in a timely manner. Thank you to the whole Milbrett family, especially Naomi, for strangely *understanding* my word pollution. Thank you to Caeli Wolfson-Widger, the celebrated author, for tearing my work and heart into tiny little pieces and thank you to Laura Myhre and Jo Ann Bernath for putting them both back together. You all helped improve this book and for that I am forever grateful!

For obvious (or less obvious) reasons of humility, thank you to the unseen for allowing all of us to exist in this beautiful playground.

Lastly, to all the trees out there that didn't realize they'd become part of this book... I'm sorry.

ABOUT THE AUTHOR

Scott Luther Larson is not a New York Times bestselling author nor will he ever be. He is simply an ordinary person who came in to this world with nothing and will leave with nothing.

He is the disappointer who never disappointed and he fears success far more than failure.

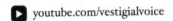 youtube.com/vestigialvoice